CALLING ON FIRE

BOOK ONE OF FIRE AND STONE

Stephanie Beavers

Copyright

Calling On Fire: Book One of Fire and Stone

Copyright © Stephanie Beavers 2014
All rights reserved

"Fairy tales do not show children that monsters exist.

Children know that monsters exist.

Fairy tales show children that monsters can be defeated."

—paraphrased from the words of

G.K. Chesterton

CHAPTER 1

The sun cast long shadows on the cemetery as it approached the horizon, silhouetting three people moving among the statues and headstones. The group had just come from a meeting with a client whose claims were…dubious.

"Well, that wasn't exactly confidence inspiring," Toman remarked dryly, his gloved hands brushing the base of each statue as they walked past. "You may not have chosen the best mission to accompany us on, Sergeant."

"I'm sure I'll live. I got you guys the job, remember?" Sergeant Gretchen Warthog's voice was equally dry.

"There might be something here. Even an idiot necromancer would know to stay away and hide if the entire village showed up with torches and pitchforks in the graveyard he was planning to raise," Esset said, fidgeting with his long overcoat.

"You just don't want to have flown across an entire kingdom to get here for nothing, Mr. Optimist," Toman said.

Esset shrugged. He paused to read the flowery inscription on a headstone. "I also feel kinda sorry for our client. Mr. Johnson, right? He just wants to protect his wife."

"Or his wife's death knocked him off his rocker," Sergeant Warthog said, glancing between the two of them.

"Would you want someone raising a loved one from the dead and turning them into a mindless abomination?" Esset asked.

"You *would* think that one of the five other groups on five separate nights would have seen something if there *were* something, though," Toman pointed out.

"That may be. But I notice we're still prepping for battle and planning to stake this place out tonight," Esset said, looking pointedly at Toman's hand, which brushed the base of the statue of a woman in a veil. Toman's was a touch with a touch of magic.

"It would be unprofessional to accept a job and not at least check it out," Toman replied.

"And impressing the pretty girl at the tavern has nothing to do with it," Esset retorted.

Toman grinned. "I know you noticed her too, what with the way you got all awkward."

Toman's words wiped the smirk off Esset's face. Sergeant Warthog lifted an eyebrow. Esset muttered a retort, but the falsehood was mostly contained under his breath.

Sergeant Warthog, walking ahead of them, rolled her eyes where they couldn't see. "This graveyard seems awfully fancy for the size of the town," she remarked, and it was true. The dead of the graveyard would outnumber the living a few times over. The community was largely agrarian, with only a couple full-time merchants serving the travelers who came through on the minor trade road running through town. In comparison, the cemetery had three small private family mausoleums and two larger, more communal ones, and that wasn't even counting the rows of statues and headstones.

"The ground was sanctified by LightBringer Ervus a century ago, which has made this a popular place to be buried, and not just by the locals. There are a number of minor nobles buried here, and a cousin of King Pyril's, Lord Escott. He lived clear across the kingdom but asked to be brought here when he died." Esset pointed. "That mausoleum is his."

Sergeant Warthog turned to look at Esset with surprise. It was Toman's turn to roll his eyes.

"He does that all the time," Toman said, tilting back his oversized, floppy-brimmed hat to see better.

"How did you know that?" Sergeant Warthog asked Esset skeptically.

"There was a plaque at the entrance. Didn't you see it?" Esset asked.

"Saw it, didn't care," Toman muttered.

"Hm," was Sergeant Warthog's only response. Toman shook his head as he stopped in front of a statue of a weeping woman and pulled a torch and firestarter from the bag slung over his shoulder. He placed both at her feet and the group moved on.

"We haven't seen any disturbed gravesites," Toman observed.

"I noticed the same thing," Sergeant Warthog replied.

"We saw plenty of undead in the war up north, and we didn't always find disturbed graveyards. Plus Mr. Johnson said it—

whatever 'it' was—was in the mausoleum." Esset said.

"Always looking for the logical—and charitable—explanation." Toman grinned.

"I do admit that none of this really looks like necromancy so far," Esset confessed. "But Mr. Johnson was at least convinced he saw something, and it put the fear of Darkfires in him. If there *is* anything out here, and it hasn't moved on already, then the tricks we learned up north should reveal it tonight."

"If not, you'll have to come with us on a different job to see us in action, Sergeant," Toman said.

"That I will," Sergeant Warthog agreed. "One way or another, I intend to see what you two are really made of. I've been giving you two jobs for a couple years now, and with good results, but that's no replacement for seeing for myself."

The two men certainly didn't look like much. They were both young, but neither was a big man, Toman with a middling build and Esset somewhat skinny, if on the tall side. Both wore long coats, practical clothes, and belt knives, but neither carried any actual weapons. Nor did either seemed inclined to brush their hair. Ever. In other words, they looked like a couple of bright-eyed, idiotic adventurers looking for glory. In fact, Sergeant Warthog had suspected as much of them when she'd first met them, although they'd later disproven her first impression.

There were oddities about them too. Esset looked to be more of a scholar than a warrior, which was not entirely untrue, and Toman had a distinct excess of pockets and belts on his person. His coat was patched up with extra, bulging pockets of various sizes, and he had belts everywhere—a few around his waist, two crossed over his chest, even a couple around his wrists and ankles. He also always wore a pair of gloves, which were subtly but ornately embroidered with dark thread.

Those gloved hands were touching yet another statue, a light brush that allowed the stone to spring to life at Toman's order. Esset didn't even need that much preparation—a few words at any time were enough to call creatures of fire to fight for him. They didn't carry conventional weapons because they didn't need them. Their individual talents were enough to keep the worst of the world at bay.

"Hey, Sergeant?"

Sergeant Warthog glanced over at Esset with a raised eyebrow, prompting the young man to continue.

"I was wondering. How did you end up being called Warthog? I can't imagine that's your real surname."

Toman purposefully moved so that Esset was between him and Sergeant Warthog—just in case the sergeant found the question impudent and wanted to take a swipe at his brother. The sergeant, however, only shrugged.

"You already know I was a career mercenary. Well, I only rose to the rank of sergeant within a merc company. Most sergeants, given their reputations, end up with nicknames. Mine suited me, so I kept it even after I went…freelance." Sergeant Warthog's explanation was simple enough. Drill sergeants were the ones who spent all their time screaming at the ranks, so it stood to reason they'd be the ones with questionable nicknames. Trust Sergeant Warthog to make it her own, though.

"Freelance? You mean when you went into intelligence-gathering." It was like Esset was begging for a reprimand, but Sergeant Warthog seemed to be in an amiable mood.

"More or less," the sergeant replied. She was what she was, and she looked it. Her garb was rough but practical, as was the sword across her back. She was past her prime, with a few grey threads in her brown hair, but she was still fit. She simply relied on her cunning and experience instead of brute strength. One eye was covered by a worn eye-patch, the string of which helped keep her hair out of her face. She may have been a battered ex-merc, but she was a *live* battered ex-merc, and a woman to boot. That counted for something, and it was only the case because she was smart.

She'd gotten out of the sell-sword business before she got too old to do it, and instead she'd built an intelligence network. She was a link between the people who needed jobs done and the people looking for those jobs—typically jobs that involved swinging swords, casting magic, or tracking down people or things. It was how she'd met Toman and Esset.

"Well, it's good you got out when you did. When you get old, you can't stay ahead of swords and arrows anymore," Esset said.

Past her prime or not, Sergeant Warthog could still deliver a lightning-quick cuff on the back of Esset's head before he could dodge it.

"You're living proof of how we 'old folk' are able to get the young and stupid to be our meatshields," the sergeant growled. "You don't think before you act any more than you think before you speak." Toman grinned—there was the admonishment he'd been expecting. "Now, how about we get back to the task at hand? What sort of plan have you two geniuses come up with?"

"It's tough to say without knowing the exact nature of the threat," Toman replied while Esset rubbed the back of his head ruefully. "This trip through the graveyard will have the statues fighting for us if there is a necromancer—or anything else. Dealing with undead doesn't typically take finesse. We'll wait outside the graveyard until one of the statues sees something—that sentry will light a torch and we'll come running. Esset can summon up a few horses to get us here fast. Then we fight whatever's here. Fire and stone are pretty effective at making undead problems go away."

"And I'll be standing out of the way, letting my meatshields do their work." Sergeant Warthog's grin was a tad wolfish. Esset was deliberately walking slightly out of her range now. They passed another statue and Toman once again moved closer to it so he could brush his fingers along the base.

Sergeant Warthog glanced at the setting sun to check the time; the shadows were lengthening further, but they still had plenty of daylight to work their way through the graveyard and make it a safe distance away by nightfall. In the meantime, the sky had become streaked with reds and oranges, promising fair weather the following day. All good, since they would likely be traveling again in the morning.

Toman stopped at another statue, drawing the sergeant's attention back to the graveyard. They'd actually lost Esset a few headstones back—he was reading the inscription, a lengthy one, by the looks of it—and Toman had already noticed his brother was too immersed in reading to notice anything else.

Both young men had magical abilities that Sergeant Warthog had never encountered personally before meeting them. In fact, she'd never even heard of an animator at all, and while summoners like Esset were far from unheard of, they weren't common. She'd also rarely seen two people as comfortable with their abilities as these two. Especially to use those abilities so casually.

Unable to resist his brother's complete inattention, Toman's eyes flicked to one of the statues he'd touched earlier. Slowly and silently, the statue bent down and picked up a very small pebble. Sergeant Warthog watched in amusement as the statue gently flicked the pebble and straightened. The rock bounced off Esset's back, eliciting a startled and amusingly high-pitched yelp. Esset looked back, and Toman had the statue wave mockingly at him. Esset immediately leveled a dirty look at Toman, the true culprit. Toman smirked and deliberately turned his back and continued on. Moments later, a different projectile thudded softly against Toman's back and bounced off again.

A tiny, supernatural bat fluttered in the air for a moment, then dive-bombed Toman from a different angle. Toman was laughing so hard he could barely shield his head. He flailed a bit, but the bat bounced off him twice more before zipping back to Esset, who had caught up. Esset held out his hand and the bat landed in it. Esset patted it on the head.

It was far from an ordinary bat. It was black and ashy, leaving sooty smudges on everything it touched. Close inspection would reveal that there were fine lines of molten red in its coal-like body, and its eyes were pinpricks of fiery light, small though they were. Too far away to hear, Esset had uttered a short incantation to summon it, but it took less than that to banish it, leaving nothing behind but air and the smudge on his hand.

They didn't even bother to banter after that, although plenty of smirks and grins were traded between them—they had evened out the score. Sergeant Warthog could only shake her head at the whole display. The potential lack of maturity might have bothered her, but she'd seen the other side to these two, and their track record spoke for itself.

Still, she was cautious. It remained to be seen what nightfall would bring.

CHAPTER 2

Several hours later, the dark sky held only the barest sliver of a moon. Esset squinted up at it, then looked around, trying to decide if there was enough light to read by. Finally he pulled the book out—it was an ancient-looking thing, for it was ancient. At the same time, it was in far better condition than it should have been, given its age, the frequency with which it was read, and how it was stored and treated in general. Thank Hyrishal for magic books.

Esset opened the tome and tilted it towards the moonlight, trying to catch enough light on the pages to make out the runes. Unfortunately, although the book was magic, that fact didn't make it readable in the dark. With a sigh, Esset stuffed it away again. His actions elicited a comment, but in a quiet murmur—they were far enough from the graveyard, but it was a reasonable precaution nonetheless.

"Really? Reading in the dark?" Sergeant Warthog asked. "I actually feel inclined to agree with your brother and all his teasing about how much reading you do."

"See?" Toman whispered.

Esset's glare at his brother was unmistakable, even in the dark.

"It's how I learn more summons," Esset said defensively, nonetheless keeping his voice low. "The more I read, the more likely I'll learn a new one. I mean, yeah, sometimes summons come to me at other times—like the horses. They came to me way back when I was thinking about how Toman and I had to travel—but that still wouldn't have happened unless I'd been reading my tome, and—"

"Torch!" Toman interrupted with a loud whisper; sure enough, a freshly-lit torch flickered in the distant cemetery. Rebuttal forgotten, the next words out of Esset's mouth were inhuman as he chanted three incantations to summon their mounts.

Three fiery horses materialized into existence before them with a brief roar of flames and the powerful smell of fresh-lit tinder. Nothing could run like these summoned horses, and Toman, Esset, and Sergeant Warthog wanted to be in the cemetery now. They swung up on the horses' warm backs of cracked coal, each barely mounted before the steeds took off, flickering tails of flame streaming behind them and leaving a faint scent of ash in their wake. In a flash, they were past the outer bounds of the cemetery and streaking towards the elaborate tomb where the torch had been lit.

An even quicker flash intercepted them before they reached the torchlight. Esset barely caught a glimpse of his attacker before he was hit like a battering ram from one side. As his mount streaked away, uncontrolled, his head cracked painfully against the ground, stunning him and making his vision spin. Toman and the sergeant were carried swiftly past, their mounts flaring with excess heat as Esset lost control of them.

Something was atop of Esset; even as his vision spun, he could feel a weight on his torso. Cold hands closed around his neck, cutting off his ability to speak, but he struggled against his assailant. He struggled on two fronts to break free: first to physically dislodge his attacker, and second to clearly think a summoning incantation to call supernatural aid. He stumbled over the strange syllables in his head, making it a little further each time, but each time he made a mental mistake he had to start anew.

A moment later, he felt a rush of air as his assailant was bashed away from him. There was an inhuman screech and crunches of stone while Esset gasped for air, reflexively curling in on himself to try to recover as quickly as possible.

There. There was the incantation, the thoughts in his head as clear and precise as they would have been spoken. There was a flash of flames, then heat and the glow of embers next to him. At once eerie and fierce in the darkness, a creature of fire stood next to him.

The lupine beast had a hide like cracked coals, blackened and ashy, but crimson light glowed in the small cracks and crevices upon its body. Its claws were red-hot, and when it opened its maw, there was a flare of light; its insides were molten, its teeth white-hot. Its eyes too were ablaze, the light trailing slightly as the creature moved. And it wasn't still for long. A bare moment after appearing, it lunged away to find Esset's attacker.

"Esset!" With a shout, Toman was next to his brother and hauling him up to his feet. Esset glanced at his brother—the dirt all over his coat betrayed that he'd bailed off the fire horse as soon as Esset had lost control.

"Esset, the horses," Toman said.

"Already got them," Esset said hoarsely. What was summoned sometimes had to be unsummoned; even the relatively tame fire horses could cause a lot of mayhem if left to their own devices.

"The sergeant?" Esset asked, and the sergeant herself answered, only a few paces behind.

"Here." She held her sword loosely in one hand, ready.

"Well, Mr. Johnson was right. There's something here, but there's no way that was a necromancer or anything that had been raised. Too fast. Too strong." Esset said. He summoned another wolf, making it sound more like a curse than an incantation. The wolf streaked after the first, and in seconds they converged on their target. Toman, Esset, and Sergeant Warthog sprinted to catch up, curious to see what they were fighting.

Once they arrived, it was difficult to determine what exactly the wolves had engaged, for the only light in the graveyard came from the wolves themselves. The clearest illumination came just before their jaws opened and the light within was cast upon their target: humanoid, pale skin, fast, strong—

"Vampire," Esset finally identified the figure before them. No wonder the statue that had saved Esset hadn't been able to get a hold on it—stone was persistent, but not particularly quick. Vampires were quick.

The wolves were equally quick. Using numbers to their advantage, one of the wolves lunged and got a solid grip on the vampire's arm, creating a momentary lapse in defense that allowed the other to latch its jaws around the vampire's neck. There was an inhuman screech as the wolves' internal fire scorched through arm and throat. The vampire didn't die, however, until its neck was burned entirely through: decapitation by fire.

Esset banished one of his two wolves, and Toman called over the statue that had the torch as the three of them walked the remaining distance to the fallen vampire. The remaining wolf dashed off into the darkness, circling them, hunting for any other opponents.

"So, undead. Just not the undead we thought," Toman observed. At least they could kill with a clear conscience. Vampires were purely evil; anything good or even human in them wiped out when they turned.

Esset twitched at the inaccuracy of his brother's statement. "Actually, there's a controversy over whether vampires actually die when they transform, so 'undead' isn't really an accurate term," Esset said, unable to resist the correction. He knew Toman already knew that, but he didn't know if the sergeant did. Sergeant Warthog, however, didn't react, and Toman just rolled his eyes and otherwise ignored the comment.

"I've got that packhorse I animated earlier headed this way. The village will want proof that this is what Mr. Johnson saw— and that it's dead," Toman said.

"We had better make sure there aren't more," Esset said grimly, examining the corpse of the vampire.

"Well my sentries certainly aren't picking them up, or there'd be a lot more movement in this cemetery," Toman replied. Esset nodded.

"That being said, stone soldiers aren't particularly smart, and their senses aren't all that keen, so it's possible they missed something, especially with vampires." His explanation was for Sergeant Warthog's benefit; Toman already knew intimately the limitations of his animations.

"So it's up to me," Esset said. "I'm going to look through my wolf's eyes. I'll need you two keeping an eye out for me, since I'll be totally oblivious to my own body." Had it just been him and Toman, he wouldn't have said anything—they'd worked together more than long enough for it to go unsaid—but Esset assumed Sergeant Warthog would want to know what was going on.

Esset sat down on the ground and crossed his legs, settling into a meditative pose. It was important that his core was balanced and that he would be able to maintain the position without conscious effort. Meanwhile, Toman was calling up the statues in the immediate vicinity to come and form a protective guard around the two of them.

Every time Esset looked through the eyes of one of his summons, he was soundly reminded how unearthly they actually were. Simply inhuman didn't cover it; their perception was more than simply altered. It bordered on indescribable. Everything was afire to their eyes; there was constant motion and flickering, and everything was cast in the colors of flame, from white-hot, to blue and yellow, to red. The senses mixed; scents were not just smelled but seen and heard and felt, and every other sensation was experienced in every other combination. And further, Esset knew that "looking through his wolf's eyes" really wasn't an accurate description, for he experienced everything that the wolf physically did. There were no shared thoughts or emotions though, thank Hyrishal. It was difficult enough to learn and adjust to the altered perceptions as it was, even after the innumerable times he'd experienced this before. To share thought and emotion with the summon would have been utterly unbearable. Madness would ensue.

Esset took a few moments, as he always did, to accustom himself to the change. The wolf's head swung back and forth, taking in every little sight, sound, smell, and sensation. Esset filtered the inputs and then set the wolf in motion towards the mausoleum where Mr. Johnson had first reported seeing movement. Esset had the beast move at a lope—fast enough to cover ground but slow enough to take everything in. Even so, Esset felt like the wolf was flying, for the altered, flickering perception made their movement seem faster. The wolf paused at the entrance to the mausoleum before carefully stepping inside.

A rank smell washed over the summon's senses: the scent was an ugly brown and as discordant as nails on slate. So overwhelming was the sensation that Esset almost missed the movement inside.

Esset's consciousness fled back to his body, and he surged to his feet.

"We have to get to the mausoleum. Now." He was moving before he was finished speaking, and Toman and Sergeant Warthog were right there with him.

"More?" Toman asked as they ran; it was a relatively obvious conclusion.

"At least nine," Esset replied, not wasting much breath to answer. "Get your statues there. We can't afford to let any past us. They're still in coffins now, but they won't be for long."

"Nine is bad news," Sergeant Warthog said grimly. Toman

was already calling on his animated soldiers.

"Nine *is* bad news, but if we can trap some in their coffins, even temporarily, we can even the odds enough to get them all. They're strong enough to smash their way out of their coffins, even stone ones, but they're usually loathe to do so, since revisiting and sleeping in their original burial place allows them accelerated healing. The destruction of a coffin is the destruction of a great future advantage for a vampire," Esset explained as they ran. He wished the mausoleum were slightly closer. At least Toman had some statues ahead—they would get there first and hold them off until the three of them could arrive.

"But when it realizes that it's dead *now* if it stays in the coffin…" Toman put in.

"Then the coffin is worthless, and they'll be out in seconds," Sergeant Warthog said, easily reaching the correct conclusion.

"Exactly," Esset said. They were almost to the entrance of the mausoleum. Esset had left his wolf in place, and it was already wreaking havoc on the first vampire to emerge. Esset wasn't currently in control of the summon, but it was naturally inclined to attack anything that moved, and at the moment, there wasn't anyone around that Esset didn't want hurt. He figured the crypt's current denizens would keep it both busy and happy enough that it would stick around and do damage where it was supposed to. And if not, well, the cemetery was far enough out that Esset would have plenty of time to get it back under control before it could get anywhere else.

Esset and Toman burst into the mausoleum first, Esset with an incantation on his lips and Toman with a belt unraveling from his waist and flowing up his arm. The belt flew from Toman's hand— it almost looked like he'd thrown it, but it moved of its own volition. It whipped towards the nearest vampire, winding around its feet and trying to trip it up.

Esset's incantation spawned a second wolf, which immediately launched itself at the nearest vampire. Five coffins had statues keeping them shut by the time they'd stepped inside, and only two of the other vampires had woken up and emerged— both were engaged with Esset's second summoned wolf.

Esset chanted the syllables twice more, and three wolves ganged up on a single vampire and tore it to pieces. Inhuman screeches filled the air, and the rest of the vampires were suddenly very awake and aware of threats. Wood splintered and exploded outwards as one vampire smashed its way out around the stone sentry holding the coffin lid in place. The statue tried to grab the vampire, but the emerging creature lashed out with both feet and staggered the stone soldier for long enough to get out of reach. As this transpired, a second vampire used similar tactics to escape, only it bashed and broke the fingers of the statue guarding it so it couldn't grasp it and hold it in place. Both vampires hissed and bared their fangs when they saw the nature of their foes, seeming more animal than human as they found themselves facing fiery creatures from another plane.

The wolves snarled as they darted, snapped, and lunged, their growls reminiscent of crackling flames. The vampires were comparatively quiet, despite their efforts to escape and attack the wolves and statues. Esset kept an especially close eye on one of the two who had gotten clear of its coffin; Esset swore it kept glancing at the three humans by the door. Vampires weren't dumb, and it would be easy to figure out that killing the ones controlling the wolves and statues would solve all their problems neatly.

From Esset's left came a crunch of wood and a triumphant screech. Another vampire erupted from its coffin. The statue bracing it—a delicately-carved angel—caught it by the throat in a lucky grab, turning the screech into a gargle. The vampire flailed for a moment before regaining its self-control, and it aimed all its blows into one spot on the statue's upper arm. Under the onslaught, the stone fractured, then broke—the angel's grip slipped to the vampire's shoulder, but with a vicious yank, the vampire broke away. Still, the vampire appeared weakened, and staggered erratically as it got out of range.

Trying to take advantage of an opportunity, Esset diverted one of his wolves to take it down quickly—a mistake. The injured vampire dodged in time, and the vampire who'd been eyeing them earlier made its move. Quicker than expected, it slipped past the wolves and sprang at Esset, its fingers hooked like claws towards his face.

"Look out!" Toman's warning was slower than his action as he shoved Esset to the side, pushing his brother's body into a pillar. A statue followed up Toman's defense with a sideways swing of its spear, narrowly missing Toman to belt the vampire in the stomach and throw him back. The vampire ricocheted off a different statue but caught himself and tried to retreat, but instead found himself trapped between a statue and one of the fiery wolves. The wolf lunged forward. The vampire tried to dodge but erred too close to the statue, which grabbed him. The vampire went down in a screaming rage, held in place as the wolf tore off first its arm, then its head. The sickening scent of burning flesh flooded the room.

The scream galvanized the remaining vampires into smashing their way out of their coffins. Esset noticed an earlier escapee—it must have climbed out when they'd been distracted with their bold attacker. Toman had a few statues in the fray, but there wasn't the space to bring in more. Although Toman was cursing the close quarters, they didn't dare move the battle outside where a vampire could easily escape in the darkness.

Besides, the vampires were dancing circles around his comparatively slow statues. As he watched, one vampire ducked under the swinging arm of one soldier statue and then used it to block the attack of one of Esset's wolves. The wolf's jaws closed around the statue's arm instead of the vampire's, leaving a blackened mark upon the stone. At the same time, the vampire struck out at the wolf from behind the statue, stabbing down on its head with an ornamental dagger. The wolf vanished in a burst of sparks and ash.

The statue tried to turn and grab the vampire, but stone was too slow once more. Esset cursed and then chanted, replacing the wolf that had been taken out of play. Another wolf materialized and lunged forward, but not before the vampire managed to clamber onto the statue's back and bash the stone soldier's head off. Fortunately, the statue could operate just as well without it. The vampire hissed and leapt away when it realized it had wasted its reprieve on a useless tactic, and the game of strike and evade continued.

So intent was Esset on replacing his fallen unit that his attention to his other summon had slipped. Movement—too close—caught his attention. One of his own wolves, heedless of its summoner's safety in its quest to destroy its target, was lunging sideways towards him. Esset started to dodge, but he knew he was too slow. He raised his arms to shield his face and braced for impact, only to find a stone form between him and the wolf.

Toman's guardian statue had intercepted in time. The wolf bounced off its rocky torso, leaving a scorch mark, but otherwise neither seemed to notice the interaction. The wolf tore into its vampire target again, and the statue stood guard. Only a glance between Toman and Esset acknowledged the close call as the battle continued. Close quarters indeed.

The sergeant was still behind them, sword drawn. There was little else she could do in a battle like this. If she ventured into the battle, it wouldn't take long before she was injured—or worse—by either a vampire or one of Esset's wolves. The skirmish was simply too chaotic. She could only watch—and yell suggestions.

"Esset, we could use more wolves!" the sergeant said. She was right—two wolves per vampire would be far more effective.

"Sorry, Sergeant, four is as many as I can summon at a time. We have to work with what we have," Esset replied. The sergeant cursed as only sergeants could.

"But she's right, Toman, we need a new tactic," Esset said. More wood crunched across the mausoleum, and Esset saw two vampires grappling with their stone guards. That left only one more still struggling to become free of its coffin.

"It's arriving," Toman replied. "I've got all that rope loaded on our packhorse. It ought to speed things up in here." He'd given up on his belt earlier—the shorter length was too easy for the vampires to dodge.

True to his word, a long length of rope slithered into the mausoleum just as the last vampire burst from its coffin; it was smarter than the others, and it had kicked out the end of the coffin, getting clear before the statue could pin it down. It recoiled away from the battle, climbing up into the rafters to survey the battle-scene. Esset could see it decide that fleeing was preferable to fighting. He saw it come down just above the door, but his wolves were busy—he couldn't intercept its escape. He could only hope Toman had something up his sleeve.

Before the vampire knew what was happening, a thick rope on the ground had snaked its way up and around its body, constricting around its legs and arms to pin it helplessly so it fell over onto the ground. Three of the statues outside came forward and picked the vampire up. One grabbed the vampire's head, another its shoulders, another its legs. They tore the head off the prone vampire, oblivious to its struggles. By then, Esset had already turned his attention back to his own battles, leaving Toman to his.

That was when he noticed that both of the vampires that had been grappling with statues had gotten free—and one was missing entirely. Esset did a head count twice to confirm, then cursed.

"Darkfires, we lost one."

Sergeant Warthog cursed too.

"Well, we still have to finish this battle," she said. They'd have to worry about the other one later.

The rope-snake and the statues hadn't lingered around the dead vampire. The statues made a protective ring around the mausoleum, ready to stop any others from escaping. The rope-snake struck out at another victim, entangling the vampire. The fiery wolf it fought lunged and dragged the vampire down by the shoulder; once on the ground, it snapped its molten jaws around the vampire's neck and finished the job. Then it whirled and lunged again, this time at the back of one of its kindred's opponents.

The vampire was knocked forward into the other wolf, which made good the opportunity. It snapped down on the vampire's arm and jerked it sideways. The other wolf locked its jaws on its midriff, holding it down as the first wolf's glowing hot fangs closed on the vampire's face and dissolved it to ash.

Esset glanced up and noticed one of the vampires had escaped to the rafters to hiss down at the battle. It couldn't escape, but it knew that if it came down, it was dead. The rope-snake harried another vampire—it slithered and struck, but the vampire stayed just ahead of it. Then two wolves cornered it against the outer row of coffins; they came from opposite sides, one high, one low. The vampire charged the left one head on, defiant in the face of certain death. The wolf tore out its throat, then melted through the rest of its neck with a second bite.

Fleeing two wolves of its own, the last vampire on the floor made to join its kindred in the rafters. It leapt at a pillar and started to scale, but the wolves could leap as high; one sprang and clamped its jaws around the vampire's ankle, dragging it down. The other sprang higher and tackled the vampire off the pillar entirely. The vampire wailed as the wolves tore it apart.

The last vampire could only hiss at them from above as the wolves paced below.

"Toman, Sergeant, go," Esset said. "I've got this." The two departed to hunt the escaped vampire as Esset banished two of his wolves before they could get antsy.

In place of the two wolves, he had summoned a bird. The bird was huge, large enough to carry a person on its back or in its talons—or both. It made the small space of the mausoleum even smaller, and Esset could feel the scorching heat that flooded from its feathers. The summoner was forced to raise an arm to protect his face from the heat of the fires. Sparks flew everywhere as it beat its wings, flipping its underbelly up so it could grab the rafters with its talons. The vampire didn't stand a chance; it was too shocked by the appearance of this new foe to move, and it was only just starting to react when the bird struck out with its great beak. Moments later, it was over, and Esset let the bird hop back down and fly out of the mausoleum to spiral up into the night sky.

The summoner followed it out with one wolf beside him and another behind him, each restlessly doing his bidding. They both automatically lunged to the left, and it was all Esset could do to hold them back, knowing that their target could just as easily be his friends as the last vampire. When Esset saw torchlight up ahead, and that which it illuminated, he went ahead and banished the wolves. Toman and the sergeant looked over at him as he approached.

"You know, occasionally, the things I animate surprise me," the animator remarked calmly. They'd caught it.

The last vampire had managed to sneak out, but it had run afoul of Toman's statues. Likely by luck alone, one of the statues of a spear-wielding soldier had surprised it and had managed to ram into the creature with its weapon. The spear was impaled at least a foot deep into the wall, but not before it had passed through the vampire's shoulder, effectively pinning it in place. The only way the creature could have escaped would have been to tear off its own arm. But that was no longer an option. A second soldier, a pair to the first, had rammed its spear through the vampire's abdomen while it was pinned to the wall. That was when Toman had arrived.

The creature wasn't dead. In fact, it probably wouldn't die for a long while, if left there: a day or two, possibly longer. But nor would it be able to survive.

"Well then," Esset replied neutrally, surveying the vampire. Toman stared at it with steely determination. Sergeant Warthog kept an eye on the vampire, but she was as interested in Esset and Toman's behavior as their prisoner's.

Toman spoke to the vampire dispassionately. "You're going to die. Answer my questions, and I'll make sure you don't suffer in agony for days before your end comes about." The vampire hissed in defiance, baring its considerable fangs.

"How many of you were there?" Toman asked, ignoring the hiss. The creature spat at him. Toman ignored that gesture too. Calling the creature's bluff, he looked at the statue next to him and it leaned, shifting its spear slightly to the side. The creature screeched its unholy, chilling screech. Esset hid a wince and glanced away.

"Why should I tell you anything? You took everything from me. The power...gone now." Its glare was absolutely venomous in the flickering torchlight.

"I told you why," Toman answered. "How many?" He reached out one hand and leaned briefly on the stone spear again. Esset twitched twice, once at the vampire's screech, and once again when he caught Sergeant Warthog's measuring look.

"No!" the vampire screamed. Toman was unimpressed. The vampire gave another shriek of fury, this time truncated when Toman pulled back and crossed his arms, waiting.

"Fine!" the vampire spat. "You win. There is no victory in silence anyways." Only pride had held its tongue; pain had subdued that pride.

"There were ten of us, including our creator. You killed the patriarch first—we felt him die. Now kill me," the vampire demanded. Its teeth were still bared, but it seemed to have deflated, hanging limply against its brutal restraints.

"Not yet. How were there so many of you?" Toman asked. One or two was common, and even three wasn't unusual. Ten was rare and a dangerously high number of vampires in one group.

The vampire stared at Toman almost petulantly for a moment, but he spoke immediately when Toman feinted towards the spear.

"The patriarch—he had a plan. A small force first, he said. He plotted with us when we were still human—we agreed, all of us, to let him change us. And the power..." The vampire's tongue slipped out between its fangs to lick its lips. "It was worth it. A small, elite force first, and we'd take the town a bit at a time. Conversion or death. Enough would turn that he'd have fodder to build an army. Next, a civilization! But you..." There was a flash of defiance, and then it slipped away again. "You destroyed everything. A few more days and we would have been ready, but you stopped us. Are you satisfied?"

Unable to keep his silence, Esset blurted, "You sacrificed your humanity to become...this?" The vampire glared at him.

"I am *better* now. Or I was. I am faster and stronger. I have no remorse or conscience to slow me down." The vampire stared at Esset in contempt before looking at Toman again.

"Kill me, human. Keep your word," the vampire said. Toman glanced at his brother, who looked away. Next Toman looked to the sergeant, who gave an indifferent shrug. Toman regarded the helpless vampire for a moment, then nodded. He stepped back and another of the armed statues stepped into his place.

"Bright Hyrishal save you if you've any soul left," Esset murmured. Both Toman and Esset turned away as the statue beheaded the vampire, ensuring it would never rise again. Sergeant Warthog observed the execution without emotion.

"That seemed like it should fall on the unethical side for you guys," she remarked. Esset looked uncomfortably at Toman, then away again.

"I don't like it, but sometimes torture is necessary," Toman said. The sergeant looked back to Esset.

"Esset disagrees," she remarked.

"Yes," Esset replied, but silence followed the brief response. Behind them, the statues began to clean up on Toman's silent order. The decapitated vampire was carried back into the mausoleum to be laid neatly on the floor, its detached head propped against its neck.

Toman finally spoke.

"Vampires aren't human anymore. When a good person is bitten, they die. Bad people turn. A human being can be redeemed. When a vampire turns, anything good in them is destroyed. They're empty, acting on instinct and greed. They can control themselves when they want to, but only to protect or further their own interests. They're monsters. Even Esset doesn't have qualms about killing them. It's just the torture that upsets him."

"Torture is always wrong," Esset said quietly. "At the very least, it damages the soul of the one who is doing the torturing." This was old territory for Toman and Esset. Each of them knew the other's stance. They'd fought in a war together, and there was nothing like a war to bring out those kinds of ethical differences in people.

The sergeant looked between them again, but neither spoke again, so she changed the subject. "What about the vampire's story. Do we buy it?" she asked.

"Sure, but we verify there aren't any more," Toman said with a shrug.

"There's a chance the vampire was lying," Esset acknowledged. "But I doubt it. Its defiance was out of spite only. It caved too easily to have been protecting anything, even if a vampire could ever be inclined to protect anything but itself. It wanted to die. Telling the truth would bring death. Why would it lie when the truth would serve it better?"

"True," Sergeant Warthog said.

"I should scout the area now," Esset said, obviously disinclined to talk much more. His soul felt heavy with the night's events. Dawn couldn't come soon enough.

CHAPTER 3

"To our heroes!" One man's toast turned into many men's cheers.

"To think, last night we were unaware of the threat. This morning, we were presented with proof of its elimination. Tonight, we celebrate! The women and old folk had their fun, now we get ours!" Another cheer rose up. The sun was hardly down, but it didn't take long for the village men to get their celebrations well underway.

Toman leaned over to Esset.

"I'm not sure a small, brief gathering to thank us and give us our payment qualifies as 'celebration,' but okay," he said with a grin.

"They're men. What do you expect?" Sergeant Warthog said, but she was smiling wryly. Toman and Esset both gave her strange looks but were saved from having to reply by the arrival of the barmaid.

The cute one.

"Drinks on the house for our heroes tonight," she said, smiling as she leaned forward and placed three mugs of ale on the table. Her ample breasts threatened to pop out of her blouse as she leaned forward, a deliberate technique, since the top button was undone. Esset saw and looked away, somehow managing to keep his blush down to a faint pink instead of deep scarlet. Toman's grin only widened.

"Thank you so much, Miss…?" he prompted.

"Roberta," she replied before tossing her blonde curls over her shoulder and turning with an exaggerated swing of her hips. Toman enjoyed watching her departure, too.

"See, Esset? It's easy. Instead of blushing and looking away, just ask her name," Toman said.

"I'm not blushing," Esset said, but his blush deepened closer to red as he protested. Toman snorted.

"If you say so. You just don't know what to do with a woman

who's not in her holy day-dress—"

"Nothing wrong with modesty," Esset said.

"We all know Esset thinks he's in one of the old tales, fighting dragons to rescue princesses. Why, I doubt our scholar would settle for less than True Love." The way Toman emphasized "true love" made the concept sound exaggerated.

"Just because I like the old tales doesn't mean I think I'm in one. Besides, Toman, you said *you* wanted a woman you could respect."

"Aye, but that doesn't mean I can't enjoy the view in the meantime," Toman said, still watching the barmaid from across the room. "Sometimes I think you're too religious for your own good, brother."

"We don't have time to chase girls anyways," Esset muttered.

"*You* might not. You spend all your time with your nose buried in books," Toman said.

"If you two keep bickering, I'll make sure you have so many jobs you won't even have time to sleep," Sergeant Warthog growled. Both brothers fell silent.

"Better," the sergeant muttered, taking a swig of her ale. "But I think I'm going to step outside anyways. You two enjoy yourselves."

"I think we irritated her," Toman remarked after the sergeant had left the bar.

"You mean *you* irritated her," Esset said with a smirk. "Some ladies' man you are."

Toman frowned.

"She's just cranky." In truth, neither could begin to imagine wooing the sergeant, even if they'd wanted to. Which they didn't.

"If you say so." Esset's smirk widened into a grin.

"So do you think she'll help us with Moloch?" Toman asked, suddenly serious.

"I don't know. It's a huge risk," Esset replied, letting him change the subject.

"This felt like a test, and I don't know if we passed or not." Toman looked down at his gloves.

"Hst, Roberta's coming back," Esset said, suddenly nervous again, despite his professed disinterest in the busty barmaid.

"Fresh ale?" she asked, lifting three mugs.

"I'm afraid we've lost our third," Toman said.

"Actually, I was hoping I could join you. I'm on break," Roberta said, ducking her head.

"Of course." Toman was already scooting over so she could sit next to him. She pushed the ales towards them before smoothing her skirt and sitting.

"Now I'm definitely glad we were persuaded to stay the day before heading home," Toman said.

"It's Toman Atrix-Iiren, right?" she asked Toman.

"Just Toman," Toman replied with a nod.

"And Jonathan Esset?"

"Just Esset," Esset said.

"Not Jonathan?" Roberta was surprised.

"He thinks it's too ordinary a name. My brother here is in love with the old tales of magic and might. 'Jon' or 'Jonathan' is far too dull," Toman said. Esset shot a look at him.

"I've always thought John to be a respectable name," Roberta said, looking at Esset curiously.

"I just prefer Esset," Esset said with a shrug, trying—too late—to play it off.

"Well, I'm sorry to bother you guys—" she started.

"Not at all," Toman interjected. Roberta smiled shyly.

"But I'm so curious. Everyone says you used magic to beat the vampires. This town is so backward… I've never seen real magic before."

"Well I'd be glad to show you some," Toman said. He held out his hand, palm up, as the tiny, slender belt that was wound around his wrist came to life. It unbuckled itself and slithered into his hand before coiling upwards, its "head" up and swaying back and forth, behaving like a snake mesmerized by someone playing a flute.

"Wow," Roberta said, her voice breathy. Roberta reached towards the belt-snake, and it nuzzled against her fingers. Esset was torn between feeling jealous and wanting to roll his eyes at his brother's display.

"That's amazing," Roberta said once Toman had directed the belt to wrap back around his wrist and become a belt once more.

"It has its limitations," Toman said, exercising at least *some* humility. "I can only animate things I touch, and I have to be able to imagine them as some kind of animal or a person. The more complex the item, with more pieces, the harder it is to animate. And I can't animate living things, obviously."

"So that's how you used the statues then," Roberta said.

"Yup. Statues are easiest. No imagination required to imagine it acting like exactly what it looks like."

"I've never even *heard* of magic like yours," Roberta said. "And I love stories about magic. I always get the inn's bards to tell those kinds of tales."

"As far as I know, I'm the only animator in existence. Or rather, the only one to specialize in this kind of magic," Toman said. He had no intention of elaborating any further. "Esset's magic is pretty uncommon too. There are other summoners, but they can't necessarily summon the kinds of things he can."

"Can I see, Esset?" Roberta asked.

"My abilities aren't, uh, so innocently demonstrable," Esset said.

Roberta blinked.

"If I summon something, I'll probably burn down the inn," Esset said.

"Oh," Roberta said. Esset wasn't being strictly truthful—he had one "innocent" summon, the bat, but it wasn't exactly impressive. Roberta looked disappointed, and Esset shifted in his seat. He glanced at his brother, who looked amused. Esset opened his mouth to speak, but Roberta suddenly made an exasperated sound.

"I'm sorry, I'm supposed to get a longer break than this, but my boss is waving me over." She got to her feet and flashed a smile at them—no, at Toman.

"That's too bad," Toman said with genuine regret.

"Maybe later?" Roberta asked, taking only the tiniest steps away from them. Toman grinned his affirmative, and she scurried back to the bar. Then Toman was smirking at Esset again.

"Innocently demonstrable?" Toman asked.

"Shut up."

Dawn broke upon three fleeting shapes in the sky, rushing to greet the coming sun. Hills, trees, winding roads, and wildlife blurred beneath the three birds of stone and their riders until they reached a small lake. The massive stone birds slowed and circled to land beside the small body of water, and their riders dismounted stiffly.

"Ugh, I have to admit, Esset, your birds are a lot warmer to ride, especially at those high altitudes," Toman said as he stretched.

"It's not too bad this time of year," Esset said. "And besides, I can only summon two of mine at a time, and mine are so much faster that one person would end up being left behind."

"I know, I know," Toman said.

Sergeant Warthog had dismounted and stretched without comment and was already at the water's edge, refilling her waterskin. The two brothers joined her, filling their skins and drinking their fill before refilling them again. Toman strode back towards their mounts and stowed his away in one of the bags strapped to the stone birds. Sergeant Warthog had already stowed hers and was mounting up again. Toman was on his own bird's back before he realized that Esset hadn't joined them.

"Oi! Slowpoke!" he yelled. Esset didn't respond, so Toman had his bird tromp awkwardly over. The animator was about to poke fun at Esset again—or maybe just get the bird to poke him—when Esset spoke, eyes fixed on the horizon.

"Do you see that? At first I thought it was clouds, but now I think that it's smoke." Esset pointed into the distance, where sure enough, a faint halo nestled on the far side of the base of a small mountain.

"Hey, what's the hold up? I want to get home," Sergeant Warthog called over. Toman steered his bird back over to her, with Esset trotting close behind.

"Do you mind a small detour? Esset might've spotted something," Toman replied as Esset mounted up.

"As loathe as I am to extend this trip…" Sergeant Warthog said, glancing between them.

"It might be important," Esset said, and his stone mount burst into flight.

The closer they got, the more apparent it became that it was smoke. Only the mountain in the way had facilitated that illusion.

The wind shifted to blow the air towards them, and it brought the scent of death.

Devastation stretched out before them. Where once a small village had stood, there was now ashes and destruction. Surveying the scene from above, Toman, Esset, and Sergeant Warthog hovered, clustered together.

Fire still consumed the village's structures, slowly spreading from one house to the next across grass and hedges between the homes. Some structures were already ash, some nearly so, and only a few were untouched. But fire was the least of it. The earth was scorched or broken in places. Jagged holes and clean slices had demolished many of the buildings before the fires even reached them. And the people…everyone was dead, and no one had gone quietly or swiftly. Toman closed his eyes against a flood of memories.

"Moloch," Toman said. No one gainsaid him. Everyone knew the dark mage was behind this.

"It couldn't have been long before dawn that he'd…finished," Toman said, his voice tight. They hadn't missed him by much.

"There's nothing we could have done anyways," Esset said, but quietly, so quietly he wasn't sure his words even reached his companion's ears before being snatched away by the winds.

"Look for survivors," the sergeant ordered.

"I doubt we'll find any," Toman said bitterly.

"You survived," Esset said. Toman stared at the rubble before answering.

"Sometimes I think he left me alive on purpose," Toman said. Abruptly, his bird dove and began flying at a low altitude to survey the ruin. Esset and Sergeant Warthog joined him, searching and calling out for survivors, but there was only death.

Finally Toman landed his bird and placed his hands on the earth; it was time to bury the dead. The earth slowly began to shift beneath his fingers as Sergeant Warthog landed beside him.

"What are you doing?" she asked.

"Making something to bury the dead. I don't just animate; I can also create. It just takes longer," Toman replied. The earth swelled, promising to take shape but still amorphous. Sergeant Warthog watched for a time before speaking again.

"What happened here is terrible, but can we be sure this was

Moloch?" she asked.

"Yes," Toman said. The silence waxed long and the earth shaped in accordance with Toman's will, rising up and beginning to form four legs and the bulk of a body.

"How can we be sure?" Sergeant Warthog finally asked.

"Have you forgotten? I've seen his aftermath before," Toman replied, his voice emotionless.

"You were just a child then. A very small child, if memory serves," the sergeant said.

"Yes," Toman agreed. "But you don't forget something like that." The earthen form lengthened to include a head-like protrusion, and the legs narrowed. Toman concentrated on the figure for a few moments before continuing. The shaping of earth paused as he pointed.

"Do you see that scorch mark?" he asked.

The sergeant nodded. It was a couple paces from a prone, bloody body.

"I can tell you how that scorch mark came to be. I can tell you exactly what happened. Moloch was here," Toman said, pointing, "and black lightning arced from his fingers to that spot. He was aiming at that woman, the woman now dead on the ground. She thought he'd missed, and she'd felt an irrational, futile surge of hope as she fled. But, you see, the black lightning entered the ground and shot through it, arcing back up with fingers—claws— of glass to impale her in two dozen places at least. Her own weight snapped the glass tendrils, and she fell back, but she didn't die right away. No, she laid there for some time until she bled to death in agony." Toman could see it happening as he spoke, for he'd seen it before. The face of the newly dead simply painted over the blurred faces of distant memory.

"And that man?" Toman pointed now at a red, mangled corpse that even the sergeant had paled upon witnessing. Even had they known the man in life, there was no recognizing him now. There were no features left to recognize.

"That man was skinned alive. One strip at a time, as he was held immobile by magic. He could only move enough to scream as his flesh was stripped away. The two bodies by that nearby structure would have been his family, and Moloch would have forced them to watch before he burned the child to death in its mother's arms and then killed her with a stroke that laid her open from pelvis to throat.

"I know what happened because I survived the horrors that befell this village. I may have been young, but I'll never forget. I can't."

The sergeant stared at him, her face only neutral from long practice. Toman turned away and resumed shaping his new animation. It slowly took shape as a massive dog; Toman didn't bother putting any details or finishing touches on it—he just sent it to start digging in a field next to the town. They would need many graves.

The sergeant left to do another sweep for survivors as he started on another.

Toman stood back and watched wearily as a roughly human earthen-animation picked up a corpse. The golem tucked in the brutalized body's limbs before sliding its "hands" underneath it and lifting gently. Toman wanted to ensure that at least in death, everyone would be treated with the utmost dignity. The golem plodded to the field where one massive grave waited.

Esset descended on a fiery bird to land beside Toman. Once his own feet were on the ground, the summoned creature vanished in a small spray of sparks and ash. Esset looked at the sun, now high in the sky, marking how much time had passed. He had a dead rabbit in his hand, dangling by the ears.

"No survivors. Nothing at all alive for quite a ways. Even the wildlife is dead. I figured being harvested for death magic wouldn't impact its edibility, so I picked this guy for dinner." Esset waved the rabbit in front of Toman, who just stared at it blankly.

Esset looked away. "Or we could just leave it, if no one's hungry. It was dead anyways."

"Esset..." Toman said.

"Yeah?" Esset had to wait a bit before Toman could articulate his question.

"How does blood magic work? I mean, I know it comes from death and pain and blood, but how does it *work*?" Toman asked. "You're the scholar, you've studied this, right?"

"A bit," Esset admitted. "Honestly, we don't know a ton about magic in general, just *that* it works, and sometimes a bit of how.

Blood magic... Well, it seems to be based in life energy. Whenever blood is spilled, energy is released. The amount of magic that's produced is related to the amount of blood spilled and the amount of pain generated.

"Death magic is just a kind of blood magic. The strongest kind. There's a predictable burst of magic that's released in the moment when someone dies. Even people who can't sense magic can still find ways to capture and use that energy." Esset paused before adding, "It's an *easy* kind of magic to do." He sounded sick and disgusted when he said "easy."

"Do you think that's why he does it?" Toman asked.

"Moloch?"

Toman nodded.

"I dunno. Evil is just...evil, sometimes." Esset shrugged.

Toman waited.

"Well, I mean, the Book of Bright Hyrishal says that all men can be redeemed, and it's not like Moloch's a vampire or something, so technically he shouldn't be one hundred percent evil." Esset paused briefly. "Although with everything he's done with blood magic and everything else... It is possible he's sold his soul to the Darkfires. Why, what are you thinking?"

"I don't know," Toman confessed. "I just... I guess I don't understand how someone gets from being human to being...whatever Moloch is. I get wanting to be stronger, I do, and I can even imagine desperation driving someone to use blood magic. And I guess things could snowball from there."

Esset studied Toman for a few moments.

"But that's not what's bothering you," Esset said.

"No. It's something I heard once. I heard he was the son of a nobleman, rich and comfortable, and that they cast him out because they caught him torturing a child. He didn't need power, he had it. He just...wanted to. He enjoyed it," Toman said.

"Moloch's blood magic has kept him young, so he's too old for anyone living to have been around when he came into his power. We can't know if that's true." Esset shifted his weight from foot to foot.

"But that concept bothers you too," Toman said.

Esset shrugged, but his face betrayed his discomfort.

Sergeant Warthog strode up, interrupting their conversation.

"Well, I think we've done all we can here," she said. "As soon as your animations are done burying the dead, we should leave. We'll have to stop and spread word of this on our way, so we'll want to use as much daylight as we can." The two young men just nodded. All three stared at the destruction of the village, disinclined to move despite their agreement with the sergeant's sentiment. Finally the sergeant broke the silence.

"Do you really think you can take *this* on?" Sergeant Warthog waved an arm towards the annihilated town.

Toman looked at the sergeant, her words galvanizing him with energy. "You think we can witness this and *not try*? We're strong in our own right, Sergeant. With your help and resources, and a good plan, we can take him," Toman said.

Sergeant Warthog shook her head and stared grimly at the dying fires.

Toman waited, but when it became clear she wasn't going to say anything more, he stood in front of her and met her eyes. "First Moloch killed my parents, and then Animator Eldan Atrix, after he took me in. Moloch is the reason why I was all alone before Esset's family took me in. Moloch has been destroying lives, destroying entire *villages,* for a couple centuries at least, and he will keep doing it until he's stopped. Someone has to stop him."

Sergeant Warthog met his gaze and didn't flinch.

"Sergeant, you've seen us fight and you know what we're capable of," Esset said, stepping in, trying to be reasonable. "We're not suggesting that we rush off and challenge him to battle. You know that too. We're strong enough to take him, but not like that. We need a plan, and we need resources. *We need your help*. You know Moloch needs to be stopped—just look around. And you know we can do this."

"No, I don't know that," Sergeant Warthog said, her gaze shifting to Esset. "You boys have amazing gifts, I'll grant you that, but *this*? I don't know."

Toman gritted his teeth and held his tongue.

"Let's not make any decisions right now. We're exhausted and I, for one, am soul-weary," Esset said, voicing Toman's thoughts, albeit more politely. "You're right, Sergeant, let's be on our way."

Toman and the sergeant stared at one another for a few moments, tension present but soon giving way to exhaustion.

"Let's go," Toman finally said. Their mounts came to them, and they departed.

The loft of a barn was sufficient for sleeping quarters, especially given that the sun had set a while ago now.

"At least we notified the surrounding area. It might be pointless as a warning, but at least they'll know what happened," Toman said, sitting leaning against a bale of hay.

"Mhm," Esset agreed, but he said nothing more.

Toman looked over at his brother, who was staring at the ceiling. "I'm surprised you're not trying to jot down everything that's happened in a journal. Normally you don't wait this long."

"Too tired," Esset said, but his tone said "too preoccupied." Silence curled around them, but neither one could fall asleep.

"So, do you think she'll help us with Moloch?" Toman asked.

"I don't know. Helping us is a big risk, especially if she's not confident we could win. If we failed, and he discovered we had help, he'd go after her too. At least waiting will give us a chance to get stronger yet."

For a moment, Toman's eyes were angry, an anger directed at Esset, before he looked aside in frustration. Why did Esset always have to be so aggravatingly *reasonable*? "I know. It's just... Every moment he's alive is a moment when he's inflicting suffering."

"I know..." was all Esset could say.

Toman suddenly plowed his fist into a hay bale. "I just wish there was something I could do. All this power, these gloves give me..." He shook his hands in the air. "All this power. I could make armies—I *have* made armies, but I know that against Moloch, that won't be enough. We've planned and trained, but we both know we could easily just die before we could even get to him. Sometimes I just wish that there were some simple way to kill him. I would give my own life in a heartbeat if I could guarantee that Moloch would die in the same instant in exchange."

Esset just stared at Toman. "Don't say that—"

Toman cut him off. "Seriously? You signed up for this too—you know that one or both of us could die trying to stop him, whether we succeed or not. How could you tell me not to say that? A trade like that? To save everyone between then and now that he would torture, maim, or kill?"

"Yes, I can say that," Esset returned forcefully. "Because there's a difference between fighting and dying and giving up your life, no matter what giving up will get you. We fight, Toman. Don't you ever just give up, not for anything."

"Of course we fight," Toman replied, a bit of defeat in his tone. He'd suddenly deflated, anger gone. "There is no 'magical' option."

Esset looked away. "What about my life?" Esset asked quietly.
"What?"

"What about my life?" Esset repeated. "If we came face to face with Moloch right now, would you trade my life for his death?"

"Esset, you're—" Toman began to shut the conversation down, thinking that it was a pointless distinction to argue. Why debate the impossible?

"I'm being serious, Toman." Esset raked his fingers across his scalp. "Today, when we saw what Moloch had done, a summon came to me. There's a summon called the phoenix. And it could do...well, it could do something like that. Like a trade." Esset said.

"Phoenix? But you can already summon fire birds—"

Esset cut him off, his frustration making his speech clumsy. "Not the birds—eagles, raptors—whatever you want to call them! A phoenix. Not just a fiery bird, a *phoenix*. Summoning it would give me the power to do almost anything. Standing face-to-face with Moloch, I could kill him. But the cost of that summon is my life."

Toman stared at him, stunned. "But that's—" He cut himself off this time, and there was a long silence. He hated himself in that moment, because a little part of him wanted to say, *"Do it,"* even though the rest of his being rebelled against the idea.

Esset broke the silence. "I will tell you my answer: no. I *fight*, Toman. *We* fight. If we die, we die, but it's not because we give up."

"I'm not suggesting we rush out to sacrifice you to kill Moloch," Toman said.

"I know," Esset said with a large exhale. "I know. But just—" Esset's jaw clenched before continuing. "We're not using this thing, okay? I'm not calling the phoenix. Not ever. If we go down fighting, so be it. But we fight. If I fight, you fight. There's no easy way out, and no giving up, right?" Esset waited until Toman nodded. "Good. Then let's get some sleep. Besides, we've got nothing to worry about, right? Good guys always win."

Toman said nothing more, but he couldn't keep his mind from racing. "Good guys always win" was something they'd always said to each other as kids, especially after Toman would wake screaming from nightmares about Moloch. It had been something he'd clung to as a child.

But now… Sometimes it worried him to think that Esset might actually believe it.

CHAPTER 4

The small group had spent the daylight traveling, and now the sun approached the horizon, illuminating both the small town on the trade road and the big city a half-day further away. The town usually bustled with trade, but with sunset approaching, it was quiet. Everyone was inside, in their own homes, or in the Staggering Tankard for the local ale and chicken pie.

"Mmm, you know, Sergeant, some might say we just come here to get jobs from you, but the truth is, I also come for the chicken pie," Toman said with relish as the steaming dish was placed before him.

"I'm just glad we can sleep in real beds tonight," Esset mumbled. However, he did perk up a little when his own pie was placed in front of him.

"You boys earned it," Sergeant Warthog said with a smirk. She didn't specify whether they'd earned the beds or the pies.

"No really, I think that the Sergeant sells her services out of this place because of the pie. It's delicious," Toman said, grinning and speaking through a full mouth.

Esset frowned his skepticism at Toman, and Sergeant Warthog arched an eyebrow.

"My business attracts customers who want a place busy enough to avoid notice and far enough away from the city to be discreet. That's why I picked this place. Not the pies," Sergeant Warthog said.

"Ah, yes. The business of buying and selling information," came an unfamiliar drawl from behind Toman and Esset. They both jumped and twisted in their seats to see who'd approached them. Esset felt a prickle of unease—dislike, even—before he even clapped eyes on the speaker. Seeing the man didn't help much.

He was a tallish man, handsome and pristinely groomed. He wore his black hair in a short, tight ponytail at the nape of his neck, and his sharp grey eyes were clever and attentive. Add the goatee, and Esset thought the man's style was both cultured and slimy. The stranger's clothing also demonstrated his wealth; he somehow pulled off his maroon and dark grey outfit of excellent cut and extravagant embroidery.

"And connecting people who need things done with those who can do them," Sergeant Warthog added. Her tone wasn't very welcoming. "Hello, Erizen. What do you want?"

"M'dear lady, Gretchen, you cut me!" This Erizen character drawled his words dramatically, even placing his hand over his heart. "Can I not come by and visit my oldest and dearest friend without an ulterior motive?"

"No," Sergeant Warthog said. Erizen grinned wolfishly but shrugged.

"Can't win them all, I guess. Now really, Gretchen, darling, do put your knife away. My interests and yours align right now, I do think, and such a silly bit of metal would do you no good anyways," Erizen said with a wave of his hand. Esset glanced at the sergeant, having been unaware that she'd drawn a weapon at all; one hand was under the table while the other loosely held her mug. She appeared non-threatening, but there was the soft hiss of a dagger being sheathed beneath the table.

"You haven't changed," Sergeant Warthog remarked as the newcomer invited himself to their table by pulling up an extra chair. Toman and Esset briefly exchanged a glance—they had each independently decided that they didn't like Erizen much.

"M'dove, did you really expect me to?" Erizen smiled charmingly, leaning back in his chair and spreading his hands. He ignored Toman and Esset completely.

"I expect nature to act on all of us," the sergeant replied. Esset had trouble reading her tone—was that bitterness? Disappointment? He couldn't tell.

"Gretchen, my rose, you are as lovely as ever!" Erizen waxed. The sergeant snorted.

"What do you want here, Erizen?" she asked, bluntly driving the conversation back to practical matters. Esset was glad because he had no idea what kind of history these two had together. Whatever it was, it had to have been interesting; how had the sergeant not killed this guy yet? He couldn't see her putting up with him for any length of time.

"You mentioned connecting people who can do things with

those who need things done, and here I am. I happen to have something that needs doing," Erizen said. He looked down his nose at Toman and Esset.

"Do these two pups need to hang around, or can they loiter elsewhere?" he asked. The sergeant snorted.

"As if you'd approach me when they were here if you didn't already know who they were and what they were doing here," she said. "Since you did approach me, I imagine they're relevant somehow, so they stay. Now, I suppose your presence in the area at this time is completely coincidental."

"To Moloch's little massacre? Of course. Tasteless business, and dreadfully messy," Erizen said. Toman stiffened. Esset thought the fact that Erizen instantly knew what Sergeant Warthog was referring to was more than a little suspicious, as was the fact that the sergeant thought Erizen might be involved.

"I've heard you've been rubbing shoulders with Moloch and his ilk," the sergeant replied.

"Alliances come and go," Erizen said with a dismissive wave of his hand. "Such things cannot come between old...friends such as us." The way Erizen paused and then lingered on "friends" disturbed Esset a little. He glanced at Toman, but his brother's face was a neutral mask. Erizen continued. "After all, as has been said, I have not changed."

Sergeant Warthog looked him up and down but didn't deign to respond. Silence between them reigned. Esset suddenly realized that Erizen had lost his accent.

"You injure me again, thinking me capable of such a thing," Erizen said. Sergeant Warthog snorted in derision. Again.

"With an ego the size of yours, injuring it isn't difficult," she responded. "It probably injures your pride that the whole world doesn't worship you as a god. Keep talking."

"Well, worship would be *nice*, but—"

"About why you're here."

"Ah, yes. As I suspect you're aware, I've moved up in the world. I'm a lord now, as I've come into possession of one of several territories under the control of a council of dark mages, Moloch among them. Mostly we keep to ourselves, but some interaction among us is, of course, necessary, and we convene occasionally." *He's a dark mage.* Esset flicked his brown eyes towards Sergeant Warthog for a moment before studying Erizen again.

"I don't know that I would call joining a bunch of dark mages 'moving up,'" the sergeant remarked. Erizen tsked.

"It's not like I go around killing babies," he shot back, his manner dismissive.

"You still have the stink of blood magic on you," the sergeant replied.

"Mostly I glean my power elsewhere. Now, if I may continue?"

"I've never been able to stop you before."

"Quite. Now, as you would imagine, maintaining such relations requires something of an illusion on my part. Wanton death and destruction has never been my preference, although it sometimes has its uses. My compatriots and I disagree on that point."

"Are you going to get to the point any time soon?" the sergeant asked.

"Very well." Erizen sniffed. "I have a monster problem on one of my borders. Normally I wouldn't care overmuch, but the father of my favorite concubine happens to live in the village it's been attacking, and she's been complaining dreadfully. I could get a new concubine, but she is a favorite of mine...and highly skilled. You see, there's this most delightful thing she can do with her tongue—"

"And the monster?"

"They say it's a dragon, but I doubt it. Probably a wyvern of some kind, maybe a loose mage construct. It would be easy enough for me to dispose of, of course, but again, of course, it might then seem like I care about my subjects, and that wouldn't do at all. I'd have to go smite a village or something to even the scales, and I really couldn't be bothered. Additionally, the border it's harassing is a shared one, and I'd rather not offend the other lord. So, since I have plenty of money, simply paying someone to take care of the problem is easiest—and leaves no one else the wiser. I know you can be discreet, my dear," Erizen drawled.

"I can also pick and choose my clients," Sergeant Warthog said.

"I appreciate the bluff, dahlin', but I know that even if you wanted to turn me down, you wouldn't turn down all those poor folks getting killed by the, ah, 'dragon.'" Erizen's drawl was back.

"We'll do it," Toman cut in. Erizen turned his condescending grey eyes on Toman.

"Who asked you?" he asked.

"You, essentially," Toman said dryly. "We'd have to be morons to miss that, and we're not."

"My mistake," Erizen said in his most pleasant tone. Esset bristled and bit his tongue.

"Boys, why don't you go see if the barkeep has any local news from while we were gone and let me haggle out a price with Erizen," the sergeant said—it wasn't really a suggestion. Both of them silently regarded Erizen for a moment before picking up their meals and going to the bar.

"Okay, why are you really here?" Sergeant Warthog asked.

"Um, dark lord, politics, concubine with dexterous fingers?" Erizen reiterated.

"*Really* here," the sergeant repeated.

"Everything is what it seems. I don't *always* play games," he said. The sergeant snorted.

"Everything is a game to you. Or is that the problem? Have your games gotten a little too serious in your political position?" Sergeant Warthog asked.

"Never," Erizen said with a wolfish smile.

"Is that so? Then why would you be here? Why ask for my help? I was wrong. You have changed. The Erizen of old would have risen to the challenge of ridding himself of a pest without his fellow lords knowing. Even if you have an ulterior motive for coming here and asking for help, that's still a change." Sergeant Warthog kept prodding.

"You're as paranoid as ever, m'love," Erizen said lazily.

"Moloch hasn't broken or bought you, has he?" Sergeant Warthog let disgust and suspicion creep into her tone.

"No." The spark in Erizen's eyes bespoke truth, but it flickered too quickly for Sergeant Warthog to identify the expression as fear or anger or some combination thereof.

"Hmm. Well, be that as it may, I suppose we have a price to negotiate. Now I know you can afford rather a lot, and given the charity cases we take that need to be balanced out, I think you can afford to be generous." It was her turn to sport a wolfish grin.

"You seek to rob an old friend? For shame, mah Gretchen, for shame! I thought better of you than that."

"Nonsense, Erizen. You'd be disappointed if I didn't."

Toman and Esset weren't inclined to make small talk with the barkeep. They kept their eyes on Erizen—they didn't need to speak to know they were on the same page when it came to the man, although Toman was more pensive about the situation than Esset. Toman was musing on the implications of their visitor and the upcoming job when Sergeant Warthog waved them back over.

"It's all settled then!" Erizen said cheerfully. Toman and Esset both glanced at the sergeant, who nodded confirmation. Erizen rose smoothly and extended a hand to them. Esset automatically took it, good manners too ingrained in him to prevent the movement. When their hands closed, Esset stiffened and staggered back as a jolt passed through their extended arms. Toman's hackles went up.

"Toman!" Sergeant Warthog stopped him before he could make a grab for the mage, who now strode out of the tavern with a smug air about him. The animator looked at her sharply and then at his brother, who seemed to be recovering.

"I'm fine," Esset said, even as he shook his head as if to clear it.

"Instantaneous knowledge transfer," Sergeant Warthog said. "Irritating, but not dangerous."

"What?" Toman's eyes darted between the two of them rapidly in obvious confusion.

"I know where to go find this…monster," Esset said. "And how to get to Erizen's capital."

"What?" Toman repeated more emphatically.

"And…a few other things." A crease appeared between Esset's

eyebrows.

Toman waved a hand in front of Esset's face to try to recall him to the real world. Esset blinked and focused his gaze on Toman.

"Instantaneous knowledge transfer," the summoner said, echoing the sergeant's explanation.

"Meaning?" Toman fished.

"Meaning when he touched me, he instantaneously transferred certain knowledge to me. How very efficient." Esset moved his head sharply to look out the door after Erizen, and he winced in doing so. "And unpleasant," he added.

"As most who know him discover," the sergeant put in dryly.

"Can we seriously trust this guy?" Toman demanded of the sergeant.

"No," Sergeant Warthog replied honestly enough. "Or at least, you can't trust him very far. He's very dangerous, and very clever. He's also mostly amoral. However, if it is in his best interest to work with us, we have gained a powerful ally."

"But the moment that changes..." Toman prompted.

"Then we have a very dangerous enemy," Esset finished, but he was clearly skeptical on the ally part.

"Well, he wouldn't necessarily go straight from friend to foe, but he'd certainly hang you out to dry," the sergeant corrected them.

"Charming," Toman said.

"So it's possible we're walking into a trap, then," Esset said.

"Possibly," the sergeant admitted. "But I don't think so. Not this time. And as things stand, I'm fairly sure he won't betray you for anything in the future either. There was something about him I'd never seen before. It's a dangerous edge to walk, but I think he'll remain benign.

"Now, the odds of him *not* knowing about your plans to go after Moloch are slim to none, but I still wouldn't mention it, just in case," she warned.

"That went without saying," Esset muttered. "So what's the deal with this guy? How do you even know him?"

Sergeant Warthog exhaled heavily and put her forehead in her palm before pushing her hair from her face. "I met Erizen...a long time ago. Back before I was a sergeant. I was just a greenhorn, actually. We worked together on a few jobs. He's actually a few years older than I am. Anyways, he's very clever and resourceful, and his magic is very strong even without his cleverness to amplify it. However, Erizen is...well, you just met him. He's amoral. He likes what he likes and wants what he wants, and he doesn't let ethics get in the way of getting and keeping what he likes and wants. He's a hedonist and a narcissist, but he's not evil. Although I can't say I'm terribly surprised he's fallen in with dark mages."

"Hang on, Erizen is older than you are? He looks... Well, he looks closer to our age," Esset said. "A lot closer."

"This is one of the problems with the pair of you not being able to sense magic," the sergeant said. "If you could, you'd be able to tell he's a blood mage too. He's not a sadist, but..." She shrugged. Esset squirmed at her ambivalent attitude towards blood magic.

"So he's using blood magic to keep himself young?" Toman asked.

"I doubt it. Magic, yes. Blood magic, not necessarily. Erizen would be the kind to think that blood magic is too...well, messy, frankly. He has very likely cooked up something else. Besides, if he is a lord now, then blood magic would have his populace cowering in fear, and Erizen learned a long time ago that loyalty can be a far greater motivator than fear. Let me amend that—both is better than one or the other, but loyalty before fear. So I think his use of blood magic is likely limited...like he said himself."

"I don't like this at all," Esset reiterated.

"Look, like I said, neither do I, but we have to work with what we have." Sergeant Warthog met Esset's eyes, then Toman's. "I told you—do what you can to make sure that you and Erizen share common goals, and this can work out to our advantage. If we play our cards right, he might be able to get you boys some intelligence on Moloch, and maybe some other things."

"So you're going to help us with Moloch?" Toman asked. The sergeant's expression darkened.

"I'm still considering it," she said. Toman didn't press her.

"Regardless, it looks like we're heading to his kingdom tomorrow. Come on, Esset, let's go get ready for another trip," Toman said.

Esset's lips pressed into a thin line, but he nodded and

followed his brother through the door.

"Are we seriously considering this?" Esset blurted once they were outside the tavern.

"Considering what?" Toman asked, deliberately obtuse.

"Allying ourselves with that man. Darkfires, even doing this *job* for him," Esset said.

"I thought you'd be all over that part—we're saving a village from a dragon," Toman jested.

"I'm serious, Toman."

"I know. But yes, I'm considering it, and you should be too. You know what we're up against with Moloch—Erizen might be a gamble, but it could be a risk worth taking it if means taking down Moloch."

"He's a *dark lord*," Esset said. "And worse, a blood mage. There's no victory in defeating a bad guy if you become a bad guy in the process."

"We're not becoming bad guys just by doing a job for Erizen," Toman said, actually a bit exasperated by the overly slippery slope Esset had set up.

"Not this job, maybe, but the next?" Esset challenged. "If we ally with him for the fight against Moloch? This is assuming he doesn't turn on us, which is far from certain. What if he's just using us in some power play against his rival lords? What if Sergeant Warthog is wrong about him and he's just gonna hand us over to Moloch?"

"I trust Sergeant Warthog, don't you? If she thinks we're good on this one, we're good. And maybe he is using us, but as long as we're saving innocent people in the meantime, does it matter? It sounds like Erizen is a better alternative than the other dark lords, so it's a lesser evil. We're not doing anything unethical, and the end result is an improvement over the current situation. As long as that's true, we're good. If it doesn't turn out that way, we make it right. If we have to take on Erizen too, so be it. We'll use this job as an opportunity to gather what information we can on him and go from there. I know Erizen rubs you the wrong way, but you need to be objective about this, Esset."

Esset scowled fiercely. "Fine. Let's go get ready then." Two garbled strings of syllables later, they each launched into the air on the backs of fiery birds. A local woman stopped and stared; Toman and Esset were common enough visitors, but the birds were a sight to behold.

Toman let the cold air clear his head even as the heat from the bird kept him warm. Their trip was a short one, just over the hill and well off the trade road. To anyone but the two of them, there was nothing to witness but a bit of low scrub on the ground below them and a few boulders and an abundance of rocks and tough grass; Toman and Esset alone saw the castle.

Small for a castle, it was nonetheless impressive. The walls were high and thick, embedded with a lattice of huge iron snakes and topped with square ramparts. Each corner of the walls was furnished with a tall, cylindrical tower, and each tower had two rows of snarling gargoyles ringing it, one row level with the wall-tops, the other gracing the top of the tower. The peak of each tower also held a rearing, winged horse of stone. There was a fifth tower, the keep, at the center of the castle. It jutted up higher than the rest. It was adorned similarly to the other four, only it had three winged horses with their backs to each other and a tall flag at the center. The flag was black with a glowing white hand in the center.

They landed in a wide, open courtyard, its cobbled expanse interrupted only by two rows of statues, which created a pathway from the gates of the outer wall to the big double doors into the keep. The statues alternated; the lines were composed of a spear- or sword-wielding soldier, his mount, and a large dog—the breeds varied. As they landed, the door to the keep swung open to admit them without any sign of anyone to open them.

"Arxus, did anything interesting happen after we left?" Toman asked as he and Esset walked down the path toward the keep.

"No, Master Toman. There were a few stray travelers that I directed around me and towards the trade road, but nothing more." The uninflected male voice came from one of the stone dogs, an intimidating mastiff that came to life as they walked past. At the shoulder, the big dog reached a grown man's waist. Its pointed ears were pricked towards them as they walked.

"Thank you, Arxus," Toman said absently.

"Here's a thought," Esset said in a tone that made Toman anticipate an argument.

"Run this plan past Arxus. He's intelligent but unbiased, since he has no emotions. He should be able to fairly weigh the pros and cons."

"You want to ask the *castle's* opinion?" Toman asked. "Just because he has no emotions doesn't mean he's unbiased. He was created to protect the current animator, remember?"

"True. But it's still a valid exercise," Esset argued. The double doors of the keep swung open before them without visible aid and shut behind them after they passed through, leaving them in the great hall.

"Although advice is not my primary function, it is a service I can provide," Arxus said blandly. Toman rubbed the bridge of his nose, shook his head, and stared blankly at the great hall before them. Massive tapestries lined the walls, and the ceilings were high and vaulted, lit by torches along the walls and an expansive chandelier high above. The hall stretched to the end in a raised stage-like structure that had a grand chair on it that somehow managed to barely avoid looking like a throne—at least to most eyes. Toman knew Esset thought the piece of furniture deserved that lofty status.

Eyes didn't usually linger on the chair, however, for behind it was an impressive tapestry of an imposing man. He wore a strange, full-face mask; it was white and had threads of color that spread around the eyes and up the forehead and then fanned down onto the cheeks. He also wore a cape and a pair of gloves that were heavily embroidered to match. The rest of his clothes seemed to be of fine make also, but they weren't notable like the mask, cloak, and gloves. He was known as the First; he had created three castles like Toman's and two other artifacts besides Toman's gloves, which endowed Toman with his animating abilities.

The abilities that Toman felt he *had* to use to make this world a better place, just as Esset did. When had that become so complicated?

"Arxus, please round up any rope or chain we've got around and leave it by one of the winged horses. We'll be needing it for our next job," Toman said.

"Yes, Master." The stone mastiff didn't move, but in other

parts of the castle, the stonework was coming to life to fulfill the request.

"It's a good thing we restocked before the last mission," Toman said, rubbing the back of his neck.

"Toman, you're avoiding—" Esset began.

"I know. Fine, whatever, ask him. It won't make any difference," Toman said. He headed off down a side passage towards the armory, hoping to brainstorm more tactics to use against a dragon-like creature—and leaving Esset behind.

"Hey!" Esset called after him. Toman knew his brother had intended that he stick around for the "debate," but Toman was taking advantage of the fact that he hadn't actually agreed to that. He wanted to think things over. He heard Esset mutter under his breath, but since his brother didn't follow him, he didn't stop.

CHAPTER 5

Two fiery birds swooped low before depositing Toman and Esset on a remote hillside around noon. The birds vanished in a small spray of sparks, and the two young men pulled travel rations out of backpacks and sat down for lunch.

"I never asked—what did Arxus have to say about all this?" Toman asked before tearing into his meal.

Esset mumbled under his breath.

"What was that?" Toman asked through a full mouth.

"He agreed with you. But really, how can you expect a magical construct to understand ethics, especially when he has no emotions." Since Esset's words weren't intoned as a question, Toman didn't answer, but he did grin.

"I still have reservations about this," Esset said. Toman swallowed and sighed.

"I know. And I do too, but I think this is a risk we need to take." Toman took another bite, and they both ate in silence.

"Oi, there they are!" Esset said, pointing with what was left of his sandwich. Two dark specks were visible in the sky, back the way they'd come.

"Right on time. Finish your food and we can get going," Toman said. He stuffed the last of his own in his mouth and stretched.

"We should reach that town tomorrow, right?" Toman asked.

"Midday or so," Esset confirmed. "We should be crossing into Erizen's territory today though, so we should switch mounts now. No need to announce our arrival any more than we need to."

Toman just nodded and watched as the two specks in the sky grew larger. Within a minute, they were clearly recognizable as a pair of stone, winged horses. Each was laden with supplies—one mainly with chains, the other with rope and a harness bristling with sheathed daggers. Toman had figured these would be the most effective weapons against the dragon—or whatever it was.

The twin horses descended, and Toman hung onto his hat.

They landed with plunging hooves and thrashing wings that blasted the area with their own wind.

"You'd think that since magic enables their flight, not their actual flapping wings, that they could land with less of a stir," Esset said dryly when the horses were still. Toman shrugged. Gripping the harness of the knife-bearing horse, he swung up on its back with practiced ease. The stone was cool to touch, but the stone shifted like the muscles a real horse would have. He'd found, with his animations, that the more detailed he made them, the more nuanced their animated behavior was. Fortunately, even with their enhanced appearance, he never had to worry about misbehavior from his artificial companions.

Esset was still mounting when Toman cued his own mount into the air with a thought. The winged horse leapt skywards, pumping its wings for altitude and gaining height despite the fact that its solid stone weight should have prevented such a creature from becoming airborne—Esset was right about them being moved by magic rather than nature.

Toman glanced back to make sure Esset was following—he was, and only a few wingstrokes behind—before setting his eyes on the horizon. His stone creations were slower than Esset's summons, and they weren't as warm, so they couldn't fly as high without freezing their riders. On the other hand, if his concentration slipped, they would just keep doing whatever they'd last been told to do. If Esset's concentration slipped, the summons would do anything they pleased. Usually that just meant they went off course or got up to some antics, but they could also choose to turn on their riders and burn them or dump them. Toman was never quite able to relax when astride Esset's summons. But stone—stone was reliable. It was also far less obtrusive flying overhead than the glowing monstrosities Esset called upon, which was why they'd switched mounts.

Toman closed his eyes and focused on the physical sensations: the wind grasping at his hair and battering his face; the worn leather of his hat, firmly held against his torso so it wouldn't be ripped away; the living stone beneath him, replicated muscles shifting and straining in the rigors of flight; and the two rigid lumps against his knees where they pressed up against daggers sheathed on either side of his mount.

Toman opened his eyes again, and the first thing he saw was flashing stone wings close on his right; Esset was flying far too close to him for comfort. Instinctively, he steered his mount a couple feet further away, but then he noticed that Esset was waving wildly at him. Toman cast his eyes ahead and then at the scenery before him. He nearly fell off his mount.

The world ahead was grey. Although there were a few clouds in the sky, it wasn't overcast. The greyness was not due to weather. But even had it been, it would have been remarkable. It wasn't as though they were traveling through a wasteland; there were copses of trees about, and although the vegetation was sparse, there was still some that should have been colorful.

But instead, everything was grey. The sky was grey, and the clouds in it. The earth was grey, with no brown or other hint of color tinting it. Only the plant-life had any color at all, and it was faded, greens or browns or yellows heavily tinted with grey.

Toman looked down at himself, half wondering if something had gone wrong with his eyes, but his own clothes were still their usual brown, his skin its proper color. Toman looked back. Just the land and sky were grey. Ahead was a stream; the water was grey too. Something had turned this entire area grey.

Toman pulled up his mount to hover in place before the grey line on the terrain. Esset did the same and they both hovered there and stared in disbelief for a time. Finally Toman waved to Esset, and they both descended to a small hill on the greener side of the line. Even then, they stared at the grey line on the scenery for a good stretch before speaking.

"Magic. It has to be," Esset asserted. Toman nodded slowly. That much was fairly obvious.

"But how? And why?" Toman asked.

"And who? I'm willing to bet Erizen," Esset added.

"Considering that I'm pretty sure we just passed into his kingdom, that line of reasoning would make sense. But we shouldn't jump to conclusions; this could be the result of an attack or something directed at him," Toman said. In all fairness, they didn't have enough evidence or facts to come to Esset's conclusion with any certainty.

Esset's silence spoke volumes.

"I do admit that I'd like to know for sure, though," Toman said.

"Whatever this is, it doesn't look good."

"Should we avoid it?" Esset asked, his uncertainty clear in his voice.

"Maybe... No, look," Toman said, pointing. A herd of deer, distinctly *not* grey, browsed on the colorless vegetation. A fawn frolicked around one of the does.

"Hm." Esset said. He didn't look convinced.

"Well, let's stay along the border for awhile, but if we don't see anything dead or unnatural, we should probably see what happens when we cross," Toman said. "After all, the village we're supposed to be rescuing is going to be inside the grey area, if it does in fact cover all of Erizen's territory."

"We'll see," Esset said, and his mount leapt skywards.

With an uneasy feeling in the pit of his stomach, Toman followed suit.

It was morning of the next day. They'd lost a little time detouring around the grey area, but not too much. Now they stood just at the edge of the grey border, their mounts still beneath them.

"Well, the village is in there somewhere, so we'll have to cross eventually," Toman said, waving at the grey expanse. "We've seen plenty of wildlife in there, and they didn't seem to suffer any ill effect, not even greyness," Toman said, sounding like he was trying to convince himself as well as Esset.

"No people, though," Esset replied.

"We haven't exactly been near anywhere people would normally be," Toman pointed out.

"Maybe I'll summon something and send it across. See if anything happens," Esset said.

"That's a pretty good idea," Toman said. Toman and Esset looked at each other and laughed, realizing that neither of them wanted to go first.

"Okay, here goes," Esset said. He muttered a quick prayer to Bright Hyrishal that everything would go fine, and then he incanted a summon. A tiny bat appeared in the air by his head, then zipped across the grey border.

Nothing happened. Toman and Esset exchanged looks again. Esset sent the bat a little farther in, then banished it.

"Okay, so the summons seem fine," Esset said. "I guess I'll go first, so you can haul me out if need be." Despite his words, he spent a few moments steeling himself. Thankfully, Toman didn't tease him about it. Finally, he urged his mount across the line.

Esset had expected something to at least *feel* different when he crossed the border, but everything felt exactly the same. He looked down at his hands and his clothes, but they all retained their original color. Turning in the saddle, he looked at Toman and shrugged.

"Your turn," Esset said.

Toman crossed with less hesitation than Esset had shown and drew even with his brother's mount.

"Your gloves!" Esset noticed immediately; normally Toman's gloves were brown and black, but the second they'd crossed the grey line, they'd gone grey.

Toman kicked his mount and it pivoted and leapt back across the line. Instantly, Toman's gloves turned brown again. Toman breathed a sigh of relief and edged back up to the line. He stuck one gloved hand across it, and the glove turned grey—the other was still brown.

"I think it's their camouflage thing," Toman said after moving his hand back and forth across the line and watching the glove consistently change colors. He rejoined Esset.

"What?" Esset asked.

"Remember that one time, when that lord insisted we get all dressed up for his celebration, and loaned us those ridiculous outfits?" Toman asked. "And my gloves changed color to match that ridiculous shade of blue? They were changing to fit in, I think, and I think that's what they're doing here."

"Oh yeah, I'd forgotten about that," Esset said. "That had explained why the gloves in the picture of the First look slightly different too."

"And they've changed size to fit my hands since I was a kid, so why not color?" Toman asked.

"True," Esset said. He hoped that was all it was.

"Why do you think nothing else has changed though? The rest of our clothes are still normal." Esset said. Toman just shrugged.

"I don't know, but we have a village to get to," he said. Even had Esset wanted to object, he couldn't have, for Toman had urged his mount skyborne again.

As he followed, Esset acknowledged that they had probably lost enough time already. He knew his reservations were well-known, so he resolved to hold his own council unless something new cropped up.

Still, Esset kept a close eye below as they sped over the landscape. A distant smudge of smoke grew clearer, until it was distinguishable as multiple plumes from a few chimneys: a forge, a smokehouse, and a couple homes. The village was small, but necessarily self-sufficient. By the time they were close enough to make out individual people, they'd been spotted themselves, and all of the residents fled indoors and hid.

Toman and Esset landed in what could have been a ghost town.

"What do you think? Do we play hero, or pretend we're exotic hunters only, tracking a rare beast?" Esset asked, keeping his voice low so only Toman was near enough to hear.

"My abilities are well-known to Moloch, thanks to my predecessor," Toman said. "Any deception on our part will only point to conspiracy if Moloch catches wind, and we want to keep Erizen clear if we can."

Esset nodded; that made sense. It was just as well, since he preferred simply being who he was.

"Think we can persuade them to help us help them?" Esset asked. Toman looked around the seemingly deserted village.

"Tough to say. We can't tell them Erizen sent us, and they may fear his reprisal for speaking to outsiders," Toman replied. It was too complicated a situation for his taste.

"I guess all we can do is try," Esset said.

Since no one seemed to want to come greet them, they finally dismounted and approached the biggest house in the village—odds were good someone important lived or worked there.

Toman knocked. Esset thought his knock was a little overly assertive, but then, that was probably why Toman was doing the knocking. When no one answered, Toman knocked again, even louder. Finally, the animator pounded on the door and yelled into the house.

"Hey! We hear you have a dragon problem!"

Still nothing.

"I really hope they're not going to make us drag them out of there," Toman muttered. Esset eyed him; they wouldn't really do that. Probably.

Toman raised his fist to pound on the door again.

"Hey—"

The door opened. Toman froze, fist in the air. He slowly lowered it. The man in the doorway was short with a frizzled grey mustache and a sagging belly. His clothes and everything on and around him were grey, but his skin was still the proper color.

"Good noon, m'lords," the man said.

"Good noon, but we're no lords," Esset said, taking the lead now. "I'm Summoner Esset, and this is Animator Toman. We heard you're having some trouble, and we've come to help."

"Beg pardon, m'lords, but only the dark lords have magic in these parts, and our Lord wouldn't take kindly to us talking to you," the man said with a bow. He was sweating profusely. Toman and Esset exchanged looks.

"What's your name, sir?" Esset asked.

"Kerby Carver," the little man replied, his eyes shifting from side to side almost in time with his feet.

"Be at ease, Mr. Carver," Esset said. "All we want is to hunt your monster. You don't have to say a word else to us, if you're worried we're spies. Just tell us what you know about the monster only. How could that hurt your lord? It could only help him, by us getting rid of your monster so your fine village can thrive again."

"Er, I suppose just telling you about the dragon can't hurt, m'lords," the man said, but he still shifted nervously from foot to foot.

"Good. Tell us what you know, and we'll leave and only come back if we kill the monster," Esset promised.

"Okay then, m'lords." Despite Mr. Carver's agreement, he still glanced around before continuing. "Well, it's a dragon, sure enough. It's massive, especially its head and jaws, but its forelegs are tiny, not useful for much of anything. It doesn't need them though. It just swoops down and picks up whatever it wants in its jaws—livestock, people, deer, it makes no difference," the man said. Toman and Esset exchanged looks again. "Massive" was a fairly general term for describing size, but it had to be big to carry off livestock without a problem.

"How big, sir?" Esset asked.

"The size of my house, m'lord, easily! We've all seen it. We've lost three people and over a third our herds since it first came."

"And you say dragon—can it breathe fire or anything?" Esset asked.

"Not that I've seen, m'lord, despite all the old tales saying they can," the man admitted. Esset was certainly glad to hear that.

"But you should know, m'lord, old farmer Erikson tried to shoot the beast and the arrow bounced right off him. Scales of steel, he has," Mr. Carver told him.

"Thank you, that's very helpful," Esset said. "Do you know where the beast lairs?"

"I don't, m'lord, but he always heads west, into Lord Koris's kingdom. And he always comes from the west, from behind the mountain. Like as not, he lairs somewhere over there, m'lord," Mr. Carver said.

"Anything else you can think of that might help us, sir?" Esset asked. Mr. Carver thought for a moment, then shook his head.

"Sorry, m'lord, that's everything I know. Likely all anyone knows," the short man replied. Esset looked over at Toman, who shook his head—he didn't have any further questions either.

"Okay, we'd best be on our way then," Esset said. He turned to go, hesitated, and then stopped. "I don't suppose you can tell us why everything is grey here?" he asked.

Mr. Carver looked surprised. "Why, everyone knows that, m'lord. 'Tis Lord Erizen's Greymaker."

"Greymaker," Esset repeated.

"Aye, it's—well, if you don't know, maybe I shouldn't be telling you, m'lord," Mr. Carver said, thinking better of an explanation.

"Right, sorry," Esset said. "We'll be off." He and Toman exchanged another look but returned to their mounts. A quick survey of the village indicated that everyone else was still closeted away, without so much as a ruffled drape.

"Let's go," Toman said. They did.

"Well, what do you think?" Toman asked as soon as they

landed on a hillside overlooking the town.

"Definitely not a real dragon," Esset said. He was simultaneously disappointed and very grateful, but Toman just gave him a blank stare.

"You know more about dragons than I do," Toman finally said.

"Oh. Right. Well, dragons are incredibly powerful, magical, and intelligent creatures. This one sounds strong, but not especially magical or intelligent. Also, physiologically speaking, dragons are well-proportioned, even beautiful creatures. They certainly don't have itty bitty forelegs and massive heads. It's also pretty rare for them to eat people, or really to be evil at all. The exceptions to that are usually very notable, but they really are rare," Esset explained.

"Uh huh. So what is it then, if not a dragon?" Toman asked.

"A monster. I can't really be more specific," Esset admitted. "I mean, it might be a relative of the wyvern, which is dragonish in appearance while still being just a beast, but wyverns rarely have forelegs and their necks are too snake-like and heads too small for them to fit Mr. Carver's description."

"Monster," Toman repeated. "That's disappointingly non-specific."

Esset shrugged. "That's it for my knowledge of naturally occurring dragon-like species."

"So you're saying it might be a mage-construct. Erizen did mention the possibility," Toman said.

Esset nodded. "That means it might have some unexpected traits, but there's not much we can do to prepare for that," Esset acknowledged.

"So what's our basic plan then?" Toman asked.

Esset shrugged again. "Find the lair. If it's a cave, we might be able to trap it inside with a cave-in or something. That would be easiest. If something goes wrong, we did bring supplies. We can't make much more of a plan without more information, but unless it has abilities far beyond what we're aware of, this should be relatively easy."

Toman nodded his agreement. "Can we still call it a dragon? Just for simplicity's sake?"

Esset grinned crookedly. "But I want to call it a semi-drakish monstrosity."

Toman gave an exaggerated wince. "Let's go find that lair."

CHAPTER 6

They could have found the lair by smell alone. The unfinished remains of rotting carcasses—and corpses—littered the ground around the mouth of the large but relatively shallow cave, which was more of the underside to an overhanging cliff that a true cave. Esset supposed that, given how large the creature supposedly was, it would be difficult for it to find *any* cave large enough to accommodate it. And if the monster was as big as the size of the lair suggested, then Mr. Carver hadn't been exaggerating.

They'd found the place by flying grid searches in the general direction that Mr. Carver had indicated. It had taken them beyond the grey area and into the neighboring territory. Now they flew lower to investigate more closely, since there was no sign that the beast was home now. As he drew nearer, Esset noticed some odd markings in the rocks around the lair. He gulped. The odd marks were gouges in the stone—gouges furrowed deep by claws that were likely as long as his arm or better. Between the gouges and the decomposing bodies of man and beast, there might as well have been "Here be monsters" written on this spot on the map.

"Good, it's gone," Toman said beside him. "You go keep an eye out for it in case it comes back. I'm going to see if I can't make some preparations."

"Sure thing. You be ready to fly if we need to," Esset said unnecessarily.

"Brother, I ain't even gonna dismount," Toman said, laughing. He was intimidated by the claw marks too, but he was still fairly confident.

They could easily handle the vast majority of creatures without magical abilities, Esset reminded himself as he took to the skies. No matter how big and fierce this monster was, it was still well within range of their abilities. With their particular skillset, he and Toman excelled against purely physical threats. It was when they were up against magic-users that they struggled, since they had little defense against magical attacks.

And that was why he worried about the possibility that this was a mage-construct. Just because there was no trace of a master behind the beast yet didn't mean there wasn't one, or that he wouldn't show up at an inopportune moment. But as he and Toman had already agreed, there was little they could do to prepare for such a possibility.

Esset glanced down at Toman, who had his hands on the rock of the cave's ceiling and his eyes heavy-lidded in concentration. He could guess what his brother's plans were, but he'd find out for sure later. For now Esset kept his eyes on the skies as well as the ground below. The ground was remarkably sparse on wildlife, he was unsurprised to see. Some tiny movements betrayed a marmot, but the larger wildlife would have learned to steer clear of the beast's lair by now. The only other creatures around were birds, which made sense to Esset, since he couldn't see something the monster's size being able to catch such tiny and fleet meals.

Esset circled Toman's location continuously, even checking the skies above—just in case. He started going through mental exercises to keep his mind from wandering, as it was wont to do, but he still found himself wishing that his brother's abilities didn't require quite so much time to prepare for a battle. And despite his attempts to keep sharp, Esset found himself surprised and unprepared when his mount suddenly started descending without his instruction.

Esset panicked for a moment, cueing the animated stone to pull up several times before he saw Toman waving at him from below and realizing his mount's disobedience was of his brother's doing. He relaxed and waved back, curious as to why Toman was bringing him down.

"Hey, nitwit, you've got all my chains!" Toman called when he was in earshot. Of course.

"Well, numbskull, you should've taken them before I took off," Esset retorted good-naturedly. His mount's stone hooves clattered against the rocks as the chains wound around it slithered off.

"So are we almost ready to go?" Esset asked, scanning above them in case the monster was returning.

"Yup. I figure we can hide over there," Toman waved an arm at the rocks overlooking the cave, "and wait for the monster to enter his lair. When it does, I have a golem already posing as the ceiling. It'll drop down and crush the monster. With luck, that's all it will take, but if not, a bunch of these boulders I've animated into snakes can wrap around it and crush it. We shouldn't even need these chains, but I'll have them hide around here too. At the very least, me and mine should be able to keep the beast from taking off, which means you can summon your beasts to fight it."

"Sounds thorough. But I still don't know why you brought *daggers* along," Esset said, waving at Toman's mount, which bristled with the weapons. "Those tiny little blades aren't going to be much use against the monster's tough hide."

Toman gave him a broad grin. "Nothing has a tough hide on the inside," the animator said. "And they're small enough to fly inside the mouth of pretty much any large creature."

"That's disturbing," Esset said, nonetheless impressed with his brother's ingenuity.

"Effective," Toman argued.

"And this looks like it'll be easy," Esset said. "Come on, let's get to our hiding place." His winged horse took off, angling up towards the adjacent hill. The surface of the hill was jagged and littered with boulders and crags—perfect.

Toman and Esset dismissed their mounts so they could hide further away—the stone winged horses were rather noticeable, after all, and Esset could summon new mounts if they had to move quickly. Toman animated two stone boulders into giant bears that crouched overtop of them, hiding them from sight and disguising themselves as the boulders they'd once been.

And they waited.

And waited.

"I hope it's not off terrorizing a village right now," Esset murmured, shifting against the rocks. He rubbed his hip bone—it felt like a permanent indentation had been created by a particularly pokey rock.

"This is the best way to deal with the creature," Toman said, but he shifted too.

"I know," Esset muttered.

"With luck, it's just sunning itself somewhere," Toman said, and Esset knew he worried too.

But what Esset said was, "What sun?" The sky overhead was

a uniform grey, almost making it feel like they hadn't left the grey zone. When Toman didn't say anything, Esset spoke up again. "What do you suppose the Greymaker does?"

"Make things grey."

Esset threw Toman an exasperated look. "But why? There must be a reason," Esset insisted.

"Given that we didn't turn grey immediately upon entering, it likely makes it easy to spot outsiders," Toman said.

"Do you think that's its whole purpose though?" Esset asked. He didn't think so.

"I think we should be quiet in case our dragon comes back," Toman said. With a sigh, Esset fell silent. He debated pulling out his summoner's tome to study up, but he'd left it in his mount's saddlebags, not anticipating such a long wait. He shifted against the rocks again. Now there was a rock digging into the side of his kneecap. He adjusted again before trying to lie still.

They had a small gap to watch the world through from underneath the bears. They could see part of the sky, but mostly just the lair below. Esset wished he could see more—Toman was right, speaking had been foolish. If the dragon happened to come up behind them, they wouldn't be able to see it. It wouldn't be able to see them either, but still.

Esset was shifting again—this time a rock was digging into his arm—when Toman gave an urgent whisper.

"There!"

Esset squinted, but it wasn't until the monster swooped down towards its lair that he saw it. The monster landed with a graceless thud, back legs and tail first before dropping down to support itself with its wings. It had forelegs, but they were tiny and held close to its chest. Its lizard-like head was oversized, sporting massive jaws and tiny eyes. It was a muddy brownish-red with heavy, plated scales all over its body. Esset had never seen a creature like this before, not even in his books. "Semi-drakish monstrosity" really *was* the best description he could come up with.

The beast sniffed and gave a large *whuff*, spraying dust around its feet. It repeated the motions twice more before swinging its head in Toman and Esset's general direction.

"Toman..." Esset whispered quietly. He glanced at his brother and saw him grimace, but didn't spare more than that. He knew why Toman was hesitating—the beast wasn't directly beneath his trap. It was still half outside the cave, so Toman's animation wouldn't get a clean grab.

The monster sniffed, then turned its whole body in their direction. It reared up on its hind legs and lifted its nose into the air, and then it sniffed again. As the dragon-beast crouched to launch into a spring, Toman gave the command. The stone bears guarding them exposed them, and the ambush below was sprung.

Toman's humanoid golem separated from the lair's ceiling and dropped onto the monster's hindquarters, botching its launch toward Toman and Esset but failing to restrain it. The beast thrashed and threw the golem off, but by the time the massive creature was facing its attacker, the golem was already on its feet. The golem swung its rough fist back and ploughed it into the side of the monster's head. With an explosion of rocks and dust, the golem's arm shattered up to the elbow, leaving the dragon-like monster looking seriously annoyed. A low, rumbling growl emitted from a cavernous chest, building until it erupted into a full blown roar as it launched itself at the golem, clamping its jaws down around the stone creature's torso.

The golem's chest was so thick the monster's jaws barely fit around it, but stone cracked and fractured under the immense pressure. The golem pounded on the beast's head ineffectively, prompting the dragon-like creature to pick the golem up and slam it against the rocks.

Esset gaped as the golem cracked into three pieces—Toman's animating magic was turned useless with the disassembly of his creation, but his other animations had reached the monster. Three rock snakes wrapped themselves around the beast, trying to disable it. One wrapped around a wing, constricting near the base and trying to crush the wing-bones—or at least tear the tough wing membrane. Another snaked around a hind leg and the base of the tail, handicapping its maneuverability. The third tried to wrap around the other wing, but the monster caught the snake's tail in its jaws and yanked it off.

Esset jumped when something bumped him in the back—his mount. Toman was already mounting his own, getting into position in case they needed to move, which it seemed they might. Shaking himself, Esset started chanting as he mounted.

As the monster stomped the snake it had caught into a fine powder despite its other hindrances, a fiery panther materialized before it. The cat was dwarfed by the monster before it, but the stone beneath its paws was scorched black with the slightest contact. Small flames licked about its paws, but they were nothing compared to the white-hot heat of its claws. Its lashing tail flickered and jumped, tendrils of flames licking off of it, and its body was like a mass of cracked and blackened earth with molten lava just beneath, ready to gush forth at any moment but constrained by the might of pure fury. Its eyes were burning pits that even the beast's summoner wouldn't meet for fear of the onset of madness. When it opened its massive maw, there was a flare of light on the rocks, and its roar sounded like a tree exploding in a forest fire.

Not that the cat remained still for more than a moment—it sprang at the monster, its molten claws raking across the side of its face. The dragon-like beast roared in protest, but the attack seemed to do little more than leave black scorch-marks on its hide. The monster snapped at the cat but missed as it darted away, then sprang again. The panther tried to claw the beast's eye, but the monster jerked its head up so it only raked the other cheek.

Esset was mounted before he summoned a second cat, and Toman had taken off and was hovering closer to the battle, sending the chains in to try to wrap around the monster and hinder it further. A fourth stone snake joined the fray, succeeding where its predecessor had failed and wrapping around the other wing. There was no way the monster could take flight without removing them first.

The two fiery panthers harried the beast, keeping ahead of its snapping jaws and forcing it keep moving to avoid their attempts to blind it. Finally the monster reared up and bellowed its frustration before dropping and charging forward. Its run was ungainly, but it forced the panthers to scatter momentarily. When it reached the back of the cave, the monster flung itself at the cave wall, aiming so the snake wrapped around its left wing would strike the rock face first. The monster seemed crazed as it began thrashing unpredictably.

Esset sent one of his cats to attack it, but after a few unrestrained hits from flailing limbs, it sustained enough damage to be banished back to its own plane. Esset held the other panther back—it growled in frustration, its tail lashing against the inactivity. Esset bit his lip—he could see a crack on one of the snakes binding the beast's rear leg; it wouldn't be much longer before that stone creature was cracked in half, but the beast's rampage was keeping him from doing anything about it.

Esset glanced over at Toman, and the crease between his brother's eyebrows betrayed thoughts along a similar line. Then the animator shook his head to himself, and Esset looked back to the monster just in time to see the snakes releasing it.

"Get back, Esset!" Toman yelled.

He's mad, Esset thought as his mount back-winged.

The dragon-like beast immediately righted itself and roared at the retreating snakes—the stone reptiles didn't go far, but they weren't attacking, either. Esset's heart nearly stopped when Toman steered his mount *toward* the monster. He saw his brother's hand thrust forward, and something metal leave it—the dagger flashed in the air and disappeared into the beast's mouth.

The beast was coiling it's haunches to leap into flight, but its roar was abruptly silenced. Its jaws snapped shut, then opened again, issuing another shorter, smaller roar. Toman's hand flicked forward again—Esset knew his aim and arm weren't *that* good, but his magic ensured that the second dagger, too, found its way into the monster's mouth.

Esset sent his fiery panther in to attack, knowing that the gesture was likely superfluous. The scorching feline pounced and finally succeeded in raking its claws over the beast's eye. Another strangled roar was met with another dagger, and when the monster's jaws opened, Esset could see blood collecting in its mouth. The monster staggered forward, its head dipping close to the ground, and the fiery panther sprang and completed its work, blinding the creature. The monster made a pitiful sound, more whine than roar, and collapsed onto the ground. The panther began attacking it with abandon, gouging at its eyes, not caring that there was little damage left to do. Esset banished his bloodthirsty summon when the dragon-like monster stopped moving completely.

Even so, he descended towards the dead beast slowly. His mount touched down gently and walked over to stand beside

Toman. They stared at the dead beast for a long while before Esset laughed with a slight edge of hysteria. Toman looked at him like he was crazy.

"All according to plan," Esset said.

Toman stared, then joined his laughter. "Yeah, Plans A through E," Toman joked. They laughed again before composing themselves and looking around.

"Well, you'd better get a couple of your creatures to saw off some claws or fangs as proof of death. There's no way we're bringing back a whole head as proof, that's for sure," Esset said.

"I hate taking trophies back anyways," Toman muttered. Esset had to agree—it was more gruesome than most people thought, for most people had never seen a real severed head, even that of a beast. Neither Toman nor Esset would ever desecrate a human body that way, but they had brought back heads for a few monsters and beasts in the past, despite their reservations.

Toman's snakes were trying to flip the massive monster over to get at the hind claws, but they weren't large enough to manage it.

"Maybe get your chains to snag the far leg and wrap the other end around your mount," Esset suggested, sitting back and watching. Toman frowned at him but took the suggestion. The carcass flopped over onto its side, and Esset trotted his mount over to take a look as the stone snakes attached to the beast's feet.

"Hey Toman, look at that," Esset said, pointing under the creature's tail.

"Uh, no thanks," Toman replied, looking at his brother askance.

"No, *look*," Esset insisted.

"I think I can live without seeing monster-junk," Toman said.

"But that's just it, it doesn't have any," Esset said.

"It's a girl?" Toman said, still not obliging Esset's suggestion to look.

"*No*," Esset said, not bothering to hide his exasperation. "It's not either. You know what that means, right?"

Toman took too long to respond, so Esset went ahead again.

"Everything in nature has a way to reproduce. This doesn't. It's a mage construct."

Esset and Toman stared at each other until one of the stone

snakes fell backwards as a claw gave way.

"You know what, one claw is enough. Let's get out of here before the mage shows up," Toman said. Taking on a mage without preparation was a bad idea.

"I'll scout the area." Esset was already steering his mount out of the lair, fully intending to get some altitude to keep an eye out for anyone incoming on their position. Toman leaned over and took the massive claw the rock snake was extending to him as his chains slithered over and began looping themselves around his mount.

Esset's winged horse pumped its wings in artificial effort, lifting them between the rock faces. Just as he was clearing the cliffs, he caught a glimpse of a disheveled white beard, a thin frame, and red robes.

"NO! What have you done?" The words were formed through an enraged screech. Esset twisted to look again, but he kept his mount fighting for altitude.

The man—a mage, no doubt—was staring at the carcass of his creation, his expression torn between disbelief and rage. Toman had frozen for a moment, surprised in spite of himself, but then his mount pivoted on one hoof and took off at a gallop down the ravine. The action drew the mage's attention, and Esset saw crackling energy build around the mage's cadaverous hands. Esset turned his mount in the air and hovered.

"Toman, look out!" Esset yelled. The mage whirled and threw his hands out before him, and Esset could hear the buzzing of high voltage as an energy bolt streaked towards him instead of his brother. Esset had just enough time to pull up on his mount. The bolt hit the stone horse in the stomach, and it exploded in a shower of dust and sharp pebbles. For a moment, Esset struggled for breath; his lungs couldn't seem to draw in any of the air that ripped and tore at him as he plummeted earthwards. Unable to speak, Esset closed his eyes and chanted the words in his head.

A rush of heat impacted lightly against his body as the fiery bird materialized beneath him. Esset sucked in a breath and grabbed for the base of each of the bird's wings. One hand found purchase, and Esset's downward momentum was shifted into horizontal movement. His other hand slipped, and for a moment, Esset thought he was going to fall again. His summon didn't care if he caught his grip or not. But no, the bird was under *his* control. It veered to swing him the other way, and he caught the other wing and pulled himself into a more secure position on its back.

It wasn't a moment too soon. Esset barely caught sight of the second incoming energy bolt as the bird dodged it. The hair on Esset's arms stood up as it passed too close with an ominous buzz. Esset didn't have time to gawk as his bird went into a dive, using gravity to aid its speed as it zigzagged around the energy bolts flying towards them. They'd almost completely used up their distance to the ground when the attacks stopped. The fiery bird pulled up and climbed into the sky again.

Esset confirmed a guess when he was able to catch a glimpse of the mage fighting the two stone bears, flinging more of those energy bolts as the animated boulders pounded on a glimmering mage-shield. Doubting Toman's animations would be enough, Esset summoned a fiery panther to join the fray.

The cat roared and flung itself at the glimmering shield, making the mage inside jump and whirl around, his eyes widening at the sight of the molten creature. Ignoring the stone bears that still pounded on the shield, the mage concentrated on the cat, pummeling it with energy bolts from too short a range for it to dodge. The bolts burst against its skin, but the cat seemed to simply absorb the energy. Unfortunately, Esset knew that was an illusion; his summons only *seemed* undamaged. Once they absorbed enough punishment, they were banished all at once. Fortunately, the mage didn't know that. Esset could see him panicking, his eyes wide and wild as he looked around for a way out and found none.

A nimbus began to build around the shield, a faint yellow glow that began pale but was slowly intensifying. Eyes narrowed, Esset maneuvered further away, landing his bird behind a boulder. He looked around for Toman, but he couldn't see him. He wasn't too concerned—Toman knew as well as he did that it was better not to be a target. Let the mage fight their minions and minimize the chance of him realizing the fight was over if he took out the animator and the summoner.

Esset glanced back at the mage, but the light had grown so bright it hurt his eyes. Suspecting what was to come, Esset hid behind the boulder just as the light exploded. With a high-pitched squeal, the light washed over everything in an eye-blink. Esset felt his creature vanish, and he doubted Toman's stone bears had survived either. A quick peek confirmed the guess. The mage stood alone on the rocks, now looking more angry than afraid. For a moment, Esset simply watched, wondering what he'd do. As far as the mage knew, he had no opponents left, and Esset was fairly certain he didn't know his or Toman's exact locations.

That was a mistake. The mage closed his eyes, and a second later, light spilled from his hands. The dazzling light coalesced into two green balls that sped towards Toman and Esset.

Esset summoned the first thing that came to mind—a wolf. It leapt out of the air in front of him just in time to snap its jaws closed around the ball of green light. With another dazzling flash, both orb and wolf were obliterated, leaving Esset with his heart hammering in his chest.

Quit standing around. Esset kicked himself into action. He couldn't hear anything from Toman, so he assumed his brother had blocked the attack as well. And, fortunately, Toman hadn't been snoozing the way Esset had been. *Wait and see what he does...idiot.* Esset cursed himself as two rock snakes flung themselves at the aged mage. The mage barely even looked worried as the glowing bubble of his mage shield appeared around him.

Esset was uttering another incantation when the mage turned—and stepped off the edge of the cliff. The words died on Esset's lips as he rushed to the edge to see the mage floating down gently until he was next to his dead construct. The rock snakes, meanwhile, were forced to slither around the long way.

Esset's eyes widened and he ducked just in time to avoid a crackling magical projectile. The bolt shattered against the rocks, sending loose stones down the rock face. He waited a second or two, then peeked over the edge. He nearly got his head blown off by another bolt, but he thought he'd seen a sickly green glow surrounding the construct. Twice more he tried to get enough of a look to summon a cat down by the mage, but the mage seemed very determined to keep him hunkered down. He was about to go for a fourth look when a flash of movement coming from a different direction entirely caught his attention.

A tiny, crude parchment bird was flapping pathetically before him. Toman had simply mashed a piece of parchment into a rough semblance of a bird, far more concerned with practicality than aesthetics. Esset snatched the bird from the air and flattened the paper to read the rough scrawl on it.

Necro. Summon NOW, the note read. Esset huffed. As if he hadn't been *trying* to summon something down there. But Toman had figured out what Esset had been unable to—the mage was down there by the construct because he was a necromancer. He was going to raise his own construct from the dead, and that was motivation enough for Esset to get creative. He did *not* want to fight that thing again, especially not as a zombie. Hopefully Toman had a plan.

Esset summoned a bird and sent it straight up into the sky. It gave a piercing screech as it climbed, dodging the projectiles the mage sent its way. Esset tried to peek over the edge, but the mage was still paying attention, and Esset only barely remained unsinged. Had he been wearing a hat like Toman, he would have lost it. Frowning, he summoned another bird and sent it into a climb just as the other began to dive.

The birds were *fast* when they dove—faster than they had any right to be. Esset tracked its trajectory as best he could until it was out of sight—by that time, the second was in a dive too. Only then did Esset risk a peek—the mage was distracted, and Esset could see Toman's snakes already battering at the mage's shield.

Two birds was the most he could summon at a time, but Esset had a feeling that wouldn't be a problem for long. Both birds swerved nimbly in the air to avoid the mage-bolts flying at them, narrowly avoiding each projectile without slowing their dives. However, the closer they got, the harder it was to dodge, until one crackling bolt of energy caught one of the birds head on and it vanished in a spray of sparks. That was Esset's opening.

Esset quickly summoned a cat. It mauled at the shield in a fashion that *looked* ineffective, but Esset knew it put considerable strain on the mage to keep the shield intact. Especially when the bird slammed into the shield, effectively destroying itself and allowing Esset to summon a second cat.

The glow around the construct faded slightly, and Esset thought he saw the mage frown—it was difficult to tell through the glimmering mage shield at this distance. But it was easy to see the light building around the shield again. Evidently the mage again planned to use the same wave of light that had obliterated Esset's summons before. It was Esset's turn to frown as he wondered what his brother's plan was. Even as the light intensified, he could see the dragon starting to twitch.

Esset ducked when the light burst outwards, but he darted up again, an incantation on his lips so he wouldn't lose the advantage. Maybe he could summon something before the mage put his shield back up. He looked just in time to see two daggers dart from the dragon's mouth and impale themselves in the mage's chest. The mage gaped at them, uncomprehending. Esset gaped too—he'd forgotten about the daggers that Toman had left embedded inside the dragon after he'd killed it.

Esset saw Toman rise from his hiding place in his peripheral vision, but he couldn't take his eyes away from the mage as the old man slumped to his knees, then his side. Death left a wide-eyed, slack-jawed expression on his face. Toman came to stand by Esset's side.

"We got lucky," Toman said. Esset just nodded.

Lucky the mage was old and uncreative. Lucky the mage had chosen to use an attack that left him exposed, if only for a second. Lucky any number of the mage's attacks hadn't met their mark. Lucky it had been just this man, alone. Lucky the mage hadn't seen *how* they'd killed his pet. Taking down a mage took either a great deal of preparation or a great deal of luck. Or both, but they'd only had luck.

Esset shivered. "Let's get out of here." The next words he spoke were incantations.

CHAPTER 7

"You did *what*?" Mr. Carver squeaked. He'd been offering food, ale, and lodging to the pair a moment before, in return for killing the monster that had plagued them.

"We killed the 'dragon' *and* the mage that created it," Esset repeated with a hint of pride. A murmur rippled through the small crowd that had gathered upon their return. Toman didn't like the feel of that murmur, but Esset didn't seem to notice.

"B-but, that'd be Dark Lord Koris," Mr. Carver stuttered. "One of *the* dark lords."

Esset shrugged. "He was an old man in red robes with a white beard." The crowd visibly drew back an inch or two. A few at the fringes even scurried away.

"You killed a mage lord. Oh no." Mr. Carver suddenly looked very afraid. More people hurried away.

"Look, we're very grateful that you killed the dragon, but you have to go now. Right now. Go." Mr. Carver actually made a shooing motion with his hands before looking shocked at his own actions. When he looked Toman in the eye, briefly, by accident, he looked afraid of *them*.

"Please go," he whimpered. Then he turned and the last of them almost flat out ran away, shutting their doors behind them. Toman even heard the small *thunk* of a bolt sliding home.

Toman and Esset stood, bewildered, in the street.

"Well," Toman finally said, looking around.

"That wasn't the reaction I was expecting," Esset said, almost sounding a little hurt.

"Nor I," Toman admitted, but he was mildly amused by Esset's response.

"I guess it's time to go see Lord Erizen," Toman added, dropping his volume so only Esset could hear.

Esset shot him a disgusted look. "Why would we do that?"

"To get payment, I imagine. Why else would he give you instructions to his castle? He certainly didn't leave our reward money here," Toman replied.

"Forget the payment, we ought to just leave now," Esset said.

"I think we ought to go. And you said yourself that Erizen was planning to provide us with transportation to his castle," Toman said.

"If we go to the next town over," Esset grumbled. He was the one who had received the information from Erizen, after all.

"Then let's fly as far as we can without being seen and hoof it to our rendezvous point," Toman said. Esset frowned. "Come on, hero, cheer up. We just saved a village from a dragon! Surely that's enough like an old tale to make you happy," Toman goaded him, but Esset did seem to lighten up a bit.

"The best tales had heroes rescuing fair maidens as well as villages...but sure," Esset conceded. But despite his lightened demeanor, he added, "I still don't like anything to do with Erizen."

As if there had been any doubt.

The sunrise looked truly odd. It was bright, and the rising sun cast the sky in many different shades of grey, but it remained as colorless as ever. Even Toman would have had to admit that it was mildly disturbing, but his brother just scowled at the sky and said nothing.

They trekked the remainder of the distance to the town from their campsite on foot—the fewer eyes that saw them, the better. There was movement, certainly, but mostly it was faint smoke hovering over chimneys and the brief glimpses of people behind curtains. That, and the arrival of a tiny courier wagon. Toman and Esset picked up their pace to greet it.

"Good morning." Esset greeted the man stepping down from the driver's seat. The courier didn't even seem to notice them. Esset regarded him curiously before trying again. "Good morning," he repeated.

Once again, the courier ignored him. Esset glanced at Toman, but he could only shrug. The courier retrieved a large package from the interior of the vehicle.

"Do you need help with that?" Esset offered, stepping forward with his hands outstretched. The courier stepped around him and headed for a nearby building. Esset's hands fell to his sides.

"What do you remember from Erizen's instructions?" Toman asked in a hushed tone. Given the courier's odd behavior, he was fairly certain that Esset had missed something.

"Just...get in the courier wagon," Esset said with a shrug, looking at his brother after one last puzzled look after the courier.

"Sounds like we should just get in the wagon then," Toman suggested. The door had been left open. Toman leaned in the door and peered inside—it was completely empty. Normally couriers didn't take passengers, as far as Toman knew, and the carriage was small, designed for speed and sturdiness rather than comfort.

Esset peered over his shoulder into the interior. "Looks uncomfortable."

"But it should be inconspicuous. No one will see us if we keep the curtains drawn." Toman stepped up into the carriage, and Esset followed him. As Toman closed the door, he saw the courier return. The man again ignored them, and Toman felt the carriage shift as the courier climbed to his seat. A moment later, there was a snap of reins and an encouraging sound to the horse and they were off towards Erizen's capital.

"Thank Hyrishal. There's the castle," Toman said, peeking through the slit between the curtains covering the tiny window.

"It's about time. Next time let's just use your animations and fly by night," Esset said. "Then we don't have to stay days squished in this ridiculous carriage."

"I'm...actually inclined to agree," Toman said. "The less time we spend in all this grey, the better." He took off his hat and scowled at it. "The color had better come back when we leave this place, or I'm going to be really upset."

Esset just looked down at himself. Everything not biologically attached to them had turned grey. Esset really wasn't happy about that either—he liked the colors of his clothes. That was why he'd chosen clothes of those colors.

The warm coil of tension and anger still boiled in Esset's gut.

"I'm ready to tear a strip off that man. Could you imagine having to *live* in this kingdom? Grey *everything*. It's depressing, and there's no way it's benevolent. We shouldn't be getting involved with him, not even this far. He's on the wrong team. We should turn around and leave."

"We're here. Let's see it through," Toman replied, almost by rote. They were already rattling through the city below the castle. Absolutely everything was grey, and the populace was as subdued as the color. That had been a common theme they'd witnessed on their way here; no large gatherings of people, no voices above a normal speaking voice, and even the children played more quietly than Esset could recall anywhere else.

The courier took them right through the city and up to a well-fortified castle on the hill above it. When the carriage stopped, a liveried footman came up to the carriage door and opened it before gesturing that they should disembark from the small vehicle. Esset was first out, with Toman close behind him. They both wanted to stretch and shake the stiffness from their cramped bodies, but they settled for just a few modest stretches so as not to make a show of it. They were led from the courtyard towards the main doors, which were open to admit them.

The exterior of the castle may have been austere and highly practical, but the inside was downright sumptuous. A fortune in elaborate tapestries adorned the walls, the scenes depicted ranging from great hunts to glorious battles to… Esset blushed, for the wall hangings also illustrated rather explicit bedroom scenes. The floor was even laid out with a ridiculously expensive red plush rug, a massive one that ran the length of the hall. Torches adorned the walls in the gaps between tapestries, and where their light did not reach, there were tall candlesticks on the ground. There were also chandeliers glittering brightly above them, hanging from high, vaulted ceilings.

In the face of such excessive luxury, Esset almost missed the blindingly obvious: nothing inside was grey. He thought back. Yes, the exterior of the castle had been grey, but the interior was awash with intense colors. Whatever was making the rest of the kingdom grey, it didn't reach within these walls.

The liveried man leading them wasn't affected either—that uniform of his had that same distinct shade of maroon in its trimmings as Erizen had worn when they'd met him at the Staggering Tankard. From that, Esset inferred that one would have to spend an extensive amount of time outside the castle for color to be drained from one's clothing. Once again he found himself hoping that the color in their clothes would come back once they were out of the grey zone for long enough.

Esset brought his thoughts back to the immediate future and away from the decadence around them. They'd reached a second set of double doors. Ornately carved of a deep, rich brown wood, the doors were pulled open by two guards standing watch. Apparently they had been expected...if only they could have expected what laid within. Even Toman couldn't hide his surprise when the doors opened to reveal the contents of the room beyond. The scene before them was too bizarre and too unexpected to be faced without at least a momentary betrayal of emotion.

It was difficult to say which side of the room drew more attention. The answer would probably change depending on who stood in the doorway. Along the left-hand wall were a row of bizarre creatures, all tethered to the wall on chains just short enough that they couldn't reach anything. They reacted to the newcomers with varying degrees of placidity: some merely glanced towards the door, but others rose snarling and snapping to strain at their chains. The most active creatures were typically the most monstrous. None of the creatures looked like anything Toman and Esset had ever seen before, for none of them were natural. It was easy to tell that they were creatures shaped by magic. How else could one animal have three sets of jaws on one head? How could a panther-like creature have a pelt of those radiant, glowing colors? They were all of them a strange mix of multiple animals combined into one, parts of which the brothers could recognize, but not in the manner in which they were...assembled. One reptilian creature had too many bulbous, blinking eyes to possibly be born of nature. Some were beautiful, but most were ugly, and almost all of them looked intimidating. The implications of these chimeras horrified Esset.

The other wall also sported a row of chained captives, but they were captives of an entirely different sort: women. Very scantily clad women. Although they weren't clad in much, what they did wear was expensive—light silks and gossamers, all in a startling array of colors, from pink and purple to red and orange or greens and blues. Even the collars and chains that held them captive were elaborate, with some made of gold, and most with links in fancy patterns. Some smiled or gestured welcomingly, lasciviously, at the duo, their poses provocative. Others danced as far as their chains would allow, dances that typically made men think with organs other than their brains. Esset hated that he felt his color rising, and it didn't help to be embarrassed about being embarrassed. But then he was angry, and that helped a very great deal with the embarrassment. How dare Erizen keep slaves like this? To keep slaves at all was bad enough, but to demean these women by making them display themselves like that...

That devil himself was reclined on a massive, red-upholstered chair at the end of the long hall, one leg thrown over an armrest to face mostly sideways. Erizen had two of his captives fawning over him, feeding him bits of fruit from a bowl on the stand beside his throne—for that's what his chair was. The mage looked so much the part of a storybook villain. He made no secret that he looked at the bodies of the women serving him as much as their faces, and Esset had no idea how the women could pretend to be so happy. So much so that he wondered what happened if they weren't.

Erizen ignored them in favor of his "ladies," blithely enjoying their attentions instead of greeting his guests.

"Okay, Erizen, we did the job. Now where's our pay?" Esset asked. Upon his words, the two ladies gave him instantaneous and identical glares, surprising him.

"That's *Lord* Erizen," one of them corrected acidly, a woman with luscious black hair that fell over her shoulders in thick waves. A sheer veil over her body hid nothing at all, leaving her modesty to three scraps of red cloth that left her minimally decent. Esset's surprise at the correction from her—and, as far as he could tell, the genuine glare—left him silent for a moment.

Erizen watched him with amusement.

"Are you going to stand by our deal, Lord Erizen?" Toman challenged the mage to help Esset save face.

"Such doubting allies," Erizen drawled lazily, exciting a titter from the second woman, who was clad in pale pink. "I have just welcomed you into my home. Does that not speak to my goodwill? Fear not, your reward is on its way. In the meantime, what do you think of my domain so far?"

"Do you really want me to answer that question?" Esset asked, his anger still simmering. Erizen hadn't been very open to criticism so far.

"You've noticed the effects of the Greymaker, no doubt," Erizen continued, blithely ignoring Esset's question.

"It was difficult to miss," Toman put in dryly.

"I will have you know that it is my own ingenious invention," Erizen preened.

So far, Esset didn't see what there was to be proud of. "So what does it do?" the summoner asked bluntly.

"I'm so glad you asked," Erizen replied with a wolf's grin, his voice suddenly unaccented. "Did you know that there is ambient power everywhere, a power that normally just floats around, completely untapped and wasted? Well, *I* have discovered a way to gather it and make it available for my use no matter where it is. The only side effect of the machine is what you have seen—and, of course, how it got its nickname. Over time, it saps the color from all inanimate things within its boundaries. I would say that it's the secret to my success, but in actuality, I was successful even before I built it."

Such modesty, Esset thought. He might have said something, but just then, one of the scantily-clad slave girls along the wall grasped the chain where it attached to her collar, unclipped it, and walked down the hall before exiting through a servants' door. He blinked, surprised. Wasn't she a slave? Chained against her will? He looked quickly back at Erizen, whose gaze was openly mocking.

"Admiring Orchid's derrière? She does have a rather lovely behind. Perky." Erizen knew perfectly well that wasn't what Esset had been doing, just as he knew what he was thinking just then. He said it instead to laugh at the color that rose in Esset's cheeks. Then again, there had been a rather suggestive swing to Orchid's hips…

At the very least, Esset didn't give Erizen the satisfaction of a response.

"If you'd like to stay the night, I could send her to your rooms," Erizen offered with a sly smile. Esset bridled at the thought of the poor girl having no say in whom she slept with, and this time anger won out over embarrassment.

Toman spoke up before Esset could respond. "We weren't planning on staying long. If this single job is to conclude our business, then we will take our payment and move on before nightfall," Toman said.

"Surely you have never enjoyed such luxurious accommodations as I have to offer, and I insist you stay the night to enjoy them," Erizen objected grandly. "It would be unforgivably rude to refuse." Esset clenched his jaw, but Erizen continued.

"There is also a matter I wish to discuss, and I'm afraid I'm quite tied up tonight… First thing in the morning, we can convene, and then you can be on your way," Erizen said, never once taking his eyes away from the women fawning over him. "There are guest rooms prepared for you, if you are amicable." Just then, the woman who'd unchained herself and left returned. She waved a little finger-waggling wave at them as she returned to her post, clipping the chain back onto her collar.

"We look forward to it," Toman replied blandly. "But our foremost concern is our payment for the last job."

"But of course," Erizen replied easily. He gestured to someone behind them. "Here is Julliard with your reward now." Sure enough, the liveried servant from before walked up behind them and then drew even, a small chest in his arms.

"Julliard can show you to the dining hall—you must be hungry after your long ride. He will take your payment to your rooms and be back by the time you are done eating to show you to them as well," Erizen said, obviously growing increasingly bored with the proceedings. The woman in red had begun to demand more of his attentions, and he obliged her, making a somewhat sickening show of it.

"Thank you, Lord Erizen," Toman replied neutrally, and the two brothers followed as the servant Julliard led the way.

Julliard led them to a table laid with a fantastically delicious meal. It was probably wasteful and excessively decadent, but neither brother had ever eaten anything like it before, and they couldn't help but be impressed. They practically had to waddle back to their rooms.

"I might not like our new 'friend' very much, but I have to admit, he serves good food," Esset confessed happily as Julliard led them to their rooms.

Toman chuckled. "I agree, that was great. Although I also have to admit, I'm looking forward to bed even more. We spent too many nights in that cramped carriage—it'll be nice to stretch out on a soft surface again."

Esset agreed vehemently with that as well. Then the liveried servant leading them spoke up.

"Here you are, sir," Julliard said, stopping at a guestroom door and turning to face them. "These are your quarters for the night. Yours, sir, are the next door." He gestured to his right.

"Thank you very much," Esset responded with a smile.

Toman settled for a briefer, "Thanks."

The servant inclined his head to them. "If you should need anything, someone will be nearby. Have a good evening, sirs." With that, the man departed.

"Well, g'night," Toman said to Esset, turning away to head to his room. He waved over his shoulder.

"G'night, Toman, see you tomorrow," Esset replied as he opened the door to his own room. Looking over his shoulder to bid his brother goodnight, Esset was a full five steps into the room before he saw her. The woman from before, the one who'd unhooked her chain, left, and returned to the great hall, was here in his room, sitting on his bed, waiting for him. She had beautiful blonde hair, long silken strands that flowed down to her waist. In fact, her hair did more to cover her body than the purple "garment" that she wore.

"Oh—I'm sorry, I thought..." Esset looked around nervously as he began to back out of the room.

"This is your room," the blonde said. Esset's mind raced. *Orchid? Yes, her name had been Orchid.*

The beautiful woman smirked wryly at him and rose fluidly. Her hips swung as she stepped softly towards him, beckoning. "Won't you come in? Relax, make yourself comfortable."

Esset had stopped his retreat when she'd said he hadn't mistaken the room, and that mistake had allowed her to trap him. She was almost upon him when it occurred to him to start backing up again. "Um, no really, that's fine. Uh, shouldn't you...?"

Orchid slid right up to Esset as he stammered. Reaching past him, Orchid's slender hand pushed the door shut to hinder his escape. Esset tried to turn to catch it, but Orchid crowded him until he was pinned against the closed door. Esset tried to raise his hands defensively in front of his chest, only to have her press up against him, planting her breasts firmly into his palms. Esset turned beet red. She smelled amazing, like the sweet breath of blossoms on a spring day.

"My, but you are adorable," Orchid breathed softly into his face. Her smile was teasing as she drew away again, but with her hands on his upper arms to bid him to follow. He tugged against her a little bit, but without rudely yanking away, he was unable to extract himself.

"Ah, this is all, uh, entirely unnecessary, really," Esset said awkwardly. "I was just going to, uh, get some sleep, y'know. Big day tomorrow and all that."

"Mmm?" The sound she made sounded almost like a cat's purr. "Nothing else you want?" She lifted one hand from his arm to brush his cheek.

"No, thank you," the summoner said.

"Really?" she asked. There was a trace of genuine surprise. Her grip loosened, and Esset took the opportunity to step away.

"Really," Esset responded; his tone almost sounded placating.

"Huh. He was right about you," Orchid said curiously, tilting her head a bit. The gesture made her hair ripple as it readjusted over one breast. Esset quickly looked away.

"Uh, who was right about what?" he asked in a rush. Anything to change the subject.

"My lord said you wouldn't take me," she replied bluntly.

"Wait, what?"

"I thought for sure he was joking. All of Lord Erizen's guests like company in their beds at night." The way she looked at him made Esset uncomfortably certain that she was wondering if there was anything wrong with him. Only after an uncomfortable silence had passed did she speak again. "He gave me the usual orders, but I'm not sure what he meant by them this time," she finally admitted.

"Orders?" That reminded Esset that he should be mad about this, mad at Erizen. "I think it's deplorable, how that man treats you."

Orchid looked surprised at his vehement assertion, but then

there was a look of dawning comprehension. "Ah, I get it now," she said. Stepping back, she sat down on the bed so she could be more comfortable.

"Get what?" Esset was confused again.

Orchid smiled again, her confidence restored. "I will explain, but you have to promise to listen, okay? You really have no idea how things work around here." Esset looked at her, not entirely sure what he would be promising to listen to, but not objecting, either.

She decided to continue. "We love him, our Lord Erizen. All of us, his women, do. He wouldn't keep us around if we didn't, and those who don't fit in find a place elsewhere—they're cared for, believe me. Lord Erizen is arrogant, yes, but doesn't he have a right to be? He's rich, powerful, and amazingly clever. Yet he changes our names and color codes us so he can remember them." She laughed gaily. "It's more than that, though. We're lucky to be his people—every person in this kingdom is."

Esset looked like he wanted to object, but she lifted a finger and shot him a warning look to silence him. He subsided.

"Contrary to the great show he puts on, Erizen takes care of us. Know that this territory and all the ones surrounding it have been under the control of dark mage lords for…well, I don't actually know how long, but generations, at least. The lord before Erizen was…not so kind. These lords, they show their power through cruelty. Life was horrible under them—is horrible under the others. So…we put on a show. Here, in this kingdom, life is pretty good. But we can't let any of the other mage lords know, or they would think Lord Erizen soft and destroy him. Everything must seem just as it is in other kingdoms. Thus, the gloom of the Greymaker. Even a healthy peasant looks put-upon under its pall. And thus the chains in the hall." She smirked. "Although I think my lord likes them anyways."

A bit of red colored Esset's ears. "I dunno. This doesn't at all match with what I've seen of Erizen." Esset wasn't quite ready to be convinced yet.

"Then you aren't listening," Orchid said bluntly. "Lord Erizen is practical—he likes power and pleasure. How does he get that? Seizing this territory gets him power. The Greymaker makes him power. Gaining the loyalty of the people keeps him that power and increases the pleasure he can receive from us. We will give him more in return than any other mage lord could possibly get from his people. Are those narcissistic enough reasons for you to accept?"

Orchid laughed at Esset's expression, and then continued. "You think me unaware of how self-centered he is? You think I think he does good because he has morals?" She laughed. "I know the truth, as do you now. The difference is, I love him anyway."

Esset didn't know what to make of this extraordinary woman whom he'd found in his bedroom. He'd met women who were scholars, warriors, or simply wives, but he'd never met anyone like this. "That... I guess that does make sense," he finally acknowledged.

"Lord Erizen will be pleased," Orchid said happily.

And that reminded Esset: orders. She'd said she was here on orders. The "usual" orders. "So... what were Erizen's 'usual orders?' You mentioned them earlier," he asked delicately.

"We are underestimated," Orchid replied readily—and proudly. "Being what we are. And our clever lord knows how best to use that, and us, to his advantage. He said, 'Give him what he needs to see things my way.' Normally that means we're to bed his guest and then pillow talk them around to coming to the decision that our lord wants. But I was confused by what he said next: 'Heads up, doll, he won't bed you.'" She did a passable imitation of his drawl.

Esset couldn't help but smile. He still didn't like that she was being used as she was, but he could see her point of view, at least.

"But you... You're different aren't you? Very different from our lord's usual guests. You don't need sex and wiles... You just needed the truth." There was just a hint of wonder in her gaze; it was that foreign a thing to her. She looked at him curiously.

"I've always been a believer in truth," Esset admitted with irony.

"Well, Mr. Truthful, you sure you don't want me to...hang around?" She rose fluidly and stepped in very close, making him once again draw back in surprise.

"That's, uh, not necessary, no." He was back to stammering again. Orchid clearly took delight in how easy it was to fluster him.

"That's actually a pity. Like I said, you're adorable." Orchid brushed past him and opened the door. Her blue eyes glanced back at him one last time before she closed the door behind her.

CHAPTER 8

Toman felt a bit of the tension drain from him as he peeled off his coat and hung it on the stand beside the door. Beneath the coat he wore an ordinary, brown, short-sleeved shirt, and of course, he kept on his gloves. He washed and slept with them on regularly anyways, but to take them off in the home of one who was a dubious ally at best—that would be foolish.

Spying a wash basin, Toman dumped the ready pitcher of water in and washed his face. When he was done, he patted his face dry with the small, plush towel left there for that purpose. Exhaling heavily, he buried his face in the soft towel for several long moments as he consciously relaxed his muscles, working his way through his neck muscles, down his shoulders, and into his arms. He was about to put the towel down when he thought he heard the door open.

There—a soft scuff on the floor betrayed the intruder's presence. Toman didn't even pause. His coat came to life next to the door, leaping at the intruder and wrapping the sleeves around her.

"Oh!" The exclamation was definitely feminine. When Toman laid eyes on her, his exhale was one of frustration. It was one of Erizen's girls from the throne room: Orchid. She struggled weakly against the coat, unable to free herself and looking rather pathetic in her attempts. Toman made it release her and return to the hook by the door.

"You really ought to knock before entering. Orchid, right?" Toman asked, dropping the towel over the edge of the sink behind him.

"I am so sorry, my lord," Orchid said, curtseying and eyeing the coat nervously yet. "I had no idea, I mean, I thought—"

Toman arched an eyebrow. "It's quite all right. My abilities are completely under my control, and I have no reason to harm you," he said to ease her fears. "And I'm no lord. Just Toman."

Orchid visibly collected herself. "My apologies, sir. You are correct. I should have knocked. I have been sent here to serve you as you please." Toman watched as Orchid consciously shifted her body language to something more demure.

Toman chuckled. "Why am I not surprised? You're lovely, Orchid, but no thank you." Orchid looked only slightly surprised—probably more by the nature of the refusal than the refusal itself. Far more than surprised, however, she looked intrigued.

"So you are like your partner, then?" Something suddenly seemed to occur to her. "You are not lovers, are you?"

Toman almost choked. "No, no, definitely not. Brightfire no. We're best friends, brothers. We grew up together."

"Huh. The last time two men rejected me in one night, they were partners in a far more intimate way than the way you and your partner are," Orchid said.

"That's, uh, very...informative, but no," Toman reiterated. He couldn't believe that this woman had managed to get him flustered. Although her precise timing had surprised him, he'd guessed that Erizen might try sending his women to them. Despite that foresight, she still had him off balance. It was...impressive.

"I apologize for the misconception," Orchid said.

"I don't think you're sorry," Toman said bluntly, his frankness surprising Orchid into looking him straight into the eye.

"I beg your pardon, my lord?"

"I don't think you're sorry," Toman repeated. "I think this has played out quite the way you planned. Your first reaction," he pointed at his coat, "was quite genuine. I don't think I've seen a genuine reaction since. You just came from visiting my brother, yes?"

"I don't—"

Toman cut her off. "Yes?" he demanded.

"Yes," she replied. There was no point in denying it.

"And your act was consistent with that. Nonetheless, I know Erizen sent you here to play us. He wants us to be assured of his...well, I don't know what you'd call it exactly, but let's just go with calling it his 'good side.' My brother is quick to judge, but I've seen more than that going on here. Erizen likes to play games and push buttons, and I get that too, but I don't like being played. So, will you drop the act?"

"My lord, I'm sure—"

"I'm afraid you tipped your hand when you 'misconstrued' the relationship between my brother and me just now. That's not a normal conclusion to jump to, and you immediately sought to justify your 'mistake.' The reason you pretended to make that mistake was to discomfit me and to put me in a space where it was easier for you to tell which of my reactions were real and which weren't. Let me guess. Erizen uses you to assess how much of a threat we are, if at all, and whether we can be shaped to his ends— or at least used to his ends. Am I right?"

Orchid looked perplexed by his monologue. Either she was genuinely confused—he doubted it—or she was stalling as she debated internally whether to speak plainly. There was a third, more frightening option as well: it was possible that there were painful consequences for her having been caught, and trying to preserve her cover, no matter how flimsy it was, remained her only hope of saving herself. And if that were the case...

Occasionally Toman wished that his compassion wasn't such a handicap sometimes. For if that were the case, he didn't want to jeopardize her. He didn't think Erizen would stoop to that, but on the other hand, he wasn't confident that his educated guess on that front was accurate.

"Okay then," Toman continued. "Now that we each know where the other stands, shall we continue our little charade?"

"I—" Orchid began.

"Don't." Toman stopped her with a shake of his head. "Unless you're admitting something, just don't." Orchid's silence spoke volumes, although the perplexed expression that she maintained kept her cover story consistent, at least.

"Okay then," Toman said again. "Let's pick up where we left off. Why don't you tell me what you think will reassure me about your master?"

"Um... This is all very unusual..." Orchid stalled, looking at him strangely. She bought the time to gather her thoughts and then moved on, as he'd requested. "My lord Erizen did send me to you, of course, and I will admit that he wanted you to know the truth of his kingdom: that is, about the Greymaker and the true nature of his relationship with his people, and with the relationship with the other dark mage lords..." From there, she told Toman much the same information as she'd shared with Esset.

Toman paid attention, but he also mused that Esset had likely fallen for her act, at least partially. Esset was more book smart than he was, but when it came to people... Well, Toman was better at people.

"So, did you have an interesting visitor last night?" Toman asked Esset. He was sitting on the end of Esset's bed as the latter shaved over a basin. Esset nearly nicked himself as he looked over sharply at his brother.

"I take it you did too?" he replied. Thankfully Toman had waited until he was almost done to bring this up, so Esset finished the last stroke and then began to wipe his face on a small towel.

"Orchid," Toman said. Esset nodded, indicating his visitor was the same.

"Maybe Erizen isn't as bad as we thought," Esset said, hanging the towel on the edge of the basin.

"Maybe. But he's very canny, and we both know we're getting involved with someone who could be very, very dangerous to us."

"Of course. But the sergeant made some very compelling arguments too."

"So she did. Well, I guess nothing's changed then. We've just confirmed what we already knew."

Esset nodded his agreement to that statement.

"Shall we, then? I do believe we have an appointment with Lord Erizen this morning," Toman added. He wore a grin, one with just a hint of cheekiness.

"We shall," Esset agreed.

"Ah good, there you are," Erizen said once Julliard had led them into the small study and left, closing the door behind him. "Don't worry. You have my personal assurance that not a soul other than ourselves will be able to know anything that is said between we three for as long as that door is closed." Erizen waved at the door Julliard had just departed through.

"That's reassuring. Although our arrival wasn't exactly a secret yesterday," Esset pointed out. Erizen grinned a broad grin, a grin that suggested he found grinning at Esset's statement particularly appropriate. Esset couldn't help but scowl slightly at the response.

"Let me tell you what happened yesterday," Erizen replied. "Yesterday, two colorless merchant's sons arrived just as public audiences were ending, and they were enlisted into my castle guard. Registers show two new recruits today, and a count would confirm that. They are of your general description, and everyone knows that I interview each new member of my personal staff individually. So, no problems there. And as for our conversations, well, I keep very thorough sound-scrambling spells throughout all the rooms in my castle. Anyone hoping to eavesdrop would have failed horribly. See? No problems at all."

"I hope so," Esset conceded.

"I know so. Now, we need to discuss how you killed my neighbor, Lord Koris." All the humor in Erizen's eyes had vanished.

"He created the 'dragon,' and he was part of the threat against the village you asked us to protect. He is no longer a threat," Toman replied.

"So it would seem," Erizen said. "However, the council of dark lords maintains a balance that is precarious at best. In removing Koris, you have disrupted that balance. I believe I can maintain my own position despite that upset, but only because Koris was such a minor player. I would warn you against disrupting it again." His voice had a threatening edge to it.

"I don't see why you would be worried about that," Toman said. "We would already have been far away from these kingdoms if you hadn't called us back here."

"Indeed." After a pregnant pause, Erizen's tone lightened. "I must admit, however, that I'm surprised you managed to kill Koris at all. He may not have been the strongest among us, but even the weakest dark mage lord here is a very formidable opponent, both in terms of strength and intellect. Otherwise he would not have been able to survive."

We were surprised too, Toman thought, but he didn't say it aloud. "We are formidable opponents ourselves," he said instead.

Erizen looked him up and down. "Evidently." The mage seemed to be considering another statement, and Toman was sure he knew they intended to take out Moloch too…eventually.

"Well then, it seems our business is concluded. I know these kingdoms must look rather tempting to a couple of *heroes* like you," Erizen made "heroes" sound derogatory, "but as long as you leave well enough alone, we can remain friends. Perhaps we can even do business again in the future. Please, feel free to remain as my guests as long as you like, although I imagine you'll be departing once night falls."

Both Toman and Esset nodded.

"Excellent. Enjoy your day." Erizen waved his hand and the door swung open. Toman and Esset took the hint and left, waiting until the door closed before speaking.

"He knows," Esset said.

"Oh, definitely," Toman agreed.

"I can't wait to get out of here."

"Yup."

"Two chicken pies!" Toman waved two fingers at The Staggering Tankard's barkeep, who scowled at him—the waitress was the one who took food orders, not him. But the waitress was just coming out of the kitchen, and she smiled and waved an acknowledgement at Toman and then said something to the barkeep, making him smile.

"Hey boys," Sergeant Warthog called from the back of the room. They went and joined her at her table.

"So how did it go?" she asked once they were sitting.

"Well, we killed the dragon—" Toman began, but Esset cut him off.

"It wasn't a *real*—"

"We killed the not-dragon," Toman amended. Esset frowned but let him continue this time. "And then we killed the mage that created the monster."

Sergeant Warthog's eyebrows flew up towards her hairline.

"We got lucky," Toman said frankly. Just then their chicken pies arrived, and there was a brief silence as the two young men wolfed down their food quickly, as only young men could.

Sergeant Warthog watched, her lips twisted in wry amusement, until Esset happened to glance up. He put down his fork with a sheepish face.

"Ah, yes. Well, after we killed the construct and the mage, we had to go to Erizen's castle to pick up our payment. The visit was…interesting." Esset and Toman exchanged a glance.

"You tell her," Toman said. "You're better at explaining things."

Esset described the Greymaker and what little they knew of it, and he told her of the brief conversation they'd had with Erizen the morning they'd left.

"Well, that all but confirms that Erizen knows you two plan on tackling Moloch, but that's hardly news. This whole thing was probably his way of taking your measure. He has a nice little setup for himself there, and he wants to know if you're even capable of disrupting it. I'm guessing you put him off balance, killing that mage. We might yet have an ally in this fight against Moloch. Hopefully we do, because we don't want an enemy." Sergeant Warthog frowned then, but at Esset's curious look, she gave a dismissive wave.

"Regardless, when we start gathering information on Moloch, we'll want to get as much as we can independent of Erizen. That way we won't have to put all our trust in him, we'll know if he tries to play us, and even if all is well, he'll be that much less likely to get caught as a traitor by the other dark lords," she concluded.

"Do you know when we might start gathering information?" Toman asked, a bit guarded. She had said she'd help them when she thought they were ready, after all. And while they wouldn't be able to walk up to Moloch's front door and challenge him immediately, Toman thought they were at least nearing the point where they should be collecting resources and information to use against the evil mage.

Sergeant Warthog gave them both an appraising look. "We'll see," she said.

Toman was less than satisfied with the enigmatic response, but he hid the reaction as she continued.

"You know, if you want me to help you strategize fighting the most powerful mage in history, you might want to give me more detail about your battles so I can give you advice for future ones,"

Sergeant Warthog remarked.

"Of course," Esset said, and he launched into his explanation.

Esset was yawning by the time he'd told the entire story and the sergeant was done analyzing it and sharing her advice.

"You boys get some sleep," the sergeant said, stifling the yawn that rose in response to Esset's. Toman didn't bother trying to stop his yawn.

"Come around again mid-morning, and I'll probably have a job for you. I heard a merchant is due in first thing tomorrow, scouting for guards for a big caravan," Sergeant Warthog told them.

"Speaking of yawning," Esset muttered.

"Hey, I'd rather guard a boring merchant train than venture after more of those giant scorpions we eradicated last season," Toman said. Esset shuddered.

"Dark caves, skittering feet, clacking pincers..." Esset shuddered again, harder this time. He didn't look quite so sleepy anymore.

"I wouldn't say no to driving off some bandits though," Toman said hopefully.

"Or other, non-arachnid monsters," Esset put in.

"It's not like I create the jobs," Sergeant Warthog said wryly. "I give you what comes along."

"Merchant trains..." Esset muttered.

"Do you want the job?" the sergeant asked.

"Yes," Toman said, shooting his brother a look.

"Yes," Esset echoed obediently.

"Good. See you in the morning."

CHAPTER 9

"Thank goodness that's over and done with. I swear, if she gets us one more job guarding a boring old merchant train…" Esset began as they walked up the front steps of the Staggering Tankard a couple weeks later.

"Oh, don't start. At least these kinds of jobs are good money," Toman retorted, shoving the door open with his shoulder and entering first.

"Yeah, but bor—" Esset ran smack into Toman's back as he stopped abruptly in front of him. "Oof. Yoohoo." Esset shoved his best friend to the side, then stopped to stare for a moment himself. To their credit, they didn't stare long, but instead quickly continued on their way to report their latest mission to the sergeant.

As it turned out, Sergeant Warthog's present company wasn't of the usual variety. Toman and Esset were accustomed enough to seeing some non-humans; they'd fought plenty of vampires and undead, and they'd worked both alongside and against the Tahr, who were more bulls than men, and the Elth, the tall, slender folk with cat-eyes and pointed ears who preferred the company of nature to humans. Even so, neither of them had ever seen anyone like the snake-lady ahead of them now.

From the waist down, she was a mass of scaly coils, a dull teal in color. It was difficult to tell how…well, how *long* she was, due to the fact that her coils were wrapped around each other, creating a comfortable position to keep her torso upright. Waist up, she was rather less snake. She was still covered in scales, but they were smaller and finer, especially on her hands and face. Other than the scales, she looked the same as any human female. Except that she wasn't wearing anything, not really. She had incredibly long, thick, black hair that covered her back and chest, and it was braided rather skillfully—and strategically. Her hair was basically her clothes; it was woven to cover her breasts, but the intricate pattern still left most of her chest and stomach exposed.

Technically she was decent, but Toman and Esset were still

getting far more of an eyeful than they were used to, even after their stay with Erizen. And she was remarkably curvy and beautiful…if one ignored the scales and the coils below and the two black indentations on either side of the bridge of her nose. Her eyes could be slightly unnerving too—there was something not-quite-human about them. They were a bright teal, the same shade as her scales, but brighter, and they were reptilian, not human; it was clear those pupils would change into slits under the right lighting conditions. In the dim evening light in the tavern, however, her eyes could almost pass as human.

"Boys, this is Lady Nassata of the Nadra. I gather from your stunned expressions you've never met anyone from her race before," Sergeant Warthog said dryly.

Esset coughed, trying to regain lost composure. "Ah, no. It's a pleasure, Lady Nassata. I am Summoner Jonathan Esset, and this is Animator Toman Atrix-Iiren." Esset offered his hand, intending to take her hand to kiss it as he would any lady's, but she took it in a clasp instead. Toman took off his floppy-brimmed hat in respect as he greeted her, and she clasped Toman's arm immediately afterwards, speaking as she did so. Her voice was soft, but not very feminine, and unusual; it rang a bit hollow, with additional sibilance.

"Gretchen is ever introducing me as 'Lady,' insisting it will grant me more respect here than my true title of 'Warrior.' Please, Warrior Nassata, or simply Nassata, will suffice," the Nadra replied. Her tongue was briefly visible as she spoke; it split into a fork at the end and was a shade similar to her scales, but a bit darker.

"Well met," Toman responded. "I'm Toman, he's Esset." He jerked a thumb at his brother. It was only then that they noticed her weapon, which she'd left leaning against the side of table. It was a long spear, forged entirely of some strange, dark metal that neither of them recognized. There was also a bag made of what looked like snakeskin on the ground beside her.

"Better," Nassata agreed. "Now, Gretchen tells me she intends to recruit the two of you to help me and my people." She glanced sidelong at the sergeant.

"They have a rather unique skill set, one that will hopefully be useful," the sergeant replied. "If you describe your problem to them, I think they'll agree."

"I came prepared to hire a group, even a mercenary company…" Nassata objected, clearly not understanding how these two people would be of much use to her.

"Trust me, Nassata. Tell them your troubles," Sergeant Warthog replied, placing a hand on the Nadran warrior's shoulder. Nassata regarded them seriously for a moment before speaking.

"We Nadra are normally self-sufficient, and this tradition has made us proud. It was difficult for us to admit that we need help, and even then, it was only after I suggested we speak to Gretchen, whom we know and trust, that the others agreed to ask for aid." She paused for a moment, almost seeming to expect a response. Esset nodded and was trying to think of something to say when she finally decided to continue.

"For as long as we can remember, the Reshkin have shared our underground living spaces. For generations, they have been pests, but nothing more. Recently, however, they have undergone changes that we do not understand, and we find ourselves in serious danger from them. Their bite has always been venomous, but never fatal. Now anyone who is bitten, no matter how strong of constitution, will die over the space of a week.

"They have always been ingenious at evading our attempts to eradicate them, but now they seem to have a kind of hive mind and exhibit far more intelligence than they ever had before. And their aggression—they used to flee at the sight of any group of three or more persons, but now they will attack any size group if they see an opportunity. Their exoskeletons have always been tough, but now they can deflect minor blows, and they are even slightly larger than they used to be.

"Something has changed the Reshkin, and now they are attacking my people. They are more than we can handle, alone. We lost many warriors when we were unaware, before all of their changes became apparent and the true war began. Now, even with full awareness, we find ourselves pushed back. There are even areas of the city that we've been forced to abandon to the creatures."

She paused, and Toman took the chance to ask a question. "These Reshkin—what do they look like?"

"They are… You would likely describe them as a cross

between an ant and a spider, only much larger. They are the size of your average dog, with eight legs and a body separated into three pieces and ridges on their backs. They have numerous eyes and very venomous mandibles."

"Delightful," Esset murmured. Then he added, "What tactics did you use when fighting them in the past?"

"Nadra favor hand-to-hand combat, but against the Reshkin we typically use our spears. Piercing attacks were always effective prior to their recent development," Nassata replied.

"But now, with increased armor, the effectiveness of that type of attack is reduced," Toman interjected.

Nassata nodded. "But we are ill-suited for heavier attacks. We have begun training in the use of maces, which seem most effective against them, but in the meantime, the Reshkin take more territory," she added.

"What about fire?" Esset asked.

"They do not like it, of course. Few cave denizens do, including us Nadra." Nassata regarded him curiously, catching something about the pointedness of the question.

"To what degree, though? I can understand not liking it, but surely you must use fire in an underground civilization," Esset persisted.

"Of course, but only when necessary. We don't like it, but we don't fear it. But the Reshkin are different—they fear it, and shy from it when they can," she explained.

"Perfect." Esset looked at Toman, who nodded, and then both men looked at her. "I think we can help."

"That is well and fine, but you have not yet explained how," Nassata said, with only the slightest trace of impatience in her voice.

"Well, you need a small army, right? I can create one for you," Toman replied. "I can animate non-living objects, and even create things to animate from scratch, if need be. I could make you soldiers of stone or earth to fight these creatures."

"And I can summon fire creatures that should be relatively effective at combating the Reshkin as well. Between the two of us, we should be able to take care of your problem," Esset finished.

Nassata glanced sidelong at Sergeant Warthog for verification.

"They've done quite the number of jobs for me in the past while, and they've performed admirably," the sergeant assured her.

"With your recommendation, then," Nassata conceded. "I have been authorized to negotiate a price."

"Ah, yes. Well, I assume you want to get going as soon as possible, correct?" Esset asked, glancing at Toman briefly but otherwise focusing his attention on the snake lady.

"Yes, of course, but—"

Esset didn't let her finish. "Perfect. Sergeant, if you don't mind, we'll leave the negotiations to you. Toman and I will go pack some things and meet you back here."

"Of course," the sergeant replied, giving them a little nod of permission. "The journey is two weeks on foot." Esset flashed her a quick smile of thanks, but the young men wasted no time in taking their leave, although they each gave a little half-bow to Nassata before retreating quickly out of the tavern. They wouldn't be gone long; they knew how to pack efficiently. Nassata would have just enough time to settle negotiations and get a bite to eat before they returned.

"They are very young," Nassata remarked, looking after them and only speaking once they had departed.

"Tell me about it," the sergeant replied with a gusty sigh. "But they're more experienced than you'd think, and…well, to be honest, you sometimes forget that we humans don't live as long as your kind do. Few enough humans live to see sixty-five, and among us warriors, thirty is cursed old. Most Nadra see a hundred and fifty easily. They seem young, but they are being viewed through our old eyes."

"Perhaps," Nassata conceded. "But I do not feel so old."

Sergeant Warthog laughed. "Well you may have seen more years than me, but you are still younger than me. But just you watch yourself—thinking others look young is a sign of old age."

Nassata hissed her amusement.

"But they won't be gone long," the sergeant said, calling her companion's attention back to business by rapping her knuckles on the table. "Fortunately, I doubt we'll be long either. Let me order you some food, and we'll haggle this out. I hope you know that part of the deal is that when this is all over, you have to come back for a proper visit so we can reminisce about old times and catch up on everything since then."

Nassata gave another little hissing laugh. "Agreed."

Toman and Esset returned with everything they needed for the trip in less than half an hour.

"Sergeant. Hope to see you soon," Toman said, throwing her a lazy salute—none of them knew if it was habit or a standing joke that kept him and Esset treating her like a commanding officer. Nassata picked up her spear as they spoke, as ready to depart as they were.

Esset was fascinated by how she moved. Her movements were snake-like, which was as appropriate as it was obvious. She moved very quickly or slowly, with nothing he would have considered a moderate pace in between.

"Gretchen, I hope to see you again before long," the Nadra said, leaning forward. She traced down the sergeant's arm with the back of her first two fingers, a farewell gesture and a distinctive mark of an alien culture. In return, Sergeant Warthog placed the front of her first two fingers against her lips. Esset was curious about the history between the two women, but there was no time to pursue that line of thought or ask for clarification.

With abruptly quick motions, Nassata was suddenly slithering past the two young men who'd been waiting for her a moment before. Toman reacted first, falling into step beside and behind her—even with the back half of her tail, actually. Esset was still so mesmerized by her scales and the way her coils moved, he had to take a couple quick steps to catch up with his brother. He was glad they were traveling with Nassata—it would give him a chance to unload some questions before they met a whole lot more of her kind.

"We thought we'd make the best time with horse and carriage," Toman was saying as they left the tavern. "If you're not averse to the idea, we can travel nonstop. The nice thing about stone horses is that they don't need to rest."

Nassata stopped by the carriage and took a second look.

"I thought they were real," she said. Toman beamed—that was a compliment both to his craftsmanship and his animating abilities. He'd intended for them to blend in, after all.

"They're just paint, stone, and magic," Toman said as Nassata placed her hand against the cool, smooth hard surface of the nearest horse's flank—to the touch, it was clearly not alive. Nassata withdrew her hand as the stone horse stomped one foot, making the animated creature's flank shift slightly beneath her palm.

"Remarkable," Nassata said.

"That's more or less how I can create an army, if need be," Toman replied.

Nassata turned her face to him and gave him an unreadable, inhuman look. The sunlight had made her pupils narrow, and the change made her seem that much more alien.

"Of course," Toman continued, "we probably wouldn't waste time painting anything I animate. These are only painted so we don't draw too much attention when traveling...in a more conventional manner."

"That is probably wise," Nassata conceded. She turned to the small carriage that the two horses were harnessed to. Of medium size, the carriage would comfortably fit the three of them, with little room to spare. It was relatively plain and made of some dark-colored wood with little shuttered windows.

With a quick, reptilian motion, Nassata propelled herself back towards the carriage door. She shifted her coils, raising her torso easily, bypassing the need for the step to reach the door. With similar ease she slithered up into the space within.

Toman noticed Esset's entranced expression and grinned at his brother; the look on his face foretold the unleashing of way too many questions. He just hoped the Nadra were a relatively tolerant race—or at least one that wouldn't be too insulted by too many questions.

The animator shoved Esset out of the way so he could get in the carriage first, ignoring the glare his best friend shot at his back on the way up. The summoner had smoothed his expression by the time he got in, however, and he was back to his old self in scant moments. He shut the door behind him, and Toman directed the horses to set off at a trot; the horses had enough instructions to avoid any accidents and whatnot, so he was free to leave them without a driver out front.

Esset opened his mouth to ask Nassata a question, but Toman interrupted him. "So, which direction, Warrior Nassata?"

"Follow the northwest trade road to start—when it splits, take the left branch. I will direct you after that," she replied. Toman nodded and the horses began navigating down the streets to leave through the correct gate.

"Fair enough. I'll give you a heads up when we're in need of further directions so we can just keep moving forward. Unless you think differently, we were thinking we'd only stop for the, uh, call of nature," Toman explained.

Nassata nodded. "Thank you. I would like to see us back with my people as quickly as possible, that we may end this war." She sat back, settling herself against the cushioned seats. "Now, then, I suppose we have a long, confined trip ahead of us."

Esset seized the opportunity. "Actually, I was hoping I could ask—"

Nassata fixed Esset with a look before he could finish his segue. "Gretchen saw fit to warn me about you. She said that you would likely ask an insufferable number of questions and that I could tell you quite clearly that I will not answer any question I do not wish to. So, let me make myself clear. I am not averse to conversation, but I will not tolerate an interrogation, however benign."

"Ah..." was all Esset could manage in the brief pause. His intense curiosity seemed to have deflated somewhat.

"She said especially that you would be curious about my race, and our physiology in particular. Let me tell you now that there are really only two things you need to know. These," she placed one of her index fingers next to one of the dark indentations that resided on either side of the bridge of her nose, "are called pits, and they allow us to detect heat rather accurately. This means that even with my eyes closed, I know where you are. The only other thing you need to know at this time is that no Nadra is ever unarmed."

From outside, there was a slight but visible wobble of the carriage as there was a sudden shift of weight within. Nassata lurched forward, her one hand striking towards Esset. Her hand was open-palmed and stopped bare millimeters from his face, but the real danger lay below. From her wrist jutted a sixth digit, previously concealed. It was a very short, finger-like appendage with a conical claw at the end; the claw was tipped black, and pointed directly at his throat. Esset blinked and froze, knowing that if she'd wanted to kill him, she had him dead to rights. Toman had frozen too, clearly ready to act if needed, but uncertain about what, exactly, to do—Nassata was not an enemy...surely?

"Of course, had I really wanted you dead, a grip on your throat while striking with my poison claw would be far more effective." She smiled, baring teeth that were normal except for the extended, pointed incisors. The expression was very eerie, given the context. Nassata lowered her hand and flowed backwards, away from Esset and back into her previous position. The claw sank back into her wrist with a complicated collapsing motion. Now that they knew where to look, Toman and Esset could see where it hid—it simply looked like a rather large, inwardly-turned belly-button, with the sides of the skin pressed together in a long slit.

"So ask away," Nassata said after giving Esset a chance to shift position uncomfortably and raise a hand to rub his untouched—but recently imperiled—throat. "But remember that lesson if you ever see a Nadra begin to grow irritated."

Now that Nassata had withdrawn, Toman smirked at Esset.

"Really though, you shouldn't be overly concerned with Nadran physiology and abilities," she continued when it was clear Esset wasn't going to speak—let alone ask any questions—for the moment. "After all, you will be fighting with us, not against us. However, should the need arise, I will of course inform you of anything you need to know. And a little idle curiosity is harmless enough." Her lips quirked in amusement at Esset.

"Y'hear that, Esset? You'll have to pare down that list of questions you've got stored up in your head, and by quite a bit," Toman laughed. Esset shot him a glare, and a degree of normalcy returned to the atmosphere.

"So you seemed to know the sergeant from previously," Toman asked Nassata, trying to start a more normal conversation. "Do you mind me asking?"

Nassata gave a genuine smile. "Not at all. About a decade ago,

I did some traveling abroad. I found myself in a bit of trouble, and Gretchen helped me out. We traveled together for a while—did some fighting too, for that matter—and found ourselves to be something of kindred spirits. Unfortunately I haven't seen her since, not before today. I would have liked to have come for a visit under different circumstances and stayed longer, but such is life. We had each promised to call on the other should help be needed, so it was quite natural to go to her when I heard what it is she now does. She is a good person in a business where there are few good people."

"That's the truth," Toman agreed. "She's done a fair bit for us too, although we try to reciprocate."

"Maybe when this is all over you can go visit her," Esset suggested, looking over at Toman. "I imagine that we'll be heading back this way ourselves, and we could cut your traveling time and whatnot again."

"I wouldn't have a problem with that," Toman agreed with a small nod. "I'm afraid we have a bad habit of seeing her as a sergeant, with no life beyond her work. We know that's not right, but..." He shrugged.

"But she has never been a person to discourage that perception," Nassata added insightfully.

Esset blinked. "That's true." Maybe she wanted to be seen that way, but it still didn't seem right to him.

"I thank you for the offer," Nassata added. "I may take you up on it, but it remains to be seen how things will unfold."

"Yeah." Esset leaned in. "Speaking of which, I imagine we'll be wanting to get to work right away when we get there. What can you tell us about the current situation that would be helpful?"

Nassata shook her head. "It will be far more effective to wait until we reach Salithsa. Our underground city can be difficult to comprehend without maps, and we will be better able to strategize once we fully understand your capabilities."

"Fair enough," Toman conceded. "We'll have to wait until we get there then."

Conversation shifted to mundane topics until evening. After dark they shifted around and distributed blankets so they could each sleep comfortably while the carriage moved endlessly towards their destination.

It was their third day of travel. Over the past hour or so, Toman and Esset had noticed the terrain growing rougher. They hadn't paid it much mind, however; the roads varied in quality depending on the area and local ruler, and there had even been a few occasions where the carriage had detoured off-road and through fields.

Toman and Esset were relaying a humorous story of a job they'd done a year ago. They were concluding the tale when Esset felt something suddenly slip around his ankle. He jumped in surprise and looked down in time to see the tip of Nassata's tail vanish back into the mass of coils that filled most of the floor space in the carriage cabin.

"Ah—I apologize," Nassata said, bowing her head slightly. "I did not intend anything."

"Uh, s'all right," Esset stammered, obviously feeling awkward.

"My people are very tactile, and it is a cultural quirk of ours that we like to be in physical contact with those we are conversing with. I'm afraid I have spent so little time away from my people recently that habit took over while I was engrossed in your story. When I went abroad in the past, I was much better at restraining such habits."

Esset noticed that she really did look sheepish. It was also readily apparent to him why she hadn't tried the same with Toman; she and Toman were on the same side of the carriage, so there was no preventing her long tail from being pressed up against his leg already.

"There's nothing to be sorry for," Esset replied, relaxing now that he understood. "I'll try to restrain from jumping next time." He smiled crookedly at her, and she gave a little hiss of a laugh.

"I do not know how my people will react to you, however. I would say you should accustom yourself to such things, but in truth, your reception may be less than warm. Few humans come to our home, and few of us travel abroad, so most will likely be rather wary of you." Her tone was still somewhat apologetic.

"Well, it's nice to know either way," Toman replied seriously.

"We don't want to offend anyone unintentionally."

"Hopefully that will not be an issue. The upside of having so little exposure to outsiders is that we are very aware that our customs are not theirs, and theirs not ours. No one should expect you to know our ways, much less our etiquette and habits."

Esset was nodding seriously at her words. He was about to add something when the carriage slowed and, for the first unexpected time in three days, stopped.

There was a moment of mild surprise from all of them before Toman stated the obvious. "I think we're here."

Esset leaned over and opened the door. They'd passed through the rough terrain to their destination. They'd stopped near a large, rocky outcropping, the furthest the carriage could go. They would have to proceed on foot.

"Finally!" Esset hopped out of the carriage and indulged in an exaggerated stretch. Nassata emerged next, taking in a deep, appreciative breath of fresh air. Toman came out last, and he smiled, glad to finally be free of their confines as well. After closing the door behind him, he looked around and directed the horses to a spot where they and the carriage would be mostly concealed until the brothers came to retrieve them. And if anyone tried to steal them in the meantime, the horses had directions to lead the would-be burglars on a merry chase and then return to the spot. Meanwhile, Esset retrieved the packs they'd be taking with them.

"Okay, let's go," the animator said when he was finished. Nassata had taken the opportunity to get her bearings and now headed off to lead the way. The landscape became very rocky, and she led them up a narrow path that wound through the rocks. They climbed quite a ways in before stopping at the top, where a concealed cave entrance waited.

"Here," she said. "This leads to Salithsa, the home of my people." She seemed all too eager to plunge into the darkness. Toman and Esset both cast one last, wistful look at the sun and followed her into the dark tunnel.

CHAPTER 1⊖

They hadn't made it a dozen paces in when Esset tripped and almost landed on his face. Nassata's hand darted out and clamped around his bicep, saving him from the faceplant.

"If we stop, I can light this lantern," Toman said. A rustling sound betrayed that he was already rummaging in his pack. The rustling continued for quite a while, the only noise in the dark of the cave.

"Here, let me help," Nassata offered, and her scaled hands took Toman's bag away from him.

"I take it you can see just fine," Toman replied wryly.

"Compared to our day vision, we Nadra see poorly in the dark, but our heat sense helps us," Nassata replied. "I had forgotten that humans are blinder yet without light."

Light flared bright, then settled to a soft glow as Nassata lit the wick of the lantern. The Nadra was tilting her head to the side thoughtfully.

"Although…perhaps we are simply more used to it. Our tunnels are far more softly lit than the outside world, and when we warriors patrolled uninhabited sections of Salithsa, we often went without any lights at all. Now, of course, with the Reshkin…" Nassata broke off with a sigh and passed the lantern to Esset. "Well, you'll see. Let's continue."

Knowing more information would come, Toman and Esset fell into step just behind her.

They hadn't gone much further when Nassata suddenly said, "Ah, the sentries," and thrust the haft of her spear towards Toman. Surprised, Toman took the weapon from her purely out of reflex as Nassata lunged forwards, away from them. There was a thud of scales hitting scales and the dry sound of their bodies struggling on the stony ground.

Bewildered, Toman and Esset quickly moved forward a couple steps so that their lantern-light illuminated the scene; Nassata appeared to be fighting with one of her own kind. A third

Nadra slithered out of darkness, holding a spear with a metal haft. He was a powerful-looking creature, his bare, scaled chest and arms muscular and rather intimidating. He had no hair to speak of, and his scales gleamed a dark green while his eyes glinted emerald in the lantern-light. His gaze wasn't entirely friendly, and it was fixed on Toman and Esset. He completely ignored the pair struggling on the tunnel floor.

The pair of young men froze when they saw him, but he simply stood ready. His spear was held vertically, so they were relatively certain he at least wasn't overtly hostile towards them. His disregard for the fighting pair convinced the young men that it was more a spar than a fight. Esset kept his eye on the green Nadra, but Toman snuck a look at the fight going on at the edge of their circle of light.

Nassata's opponent appeared to be another male of her kind, this one appearing a bit younger—from what Toman could see—and of a somewhat lighter build than the other male. His scales were a pale yellow, and like the two other Nadra that Toman and Esset had seen so far, his eyes, when they caught the light, gleamed a brighter shade than his scales, making them a bright yellow topaz. Unlike the green Nadra, the yellow male had ridges along the sides and back of his head, giving him a fierce appearance despite his smaller stature.

Toman couldn't help but be impressed by their struggle. They were incredibly fast when they moved in striking motions, and their style of fighting made full use of that strength. The fighters moved constantly, but their flowing movements were punctuated by sudden, abrupt striking motions that Toman's eyes could barely track at times. Their battle was about speed and leverage, far more so than strength. He had no doubt that either of them could overpower him if they chose, but he had a feeling that wouldn't be a tactic that either would choose.

"Tsan! Were I foe, you would be dead!" Nassata taunted as they suddenly broke apart, raising her torso high and her arms higher, her fingers crooked into claws that were pointed at Tsan. The yellow Nadra bared his teeth at her, but he was smiling.

"Nassata, you are softer than I remember—has so little time away made you lose your luster?" he taunted back. There was another thud of scales-on-scales as the pair both lunged and crashed together. They grappled and their bodies jerked from side to side in a match, not of strength, but of who could topple the other with a sudden, unpredicted movement.

"Tsan, Nassata." The green Nadra's voice was deep, slow, and deliberate, but elicited an instant reaction from the pair. Their grips on each other loosened, and Nassata slipped one arm around Tsan's waist as she turned to face the green Nadra, shifting her coils atop Tsan's and moving behind his torso until she was looking at the green Nadra over the yellow Nadra's shoulder.

"Yes, Asiran?" she said, surprisingly demure as she placed her chin on Tsan's shoulder. To Esset, it seemed like a strangely intimate gesture, and he wondered if there was something between them. Then he remembered what Nassata had said about the Nadra being an extremely tactile race, and he wondered if that was all it was.

"We expected you back later," Asiran replied. He had yet to take his eyes from Toman and Esset.

"I made decent time there, and excellent time back," Nassata replied, shifting to look at Asiran from over Tsan's other shoulder. Tsan reached one hand back to slide against her scales as she moved off from atop him on his other side and then away from Tsan completely, towards Asiran. "I did not want to take any longer than necessary."

"I expected something...more," Asiran replied, looking Toman and Esset up and down. Esset knew how they looked, himself especially. Young. Weaponless. Skinny—especially next to the lithely muscular Nadra. But the pair had practice at not taking offense to others' hesitation, since it wasn't an uncommon reaction. Neither one of them looked like he could deal much damage.

Nassata slid up beside Asiran and ran a hand up the arm holding the spear before ducking under it and pressing her back up against his chest as she looked up at him and replied. Asiran placed one hand on her shoulder in response.

"Gretchen assured me that these two can help us better than a mercenary company," she said. "And I believe her. I've seen some of what one of them, at least, can do." Now Asiran looked down at her.

"Very well," he replied. "Retrieve your spear and proceed."

Nassata flashed a smile up at him and slithered back towards Toman and Esset. Asiran let his hand run down her arm as she pulled away. *Yes,* Esset decided with a tilt of his head, *this is just the tactile tendency of the Nadra that Nassata had mentioned.*

"Come," Nassata bade them to follow her, holding out her hand for her spear. Toman happily handed it over as they stepped forward. Tsan had vanished for a moment and reappeared with a spear of his own, just in time to salute them with it as they passed. Esset was all too aware of Asiran's eyes on them as they passed him and continued down the tunnel again. Nassata had mentioned that they might not be welcomed by every Nadra...

The three didn't encounter anyone else until a glow of light had appeared ahead. By the sound and light radiating from the end of the passage, Esset guessed that the city was just beyond the curve, but they stopped to greet two more sentries that stood there.

"Tseka, Sokess." Nassata slithered forward and both sentries took turns clasping her forearm in a warrior's clasp. Then one of them locked her red eyes on Toman and Esset.

"So, these must be our...saviours." She sounded distinctly less than welcoming. The warrior—Nassata had greeted her as Tseka—was very striking, with brilliant scarlet scales burnished to a dull sheen. Her eyes were utterly fearsome, a vibrantly bright shade of blood-red. Her hair was a startling orange-red as well, and it was pulled back in huge, thick braids and wound around her body in a harness around her torso.

"Toman and Esset." Nassata introduced them.

With a very sudden movement, Tseka was next to the two humans, quick as a striking snake. She raised her torso up on her coils so that she towered over them, deliberately looming in an intimidating fashion. She bared her teeth and hooked her fingers into claws.

Toman and Esset both stepped back and braced themselves, but their faces only hardened in determination—there was no trace of fear. There was a long moment where neither moved. Toman and Esset were unwilling to take preemptive action, and although Tseka was being hostile towards them, she hadn't actually attacked them yet—although given how fast she moved, neither was entirely sure they could stop her in time if she chose to attack.

"We've no quarrel with you," Toman finally said after the conflict had stretched on long enough.

"Huh." Tseka suddenly relaxed, her torso sinking back down into her coils until her head was level with theirs.

"Well, they're not a waste of time at least," Tseka suddenly said to Nassata over her shoulder, her smile slightly malicious. Esset looked slightly disconcerted.

"Oh, come on, I was just playing with you," Tseka said, slapping them both on the shoulders; Esset winced. Tseka didn't apologize.

"Tseka likes her...games," Nassata said, directing her explanation at Toman and Esset. She looked like she was considering apologizing on Tseka's behalf, but she didn't. "Come, you must see the city."

"I'll catch up with you later," Tseka promised, but it was ambiguous who she was speaking to; she had already returned her gaze down the tunnel she was guarding.

Toman and Esset weren't given any time to consider the semi-hostile exchange, for the tunnel had opened into a massive cavern, and they were struck by the sight of the underground city.

"Our city is beautiful, yes?" Nassata asked proudly. They both nodded dumbly. They stood in the entrance to the cavern, and a few meters in front of them was a ledge, beyond which dropped the bowl of the cavern. The ledge spiraled down the cavern walls, creating a walkway for the Nadra down the tiers carved into the stone bowl that was their city.

"You see the entrances along the various tiers?" Nassata asked. Esset nodded. "Some are simply rooms or suites, but others are tunnels that lead to other parts of the city. Our tunnels intersect many times. This is only one of three great caverns, which act like a nexus."

Esset noticed that there were no doors to any of the rooms, homes, shops, or tunnels; there were only curtains, some made of cloth, others of beads and the like. The stone beneath their feet had been polished so smooth it practically glowed. Generations of Nadran scales slithering across it had polished it more perfectly than any artisan could ever hope to.

"Look up," Nassata suggested. They did, and they saw that they weren't on the top floor. Several tiers were yet above them, and the ceiling arced higher yet. The whole place was illuminated by a remarkably clear and bright light that emanated from the ceiling. The roof of the cavern was covered in stalactites, jutting down in various lengths and diameters. Esset thought they'd been polished and hollowed out, then packed with some kind of bioluminescent organism—moss or lichen, most likely, or perhaps some kind of bug. Before he could ask, Nassata was speaking again.

"The art in our city is the pride of our people," she remarked. "It is a great honor to maintain it or paint new sections." Esset could see why. Somehow, thoughts of caves and caverns and all things underground brought to mind thoughts of washed-out colors and monotonous surroundings. Not so in the Nadran world; Salithsa was a painted city.

The snake-people didn't favor murals, paintings depicting scenes, events, or images of concrete things. Instead they seemed to favor geometric patterns or more abstract swirls of color. But each painted section flowed into the next with no jarring transitions or apparent asymmetry. And they used every color imaginable—their underground world was rich in minerals with which to make paints of every kind and color.

The last thing Esset noticed was how warm it was; again, the typical thought of a cave evoked a damp coolness that was lacking here. In fact, if anything, he would have described it as the exact opposite: a comfortable, dry warmth. It was rather pleasant in the underground city.

"It's a good thing neither of us is too afraid of heights," Esset remarked, peering warily over the edge. The foot-high lip provided reasonable containment for Nadran coils that could mistakenly err over an edge, but for a human or other biped, it would be a simple matter to step or worse, trip, over the small ledge. As he looked down, however, he noticed for the first time a large pool of water at the very bottom of the cavern. The last tier circled around the great spring. Well, that explained where the city got its water supply.

"Nassata!" an excited, breathy soprano called from behind them. They turned, and both Esset and Toman blinked when they actually saw the female speaker.

The Nadra they'd seen so far had all been dull of scale and

muscular of form—this delicate thing before them was neither. She was very slight, with fine features and a shy air about her. She had long, curly hair so black it had a blue sheen. Unlike Nassata's hair, however, hers simply hung loose—and, thankfully for the two modestly brought-up young men before her, it covered her otherwise bare scaled breasts. Her eyes were a bright sapphire blue and her scales matched. Her scales weren't dull, but rather polished bright and painted as colorfully and intricately as the city itself.

"Kessa!" Nassata slithered over to hug the smaller Nadra, giving Esset a chance to covertly study Kessa's scales. The geometric patterns on her scales had to have taken hours to paint, and hours still to maintain—each shape was no bigger than her own pinky-fingernail. The colors looked like they were made of rich enamels—or something like it, Esset was no expert—and in colors that complemented her scales: blues, purples, and a few bright yellows as accents.

"It's good to have you back," Kessa said to Nassata. "We expected you go be gone longer. I came to meet you as soon as I heard you had returned."

"It is good to be back," Nassata responded. "I was fortunate to find help so quickly, and help with quick transportation at that."

"But they can help?" Kessa asked, her eyes wide. There was something innocent about her, something almost helpless.

"Yes, they will help us," Nassata reassured her. Then Nassata turned her face towards Toman and Esset.

"And in turn, Kessa will help you. She can be your guide when you are not with the warriors, and if you need anything, just ask her. She will also bring you food and any other necessities you will be needing here."

"Thank you, Kessa," Esset said to the blue Nadra, giving her a smile and a nod; Toman smiled and nodded to her as well. Kessa ducked her head meekly in response, and Esset thought she seemed almost embarrassed by the attention.

"Kessa, please let the warriors and council-members know that I am back with help," Nassata instructed her cousin kindly.

"Yes, Nassata!" Kessa responded eagerly. The little Nadra darted away quickly, moving with startling speed towards a lower tunnel and then vanishing into it.

"Come," Nassata bade the two young men, beckoning with

one hand as she headed in a different direction.

Toman and Esset soon saw many more Nadra with scales painted and polished to the nines, creating two distinct sets within the race—those with painted scales and those with dull scales. Esset had a hunch about what the difference signified, but he asked Nassata about it anyway.

"We warriors are set apart from the others," Nassata replied, confirming his hunch. "Painting our scales is not a practical pursuit for us, and few of us have any desire at all to try. We dull our scales instead—it is better should we need stealth, after all, and far easier to maintain."

"That makes sense," Toman replied. Esset felt a little flush of pride that he'd guessed correctly, but he was immediately distracted as they passed close by a light-source bracketed to the tunnel wall. It was like a lantern, and it emitted the same light that had filled the main cavern they'd now left. The surface of the lantern was translucent, however, keeping him from being able to tell exactly what was giving off the light. It certainly wasn't fire. They passed any lanterns too quickly for Esset to really get the chance to ask.

"I think it best if you show something of your abilities before we meet with any council members and other warriors. I will take you to a sentry post where the Reshkin will be near," Nassata said.

"That seems wise," Esset agreed. "We can cut down on politics that way, and you'll have a better idea of how best to utilize us."

"Indeed," Nassata responded as they moved. Toman and Esset almost had to trot to keep up with her; Nassata made very good time in the tunnels, and both got the sense that she was holding back so they wouldn't have to jog to keep up. Toman found himself wishing they hadn't been forced into inactivity in the carriage the last few days; he'd be better prepared for the grueling pace. He wondered if other Nadra would be so considerate, or if they'd be doing a lot of running in this place.

When they reached a sentry point, two warrior Nadra, blue and green, stood with lanterns at their backs, keeping eyes on the darkness. Only one glanced back to look at them—the other remained intent ahead.

"Nassata," the female sentry greeted their Nadran companion.

"Eska. I have brought help." Nassata pointed down the tunnel for Toman and Esset's sake. "The creatures are just down there. We can see their heat signatures."

"I thought the Reshkin were insect-like," Esset said, a hint of confusion in his voice.

"They are," Nassata responded, unsure what he was getting at.

"But insects aren't warm-blooded, so how can you see them?"

"It's true, they are more difficult to detect than, say, you, but it is not just heat that we detect." Did Nassata sound…amused? Esset finally shrugged and set the thought aside before getting back to the task at hand.

"Okay. You've seen what Toman can do. He requires preparation for a truly effective assault. Instant battle is my specialty, so now you can see what I can do," Esset replied. Toman rolled his eyes at his brother's bit of ego shining through, but the gesture went unseen in the darkness.

"You might want to shield your eyes for a moment to protect your night vision," Esset added as an afterthought. He didn't waste any more time before speaking the incantation.

A fiery wolf materialized just ahead of the two sentries and sprang into the darkness. The sentries hissed in surprise at the creature's appearance. Esset had to stifle a gasp of his own at how close the wolf's target was. Eerie firelight flashed off a shiny black carapace less than two meters beyond the ring of light cast by the lantern. The Nadra had known it was there, but for Esset, it had been completely hidden by the darkness.

The wolf growled and clamped its jaws over the Reshkin's head, crushing it and instantly killing it. The next Reshkin skittered forward on too many legs, with two companions in its wake. When the wolf snapped at them, its open mouth created reflections of fire on their exoskeletons. Esset could hear the tapping and skittering of even more Reshkin in the darkness as the wolf lashed about, snapping and snarling and taking down three more of the insect-like creatures. The Reshkin rushed the wolf and bit back, but their poison was ineffective against fire. Still, they kept biting and stabbing with their smaller forelegs as more of them flowed out of the darkness. Esset counted five Reshkin corpses before they swarmed his summon completely and forced Esset to banish the wolf.

"Remarkable," Eska murmured, opening her eyes once the wolf's heat signature vanished. Both sentries were ready to act if the swarm moved forward, but instead, the Reshkin collected their dead and receded, since the one who'd attacked them had "died."

"I can summon up to four wolves at one time, but I think, in these close quarters, I would be better calling on a stronger summon that I can control fewer of," Esset commented. He was proud of himself, yes, but it had been a small display of his abilities.

"I think Gretchen made the right call," Nassata mused. Then she turned to her fellow Nadra. "You will be okay here? The Reshkin do not seem inclined to attack."

"We will be fine," Eska replied. Esset didn't envy their duties, keeping watch in the darkness for an enemy that outnumbered them and could kill them with poison. Nor did he envy the current conditions: the tunnel was now choked with the smell of burnt insect.

"Esset, Toman. It's time to return," Nassata said, turning back down the tunnel. "The others should have gathered by now." Esset suppressed a shudder as he cast one last look down the darkened tunnel before turning his back on it and following Nassata.

The three of them headed back to the main cavern and then down a few spiraling tiers before going down a different, shorter tunnel. The tunnel ended in a room adorned with many maps of the underground city and a massive circular table in the center of the room. At least a dozen Nadra were already around the table, awaiting them. Little Kessa was by the door and smiled at the three who entered, reaching out to brush her fingers against Nassata's arm as she passed.

"Warrior Nassata. I hardly believed it when word went around that you were already back with help," the nearest Nadra said, moving forward to take Nassata's hands in her own. She was a vividly-colored Nadra, even for her kind. Her long, loose hair blazed a bold red-orange, matching her blood red scales, which were painted in sunset colors in fluid swirls.

"Councilor Ksendra, I met with much good fortune," Nassata replied.

"If you could please introduce our guests," Ksendra requested with respectful nods to the two men.

"I am Summoner Jonathan Esset."

"Animator Toman Atrix-Iiren."

"It is good to meet you. Warrior Nassata, please, tell all," Ksendra said.

Nassata launched into a brief explanation of how she'd found them and what she'd seen of their abilities. It didn't take more than a few minutes. When she was through, those gathered appraised Toman and Esset in this new light.

"Animator Toman, Summoner Esset, now that you have seen our tunnels and our enemy, do you have any ideas on how to rid us of the Reshkin?" Ksendra asked. Toman and Esset glanced at each other, and Toman stepped up.

"Nassata gave us a little information on our way here of what to expect, and it matches with what we've seen so far. Esset and I think that the most efficient use of my abilities is to build you a stone army. Soldiers made of stone can't be hurt by poison, and they can carry clubs, something Nassata tells me the Nadra are not fond of wielding. Building an army will take time, however—a few days, at least, and I'll need a great deal of raw stone to do it. If there's no place down here where material might be available, I can always work aboveground and send my soldiers down."

"Soldiers?" one of the other Nadra asked nervously. He had violet scales painted with jagged green patterns.

"Yes," Toman replied. "I would send the first to reinforce your sentries, then build a strike force to attack the Reshkin. Stone soldiers might not be the brightest or quickest, but they never suffer from weariness or inattention. They'll be of great help to your sentries."

"And what's to stop you from turning those soldiers on us?" the violet Nadra asked, slightly bolder this time. He gathered his coils beneath him to raise his torso and glanced around at the council. Esset saw concern on more than a few faces, but none of them spoke up.

Toman opened his mouth to respond, but Nassata spoke first.

"My friend Gretchen vouched for them, and that counts for much. You also know I have seen much of the world, and I am a fair judge of character. After traveling with these two to our city, I vouch for them as well." The teal warrior's tone was reasonable, but a determined light shone in her reptilian eyes.

"And have you forgotten the threat that awaits us in our own tunnels?" Nassata continued. "We need them. We are at war with the Reshkin, and we need warriors to fight. Ours alone are not enough, and we voted to seek help. We *need* them to help us, so I hope you do not antagonize them further."

Toman and Esset exchanged another glance as the violet Nadra who'd spoken out lowered himself back to the normal level and averted his eyes. Nassata turned to them then.

"My apologies for the interruption. Please, continue." Nassata lowered herself to the normal level as well.

"No apology necessary," Toman replied, taking the floor again. He looked at the painted violet Nadra and then swept his eyes around the table. "I know you don't know us yet, but I hope you'll come to trust us once we've proven ourselves. We're here to help you."

Ksendra inclined her head to the brothers, and while Esset saw there was still concern and even fear lingering in the eyes of many, Toman continued.

"Esset and I were also thinking that chains could make for effective 'soldiers' of sorts. I can animate chain—or even rope— to entangle the Reshkin and make them easy targets, if not render them immobile."

"Chain and rope we can supply," a painted green Nadra replied. A few others nodded.

Now Esset stepped forward. "In the meantime, you'll have to make do with just me. Nassata saw what one of my summons can do in the tunnel just before we came. The wolf is just one of the things I can call on. I'm thinking, however, that I'll be better off calling on panthers to aid me—they are much stronger, but I can only summon two at a time. Given the close quarters, however, that shouldn't be a problem. Larger numbers would only get in the way of each other.

"Like Toman's animations, my summons aren't harmed by poison. They're far from invincible, but even without Toman's help, I should be able to do some damage. If there are any particularly bad areas, I can start there while Toman's building your army. I'll be wanting back-up, just in case, but given how the Reshkin responded to my last summon, I hope that will be a precaution only. I should be able to simply send my summons ahead without endangering myself or any Nadra who comes along."

"You seem very confident," another Nadra said, a pale yellow warrior this time. "But you also say your...'summons' are far from invincible. How do you mean?"

Esset thought that was a fair enough question. "When my summons do battle, they don't *seem* to get hurt, but once they've taken enough damage, they are banished back to where they came from. As such, they're not as durable as one of Toman's stone soldiers, but given their, ah, fiery nature, they should be able to do a great deal more damage individually. And, of course, I can call them as needed, so we can start immediately," Esset replied. The yellow Nadra appeared satisfied with the answer.

"Any help will be much appreciated," he said. "Here, look at these maps and we can prepare an attack plan."

Both Toman and Esset leaned in to look.

An hour later, Toman and Esset had a fairly good picture of what was going on in the underground city. They'd come up with some rudimentary strategies for an endgame and more detailed plans for Esset while Toman was building their army. Within another hour, Toman had been led back up to the surface by Kessa, and Esset was deeper in the tunnels than ever.

Kessa settled back on her coils to watch Toman and wait. The animator crouched a few feet away and put his palms flat on the ground. He closed his eyes to help him concentrate, but that didn't deter Kessa from putting forward a question.

"Do you worry about your brother?" she asked.

"Of course. But he's strong, and he's smart, and we need to play to our strengths. It would be foolish for him to sit around while I'm preparing, especially when your people need help now," Toman replied.

"I guess," she replied, casting her slitted eyes downwards and hugging her arms tight to her chest. "It just worries me sick that any of my people are in danger...but especially Nassata."

"You're close to her, then?" Toman asked without opening his eyes.

When Kessa glanced up, her eyes almost bugged out of her

head completely as the ground in front of him bulged and swelled upwards like a chunk of modeling clay being withdrawn from a bigger piece. There were a couple of silent moments before Kessa realized Toman had asked her a question and retrospectively absorbed the meaning of the sounds.

"Yes," she replied. "Especially since the Reshkin changed and started attacking." There was a little pause, and then she added in a small voice, "She saved me from them."

"She seems like a remarkable individual," Toman replied. There was a tiny crease of concentration between his eyes as his attention was divided between the conversation and his work. The bulge was growing slowly but steadily before him.

"So, you and Summoner Esset—you are brothers?" She was not the first to notice that while they acted alike, they didn't really look alike.

Toman chuckled. "Might as well be. We kind of adopted each other when we were really young, and we grew up together. We don't share blood, but we're brothers in every way that matters." He still had his eyes closed, but he could feel her curious gaze on him. He knew she had a question, so he simply waited for her to ask—he had too much else demanding his concentration to anticipate it. Not that he could've anyways.

"You're not at all like I expected." It wasn't a question, but it begged an answer nonetheless.

Kessa's confession evoked a laugh from Toman. "We rarely are," he replied. "But what did you expect?"

"Well... When Nassata left, she said she was going to bring back warriors, but that human warriors were different from Nadra warriors. She said the warriors she brought back would be merss... mersens..." She stumbled, trying to recall the unfamiliar word.

"Mercenaries?" Toman supplied.

"Mer-sen-aries," Kessa repeated slowly. "Yes. She said mercen-aries just fought for money, and love of war. She said most weren't very nice, but we needed help."

"For the most part, she's right," Toman replied. "Mercenaries, as a group, are typically not the best members of society. I'm not sure Esset and I could be considered mercenaries, but that might be a moot point. What it comes down to are our reasons for fighting. We fight because we want to help people. We take money because we need it, and we never take more than we need or a client can afford. And...we fight because there is an enemy out there that needs to be defeated, and we need to grow strong enough to do it. But we never abandon our ethics, and we will never abandon each other or someone who needs our help."

"So...you fight for peace?" Kessa asked.

Toman laughed again, but it wasn't at Kessa or the essence of the question. "Don't ask that when Esset is around," he laughed. "He'll engage you in a philosophical debate about what peace is."

Kessa frowned, clearly thinking the definition obvious.

"But it's something like that," Toman continued, to answer her question. "We fight because there many people who can't fight for themselves."

"But you hate fighting, right?"

There was a long pause before Toman answered that question. The growth of his creation had slowed considerably as his attention was drawn away from it.

"I wouldn't say that. I don't like the necessity of what we do, but I love the rush of running into battle. I love animating, even it's for war, and I know Esset loves summoning, even though half the creatures he summons are the blood-thirstiest creatures I've ever seen."

After that, there was a very long pause. Preoccupied as he was, Toman didn't realize how long it was until it had drawn on very long indeed. When he finally noticed the silence, he paused to crack an eye and read Kessa's body language. He'd had trouble reading Nassata, but Kessa was an open book. Assuming Nadran body language was mostly like a human's—and so far that seemed to run true, once you adjusted for anatomical differences—she looked mostly uncertain, perhaps even afraid, or...disappointed?

"What's wrong?" Toman asked, closing both eyes again and resuming his work.

"Wouldn't you rather not fight?" she asked after a moment.

"I would rather not have to," Toman replied. He had a feeling he was missing something, because he wasn't entirely sure where she was coming from. *She's not human,* he reminded himself. *You've seen already how different their culture is, are you surprised there are other differences?*

"Isn't peace the most important thing?" she asked.

Toman had to stop and think about that one; even without an unknown cultural context, it was a difficult question. There was something else he remembered then, something Nassata had said: "We warriors are set apart from the others." It seemed that, perhaps, peace was held as an ideal to the Nadra. They recognized the necessity of warriors, it was clear, but they seemed to hold peace as far higher a value than most human cultures.

"No," Toman finally replied. "Peace is something that we should strive for, but I wouldn't say it's the most important thing. I know I wouldn't trade this life for one of peace where I never met Esset."

"But war is wrong! Fighting is wrong! Every Nadra knows that," Kessa persisted.

Toman was finding it difficult to carry on this conversation and animate at the same time. It was making work go very slowly.

"Yet the Nadra, as a people, have warriors," Toman pointed out, slitting one eye open in time to see Kessa scowl. He waited for a few moments for a response, but she seemed to be mulling over what he'd said, so he let her. He concentrated on his creation again, and the stone that had swollen up from the ground now began to take on some rough approximations of arms and legs.

After a minute he was completely consumed in his work again, and he had almost forgotten she was there. As such, he received an internal jolt when Kessa suddenly spoke again almost ten minutes later.

"What's it like, having legs? It seems terribly unstable," Kessa finally asked, eying his semi-human work-in-progress.

"What's it like having coils instead? It seems terribly cumbersome," Toman asked back with a slight smile. He cracked an eye in time to catch a flash of body language and facial expression conveying embarrassment.

"Well?" she persisted. He liked her boldness.

"It's not something I've really thought about. I haven't known it any other way, so anything else seems odd. That's why I asked you an equivalent question. Can you really answer my question any better than I just did yours?" Toman asked, without aggression.

"Hm... I suppose not," Kessa replied. "But it does seem unstable."

"I guess, compared to Nadra," Toman admitted. "But there are convenient things too. For example, Esset and I argued about how to get here fastest with Nassata along. After all, could a Nadra ride on the back of a horse or a giant bird? It didn't seem likely, or at the very least, it seemed impractical or inefficient. Not to mention uncomfortable."

"I guess," Kessa echoed. "There are pictures of ancient times where Nadra rode in chariots. Mostly we just travel on our coils, without aid of beast or machine."

"And that works for you," Toman pointed out. "Especially with the society you've built here. And our ways work for us. Both our races have adapted ourselves and our surroundings to our needs."

"What's human society like, then?" Kessa asked.

"That's an awfully broad question," Toman replied. He was enjoying the conversation, but at the same time, he was thinking that his work wasn't going to move very quickly if they kept up like this.

"Well then... what's the place you grew up like?" Kessa compromised.

"That's better. We humans have a lot of cities, and a lot of different societies, even. That being said, going north to Baliya wasn't nearly as different from home as this place is. Hm... Home.

"Well, for me, things were a little different. Esset grew up in the city, but I wasn't from the city. I...kind of inherited a castle when I was quite young, and I lived partially there and partially with Esset while I was growing up, so things were a little different for me. Still. The city was a pretty good place to grow up. It was a good place in general. The king lives in the city, and he is a good king. Laws protected and even helped the people, so it was a relatively safe place for kids to grow up. We played all over that city when we were young. Outside it too, since we were at peace with our neighbors.

"The church was also a big part of our lives—it governs the school system, so we had classes there, and of course once a week were the main services in the church, and then every day there were other optional services to attend, almost no matter the time or day or night. The thing with cities is that there seems to always be something happening somewhere."

"What's church?" Kessa asked. The word was easy—unlike

"mercenaries"—but it was clear that it sounded very odd to her.

"Oh dear. Religion?" Toman tried.

"Of course I know what religion is," Kessa responded, sounding almost contemptuous.

"Sorry. A church is a building or organization that runs a religion, or is a religious center...that sort of thing. Sort of. You'd get a better answer from Esset. Although it would be a very long answer..." Toman replied, trailing off at the end.

"Oh." Kessa seemed to think that odd.

"What about the Nadra? You must have some kind of religion, or at least a set of beliefs, a faith," Toman asked. He figured it was his chance to find things out. At least Kessa couldn't justifiably threaten him for asking too many questions—not with the boatloads she was asking.

"We believe in the energies that flow through the world." There was a bit of an unspoken "of course" tacked into the tone of her response.

"Energies?" Toman asked, encouraging her to continue. This didn't sound familiar to him.

"Yes." It took a second for her to realize that these concepts, so obvious to her, eluded him. "Um... well..." She suddenly stuttered, realizing she was going to have to explain something she'd always taken for granted. "It's like our city," she finally said.

"How so?" Toman asked.

"Well, you can see the energy, the way heat and magic flows in the city," Kessa said with the slightest hint of impatience.

"Kessa, I can't see heat and magic. There aren't many magics that I can sense, and even then, I can't *see* it. I wasn't born with the ability to sense magic, and I don't have your..." Toman placed his fingers on either side of his nose where his heat-sensing organs would have been if he had been Nadran.

"You can't—oh." Kessa peered at him, realizing what was obvious to her wasn't necessarily clear to him. There was another pause as she struggled to think of a new explanation.

"Kessa, I'll tell you what. How about you take your time and think for a bit. I work really slowly when I'm dividing my concentration between working and talking, so how about I keep at this while you think, and when I stop to take a break, we'll talk?" That didn't come out quite as tactfully as he'd hoped, but at least it got the point across without being too harsh. He opened his eyes to regard her as he spoke this time.

"Oh! I'm sorry," she immediately apologized, raising her hands to her mouth.

"No worries," Toman replied easily with a smile. "I'll talk to you in a bit. Keep thinking."

Kessa nodded vigorously, and he just smiled and closed his eyes again to continue his work.

CHAPTER 11

"Okay, looks like we're ready to go," Nassata said, taking the last spear off the rack and handing it to Tseka.

"Excellent," Tseka replied. She fingered a chip on the haft, and then adjusted her grip as she eyed Esset thoughtfully. There was a predatory gleam in her eye that Esset found disconcerting.

"Say, what color do humans bleed?" Tseka asked. "I heard somewhere your blood is black, not a proper red at all."

"Er, no, our blood is red," Esset replied.

"Huh." Tseka was still eyeing him, looking like she wanted to poke him with her spear to find out for sure.

"Come, we must go," Nassata urged them. Like a prayer answered, she moved between him and Tseka as they headed out of the small weapons room.

"What's our first target?" Esset asked.

"There's an armory we need to recover. As you saw, that one is a little sparse." Nassata waved a hand back at the room of empty weapons racks. "We barely have enough weapons to arm our warriors. If a weapon is lost or damaged, we have no replacements. This armory was also mostly storage for spears. While we specialize in that weapon, they're not terribly effective against the Reshkin. The armory we seek to recover is plentifully stocked with a variety of weapons. It will be good to be better equipped."

Esset turned that information over in his mind. He, Nassata, Tseka, and a small group of warriors headed towards the guarded perimeter of Salithsa's core.

"It's too bad you're not better armored," Esset remarked. The most clothing they seemed to wear were belts or weapons harnesses. "Even just metal gauntlets and bracers would help."

Nassata grimaced and opened her mouth to respond, but Tseka jumped in.

"And how do you propose a people of peace and isolation obtain such tools of war? Or did you think we were too stupid to think of using armor?" Tseka challenged him.

Esset nearly tripped over his own feet. "I—what? No! I mean, I was fairly certain you had thought of it, I just—" Esset stopped talking as Nassata put a hand on his shoulder and shot a glare at Tseka. Tseka shrugged nonchalantly, looking away without a hint of apology.

"We know you meant no offense," Nassata said. "Such did occur to us, but we don't have the means. We don't have the skills or tools to make metal armor, nor the funds to buy them in sufficient numbers. We tried some tough leather gloves for protection, but the Reshkin can bite clear through them. We are also unaccustomed to wearing gloves, and they compromised our grip on our weapons."

Nassata nodded to a sentry at the mouth of the tunnel they were headed down.

"This is the edge of the safe zone," the teal warrior volunteered. "We keep sentries at the entrances to all far-reaching tunnels, especially the ones connecting to other cave systems. If anything goes wrong further down, they can relay the alert to the city and act as a final barrier, if necessary. There are other sentries further ahead yet, so it should still be safe, but we must remain alert. We haven't lost any non-combatants since we withdrew into the center of the city and set up the sentry system."

"How do your sentries sound an alarm?" Esset asked. He hadn't seen any carrying alert horns or anything like that.

"Cries carry far down these tunnels," Tseka replied in Nassata's stead. "And if the sentries are overrun, the screams carry even further."

Esset felt a chill.

"Do you know what happens when a Reshkin bites a Nadra?" Tseka asked. Esset felt disinclined to meet her blood-red eyes, but he did so for a moment anyways.

"Reshkin venom is lethal." Esset remembered that much.

"It is more than lethal," Tseka replied. Esset realized it was getting dimmer in the tunnel, but Tseka had caught his eyes again, and this time he couldn't look away.

"If a Nadra is bit," Tseka continued. "We don't simply die. Even if the wound is superficial, we will soon writhe in agony. In fact, small bites are worse than large ones, for it takes the venom longer to kill. If a Nadra is bit, you will learn how these tunnels and caves carry sound." The red Nadra broke eye contact and looked forward. "That is why most of us have agreed to a pact. If I am bit, the others will kill me before I go mad with the pain. They will end my suffering, as I would do for any of them."

Her pact ran counter to his beliefs, but Esset kept his mouth shut and let silence fall. The tunnel was almost black now, and there was no sign of light ahead. The wall sconces no longer cast illumination in the tunnels.

Esset had a feeling it wasn't going to take him long to start missing the sky. The dark didn't bother him much, nor did the close rock walls around him. No, it was a combination of both those things, the soft sounds of scales on stones, and the knowledge that those disturbing, deadly Reshkin were out there. At least the ground was so perfectly smooth that he knew he wouldn't trip, and the swish of scales on stone let him know that he hadn't fallen behind.

"Should I have brought a lantern?" Esset asked, his voice low.

"What's the matter, can't see in the dark?" Tseka's hissing laughter came from behind him now.

"I realize you can't see as well as we can," Nassata said, ignoring the other warrior. "But you'll have to rely on us to navigate. We are almost to the sentry—ah, yes, there he is. Greetings, Warrior."

"Greetings, Warrior. And good luck," the sentry replied. Esset couldn't see him, but he roughly located his direction by his voice.

"Thank you," Nassata replied. "Now, Esset, I am at your side, as is another warrior, with the others behind. Before you is clear if you need to summon something."

"Good," was all Esset could think to say. He found himself wishing Tseka hadn't come along. He was sure she must be a skilled warrior for Nassasta to have chosen her, but he wondered if he'd be as unnerved right now if she hadn't just painted such a vivid picture of an excruciating death. Then again, these tunnels did remind him of that job they'd taken on early in their career where they'd eradicated an infestation of giant scorpions, so maybe he only had his own, overly productive imagination to thank.

Suddenly a very solid arm jarred him to a stop and back to reality, and he realized he'd fallen prey to his very bad habit of woolgathering in the field again. He mentally kicked himself as he rebooted his senses to gather every bit of information from around him that he could without using his eyes—it was still pitch black. He couldn't gather much, unfortunately. More fortunately, the Nadra were willing to help.

"Thirty of your paces ahead is the armory we lost. There are a great many Reshkin inside," a warrior whispered in his ear. Esset barely managed to keep from jumping—the Nadra were extremely quiet and he hadn't realized how close the nearest was—his mouth had been almost right next to his ear. The summoner nodded, realized it was dark, and almost replied verbally before remembering that the Nadra could "see" him anyways. He briefly wondered how the Nadra would normally proceed with an attack from here, but he saved the question for later. Instead he concentrated very specifically on the incantation that would summon him a battle cat.

The creature exploded into existence before them with the thick smell of charcoal and ash. Esset wondered what it looked like to Nadran heat-vision. Esset knew that the core temperature of his summons was incredibly high. A wolf could superheat any metal placed between its jaws until it was as malleable as dough. A panther could melt metal in its jaws. Right now the panther would be blazing like a small sun to the heat sensors of the Nadra.

The ferocious fire-cat whipped down the tunnel and into the armory, tearing into the Reshkin ahead. It was an unstoppable force of unspeakable rage and tangible menace. Since its jaws could melt metal, Reshkin exoskeletons would be no match for its ferocity.

Esset had barely released the first to attack before summoning the second and sending it down the tunnel as well. The two of them ripped into the Reshkin swarm and the stench of their opponents' burning bodies flooded the tunnel. Some of the Nadra even covered their noses against the smell, and it would have bothered Esset to realize how little the smell had come to bother him. He barely noticed the smell at all; he was so used to summoning and fighting with the fiery creatures he called upon.

In the darkness, Esset was forced to rely on his ears, and they conveyed a horror-story to him. Only the bestial, vicious nature of the Reshkin could allow him to withstand those sounds. He never could have been responsible for the similar decimation of a sentient species—or a gentler one. For all that their clacks, chatters, clicks, screeches, and hisses were totally inhuman, it wasn't difficult to discern between those that were enraged, those that were terrified, and those that were screaming in agony. There was no mistaking the cries that were cut short as lives, no matter how monstrous, were ended. And those weren't the only sounds. They could clearly hear the crack of exoskeletons, the snap of flames, and the squelches as the innards of the Reshkin were spread across the floor by scorching paws and serrated claws alike. Esset had learned a long time ago that there was no glory in battle, only horror. In darkness, the sight of the horror was spared, but it seemed to only amplify the monstrosity of the sounds. It was sometimes too little comfort to know the necessity of such battles.

"Summoner Esset." Once again, Esset almost jumped at the voice that was a hairs-breadth from his ear.

"Yes?" he hissed back.

"Can you bring back the carcass of one of the Reshkin?"

Esset gave the Nadra a curious look. Not that he could see him, not really. And it was entirely possible that they couldn't read expressions in the dark any better than he could, even with heat-vision.

"I would imagine, yes," he replied. "Why?"

"We have been unable to. And if we could study the venom, perhaps we could procure an antidote," the Nadra replied. Then it occurred to Esset—yes, the Nadra's words made sense. He remembered how the Reshkin had swarmed in and carried away the carcasses of their fallen, and how aggressive they'd been about it. Gaining a sample of the venom would be invaluable.

"If I bring back the whole body, the Reshkin might try to recover it," Esset thought aloud. "But odds are, the venom sacs are in the head, likely near the fangs. If my summon only brings that back..." He trailed off as he formulated a plan.

Up ahead, one of the panthers left this plane with a small puff of smoke and flame. Silently, Esset summoned two wolves to take its place, sending both dashing down the tunnel towards the battle. They tag-teamed, one driving live Reshkin away from a carcass, the other tearing the head off the dead Reshkin and returning to them with it. The head made a sickening sound when dropped on the tunnel floor, and the odor arising from it was foul. Esset banished the wolves then and sent another panther down the tunnel again.

The summoner sensed more than saw or heard the Nadra next to him pick up the head and pass it to another warrior at the rear of the party. That warrior raced back to the city with the prize. Esset hoped they'd be able to devise a cure—or even a vaccination—from the venom sample. Fortunately, the Reshkin didn't seem to have noticed that they'd lost part of a carcass. That had been Esset's hope in leaving the rest of the carcass behind—they seemed to be almost obsessive about collecting their dead, so he'd wanted to leave something behind for them to collect. That, and it was easier for a wolf to carry off a head, and not the entire carcass of something nearly as big as it was.

"I'm banishing my summons—I want to see if they'll retreat," Esset whispered to his Nadran guard. They didn't respond, so he assumed they were okay with that. With their usual puff of smoke and fire, both panthers vanished and the tunnel was plunged into absolute darkness.

Esset strained his ears and found himself twitching at each skitter, hiss, and click the Reshkin made in the darkness. The acoustics of the tunnel made it difficult to tell exactly how close they were, whether they were advancing or retreating or neither. He trusted the Nadra to tell him if he needed to summon something again, but it was nerve-racking to be forced to rely on them. He felt helpless in the darkness. He didn't like feeling helpless.

The sounds of the Reshkin vanished around them, but Esset remained tense. There was a long silence, a silence made longer by the darkness. Finally, after what seemed like an eternity, the Nadra next to him whispered, "They are withdrawing." Then there was another long silence before the warrior spoke normally and began moving.

"There, they are far enough away. Let us retrieve our equipment from the armory."

Esset walked forward when he heard their scales moving on the floor again.

"There will be lanterns in the armory," Nassata said behind him, much to Esset's relief. At least she was aware of how uncomfortable this darkness was for him.

"Thank Hyrishal," Esset said. They entered the armory, and Esset found that he had to step carefully—the footing was a bit slick, and part of him was glad that he couldn't get a good look at the ground. One of the Nadra found and lit a lantern, and he chose to avoid looking at his feet. A soft glow filled the room, illuminating the Nadra, who were already hard at work collecting the weapons and piling them into great wheeled crates that were already in the room. Within minutes, the four crates were packed and they were heading back down the tunnel, each Nadra pushing a crate. Esset brought up the rear, grateful to leave the haunting tunnel behind them.

As promised, Toman and Kessa resumed their discussion when he took a break. He was true to his word—he worked faster when he could concentrate completely, and he gained momentum as he worked. He had a handful of rough-hewn soldiers with stone clubs ready to command. He hadn't wasted much time on any unnecessary finer features—it was by general shape alone that they could be identified as human soldiers. Instead he just concentrated on quantity and their durability and such—considerations that mattered for the task at hand. He could care less about their aesthetics as long as they got the job done as effectively as possible.

"Phew. Well, that's a good start," Toman said, plopping down on a rock near Kessa. "So, ready to explain to me about the energies you mentioned?"

"I'd like to try," Kessa responded. She collected her thoughts and then began. "So, there are certain things that we can see in the world. There's the flow of water, that always takes the path of least resistance, but can wear away stone with enough persistence. There is heat, which flows from object to object—you can feel it at least, even if you can't see it. There's even the wind, and the sun. All of these energies we can feel through touch.

"But there are other energies too. Every time we move or do not move, there are different kinds of energy. For every emotion that is felt, different energies are created. Energies can come from color and sound, and different patterns in them. These are energies that exist but that we cannot touch with our bodies, but can with our souls. Magic is the bridge between those energies, as well as being a kind of energy itself.

"So, everything we do affects the energies around us. That is why peace is so important. If there is no peace, all the bad energies would tear us apart. Our souls would eventually become obliterated or lost in the energies. It's only amongst peaceful energies that we can not only survive, but thrive."

Toman considered her explanation and ended up nodding. "I suppose that makes sense," he replied. It wasn't a view he would ascribe to, but it certainly wasn't irrational.

"Of course it makes sense!" Kessa replied indignantly. "It's true!"

"Sorry, I didn't mean it like that," Toman apologized. "I wasn't assuming what you told me would be nonsense or something. All I meant was that these are new ideas to me, but they make sense anyways. I'm not the great thinker that Esset is. I'm smart enough, but when it comes to delving into the mysteries of our world... Well, I'm not interested like he is. I'm simpler that way, I guess. I believe in Bright Hyrishal—that's our religion— and it makes sense too. And my religion isn't something I can just abandon willy-nilly. I could give you an overview of my beliefs, but frankly, I probably wouldn't do a very good job."

"I'd like to hear," responded Kessa, a little appeased and definitely curious.

Toman sighed but began collecting his thoughts to give a summary of the Church of Bright Hyrishal. "Well, here goes then," Toman began. "Just remember, I suck at explaining things. If you still don't understand when I'm done, you should ask Esset. So, Bright Hyrishal is our deity, a god above all others who's good...and stuff. His symbol is fire—or Brightfire, rather. He's opposed by the Darkfire, which is evil. So, y'know, good versus evil. Bright Hyrishal wants people to be good, and to do good, and the Darkfire just wants there to be evil everywhere. Everyone has a little light and a little darkness inside them, but the point is for the light to win." Toman stopped. That was the worst explanation he'd ever heard, and he'd just said it. A two year old could have done better.

"I...suppose that makes sense?" Kessa replied, echoing his earlier words tentatively. Kessa and Toman stared at each other for a moment, then simultaneously burst out laughing. Something about the moment just seemed so monumentally ridiculous. There was an undercurrent of an "S" to Kessa's giggles, an involuntary Nadran addition to laughter. After a minute or two, they finally started to get a hold of themselves.

"Oh Brightfire," Toman gasped. "Really, just ask Esset. I'll only butcher it more. It'll be a long explanation, and really detailed and complicated, but at least he won't sound like a moron like me."

"Perhaps I shall, sometime. But I would not have missed that for the world," she replied.

"Gee, thanks," Toman retorted with a wide grin. "Well, since I've managed to completely humiliate myself, I'm now going to attempt to regain my pride by doing something impressive. Something I do rather a lot better than explain even the simplest elements of theology, apparently." Toman stood as he spoke, and went back to his place, crouched with his palms on the ground.

"I am sure there are many things you do better," Kessa agreed demurely, but with a slight hint of mischief in her voice.

"Brightfire, I hope so," Toman muttered under his breath. As he closed his eyes, he heard her soft hissing laughter as he returned to work.

CHAPTER 12

Another day, another dark tunnel. Esset had to jog to keep up with the quick pace the slithering Nadra kept. Nassata kept a hand on his shoulder to guide him in the darkness.

"Where to today?" Esset asked. They had just passed the first line of sentries.

"There is a choke point down this tunnel," Nassata explained. "We lost it barely two sevendays past. The Reshkin were clever in their attacks, taking advantage of a...mischance on our part. If we can recapture the tunnel to that point, we should be able to hold it indefinitely."

Esset wondered what the mischance was, but she had phrased the explanation delicately, so he decided not to pry.

"Have you heard on Toman's progress then? I haven't had time to inquire recently," she asked, delicately changing the subject.

"Honestly, me neither. This will be what, our fifth blitz attack? How long...I can't track time underground like this," Esset confessed as he tried to guess how much progress Toman would have made. Esset and the Nadra had returned to the city between attacks, leaving Nadran sentries behind at each battle-site and replenishing their numbers before heading out again. He'd also snatched a few catnaps and some food, but time seemed to flow differently without day and night to track it. Everything seemed to take longer in the eternal underground night. He wondered how long it would take to get used to the conditions—if he could get used to them at all.

He understood the grueling pace though. At this point, surprise was still on Esset's side. The Reshkin had yet to devise a way to effectively combat his summons, and both the summoner and the Nadra intended to make good on that.

"I honestly don't know," Esset finally said. "We've been underground what, two or three days now?" He felt tired enough for that to be true. He wasn't exhausted yet, but another day at this pace would probably put him there.

"We're almost there," Nassata said instead of responding, her voice quiet.

Within minutes, they met the outer sentries and then waited in the darkness as Esset's two fiery panthers ripped another hole in the Reshkin swarm. It was another sickening serenade of clattering, hissing, and roaring, complemented with the stench of burning Reshkin entrails and unsettling flashes of light on glossy carapaces. Esset was still trying to find the balance between concentrating to keep his creatures on task and detaching himself to keep from vomiting from the smells, sights, and sounds. At least he only had to concentrate on one front.

"Hie! Reshkin to the rear!"

The call snapped Esset out of his thoughts. He'd been mostly paying attention to the battle, but with little to no visual stimuli to track, it was all too easy to draw inwards while his summons fought and he waited. Good thing it wasn't the same for the Nadra.

"Pull your summons back!" A heavy Nadran hand on Esset's shoulder accompanied the order. Instead of obeying, Esset banished both and re-summoned them nearer the group, one facing down the tunnel one way, the other on the opposite side of the group, facing the other way. Esset held them in place, waiting for more information from the Nadra before letting them loose again.

"Are the Reshkin advancing from both sides now?" Esset asked, not giving the Nadra a chance to forget that he couldn't see the Reshkin coming.

"Yes, and quickly. City-side is twice the distance away than the far side, but far side has closed the distance they were at by half," the warrior replied. Esset didn't waste another second in letting the panther on the far side go. He counted to five, then released the panther on the city-side. They met the oncoming waves of Reshkin at an approximately equal distance from the group in opposite directions. Esset wasn't liking this at all. There was nowhere for the small group to go, and their position was not very defensible.

"The tunnel is too wide for one on each side to guard—watch for Reshkin slipping past the summons!" Esset warned them. He drew his dirk, knowing that it would be petty protection against a Reshkin but feeling better for it anyways. He wondered if he should banish the cats and summon wolves—he could call on four of those, after all. But two cats were still stronger than four wolves, and he wasn't sure the numbers would make a substantial enough difference, especially when swapping them out would leave a temporary gap. Deciding they wouldn't be worth it, he left things as they were.

Esset felt a sudden surge of relief as a lantern was lit behind him. He hadn't realized that he'd nearly stopped breathing from pure terror at the unseen menaces in the darkness until the light had illuminated the passage. He swallowed and breathed, trying to get his head into a space where he could fight—and not just through his summons.

The Nadra encircled him, knowing that his survival would best ensure theirs. The panthers kept the bulk of the forces at bay, but some were slipping past. Nassata swept aside a Reshkin with her spear-butt, tossing it back into the swarm just in time to skewer a second Reshkin with a precise thrust into a glittering eye. Another Nadra helped her free her spearhead with the butt of his own in a swift, practiced gesture, but they both had to dance out of the way before a third could bite them; it was driven back as Nassata's spearhead swung back around.

Esset stayed crouched in the center of the Nadra, trying to watch every direction at once so that he could dodge out of the way or press an attack as needed. He also had to keep a corner of his mind and some of his gaze on his summons, too, for them to be effective. He scolded himself for having gotten too used to sitting back and letting them fight without engaging himself as well, as he was finding the task more difficult than he remembered during the Baliyan war.

The Nadra, meanwhile, were hard pressed to kill the Reshkin that made it past the summons, given that they were trying to avoid that deadly bite. A copper Nadra fended away a Reshkin with spear-blows that bounced off the creature's carapace. He tried to stab at the creature's eyes, but he couldn't keep up with the Reshkin's darting attacks as it tried to sink its fangs into his coils. Finally another Nadra aided him, coming in from the right angle to bash the Reshkin against the wall with a mace; Esset heard a crunching sound as the impact cracked the Reshkin's carapace.

The lights reflected strangely on the battle. Beyond the Nadra, a panther opened its jaws, emitting a flare of light, but the flare was inevitably brief as those fiery jaws closed around an unfortunate Reshkin a moment later. That yellow light conflicted with the strange, colorless light emitted from the Nadran lantern. And every light cast in the dark tunnel was prone to have shadows cast from it; leaping, dashing, contorting, squirming shadows, shadows that hid monsters while seeming to be monsters themselves.

Those shadows nearly cost Esset his life. A Reshkin darted forward under the brief cover of one patch of darkness, right between the two Nadra on that side. Esset braced himself to defend, even as he knew his dirk would be next to useless in keeping those twitching mandibles away from him. The Reshkin hissed and leapt. Esset raised his dirk, and a spear darted over his shoulder. The Reshkin swallowed the point, impaled, and halted barely an arm's length from Esset's nose. Esset gulped, and Nassata swung her spear up and slammed the dead Reshkin down atop one of its advancing kindred. There was no time to thank her as the battle continued.

The tunnel was filled with the strange sounds and stenches of a battle between the Reshkin and the Nadra and the summoner. The serrated Reshkin feet skittered and scratched on the floor, and they made strange hisses and clicks as they fought. The Nadra hissed too—far louder and more varied sounds. Then there was the swish of scales on smooth stone, and the crackle of flame from the summons. Burnt Reshkin flesh stank in the air, nearly choking Esset. Metal spear-butts clattered against the floor occasionally as the Reshkin were warded away by quick, striking blows from the weapons and slashing sweeps of the spearheads.

"There!" one of the Nadra suddenly yelled, and Esset felt strong Nadran arms sweep him off his feet as they made a break to push through the Reshkin swarm. Esset nearly dropped his dirk when he was picked up, but he only let shock preoccupy him for a moment. In the next, he was pulling the panthers in close to them to help clear the way. It was wise of them not to put him down—his inability to see in the dark would no doubt put them all in jeopardy now that the lit lantern had been left behind.

Somehow, they made it through, but the Nadra didn't stop moving until they'd put a great deal of distance between themselves and the battleground. Esset pulled back his panthers on rearguard, ignoring the pain in his shoulders—both had been wrenched during their escape. They only stopped when they reached a squad of five more Nadra heading their way.

"Thank goodness you're okay!" one exclaimed. They were all visibly relieved to see them. A lantern was brought out quickly, and Esset and his guards were quickly checked for serious injury as the rest of the group went forward to stand guard in case any more Reshkin came. Esset could feel his two panther summons still in his head, fighting Reshkin somewhere down the tunnel. He saw no harm in letting them continue—the only creatures down there were Reshkin, and he wasn't feeling particularly kindly towards them at the moment.

Esset had been set down as gently as possible, and he immediately winced and began massaging his wrenched shoulders. He forestalled the apologies that the pair who'd carried him were trying to make, however. "Thank you for saving my life."

Both Nadra were clearly relieved that he had suffered no serious harm and harbored no ill will towards them, not for letting the Reshkin corner them and not for hurting him while saving his life.

"How did they get behind us?" Nassata demanded of the second group. The group's very presence indicated that they'd somehow found out they'd be in trouble. Esset was just glad he didn't have to ask the question himself.

"One of the offshoots of this tunnel. We had four sentries stationed there, so it should have been safe, but the Reshkin swarmed in greater number than usual, even for that location. All of our sentries are dead. Niyisha, Mayska, Keskana, and Stayvin. Keskana managed to raise an alarm, but she'd already been bitten."

Esset watched the various reactions of the warriors as they learned of their fallen comrades. They were wartime reactions—anger, sorrow, guilt; not in measures that they would have experienced in times of peace, but rather in measures that showed they been as desensitized as they could be to the deaths of those they knew and loved. They themselves had survived the day, but their kindred had not been so lucky. Esset watched the Nadra comfort each other—not a single one of them stood apart except for the sentries standing guard. All of them sought tactile comfort in woven arms or tails or in outright hugs. Only Esset was not included, and that was not something he minded—he would not have intruded for the world. After a minute or two at most, Nassata extracted herself to come to him.

"I'm so sorry," she began before could forestall her.

"There is nothing to be sorry for," he replied. "This is war. We do what we can do and we just keep fighting." She regarded him seriously and then nodded.

"Thank you," she said briefly, grateful he understood. She turned to the others. "Come, let us get home, comrades."

Esset picked up the lantern from the ground where it had been left, all too grateful to comply. The new group stayed where they were, as they were the new sentries for the tunnel. They were already lighting new lanterns and posting them on wall brackets to illuminate the watch-area.

Nassata, Esset, and Esset's guards made their way at a pace equal to the summoner's walk back to the main city, a fact for which Esset was also grateful. He wasn't sure he could summon the energy to go faster. *Summon...!* Esset finally reached for his summoning ability and banished the two distant summons. While he probably could have relied on them to stay and battle Reshkin, there was no guarantee, and the cats were particularly unpredictable creatures. He didn't want to be responsible for a Nadran death. There had been enough death already.

Esset had taken his shirt off to examine the damage to his arms. There were matching bruises on each shoulder—very large, very colorful bruises. He was in the room he and Toman had been given. It was smallish, with two single beds, a chair, and a wardrobe, all of rustic make.

"What in the name of Bright Hyrishal happened to you?" Toman exclaimed the moment he pushed the cloth door aside to enter. Behind him, Kessa craned her neck to see around him into the room.

"Oh!" she exclaimed. "Did you see the healer?" Esset almost jumped in surprise, having not realized she was there. Toman noticed Esset's flush of red and his shift in body language, suddenly self-conscious. Then again, there was a naked—by their standards, anyways—girl looking at him with his shirt off.

"Ah, yes. They gave me this salve to put on it, but it hurts to reach that far," Esset replied.

"I don't doubt it," Toman responded, moving further into the room and throwing his floppy-brimmed hat on the bed. He was about to offer a hand, but Kessa beat him to it.

"Here, let me," she said, moving forward quickly and taking the container of salve from Esset before he could respond. The brothers were beginning to notice that the Nadra seemed to have a very liberal view on privacy. Esset intended to object, but Kessa already had her hands in the salve. The moment she touched him, he changed his mind. The salve had an immediate numbing effect that provided instant relief, rendering him unable to speak a word of objection.

"Thank you," Esset said instead, but only after a minute of silence.

"So what happened?" Toman asked. He'd thought Esset and his entourage would only be sniping from a distance—there was no reason why Esset should have sustained injuries at all. Esset launched into a description of the day's events—their various attacks and how the last one had gone wrong. Toman studied his brother covertly as he spoke, and he noticed the strain. Esset's injuries were inconvenient, but very minor. No, something else had taken a toll on him, a psychological toll. Toman guessed it was the conditions—Esset had never been fond of insects and arachnids and the like. The summoner handled himself just fine in their presence, but afterward, they got under his skin. Add that to the darkness in the tunnels… Toman glanced at Kessa. He'd talk to Esset when she left.

Wrapping up his explanation, Esset brought up something that had been bothering him since he'd gotten back. "Toman, I've noticed that the Nadra have practically no defenses. The tunnels are wide open—they just set up sentries and rely on them to keep back the swarm. You saw how wide-spread the tunnel network was—imagine how spread thin they must be to cover all that territory." Toman nodded, seeing Esset's point.

"We need to seal off some of the tunnels," Esset continued. "I was thinking that if you could animate something like a giant snake, it could curl in the narrower points of the tunnels and block them. We and the Nadra could get them to move if needed, but otherwise they could block the tunnels from the Reshkin by sealing it right up." Toman nodded again.

"I could do something like that," he agreed. "We'll have to mention it to them tomorrow. I've got nothing left in me tonight." In fact, the surprise of seeing Esset's condition was all that was keeping him on his feet at the moment.

"I could take your idea to the warriors tonight," Kessa suggested. "That way they will have come to a decision by tomorrow morning." She finished smearing the last of the salve on Esset's shoulders and wiped her hands on a small towel before securing the lid on the container and passing it back to the summoner.

"Thanks," Esset murmured, both for the container and the help with the salve.

"Thank you, we'd appreciate that," Toman added, for the offer to pass on the message.

"I will see you both tomorrow morning," Kessa said. She sort of half started to reach out to them, then tucked in on herself before fleeing out the door. Esset very belatedly realized that she'd been reaching out in that tactile Nadran tendency. Toman made the realization even later.

"They are a strange people," he commented. He held his arm out towards the table and the excess of belts that he wore flowed off of him like so many snakes to coil atop the furniture.

"I kinda like them," Esset replied, pulling off his boots.

"Me too," Toman added with a grin. They both got ready for bed and covered the lantern; fire wasn't the light source of the lantern, and closing the shutters on it seemed to be the only way to put out the light. Esset was so tired, he didn't even try to figure it out. Once they were in bed, Toman listened to his brother's breathing for a while before speaking, knowing they were both still awake.

"It's pretty brutal, huh? Fighting those things in the darkness down here?" The animator and the summoner knew each other too well—that question was all it took for Toman to open the floodgates to Esset's fears.

It was an hour, at least, before they stopped whispering, before

Esset had vented and calmed enough to sleep.

CHAPTER 13

Morning seemed to be a very relative concept underground. Without the sun to remind them and with exhaustion dampening their internal clocks, Kessa had to come to wake them. She did so cheerfully, coming into their room with a lantern and unveiling their own to add yet more light.

"Good morning!" she greeted them cheerfully.

"What the—gah!" That was Esset, scrambling under his covers in half-wakeful confusion. Toman opened his own eyes blearily, managing to retain some composure.

"Come, it is breakfast time!" Kessa urged them, going up to Esset, who was closer, and putting her hand on his foot to tug on it.

"Oi!" Esset jerked his foot back. "Can we get dressed first?"

Kessa blinked her reptilian eyes at them. Given that she saw her own kind completely unclad every single day, it really wasn't surprising that she didn't notice they weren't clothed. "Oh."

"Just wait outside a second, we'll be right out," Toman said, having woken up faster than Esset. He stifled a snicker at his brother. He looked distinctly ruffled—Esset's hair was rarely tidy even at the best of times, but it was sticking out at some rather ridiculous angles at the moment, and his expression only reinforced the rumpled image.

"Okay!" Kessa agreed readily, vanishing out the cloth door. Toman immediately emerged from beneath the covers and started dressing—Esset took a second or two longer to rub his eyes and yawn before following suit. Thankfully, by the time they joined Kessa, he was considerably more alert—and he'd straightened his hair out, sort of.

"Good morning," Toman said, greeting her properly this time as he stuffed his floppy-brimmed hat on his head.

"Mornin'," Esset echoed.

Kessa greeted them with a bright smile. "Good morning. I took your suggestion to the council, and they said that if you think it will work, you should do it. They hadn't thought of getting you to do something like that, I think," Kessa informed them.

"Excellent. I'll get started right away then," Toman said, rubbing his gloved hands together.

"Breakfast first," Kessa said, taking both their wrists in her hands and leading them down the path. Toman and Esset both exchanged glances. They'd tried Nadran food already. It was heavy in mushrooms and other fungi, in bugs, and in some unidentifiable meat that Toman suspected to be some kind of rodent. Neither of them liked it very much. They knew they needed food, but…after days of trying to choke down the Nadran fare, it had become almost too much to bear.

"Is there…anything else to eat? Your food is rather…alien to us," Esset said delicately.

"Oh… Nassata said something about that. I will have to ask her again. Is that all right?" Kessa looked rather uncertain.

"One more meal is perfectly fine," Esset assured her with a forced smile. Hopefully it looked genuine, although both Toman and Esset felt their stomachs snuggle up a little closer to their throats.

"You remind me of Gretchen the first time she visited here." Nassata had found them, and she'd come up behind them unnoticed.

"Nassata!" Esset exclaimed, jumping a little and wincing as the movement jarred his bruised shoulders. She hissed at him, a little laugh.

"She did not care for our food either, and thankfully she remembered that when she designed your contract. I know I had forgotten. We are a due a delivery of food you will appreciate some time today," she assured them.

"Thank you," Esset replied, knowing that didn't even begin to cover the relief both of them felt at learning they wouldn't have to eat Nadran food for the entire campaign. Not that they looked forward to this particular breakfast any more than before…

"Now, the council very much liked your plan," Nassata said, shifting her attention to Toman. "We tried blocking some of the tunnels in the past, but we were always swarmed before we could complete an effective barricade. You see, we have no efficient means of sealing tunnels. We can't get enough material in place to block a tunnel before the Reshkin swarm us. We even lost five of our Shapers—our magic users—in one attempt, and we cannot risk more of them. If you can indeed seal off the tunnels in a non-permanent fashion, it would be a great advantage, and it would free up many of our sentries. We would likely still leave guards, but only one instead of the two to five in some places."

"Do you want I should create the seals on location, or should I go above and make them up there and bring them down when I'm finished?" Toman asked.

"If you made them on location, you would be taking stone from the walls there, yes?" Nassata asked. Toman nodded.

"I could take the stone from this main place or places on the way," Toman offered.

"That...may be best," Nassata said. "The sooner our defenses are tightened and warriors freed up, the better." Toman and Esset were nodding their agreement.

"I also think it best if you come along," Nassata continued, looking at Esset. "We had planned on giving you a period of rest, as we intended to rethink our plans, but with this new approach..."

"Of course," Esset responded. Rest was always nice, but it wasn't necessary yet. Sore shoulders wouldn't stop him from summoning. "If there's another ambush like yesterday, I need to be there."

"It is almost as though they are becoming more intelligent," Nassata said. "They work together now like they never have before—even more so yesterday. At the least, it's obvious in how they swarm us when we try to seal the tunnels. They've also captured some suspiciously key points. But that ambush yesterday... That was on a whole new level."

"You think there's something—or someone behind this," Toman responded, studying Nassata and reading between the lines.

"I do, but I have no evidence other than the changes in the Reshkin. This worries me," she replied. Off to the side, her presence forgotten for a few moments, Kessa began to look very alarmed.

"Oh, Kessa!" Nassata exclaimed, suddenly remembering her presence. The Nadran warrior slithered over to her cousin and wrapped her arms around her. Toman and Esset stopped to wait, a bit embarrassed that they, too, had forgotten that the other Nadra was there. Even they were aware, to some extent, of how delicate she could be.

"It's okay. I will protect you, Kessa," Nassata soothed her, stroking her hair. "We will protect our people." Kessa snuggled in against her chest, looking very child-like.

"I believe you," Kessa replied, gazing up at Nassata's face with simple trust. "But it is frightening."

"Yes, it is," Nassata agreed. "But you must be strong too, yes? Can you do that for me?" She loosened her embrace and they drew apart slightly, their hands still on each other's arms. Kessa nodded, her innocent smile returning.

"Good. You're so brave, Kessa." Nassata gave her one last, quick hug before letting her go. They resumed their travel to the common eating area of the Nadra.

"Do you mind stopping a moment? I told Tseka I'd wake her up," Nassata requested a moment later, pausing next to a curtained doorway.

"Tseka?" Esset asked with a slightly pained expression, but Toman was already saying, "Not at all," and stopping to wait.

Nassata pulled back the curtain wide, and Toman and Esset got their first look at a typical Nadran dwelling.

Had they stopped to think about it, they probably would have realized that the room they were staying in was not typical, but made especially for bipedal guests. But they hadn't thought of that—they hadn't really had a chance to—and so they were somewhat surprised. The room was very round, the floor smoothly curved and depressed into the room. Flowing patterns of color splashed across the walls, lending additional brightness to the room. Two lanterns in the room shed light on the occupants, who were gathered in one spot. A Nadra's bed, apparently, consisted of a smooth, deep depression in the stone floor that was filled with pillows and blankets in no sort of order. The "bed" was rather large, and there were four Nadra tangled in it.

The bodies of the four Nadra were so entwined and wrapped around each other that "tangled" truly was the only word to describe them. Dull scales mixed with painted, but even so it was difficult to tell which appendages belonged to whom. When the curtain opened, four heads popped out of the mix, blinking with varying degrees of bleariness to see who was calling. There wasn't a shred of self-consciousness among the four.

Toman glanced at Esset, knowing his brother would probably be a little scandalized by the sleeping arrangement. The animator wondered if the Nadra in the room were kin, but he doubted it, and even so, such an arrangement would be bizarre in their own culture—to say the least. Here, it seemed normal. Sure enough, he found Esset's expression mildly humorous, and he elbowed Esset before their hosts could see it.

"Ah, Nassata, that time already?" Tseka asked, disentangling her arms with perplexing ease to stretch.

There was some writhing movement in the bed as her companions shifted around to let her out. Tseka had no problems helping them along, either, it seemed, as she unceremoniously shoved a few coils out of the way as she extracted herself.

"Ah, our saviors," Tseka said when she emerged, eyeing Toman and Esset.

"Good morning," Toman greeted her. Tseka just kept eyeing him for a moment, not deigning to respond, while Esset blithely wondered if it really was morning or not. Finally, the red warrior looked away, placing a hand on Nassata's shoulder and giving her a nod of greeting before looking down the hall.

"We have somewhere to be, yeah?" Tseka grinned, pushing past them to head in the direction they'd been going. Toman couldn't help but notice that Kessa and Tseka didn't greet each other. In fact, Kessa had shrunk back a bit, as if trying to avoid notice. Then again, if this was what Tseka was normally like, Toman didn't blame her.

"Come, we should meet with our escort, or they will have to wait on us. We are all eager to increase the security of our city," Nassata said, increasing the group's pace. Toman and Esset almost had to jog to keep up, but the Nadra kept pace effortlessly.

"What about breakfast?" Kessa asked. She shrank a little when Tseka raised an eyebrow at her.

"We're...not hungry," Esset said, thinking of the *real* food they'd be getting later.

"Then we can get started now," Nassata said. Tseka eyed Esset and Toman, as if suspecting them of something, but she held her tongue.

"Kessa, you might as well find other jobs for the day. Toman and Esset won't be needing you until later," Nassata said to Kessa as they moved.

"Yes, Nassata. Bye everyone!" Kessa waved to them—at least there was one gesture humans and Nadra shared—and absently trailed her fingers down Toman's arm as she parted and headed off in a different direction. Toman blinked but smiled at the unconscious gesture.

"We're going to start with the east tunnels," Nassata said once Kessa was gone. "Reshkin attacks are worst from that direction."

They stopped at a small armory in the city so Nassata and Tseka could arm themselves. They met the rest of their escort there, four more Nadran warriors.

"What kind of parameters do you want my creations to follow?" Toman asked as they headed out.

"What do you mean?" Nassata tilted her head to the side.

"Well, I can have my creatures block the tunnel, but I have to tell them who to obey and who not to when ordered to unblock the tunnel," Toman explained.

"Hm... I should think that any Nadra should be able to command passage, and the two of you of course. That should suffice," Nassata said.

"*Any* Nadra?" Toman asked in surprise. "You don't want to authorize just a few?"

"*Any* Nadra," Nassata confirmed, adamant.

"But—" Toman began to object, thinking of Nassata's earlier comment that it seemed someone was behind the Nadra.

"Any Nadra, Animator," Tseka interrupted, her voice even, for once, without rancor or mischief. She and Nassata exchanged a knowing look before glancing back at the other Nadra with them.

They both believe someone's behind this, but not Nadra, Toman realized. And the others either aren't aware of this belief, or they don't share it, so Nassata and Tseka don't want to bring it up in front of them.

"Okay then." Toman shrugged. He wasn't sure there was any particular reason to believe a Nadra wasn't behind the changes in the Reshkin, but now clearly wasn't the time to debate it.

"It'll take me about fifteen minutes to shape the animation and define its orders," Toman informed the Nadra when they stopped in a vacant chamber on their way to the first choke point that they wanted blocked. Given that they had been swarmed when trying to block off tunnels in the past, they wanted their barrier ready to place as quickly as possible.

"Take what time you need," Nassata replied. It was implicit that it would be appreciated if he didn't take more than that. With a simple nod, Toman got to work. He placed his hands against the wall and closed his eyes, and the stone began to shift.

Everyone watched with fascination, Esset included. He'd seen Toman make his creations many times, but it was still engrossing. It happened just quickly enough that there was something to watch. A long shape bulged from the wall; it was long and snake-like, but it became apparent after a moment that it was being created back end first. At the front, the tubular shape split into two, until its overall form was clear—it was a massive, two-headed snake.

When the form was done, Toman stood for a few minutes, firmly implanting its directives in his creation. When Toman finally opened his eyes, he didn't seem wearied at all. The wall it had been born from was left smooth—the stone had been drawn evenly from the whole wall, so the tunnel was just slightly wider to account for the stone Toman had used.

"Let's go," he simply said. "Hopefully this works as planned." Everyone was ready to get moving again. Fortunately, it wasn't far to their destination.

"There are Reshkin further up the tunnel, but they do not seem to be moving overmuch," Tseka informed them from the lead. They'd passed the last sentries in the tunnel only a few moments ago.

"Good." They had a lantern with them, ready to cover if needed, but until then, the light was comforting for the two humans in the party.

"Warrior Tseka, could you please edge back a bit? You're right in the best spot to block," Toman requested respectfully. Tseka shot him a look—what was that, distaste? It was difficult to tell in the dark—but she moved back. The stone snake slithered forward to where Tseka had been, then suddenly swerved right. Its body slid up the wall, around the other side, and then along its own body until it had coiled perfectly inside itself, braced against the tunnel walls. One head looked at them, and the other looked down the tunnel beyond. It took a second to settle, and then it had created an airtight seal on the corridor—no Reshkin were getting through.

"I think that will work," Esset commented, looking at Nassata to see what she thought. None of them had been entirely sure how Toman was going to block the tunnel with a snake, but it now looked like it would work quite well.

"I think so too," Nassata said, slithering forward to inspect the stone snake.

"If any Nadra tells it to move aside, it will. Tell it to move back into place, and it will," Toman explained concisely.

"Excellent," Nassata replied. She finished her brief inspection, then moved back towards them. "Okay, let's keep going." They had many tunnels to block.

CHAPTER 14

They were back in the heart of Salithsa after a long day of blocking tunnels—they couldn't block them all, but they'd blocked enough to make a difference.

"Well I'm glad that went as smoothly as it did," Nassata said.

"It's a sad state when having to drive back swarms of venomous monsters counts as smooth," Tseka said.

"Yes, but thanks to Esset, we never even had to close with the monsters ourselves, and we are far safer now than we were," Nassata countered. Tseka made a grumbling sound that sounded like begrudging agreement. Toman wasn't fooled; he suspected she had actually already warmed to them.

"Man, I'm stiff," Toman said, stretching his arms as they stepped into the light of the main bowl of the city.

"Me too," Esset agreed, tenderly massaging his own sore shoulders. "What I wouldn't give for a hot bath right now."

"Why not try our hot springs?" Nassata suggested. "There is a small spring chamber not far from your rooms that is rarely used. It's a smaller spring, and only the guest quarters are terribly close to it. It should be empty now. Kessa could show you where it is."

"Speaking of—oh, there she is," Toman said with a smile.

Kessa had emerged from a curtained room and came darting towards them with a smile. "You're back! It is good to see everyone safe."

"We had no trouble at all," Toman replied.

"These two have expressed interest in visiting the hot springs," Nassata put in, slithering over to Kessa to put an arm around her shoulders. "I suggested the small one near their rooms. Could you show them the way?"

"Of course, Nassata!" Kessa agreed happily.

"I don't recall going down that tunnel before," Toman remarked. "It's guarded further down then?"

Nassata shook her head.

"The tunnel is shallow; only the hot spring is down it, and it backs on your quarters. With no other access points, there's no need to guard it."

"We should join them, Nassata," Tseka put in, her smile somewhat malicious. Toman and Esset exchanged hesitant glances at the suggestion.

"Hah! You know how small that spring is. They will find it comfortable enough, I'm sure, but we would overcrowd it. Besides, you and I both know that you do not care for the springs," Nassata retorted, letting go of Kessa to head back over to the rest of the Nadra. She gave Tseka a shove, which Tseka took with a grin.

"But think of the fun we could have with these two," Tseka wheedled. Esset shifted from foot to foot.

"You have far too much energy left after today, Tseka. Perhaps you should go help Asiran with training. I know how much you love beating the scales off the trainees," Nassata suggested.

"Have I earned no rest?" Tseka complained.

"Wicked scales must always move," Nassata quoted. She took Tseka's arm and began leading her away. They bantered back and forth as they drew away from Toman, Esset, and Kessa, with Nassata successfully distracting the other warrior. Toman and Esset didn't waste any time getting away, either. The moment the warriors began moving away from them, they turned to Kessa.

"Hot springs?" Toman asked hopefully. Esset's eager expression echoed his brother's.

"This way," Kessa replied with a bright smile, slithering away. Toman and Esset took up spots on either side of her. She took a corridor a ways before their rooms, but the way the tunnel wound about, when they finally reached the hot spring chamber, they were almost right next to their room on the other side of one of the adjoining walls.

The room might have been small by Nadran standards, but it wasn't overly so by theirs. It was spacious enough, and the spring itself was large enough to fit probably up to six humans. The water steamed, betraying its temperature and filling the room with a gentle, humid heat and obscuring most of the floor to about knee-height. Toman guessed that it must also keep their sleeping quarters warm for them by heating the wall it was adjacent to.

"Nice," Toman said when they pulled aside the bead curtain to view the room. He immediately stepped inside, stripping off his heavy coat.

"You must be starving," Kessa said once both of them were in the room. "I'll bring you some food." She vanished quickly, leaving them to enjoy the spring. Neither of them took their time getting in.

There were hooks along the wall, with only three of them presently occupied with rather large towels, so Toman hung up his coat. Everything went on those hooks except for their smallclothes, which they kept on, Toman's gloves, which he also wore, and their socks and boots, which waited on the floor. After making sure the towels were within easy reach, they dipped their toes into the hot spring and got in.

"Oh Brightfire, does this ever feel good," Esset said, sinking into the water. To his surprise, there was a ledge to sit on at about the right level, so it seemed that this chamber was also one that was normally meant for human—or humanoid—guests.

"Agreed," Toman said. He ducked briefly beneath the surface of the water, just enough to get his hair wet. He slicked it back out of his face, and propping his arms on the ledge behind him, he sat back and reveled in the heat. Pretty soon both brothers lapsed into silence, relaxing so far as to almost fall asleep in the heat and comfort.

They were jolted awake by the jangle of beads as Kessa came in. She held a tray with three plates on it, one for each of them. It was Nadran food, but Toman and Esset were so hungry that they didn't particularly care.

"Here we are," Kessa said cheerfully, putting down plates next to each of them. Then she went around the other side of the hot spring and slipped into the water herself. Suddenly both young men were glad they'd opted to keep their underclothes on, since she clearly intended to stay.

They were all quiet for a bit as Esset and Toman wolfed down their food; Kessa ate more delicately. She let them finish before starting a conversation.

"So how is sealing the tunnels coming?" she finally asked.

"Really well. It feels like slow going, since I have to create the seals and then we have to travel to where my animation will block the tunnel, but we actually made really good time today. We should get the majority of them done tomorrow, and then finish the last few the day after. But already there's a significant number of warrior Nadra freed up by the seals," Toman reported. "Now the areas that need them can have more guards, and the rest of them can get more rest."

"That's great," Kessa agreed with a smile. She was looking at Toman strangely, however. Or, more specifically, she was looking at his gloves. Finally Toman lifted his hand and wiggled his gloved fingers at her.

"Ah, sorry," the little blue Nadra apologized. Toman chuckled.

"Not at all. You're wondering why I'm still wearing my gloves in the water?" Toman asked. Kessa nodded.

"Here, take a closer look," he said, holding out his hand towards her. She reached out toward the glove, but then her eyes went wide in surprise.

"They're still dry!" she exclaimed. Toman dipped his hand beneath the surface and then lifted it again.

"Still dry," he repeated with a smile.

"That is so strange," Kessa marveled. "How?"

"Magic," Toman said, wiggling his fingers at her again. The corner of her mouth twitched in dissatisfaction with his answer.

"Why then?" Kessa pressed, crossing her arms over her chest.

"I don't ever take them off," Toman replied. "I don't need to, so it works out."

"But why?" she asked again.

"Well, it's not something I advertise, but it's no secret either," Toman said with a shrug. "I wasn't actually born with magic. My ability to animate comes from these." He held up both hands then, flipping them so she could see his gloved palms, then the backs. "They're...well, Esset would call them a magical artifact. Long story short, I inherited them, and now I'm an animator. If I take them off, I can't animate anything."

"Oh," was Kessa's only response. She was surprised and interested.

"Most of the time, they go completely unnoticed," Toman said with a grin, putting his hands down again. "But hang around me long enough, and most people notice there's something slightly odd about them." Kessa just nodded.

"So Kessa, I have to admit that your readiness to get in the water surprised me. Are you not worried about your paints washing off?" Esset asked, changing the subject.

"Not at all. They are more enamels than paints. The water will not harm my patterns," Kessa replied.

"How do you ever remove them then?"

"We have combinations of oils and minerals that take off our paints. Not that we often use them, but it is not overly difficult," Kessa replied.

"So…your patterns. Do they have any meaning, or are they just decorations?" Toman asked.

Esset glanced at him with a bit of surprise, since Toman didn't normally show much interest in other cultures' traditions. Toman normally kept his inquiries to "the practical stuff," while Esset would ask about any old thing.

"They are simply art, a way that we express ourselves," the little blue Nadra replied. "Some of us choose to incorporate meaning into our paints, with images or words or memorable patterns with historical significance, but most of us do not.

"Me, I love purple especially, which is why I paint my scales with it. The blues complement my scales, and the yellows make a nice contrast. There is little more to it than that. My grandmother taught me to paint, and I have always loved to do so."

"Your painted scales are lovely," Toman said. Kessa ducked her head in embarrassment, a Nadran equivalent to a blush.

"Thank you," she murmured back.

Esset suddenly realized that he had a Nadra to talk to who wasn't a warrior and probably wouldn't threaten him if he asked too many questions.

"So, how does your thermal detection work, exactly? Is it like vision, or totally different?" he asked, leaning forward.

Kessa blinked at the sudden change in topic. "Um… I suppose, like vision, yes. They kind of…combine? It is difficult to explain. In some ways it is much like vision, but in many ways it is like…like a different tactile sense. It is complicated. Perhaps it is totally different."

"Well… What do you see or sense now, when it comes to thermal detection?" Esset pressed.

"Not much, actually," Kessa responded. "Or actually, too much. It is very warm in here, and the steam makes it difficult. The hot water does too. I cannot distinguish anything beneath the surface of hot water. But this whole room is like that too. The hot springs are one of our sources of heat for the city, and lines of earth-heat run all through this place. Since the spring is here, this entire room is cloaked in heat-tracks. It makes our heat sense almost useless in rooms like these."

"Interesting," Esset murmured. "So you use geothermal energy to heat the city then... I'd wondered. And these heat tracks—those are the paths that the heat-energy follows?" Kessa nodded. "And they run all throughout the city."

"Yes. We have arranged them in patterns that are beautiful to behold. It just occurred to me that you cannot see them. That is a pity—they are beautiful," Kessa replied, tilting her head to the side.

"Well, we do appreciate the end result," Esset said. "It's quite comfortably warm pretty much everywhere in your city."

Kessa smiled.

"So what about the lanterns and lights? I've been really curious—"

"Good grief, Esset. Do you always have to devolve into interrogation mode? Relax, for Hyrishal's sake. Shut your brain off for a change," Toman admonished him.

"I don't mind," Kessa put in with another little duck of her head.

"I do," Toman muttered.

"Oh come on, Toman. You're not curious?" Esset coaxed his brother.

"No, I'm really not," the animator replied with a shake of his head.

"Not about anything?" Esset asked.

"Certainly not about the light fixtures," Toman replied pointedly, looking deadpan at the summoner.

Esset muttered something about enlightenment and trolls that wasn't entirely audible. Toman ignored him.

"Maybe I can ask you two some questions then," Kessa suggested tentatively.

"Absolutely," Esset responded instantly. Toman rolled his

eyes, making Kessa giggle.

"So why do you wear all that?" Kessa asked, gesturing at the clothes hanging on the hooks. Esset blinked, not anticipating that particular question.

"Yeah, Esset, why do we wear all that?" Toman asked his brother, grinning from ear to ear at the awkward situation he'd brought down upon himself.

"It seems like it just slows you down," Kessa proceeded innocently.

"Well, ah, warmth, for one, and protection, sometimes, and, uh…y'know, it's a cultural thing too," Esset stammered. "And pockets—clothes have pockets to carry things in."

There was a little sound from the entryway, like the bead-curtain had been jostled. Toman glanced that way, but with the steam filling the small room, he didn't see anything. Dismissing the tiny noise, Toman looked at his brother again, enjoying watching him squirm.

"Well you don't need the warmth here—you said yourself that it is warm enough belowground," Kessa said, her head still tilted slightly. "And just a little bit of cloth surely can't provide much protection, and it looks terribly uncomfortable."

"Well, you know, our skin isn't as tough as your scales. It doesn't keep the heat in so well either. From what I've seen, Nadra are much less sensitive to heat than humans," Esset said, defending his choice to wear clothes.

The "argument" was so absurd that Toman almost snickered— but then he caught that little sound again, and he once again looked towards the doorway.

"And your pockets are very small—surely they are not all that useful," Kessa prodded. Esset and Kessa seemed oblivious to the little sounds that Toman kept hearing. Was someone in the room with them now? Was it Tseka, up to some trick? But the sound had been so small… Maybe he was imagining things. Brightfires only knew that traveling the dark tunnels all day, on constant lookout for the venomous Reshkin, had put him on edge.

"Pockets are very useful!" Esset objected defensively. The steam behind him shifted. "They can—"

"Jonathan!" Toman yelled. The animator lunged forward and grabbed his best friend's shoulder to yank him forward. It hadn't been his imagination, and it certainly wasn't Tseka sneaking up on them. Esset cried out as Toman's hand smashed into his bruises, but that was the least of the animator's worries. Reshkin had found their way into the bathing chamber. If Toman hadn't moved when he had, Esset would have fallen to the venomous Reshkin's bite; at the last possible moment, Toman had seen the creature behind Esset, hiding in the steam.

"What—?" the question was cut short when Esset saw another of the creatures and responded with a brief prayer. "Oh Brightfire—"

"Kessa, get away from the edge!" Toman ordered the little Nadra. "Put your back against ours!" Eyes wide, she did as she was told, and they felt her tail curl around their feet under the water. They could both feel her shaking as they stood in the center of the spring, back-to-back, with a ring of Reshkin surrounding them.

But they weren't defenseless.

Esset shouted an incantation. At the same time that the fiery wolf materialized, Toman brought to life the clothes hanging on the hooks around the room. His belts shot quickly towards them, entwining in the Reshkin's legs and winding around their heads to cover their glittering eyes. Their coats flooded forwards and wrestled with a creature apiece to drive them back. Esset's dirk flew up into the air and darted around like a small bird—like a kingfisher, actually—swooping down and stabbing the Reshkin in their faces. It was minimally effective, but it was something.

Fortunately Esset's assault was far more effective. The first summon didn't stand a chance, but it had only been a first response. The steam in the air weakened it immediately, and it was swarmed almost right away. Two incantations later, however, two fiery panthers were tearing through the Reshkin like kindling. The three in the spring were forced to shield their faces against splatters and bits that were sent flying, and Kessa soon hid beneath the surface of the water. Toman and Esset could still feel her there, shaking with terror, but she was hidden from sight and at least somewhat more protected from projectiles. Toman didn't blame her—the summons added to the heat already in the room, making the place stiflingly hot. The steam choked down on them, making it not only difficult to see very far, but creating a claustrophobic atmosphere that made breathing the already scorching air even harder.

A panther roared its endless fury, and Esset prayed to Bright Hyrishal that the Nadra would hear the sound echoing down the tunnels and come to their aid. The sound cut off as the cat's jaws closed on a Reshkin head and crushed it. The two panthers darted, swatted, and bit the Reshkin, trying to drive them towards the curtain.

Steam and ash swept around, obscuring everything, so it was difficult to see what exactly the Reshkin were doing; just when Esset thought his herding tactic had worked, one of the deadly bugs emerged out of the steam, mandibles clicking. It was well behind his cats.

Toman's coat dropped atop the Reshkin. The bug skittered backwards and flailed, slicing through the thick material before shaking it free. Only a moment later, a fiery panther pounced on it, molten teeth clamping on a leg and throwing it against the far wall.

Esset gave up the herding tactic in favor of keeping his summons close enough to protect them.

"Jonathan, we've gotta get out of here," Toman said to his brother, sparing a glance to see how he was faring. Toman was trying to shape the water, but it wasn't making a terribly effective weapon against the Reshkin. It was easy to shape, but the Reshkin smashed the water-creatures easily. Toman was focusing on getting them in the eyes to distract them long enough for panthers to dispose of them, but the panthers weren't keen to get near anything excessively wet.

"Ya think?" Esset yelled back. "I'm trying, but they keep getting behind the panthers whenever I try to drive them to the doorway!"

"What about wolves? They've gotta be better herders than panthers. Strength in numbers?" "No way!" Esset objected. "They'd be overwhelmed in seconds, and that's all the opening the Reshkin would need to reach us. I'm just barely keeping them back!"

"Well I'm doing all I can over here! I don't have the time to make anything effective. I've called some of my soldiers from up top, but frankly, I doubt they'll get here in time," Toman warned.

"We'll have to hold on until help comes, Toman. We don't have any other choice!" Both brothers set their mouths into grim expressions. There was nothing more to say; all they could do was fight until help arrived.

Neither was really sure how much time had passed before they heard traces of a scuffle outside.

"Summoner! Are you in there?!" It sounded like Nassata—at any rate, it was the voice of a female Nadra. Toman guessed it was Esset she was calling since it was the summons that were making all the racket.

"We're in here!" Esset yelled back. "Thank bright, Bright Hyrishal," he prayed briefly. He reached under the water to grab Kessa's arm and pull her up. She'd only surfaced briefly a few times for a fresh breath, and there was no way she'd heard the call from beneath the surface.

"Help is here," he said urgently to her. "Get ready to move if we need to." She looked at him and nodded, still utterly terrified.

"We're coming!" they heard their rescuers yelling from the tunnel.

Just then, one of the panthers reached its limit. There was a puff of ash and smoke and suddenly there was a gaping hole in their defenses.

"Jonathan!" Toman yelled, seeing the Reshkin flood into the sudden opening. The animator managed to get the shreds of his coat to intercept the nearest, but it would hold only moments. He heard Esset chanting the incantation behind him. Toman abandoned animating the water and just splashed it—the Reshkin was so close that it was caught full in the face. It drew back for a moment as the mineral-rich water stung its many eyes—and Toman had stalled it just long enough. A massive fiery panther descended atop the creature in a spray of sparks and Reshkin blood. Toman had to duck as the panther's tail swung dangerously close to his face, but he wasn't about to complain—the Reshkin were that close, so they needed the summons that close, even though the fiery cats could hurt them as easily as the Reshkin.

Suddenly the Nadran rescue party was in the room. Tseka was unmistakable, even through the obscuring steam. She battered her way through a group of them, twirling her spear around as if it were no more than a featherweight, and not the hefty metal rod it was. She used a combination of surprise and pure ferocity to drive her way through the Reshkin mass to the edge of the pool. Without waiting on them or asking consent, she reached in and grabbed Esset by the arm, forcibly hauling him out of the water.

"Kessa! Go!" Toman yelled at the little Nadra, using a free hand to pull her around to his other side and shove him towards Tseka. Toman kept right behind Kessa, accidentally stepping on her coils under the water a few times. Then he felt her being hauled out of the water behind him. He stayed until he was sure she was out, and then glanced behind him just in time to see Tseka reach for him. He whirled and grabbed her arm to launch himself out of the water. By that time, the rest of the rescue party had joined them. Kessa was tucked between two of the three warriors, as safe as she could be.

With fewer sides to cover, the panthers suddenly became very effective at driving away the Reshkin. They managed to make a path back to the exit and the whole group managed to get back into the tunnels. There was a brief moment where Toman was absurdly grateful that he'd decided to keep his smallclothes on during his bath in the hot spring, but the thought was fleeting at best, since he was the least effective combatant at the moment. Without any effective soldiers to animate, he was almost as helpless as Kessa. He knew some self-defense, but that was useless when he needed to stay out of range of the poisonous Reshkin fangs. Esset needed to be shielded from incoming attacks too, but at least he had a powerful offense going elsewhere. Toman hated being caught off guard—he was so useless. He gritted his teeth as they fled down the tunnel. He swore to himself that he'd make his dent yet.

The panthers stayed behind to decimate the Reshkin, but with their original targets out of range, the Reshkin were suddenly uninterested in the fight. They began to retreat. The group stopped when they reached the main city, waiting just inside the tunnel to catch their collective breaths and compose themselves. Tseka crossed her arms—not an easy feat while holding a spear, but she still managed to do it and look formidable—and she looked Toman and Esset up and down.

"My, but you humans sure are scrawny. I mean, I knew it already, but without your silly coverings, it is even more obvious." She was wearing a snarky smirk, but even Esset was willing to forgive her for it, given how she'd just helped save them. Her smug little moment was ruined a moment later by Kessa. The little sapphire-blue Nadra had been keeping as close as she could to Nassata without really being in the way, but now she darted forward and threw her arms around Toman, sobbing. He was rather surprised, but he recovered quickly.

"Hey, hey, it's okay," Toman comforted her, stroking the back of her head and putting his arms around her back. She was still shaking, but he could tell she was beginning to calm down. Toman saw Esset's surprise and realized that Esset had really only interacted with warriors so far. Given Kessa's explanation of how highly prized peace was, it stood to reason that the general populace might be extra sensitive to violence. They were a close-knit bunch, after all, so hurting one of them would hurt the whole. And Kessa seemed to be particularly sensitive.

"We're all okay now, see?" Toman said, pulling back slightly and using one hand to turn her chin so she'd look around the group. "Everyone's here, and we're all fine." Down the tunnel, a panther screamed its rage, a reminder that this wasn't over, not completely.

"Nassata, where did those Reshkin come from? I thought this tunnel was a closed loop, with its only entrances to the main city," Esset asked while Toman continued to comfort Kessa.

"It is. I don't know how they got in," Nassata replied, looking into the darkness behind them.

"Well, Reshkin can dig, can they not?" Tseka asked, tapping her spear-butt on the floor.

"What?" Esset interjected, startled.

"They can dig, but not well. At best they can expand an existing tunnel, or cause troubles for our food production. They cannot dig entirely new tunnels," Nassata responded.

"Is that true of them now, or how they were before?" Esset asked. "They've adapted rather well to fight you... Is it not possible that this may be a new quality of theirs as well?"

"I'm afraid that's the only logical explanation," Nassata said, looking troubled. "But we should be able to detect them before they get close enough for an ambush."

"What about the heat tracks? Kessa was telling us about how you distribute heat to your city—could they not mask their heat signatures using your heat tracks?" Esset pointed out. Nassata looked at him seriously, disturbed by the implications of his suggestion.

"This is very bad news," she replied. "This puts the whole city in danger—security is just an illusion if they have become this intelligent. We knew they had gotten smarter, and that they seemed to have grown a hive-mind of kinds, but this... This is high-order strategy."

"Okay, but why attack these two?" Tseka said, gesturing at the young men with her spear. "Why are they the first attack like this?"

"No offense, but I think we're the first majorly dangerous individuals to target here," Esset replied. Tseka scowled fiercely at him.

"No, think about it," he said to her. "From what I've gathered, the Nadra rule themselves by council and general vote, right?" Nassata nodded, not sure what that had to do with anything.

"So if you lose any one individual, even a council-member, your government can compensate," Esset continued. "It's tragic, but it doesn't cripple you as a people. It doesn't prevent you from being able to organize and defend yourselves. The same goes for individual warriors. You're all incredible fighters, but no one warrior poses a drastic threat to the Reshkin."

"Shows what they know," Tseka muttered, but everyone ignored her.

"But then you bring us in. My summons are immune to Reshkin venom, and they pack a pretty hard punch. Toman's creations are causing serious problems for the Reshkin already by blocking their access to you, and he hasn't even really started building you an army yet. He's going to make you a huge force that's immune to their venom as well. Between the two of us... Well, we're well worth assassinating," Esset finished.

Nassata was nodding. "You are right."

"But how would they know you would be in the hot spring?" Tseka prodded.

"They probably didn't. However, the sleeping quarters you gave us are right on the other side of those walls, are they not?" Esset replied. Once again, Nassata nodded.

"And this means that we have been extremely negligent in guarding you," the green warrior said. "From now on, you do not go anywhere without protection."

"Agreed. But can I suggest something?" Apparently Toman had comforted Kessa enough. Everyone turned to look at him, and he returned their gaze steadily. Kessa stood right beside him with Toman's arm securely around her shoulders. She was still huddled up next to him, but no longer clinging.

"Some of my stone soldiers are already heading this way—I called them when we were in trouble, having no way of calling anyone else." He paused, then added, "By the way, they might have spooked your sentries. Sorry about that." His thoughtful expression turned more serious again. "My animations should do well enough. I'll keep them around whenever we're in the city, and leave them behind when we're with your warriors if you don't want them around. But they don't need sleep or food or anything, so it'll be easiest to use them as sentries while we're doing the boring stuff, like sleeping."

Nassata considered his suggestion. She didn't look entirely satisfied with the idea, having the correct impression that an animation couldn't replace a real person.

"I can also create something that can go for help if anything happens again," Toman put in as an afterthought.

"Very well," Nassata finally agreed. "Well, keep calling your soldiers. I want to go back into the spring to investigate as soon as we can, but I want to alert the council, more of the warriors, and my sentries first."

"Fair enough," Toman replied. He wasn't keen to go out into the rest of the city wearing just his boxers and gloves anyways. Esset looked slightly relieved too, standing there in his underwear.

"Hurry back," Esset suggested with a wry smile.

CHAPTER 15

Within half an hour they were carefully making their way back to the hot spring chamber. Typical of the Reshkin, the carcasses of their kin—and one of Esset's socks—had been dragged away, leaving only blood behind. The missing sock wasn't their first concern, however.

"Look at this," Esset said, kicking a rock on the ground beside the rough little tunnel that the Reshkin had burrowed to get into the chamber. "I'm guessing there's a second one out in the tunnel wall somewhere, given that they were coming from outside too."

"I don't doubt it," Nassata agreed, and she motioned for two warriors to look.

Esset glanced over as Toman picked his coat up off the floor, clearly unhappy. There was a giant rip in the back and it was covered in... He didn't want to know what it was covered in. Toman held the offending garment away from himself with one hand.

"May I borrow your spear?" he asked Tseka, who was standing beside him. Esset was pretty sure she was laughing inside, given the smirk she had on her face when she saw the state of his clothes.

"Sure," she said, passing it over to Toman, clearly curious. Toman took it for a moment and then let go; the metal staff collapsed to the ground, curling about into a pile like a snake, the spearhead its head. No sooner had it landed then it slithered over to the water and vanished beneath the surface.

"I figure it's smart to make sure none of them are hiding in there, especially since I'd like to wash my coat," Toman remarked by way of explanation.

"I'd better be getting my spear back," was Tseka's only reply, despite her obvious fascination with her spear's behavior. She was clearly impressed.

Toman didn't respond to Tseka, but in a minute the spear slithered out of the water again. It stretched out straight on the ground, and Toman picked it up and passed it back to her.

"Thank you," was all he said. The spear was once again a stiff, sturdy metal spear, with no signs of snake-like behavior. Tseka tapped it on the ground a few times to make sure.

Esset walked over to the hole in the wall, eyeing it speculatively.

"I want to see what's down there," he decided aloud. He waved Nassata over. "I'm going to sit down and go into a trance. I can look through my summon's senses that way. I won't be aware of anything around here though, so if something happens, I'll be counting on you to protect me. Give me a good shake to bring me back."

Nassata nodded her understanding and he sat down cross-legged on the ground. One incantation later, a fiery wolf was fleeing from the steamy air by way of the Reshkin's tunnel. Esset adjusted to the summon's senses on the fly, but something remained disorienting until he realized that the smell combination that he was picking up from the tunnel was unlike anything he'd encountered before. The unusual element belonged to the scent left behind by the Reshkin. He made a mental note to mention the odd qualities to Toman and Nassata when he "got back"—there was something like magic included in what he was sensing, so Nassata's theory that there was someone or something bigger behind the Reshkin was becoming less of a theory and more a certainty.

The wolf summon really didn't like the close quarters of the little tunnel, but at least it wasn't being injured by the ambient steam anymore. It was restless. There was nothing to fight but the rocks that surrounded it, so it snapped at them as it passed. It seemed like an eternity had passed before the tunnel finally narrowed to a place where the wolf could no longer continue, but Esset knew that perception was an illusion. The fire creatures that he summoned were extremely impatient, and his link with the wolf altered his own ability to measure time. He guessed it had actually only been a minute, maybe a minute and a half at most. Time resumed its usual pace when the Reshkin's scent suddenly grew strong enough to indicate immediate proximity.

Close quarters made fighting difficult, but that didn't stop the wolf. Being unable to maneuver hindered the Reshkin far more than the summon, since the Reshkin liked to gang up on foes to defeat them. The fiery wolf slashed and bit with his fangs and short claws, making quick work of the individual blocking his way. It was a hassle getting around the carcass to try to get at the next one, but at least Esset didn't have to worry about bringing the wolf back; it didn't matter where a summon was, he could banish it just the same. Which was just as well, since there would be no convincing the summon to turn around and go back down the tunnel.

The wolf had destroyed two more Reshkin when it was suddenly confronted with something different. Esset could tell it was still a Reshkin, but it looked rather different. It had an extra set of mandibles, far larger than its venomous set. Its foremost set of legs were also thicker, tougher, and sharper. It was also bigger— it only barely fit into the tunnel. The wolf attacked and killed the creature, but the carcass then blocked the tunnel completely. Esset could have let the wolf immolate the carcass by attacking and burning it until nothing was left, but he had information to take back, so instead he just banished the wolf and returned to himself.

"We have a new kind of Reshkin," he said as soon as he came to. He took a few deep breaths to get used to his own body again and stretched before standing. "Bigger, but designed for digging, not fighting. Also, there's something weird about the scent and traces the Reshkin leave behind. There's definitely magic in it. It's tough to tell what exactly, but it's looking more and more like this is all engineered."

Toman and Nassata looked at Esset grimly.

"This just keeps getting better and better," Toman responded. "Well, I better block this hole then." He was holding Esset's clothes. He passed them to his brother. They were dripping wet after Toman washed them in the hot spring, and a bit worn from the fighting, but they beat being the next thing to naked. Esset took the clothes with a quiet "thanks" and started getting dressed. Ironically, the way the wet cloth clung to his body made him look even scrawnier. Toman knelt next to the hole and started animating. Soon there was a porky behind with a curly little tail sticking out the opening.

"If anything tries to break through again, this little pig will find the nearest Nadra to sound the alarm," Toman said, leaving the animation there.

"Hopefully that should do it, then," Nassata said. "You should both go get some rest."

"I won't argue," Esset admitted.

Nassata's concerned gaze flicked between the two of them for a moment. She opened her mouth to speak, but a couple moments passed before words emerged. "Why don't the both of you take tomorrow to rest? Sleep long. Recover."

They both shook their heads immediately. "No, this is too important," Esset said. "*Especially* now that things are escalating."

"We'll be back at it first thing tomorrow," Toman confirmed.

Nassata nodded, looking relieved. "Thank you." Then Nassata placed her hands on their backs and gave them a light push towards their rooms. "Now go. Sleep. We don't wish to lose you to weariness, not when it can be avoided."

Toman and Esset did as they were bade and returned to their room, where Toman's stone sentries already waited. Since they both had a great deal of practice ignoring Toman's creations, they both simply stripped off their wet clothes and collapsed into their beds.

"Good morning!" Kessa woke them with a cheery call—just as she had the previous morning.

This morning, however, she carried a tray laden with two large breakfasts. In particular, two large breakfasts of non-Nadran fare. Esset came awake with surprising alacrity at the smell of eggs and ham. There was that and toast too, all in very generous portions.

"Your human food finally came," Kessa announced with a smile.

"Oh thank Hyrishal!" Esset exclaimed when he registered what he smelled. Within a minute both Toman and Esset were wolfing down the glorious food. Getting out of bed and getting dressed had taken a poor second place to consuming as much as they could as quickly as possible. Kessa was giggling at their reactions.

"Did you try some?" Esset asked around a mouthful of eggs,

waving a piece of toast at her.

"Yes," she replied, pulling a face. "It tasted very strange. Not all bad, but very, very strange."

Toman chuckled. "Well, at least you have a starting place for understanding what your food tastes like to us," he said. Still chewing, he got up and pulled on his clothes—a different set from yesterday, since those would need repair now. Between snatched mouthfuls, both he and the summoner got ready to depart, leaving only crumbs and messy beds in their wakes. They were heading for the door when Kessa suddenly ambushed Toman with a hug. After letting the surprised young man go, she hugged Esset too.

"Be careful," she said. The previous day had really driven home for her how dangerous it was, fighting the Reshkin. She had been frightened before, but not like now.

"We will," Toman promised. "We'll keep ourselves safe, and you and your people, too. Don't you worry." He reached out and gave her arm a quick squeeze with his gloved hand, knowing the tactile reassurance would mean more to her than words. Kessa just smiled and brushed his arm with her fingers as he headed out the door.

Toman had a hard time keeping his promise. Their group returned to the city after far too much struggle and bloodshed.

Nassata slammed her fist against the wall. Esset had never seen her so agitated.

"*Three*," she hissed. "And that's atop the two we lost earlier. Two of these Nadra weren't even warriors."

"At least we've evacuated the rest of the outlying areas. We won't lose any more noncombatants," Esset said, trying to offer what scant comfort he could.

"There's no way we could have prepared for today," Toman added. "The way they attacked, swarming the sentries... It's like you said, someone's behind the Reshkin, and whoever it is isn't about to sit back and let us get the upper hand."

"Those attacks today..." Esset said. "At least Toman had some soldiers ready-made. We'd planned to deploy them as a single force and take the Reshkin by storm, but even in losing that edge of surprise for later, we saved lives today."

"Why are they doing this?" Nassata asked, her vibrant teal

eyes filled with such sorrow that Esset felt his own heart wrench in response. The Nadran losses struck Toman and Esset hard, but it wasn't personal for them, not the way it was for Nassata and the other Nadra, who'd known the victims.

"*Who* is doing this?" Nassata's voice suddenly raised in pitch, and her coils twitched. "We are a peaceful people. We have wronged no one! Why attack *us*? Why kill us? Torture us? Drive us from our homes?"

Neither Toman nor Esset had an answer, and they averted their eyes as Nassata calmed herself. They were both ready to drop from fatigue.

"The tunnels are all sealed off. No Reshkin can get into the city without tunneling, and we're watching for that now. The city is safe." Esset's weariness was plain in his voice.

Nassata could only stare at him for several long moments. Then she seemed to shake herself. "Yes. Safe." She repeated the words as if the sentiment alone could make them true. In truth, no one really felt safe anymore.

"Go and rest," Toman suggested. "You're as tired as we are."

"Yes…" Nassata said after another long moment. "Thank you." Without waiting for a response, she slithered away.

Toman and Esset turned slowly and trudged the short distance left to their quarters in silence. A subdued Kessa met them at the curtain door with a large tray of food. Her coils brushed their legs as they passed, but she didn't even speak a greeting. She had already gotten news of the day's events.

Toman reached his bed first and collapsed onto it immediately, but as soon as Kessa set the tray down, she went over and sat him back up.

"No, you must eat first," she insisted. She picked up a plate and set it on his lap. She sent a stern look over at Esset, too. Too tired to argue, he picked up his own plate voluntarily. Kessa kept a close eye on them, making sure they didn't fall asleep sitting up.

"If you don't keep eating, I will spoon feed you," she threatened at one point. The meals were small, but both were so tired that neither would have remained awake to finish them without the small Nadra there, keeping watch.

"Okay, sleep," Kessa finally said when their plates were empty. She scooped the dishes up and left; Toman and Esset were both asleep before she passed through the curtain.

Esset could read his brother like an open book, and he could tell the night had passed far too swiftly for Toman's liking. But Toman wouldn't complain.

"We're to be your guards today," one of the two other Nadra told them when they arrived with Kessa.

"Good. I can work faster if I can concentrate," Toman said. "Let's go. The more time I have to work, the more soldiers I can make." He didn't wait for a response; his escort followed him out, everyone's expression equally grim.

"Am I needed for anything today?" Esset asked Kessa. She shook her head.

"Nassata asked that you stay in the city. It's central if you're needed anywhere in a hurry, but there are no excursions today," she said.

"Huh." Esset just sat there for a moment as the prospect of some free time sank in. Then he leaned over the side of the bed and rummaged through his bag.

"What are you doing?" Kessa asked, peering over Esset's shoulder.

"Our clothes got pretty beat up the other day. I'm going to fix them."

Kessa looked at the torn clothes lying on the bed and went over to them. She picked up his shirt and turned it around, inspecting the giant rip.

"How?" she asked. Esset blinked for a moment, remembering that the Nadra didn't wear clothes. How *would* they know anything about cloth if they never had anything to do with it?

"I'm going to sew them," he replied, withdrawing his little sewing kit from his bag and holding it up for her to see.

"Sew?"

"Here, just watch me do it," Esset suggested. He went over to the bed and sat down. He took out the needle and thread from the kit, prepared it, and beckoned for her to hand him the shirt. She did so, watching with keen interest, and he began sewing a neat line down the tear, mending it almost invisibly.

Esset had a lot of practice mending things. Toman could sew as well, but he wasn't as good at it. Esset had always been better with things that required details, and he found he had a knack for sewing—even if it had caused him to be the butt of a few jokes over the years.

The first tear he mended was small, since he just wanted to demonstrate to Kessa how it worked. He passed it to her when he was done, and she examined it with interest.

"I wondered how this stuff worked," she said when she passed the shirt back.

"The Nadra seem to be very isolated here in the underground city," Esset remarked, taking back the shirt and starting on the next rip.

"Yes… I asked, once, why we rarely see other peoples here. I was told it is the only way to keep peace and to keep the energies in balance here," Kessa replied.

"Hm… I suppose that makes sense. I don't necessarily agree with that, but I don't share your beliefs, either, so I guess that's to be expected," the summoner replied thoughtfully.

"I guess," Kessa replied, eyeing him askance.

"So tell me about Toman and yourself," the blue Nadra suggested, changing the subject. "You are brothers but not, and you are fighters who do not abhor peace. You are strange."

"It's funny that you bring up those two things together, because they kind of go hand-in-hand," he began. "I met Toman when I was eleven years old—he was ten at the time. He'd been hanging around outside the city, a little boy wearing an oversized, floppy-brimmed hat." Both Kessa and Esset smiled at the mental picture—it was rare to see the animator without that hat on even in the present. Kessa settled on her coils on the floor, actually hugging the end of her tail to her chest.

"Anyways, he was all by himself, so the city guards were concerned about him wandering around outside the city, but he would run away when they tried to get close. I was a bit of a loner back then, so they tracked me down and sent me out to find him. Long story short, I found him, and we became fast friends. He was all alone—no friends, no family, just the creations of the past animator to make sure he had food, shelter, and clothes."

"I've seen his stone creatures. They look like people, but they're not really," Kessa said with a scowl.

"Exactly," Esset agreed. "Once Toman got past his fear of

others, he was pretty starved for human contact. Eventually, my family just kind of adopted him. He and I spent virtually every waking moment together. We played together every day, and we went to school together. I had extra studies and he practiced animating, so there were—are—times when we follow our own pursuits, but you'd be hard pressed to find blood brothers closer than we are. From the day we met on, we learned to love peace."

Kessa nodded there, prompting Esset to continue.

His face grew thoughtful and a little distant. "But peace... It's a funny thing. Those raised with peace are spoiled, and they want adventure. At least, that was how it was with me. My father is a summoner, and I knew that one day I'd be a summoner too. I love to read, and I read far too many old stories about heroes and whatnot. As I grew older, I got a little wiser, and while that longing for adventure never really went away, it was tempered with logic and reason."

"What kind of stories?" Kessa tilted her head to the side.

"Oh. Right, I suppose we would have different old stories, wouldn't we? Remind me and I'll tell you some later."

Kessa nodded eagerly.

Esset continued. "Well, regardless of stories, with the power that I ended up being able to wield, I felt that I had a responsibility to use it to help people. Even though there was peace where I grew up, I knew there was a great deal of suffering elsewhere. Being best friend and brother to Toman especially drove that point home. All that and Toman himself are the reasons why I live this life now." Esset paused there, although his hands kept moving methodically, the needle dipping above and below the fabric in a pattern that Kessa watched with hypnotized fascination.

"But that's only half the story. There's Toman's half too," Esset eventually said. He tied off the thread, having finished mending the tear. Once he was done, he looked at Kessa appraisingly. At first she looked back curiously, but then she looked away and started to squirm slightly under his scrutiny.

"I'm never sure if I should talk about Toman's history to anyone. He certainly doesn't like talking about it, but he doesn't seem to mind people knowing." He finally looked away from her and started sewing the next tear. "Before meeting me, Toman's life was...well, pretty horrible. He was born Toman Iiren. His parents were weavers—good ones, from what I heard. They lived in a pretty small village in the mountains and did fairly well for themselves. Then, when Toman was seven, a mage named Moloch came. Who knows why he chose that particular village, but he did. Moloch is what we call a blood-path mage—he gets the bulk of his magical power from pain, suffering, the spilling of blood, and death. He went to Toman's village and destroyed everything. Almost every single person died that day, including Toman's parents."

Kessa was staring at Esset, eyes wide and watery with sympathy.

Esset wasn't looking at her anymore, however. He appeared intent upon his sewing; the shirt was almost mended. "There was an animator before Toman," he continued. "His name was Eldan Atrix. He had been fighting Moloch for a long time, and he arrived in the blood mage's wake. He helped the few survivors of the attack and ended up taking in Toman. That's why Toman's last name is now Atrix-Iiren. He was a father to Toman for three years.

"Then...well, Moloch is very powerful, and he's clever, and he's vicious. One day he caught up with Animator Eldan. Animator Eldan managed to make it back to a safe place and returned to Toman, but he died of his wounds. Toman inherited the gloves and the ability to animate with them. He fled...and after that, I met him. I think after losing a mother and two fathers, he couldn't stand the thought of having parents to lose again. My family adopted him in spirit, but never in name. That's why, even now, he's not technically my brother, not even by adoption. But...that's never mattered. Spirit is what matters.

"I can only imagine how he could have turned out if we'd never met. I know I would be different. In fact, I would probably be dead. But Toman... I think he would definitely be dead. Together, we might stand a chance of hunting Moloch down and defeating him. Separately...I don't think we'd stand a chance, not either of us."

Kessa had been listening, a bit horrified, a bit sad, and a bit some other garbled mix of emotions. With the last bit, however, she was truly horrified. "But revenge is wrong! You can't seek revenge!" she objected.

"But that's the thing... Toman isn't hunting Moloch for

revenge," Esset explained. "Or at least, that's not his main reason, or a major reason. We're hunting him because so far, no one has been able to stop him. All the things he does... He needs to be stopped, so Toman and I have to try. Ever since we left home, we've been fighting, doing what we can to make this world safer and better. And...we've been fighting to become stronger. We found Sergeant Warthog, the woman Nassata went to in order to find help, so that she could help us find Moloch. As soon as we can, we'll stop him. It has to be done, or else many, many more people will suffer and then die. You can't imagine the amount of pain and suffering that Moloch can inflict upon people. If we can stop him, then we have to. We can't just let him keep on doing what he's doing."

By the end of his dialogue, Esset had locked eyes with Kessa, and she found herself intimidated by the intensity of his gaze. She shrank back, and gave a tiny nod.

Suddenly Esset's intensity vanished, and he smiled wryly. "Sorry," he apologized.

Kessa unwound a bit, straightening her posture.

"Well, at least now you know why we are like we are."

"I... I think I understand it a little bit. Your beliefs are very different from ours," Kessa said timidly.

"Sort of," Esset countered. "In many ways, they're similar. We both strive for peace, and hold many of the same values, just to different degrees."

"I guess," Kessa agreed, not engaging in the debate.

"Why don't you tell me some of your old stories?" Kessa suggested then.

"Hm. Well, many of them are lengthy. They're all written down, you see. Or they're written as poetry. So I can't tell you the full stories, but I can tell you *about* them, if you want," Esset suggested. Kessa still nodded eagerly.

"Well, a lot of the stories are pretty fanciful. Lots of knights and princes fighting dragons and rescuing princesses," Esset explained.

"Prince and princess... Those are the children of rulers, yes?"

"Yes." Now that Esset thought about it, he was a little surprised Kessa knew even that much. Maybe they did have a couple of human old tales. Or maybe they were educated in human government.

"Most of the tales feature people of high social status— princes and princesses, knights and noblemen, people like that. A few are about adventurers or poor folk, but they're outnumbered." Esset seemed to be musing aloud, so Kessa poked him with one finger.

"Yes, but can you tell me one?" she asked. Esset laughed.

"Sure. Uh… how about the tale of Sir Terrus?" he asked. "It was always one of my favorites." Kessa shrugged and nodded at the same time, eliciting another chuckle from Esset. Then he closed his eyes and tried to remember exactly how it went.

"Long ago and far away, there lived a knight named Sir Terrus. He had fought many battles for his king, against both monsters and men, and he was esteemed across the country. His armor shone brightly in the sun, he wore a great, two-handed sword across his back, and he rode a stallion as white as snow."

"What's a stallion?" Kessa asked.

"A male, ungelded horse," Esset replied.

"What's 'ungelded?'" Kessa asked.

"Uh…it's not important. It was a white horse. Very impressive." Esset figured that could turn into a complicated, awkward conversation quickly, given that the Nadra didn't keep livestock.

"Okay."

Esset breathed a sigh of relief and continued. "Well, one day, they got news that the princess of the neighboring kingdom had been kidnapped by an evil mage, a practitioner of dark magic. Sir Terrus couldn't stand the thought of the princess being this mage's prisoner, and the kingdom was an ally, so he immediately volunteered to rescue the princess. Everyone begged him not to go, because the mage was so powerful and Sir Terrus was much beloved, but he would not be dissuaded. Finally the king granted him leave, and Sir Terrus set out to go." Esset paused to pin down the details of the next part in his head before continuing.

Kessa had a slightly perplexed expression on her face, but she didn't say anything.

"As he was about to exit the gates of the city, however, the king's mage stopped him. The old man came up to him and pressed two objects into his hands: a key enchanted to open any lock and a piece of chalk.

'Please, take these things, and keep them with you,' the mage begged him.

'Thank you for this key,' Sir Terrus said, recognizing the item. 'But why do I need this piece of chalk?'

"It's a key of a different kind," the mage said, but Sir Terrus didn't understand.

'Just keep it with you,' the mage begged.

'Very well,' Sir Terrus agreed."

Esset paused to take a breath and Kessa interrupted. "How is a piece of chalk a key?" she asked.

"Hush, and listen to the story," Esset said, and she quieted, waiting for him to continue.

"So Sir Terrus rode forth. Now, his is a pretty long story. The mage sends lots of monsters for him to fight along the way, but he beats them all and arrives at the evil mage's tower at the top of a tall, jagged mountain."

Esset missed Kessa's slightly amused expression as he skipped past that part of the story.

"Just as Sir Terrus arrived, he heard a terrifying roar echo between the mountains. His stallion pranced in place, raring for a fight, but there was no foe to be seen. So Sir Terrus tied his horse outside and approached the door to the tower on foot.

"'Mage, I challenge you!' Sir Terrus yelled at the tower, but no response came, so the knight tried opening the door. Now, obviously, the door was locked, but the enchanted key that the king's mage had given Sir Terrus opened the door easily, and he went inside.

"Twice more, Sir Terrus used the enchanted key to ascend through the tower until he reached the very top. The top level was one large room beneath the conical ceiling, and that was where the princess was being held. She was kept in a large cage with iron bars. Sir Terrus hurried across the room to free her, but in doing so, he crossed a series of lines on the floor.

"Sir Terrus tried to reach the princess, but he hit an invisible barrier before he could reach her. That was when he realized he'd entered a mage trap. Drawn on the floor were a series of complex lines in a full circle around Sir Terrus. Arcane symbols illuminated whenever he tried to cross the lines. First Sir Terrus tried each direction, then he attacked the barrier with his sword, but to no avail.

"Now Sir Terrus pulled out the piece of chalk. This was what the mage had meant about a 'key of a different kind.' These lines were magic, drawn to hold him in. Thanks to the king's mage, Sir Terrus had the means to change those lines. But how?"

Esset paused there for dramatic effect, so caught up in his story that he still didn't notice that Kessa wasn't as enthralled as he was.

"Now, being a knight also means being a servant of Bright Hyrishal, so Sir Terrus drew on the greatest power he knew. Kneeling next to the lines, he drew the sun of Bright Hyrishal. The fires of Bright Hyrishal warm and nurture all of creation, but those same fires can also burn away sin and scorch evildoers. They can also fight dark magic in the hands of the faithful, as Sir Terrus found. The sun he drew sent a flash of fire outwards and burned the dark sigils from the ground, freeing Sir Terrus.

"Sir Terrus immediately rushed over to the princess's cage, but before he could reach it, half the roof was torn away, revealing the sky and a terrible monster!"

This time Esset saw Kessa's amused expression at his melodramatic telling, and he faltered for a moment, giving her a perplexed look. Only when she coaxed him with a "go on," did he continue. She schooled her expression a little after that.

"The evil mage had transformed himself into a dragon." Esset's delivery had fallen flat. "A great battle ensued, but Sir Terrus prevailed and killed the evil mage. He rescued the princess and they lived happily ever after." He was red-faced by the end of his telling.

"You don't tell stories often, do you?" Kessa asked, and Esset could still see the amusement in her eyes.

"I usually just read them," Esset confessed. "And never with an audience."

"Well it was an…interesting tale. Very different from ours," Kessa replied.

"What are yours like?" Esset asked. "I haven't had a chance to see any Nadran literature."

"Ours are… Well, they are tales of finding or creating peace from strife, mostly, like Shaper Vorriss who led us to Salithsa, or about teaching life lessons, like the turtle who taught the bat patience. I don't think I know any well enough to tell, but there are rarely battles in them." Kessa didn't wait for Esset to respond.

"You said there are lots of stories you've read. What are some of the others like?" Kessa asked. Esset noticed she wasn't asking him to tell the stories themselves, just about them.

"Well, there are a series of stories about the seven knights of Agrimon. They fought monsters and rescued princesses too. They're all about deeds of heroism and knightly virtues. Each of the seven stands for a virtue: courage, justice, mercy, generosity, faith, nobility, and hope."

Esset was so busy thinking of other stories that he missed Kessa's unconvinced expression.

"There are the stories of Prince Noren, who led his country in the war against the Lokrush onslaught. There are the tales of Marix the Thief and the adventures of Kuun Fletcher. There are a bunch more, but I can't remember them all off the top of my head.

"And of course, those don't include any of the stories or parables in the Book of Bright Hyrishal. Those center around moral lessons, of course, teaching of justice, love, and sacrifice. Of course, Bright Hyrishal so loved this world that he created that he came down to earth to experience it in the flesh. In his fight against the Darkfires, he ended up sacrificing himself to save the world he loved."

Esset finally noticed Kessa's expression.

"What?" he asked, perplexed in return.

"Very strange. Very strange indeed," was all she said. No matter how Esset pestered her, she wouldn't elaborate.

The next day, Kessa woke them with breakfast as usual. They chowed down and started dressing, as usual, although Esset's curiosity was getting the better of him—as usual.

"I don't want to look a gift horse in the mouth, but I have to admit, I'm curious where you got all this food from," Esset confessed, waving the last bite of his toast at his plate before stuffing it in his mouth.

"There is a small town not too far away," Kessa replied. "We deal with the people occasionally. Not often, but often enough that they do not fear us overmuch and we can trade for some items when needed."

"Convenient," Toman remarked. He stuffed his hat on his head. "Okay then, I'm off. See you two later." He didn't waste any time vanishing out the door. Kessa and Esset watched him go, then picked up their plates from the beds.

"Well, let's drop these off at the kitchen, and then I'd like to go talk to Nassata," Esset said, heading for the door himself.

"What about?" Kessa was curious to know.

"Well, I want to run an idea past her. I think I might be able to perform a little espionage on the Reshkin using one of my summons. I don't use this particular one often, since it's not useful in many situations. Now, however, I think it would be good to get some good intelligence on where the Reshkin are gathered and whether they have any new surprises planned. They were too quiet yesterday."

Esset and Kessa actually found Nassata in the kitchen as they were dropping the dishes off—she was just finishing breakfast herself, as Toman had gotten an earlier start than most of the city. Esset managed to convince her to put together a squad so he could attempt to get some good intelligence on the Reshkin.

"Okay, let's see if I can do this," Esset said. He had his ear pressed up against the coiled snake that was blocking the tunnel. They had agreed that they shouldn't open the tunnel—they didn't want to chance a Reshkin invasion. He took a deep breath, then murmured a small incantation. The Nadra didn't see anything happen, but a moment later Esset whispered a triumphant little "yes!" Unlike the other creatures that Esset called upon, this summon's heat signature was so small they were only able to find it after looking for it.

"Okay, I managed to summon a bat on the other side of the wall. I'm afraid this is going to be rather boring for you—I'm going to go into a trance and do some scouting through its eyes," Esset was already sitting down and crossing his legs beneath himself. "If anything happens, give me a shake—I'm not going to react to anything else."

"Okay," Nassata agreed.

Moments later, Esset was perceiving the world through a very disorienting set of senses. The summoned bat was instantly careening around the top of the tunnel. It's tiny, thin, ashy wings fluttered madly, narrowly keeping its tiny, ashen body from colliding with the walls. Looking through its eyes were almost useless—it could dimly perceive things with its vision, but that was at its best. No, its main sense was hearing, but it was an experience like no other, and it had been a long time since Esset had scouted with a bat summon. It took Esset a good ten minutes before he got a good enough handle on the bat's echolocation that he felt that proceeding would be useful.

The little bat fluttered down the tunnel, well out of range of any of the Reshkin on the floor or walls. That was just as well, since Esset knew from experience that any hostile contact at all would cause the bat to vanish from this plane immediately. The little bats couldn't take any kind of hit, which was one reason why he so seldom used them. Esset directed the little creature along with almost no mental effort. Unlike the ferocious wolf or the utterly vicious panther, the little bat had no ulterior motives. As long as it didn't have to be still, it was perfectly happy to follow his directions. If left to its own devices, it would simply flutter around aimlessly.

It was grim, getting a sense of the number of Reshkin in the tunnels. Some were loosely scattered, but most of the time they gathered in large swarms. Esset actually wasn't sure what to look for—these weren't soldiers, with sophisticated organization and bases. They were... Well, they were bugs, for all the coordinated behavior they'd shown during attacks. And from what he was seeing, when they were fighting, they acted like bugs.

The bat flitted about unnoticed. The tunnel suddenly opened up into a large cavern, and it took Esset a moment or two to realize what he was seeing; at first he was just confused by the texture of the floor. Normally the Nadra traveled on flat stone, polished by the constant wear of their own scales upon it, but this part of the cave was strangely bumpy. Then he realized what was causing the discrepancy—the ground was completely covered in eggs. The revelation was such that he lost control of the bat for a few moments. Thankfully it didn't give itself away, although it did flutter down a side tunnel right away. It took Esset a few moments to steer it back to the cavern so he could investigate further.

He didn't want to risk discovery, but this was something that he wanted more information about, so the summoner had the bat swoop down closer to the eggs to get more information. They appeared to be sticky and soft-shelled. He had no idea what color they were, but that was incidental. What bothered him was how many there were—it was a massive cavern, and the floor was completely covered, without a single square inch of the floor visible anywhere. If the Reshkin wanted to go through the cavern, they navigated along the walls instead of crossing the floor. Occasionally one of the Reshkin would go up to the eggs for a moment or two to check on them, but they looked entirely too healthy to Esset. He wondered how flammable they were.

He took him a minute or two to decide to continue his surveillance instead of seeing if he could sabotage the eggs. It was just as well, since an hour later he'd found five more identical caverns and seen far, far too many Reshkin. He'd tried to memorize a map for tactical use later, but the Nadran tunnels were far more convoluted than he could confidently organize in his head. He returned to himself with a gusty exhale and a few deep breaths to readjust to his own body.

"No good news, I'm afraid," he reported, opening his eyes and putting his hand on the wall to help himself up. He briefly described what he'd discovered, but he couldn't see the reactions of the Nadra due to the darkness.

"Unfortunately I don't know anything about the life cycle of a Reshkin, so I can't tell you how close they are to hatching, or how long it will take them to mature when they do," Esset finished. "Do they have a larval stage, or...?"

When he heard Nassata reply, her voice sounded concerned. "I...think you saw it," Nassata said. "Their eggs are actually relatively small, and they always hide them. In their larval stage, they excrete a sticky substance and curl in on themselves, usually in groups..."

"That does sound like what I saw," Esset confessed.

"Too bad you couldn't tell color—the larvae are white and light grey, and the eggs camouflage with stone. It would have been easy to tell," another of the warriors said.

"I think his description was definitive enough," Nassata

disagreed.

"So how long does this larval stage last then?" Esset asked.

"About two days, with the old Reshkin we knew," Nassata replied.

"Well, larger organisms tend to have longer life cycles," Esset put in.

"Yes, but we don't know how long they've been there. They could hatch today, for all we know," Nassata pointed out.

"I know," Esset conceded. "And we don't know whether there are even more caverns like that. There are probably more. A lot more. Reshkin in those numbers... I couldn't hold them back, nor Toman."

Nassata stared at Esset.

"We'd have to abandon Salithsa," she finally said.

"Or face extinction." Esset rubbed the back of his neck. "Well, I can't get to all of them, but want me to see if I can send a summon to do what damage I can to the first cavern?"

"From what you've told me, your summons will be swarmed before they can get close enough to do damage to the larvae," Nassata said.

"True. There probably isn't anything I can do with one of the bats, which is probably the only summon that could get there unnoticed. I can't summon a bird underground, and both the wolves and panthers, while being fierce fighters, probably would be too outnumbered to get far enough. I wasn't thinking of a combatant summon, however. I can summon horses, and they are very, very fast. They love to run, so if I sent one streaking down the tunnel, it might just make it to one of the caverns, and then trampling should work well enough." There was a pause before Nassata replied.

"That might work," she acceded.

"Worth a try, anyways," Esset put in. At least he could find out if the eggs were particularly flammable. He sat back down with his back pressed up against the animated snake.

One incantation later, a fiery horse appeared on the other side of the barrier and immediately leapt into motion. Esset synced his senses with it on the fly. The fiery beast didn't pause or slow but hurtled down the tunnel, leaving sooty hoof-prints on the stone floor. Reshkin scattered at first, then tried to coordinate a defense, which the horse either dodged or leapt over or bowled straight through, depending on the tactic the enemy used.

Sometimes all it took for someone to accomplish something was the absolute belief that success was the only possible outcome, and Esset always got the impression that his summons had that. The wolves and panthers believed that they were invincible warriors, the birds that they were the fastest and best hunters and fliers, and the horses that they were faster than the wind itself and completely unstoppable. It was easy to believe along with them, as Esset did with the horse as it blazed down the tunnel; the Reshkin were no more consequential than ants around its feet.

But sometimes belief was not strong enough to defeat reality.

Esset knew the cavern was close, but when he saw what lay ahead, he suddenly knew the horse wasn't going to make it. The Reshkin had swarmed and amassed in the tunnel ahead—there was no going around or leaping over. The horse tried to plow right through, but the Reshkin slashed at it and clung to its legs. They pulled the summon down before it could get halfway through. Esset banished the horse before they could climb all over it and force it out of existence. The summoner snapped back to himself with a sharp intake of breath.

"Sorry," he said immediately. "It couldn't get there. It was close, but... not close enough." And a second attempt would only see them better prepared.

"You did what you could," Nassata reassured him. "At least we have a better idea of what we're up against."

"But now they know we know," Esset said. He kicked himself mentally—he should have left well enough alone. Half the advantage from intelligence came from your enemy not knowing you had it, and he'd blown that.

"I think it makes little difference," Nassata said, dismissing his unspoken feeling. "Come, we've done enough here."

"I guess," Esset said with a gusty sigh, not feeling much better. He got to his feet again, using the wall to steady himself. It was all up to Toman and his stone army now. They had two days at most before the larvae hatched. Two days until the evacuation of Salithsa—or the extinction of the Nadra.

CHAPTER 16

By noon the next day, Toman had finished creating an army of approximately two hundred and fifty soldiers. An hour later, they were standing by to attack. Toman and Esset were part of a squad with Nassata, Tseka, four other Nadra, and a large beast-of-burden-like animation with a massive Nadran lantern on its back—the more they could see, the better they could attack, and the lantern flooded the tunnel with light.

A variety of animations stood with them. Most were two-legged soldiers, but some were Nadra-like. They also had a few animated chains and ropes; the Nadra had come through with all the rope and chain they could find or make, and it had taken only a matter of minutes for Toman to animate the whole lot, since he didn't have to shape anything.

A Nadran messenger slithered up to them and thumped her spear-butt on the ground.

"All points of attack are in position. Unit leaders are ready to give orders to animations if needed, but we await your order to begin, Animator Toman."

"Thank you," Nassata said with a nod.

Toman and Esset's squad waited just before the tunnel seal leading to the larvae's cavern. Esset sat on the floor, his mind far away inside a summoned bat.

"How is it that you can control so much at once?" Nassata asked Toman as they waited for Esset to finish scouting.

"Because I'm not consciously controlling it all at once," Toman replied. "When I animate something, I give it a set of instructions, and the animation will follow those instructions to the best of its ability until it's told to stop or do something else. Animations are most efficient if I can see them and direct them individually, to respond to individual circumstances, but they can still act and fight without direct guidance. Especially if I key them to particular orders, like 'stand,' 'attack,' and 'retreat.' It takes more time to prepare, but it makes them easier to control later."

"That…is a frightening amount of power."

Toman nodded grimly just as Esset opened his eyes.

"The good news is, the larvae are still larvae. The bad news is, a few are starting to wiggle. We can't afford to wait any longer, so it's a good thing we're attacking now," he reported.

"I'll give the order," Toman said, and the tunnel seals opened, and all his animations attacked simultaneously. The stone Nadra led the assault. Esset was impressed with his brother's ingenuity—the Reshkin on the other side were crushed when the Nadra began thrashing their snake-like bodies when they reached their foes. It was a maneuver that wasn't realistic for a real snake-person—any Nadra trying it would end up too bruised and battered for it to be effective, never mind the risk of sustaining a bite from the deadly Reshkin—but for the animations, it was very effective indeed. Behind the wave of stone Nadran warriors came a few rows of humanoid stone soldiers with clubs—they filled in the gaps left by the Nadran animations. Those that they missed were immediately devoured by a pair of Esset's fiery wolves.

Their initial pace was faster than Esset had anticipated, but then the bugs rallied, and the attack party had quite a bit more to do. The statues bore the brunt of the attack, but it wasn't long before Reshkin were slipping by them by skittering along the walls. The Nadra worked with Esset's wolves. Tseka swiped at a Reshkin with her spear, caught it under the carapace, and swung it right into the waiting jaws of one of Esset's fiery wolves. A second wolf leapt right at the wall, a flickering blur as it cracked and melted holes in the carapace of its victim, leaving a scorched and stinking carcass behind. Another warrior, wielding a club, crushed the head of a Reshkin that got within range.

Before long, the ground grew treacherously slick beneath their feet, but fortunately the Nadra were unhindered. Reshkin carcasses were shoved unceremoniously up against one wall as they progressed through the tunnel, some of them still twitching in death.

Esset fought through his creatures, the rational, human part of his mind detached and distant while his animal side, his instinctive being, was in full control. There was nothing beautiful about war, nothing glorious, but Esset—and every other warrior in those tunnels—was consumed by it. There was something horribly marvelous about engaging in battle; the heightened senses, the rush, the exhilaration, the satisfaction of seeing those who would do you pain instead have pain done upon them. The self became a distant third person as the senses were enveloped in the madness.

The Reshkin were like the drops of water in the sea—a single drop was nothing to worry about, but a tidal wave could wipe a coastal town off the map. Even after all the scouting forays and skirmishes, it was shocking to come up against the full force of the Reshkin. To one side, a terrible scream rose from the throat of one of the Nadra—he had been bitten by one of the Reshkin. As Nassata had told them upon their arrival, the Nadran warrior was doomed. Esset felt a cold shock when the scream suddenly cut off—Tseka had slit her comrade's throat to end his suffering. Esset had to force the brutality from his mind—if he became fully conscious of everything going on around himself, he knew he would freeze up. It was a lesson he'd learned long ago—even though he'd pay for it later, he had to block everything out and embrace that terrible joy of battle until there was no fighting left to be done.

The shadows were surprisingly stable for a tunnel illuminated by a giant lantern on the back of a stone beast, but the light still sometimes shifted. Nassata stabbed at a movement in the shadows, but her spear met nothing but air.

Esset flinched, but Nassata didn't pause; she swung her spear around again, thrusting at an advancing Reshkin. The attack failed to pierce its carapace, but it did shove the creature back long enough to facilitate a second, more accurate thrust into its eye.

Another movement in the shadows; Nassata thrust at it, and the shock was even greater when her weapon made contact. How many times had she stabbed at shadows when nothing was there? Every unneeded thrust was made worthwhile when this one destroyed the enemy that could have taken a life unseen.

Toman and Esset mostly had to trust the Nadra to keep them safe. Both of them were dealing huge damage to the enemy as a whole, but individually, they were ill-equipped to defend themselves. Esset's wolves lunged back and forth behind the rows of stone soldiers, decimating most of those that managed to pass their lines, but too often they were too far away to directly defend the summoner or the animator, so the two young men kept themselves within a circle of Nadran guardians. Esset directed the summons where needed and summoned and dismissed extra summons as they were needed.

A slight flicker of movement overhead caught his attention, and Esset looked up just in time to see a Reshkin directly above the silver Nadran warrior next to him. The warrior hadn't seen it yet; the incantation was already finishing in Esset's mind as the Reshkin let go of the ceiling and dropped towards the warrior. Halfway there, a fiery wolf materialized in the air between the warrior and the deadly bug. Molten jaws closed around the Reshkin's head, but the mass of the wolf pulled it earthwards, and it landed atop the Nadra. Scorching paws hit the warrior's shoulders, burning scale and skin before Esset could banish the creature again. The warrior cried out in pain, and Esset stepped forward, catching the warrior's spear as the silver Nadra thrashed before getting a hold on himself.

"I'm so sorry!" Esset was apologizing as he dug bandages out of his side bag with one hand. A scaled hand on his stopped him.

"Thank you. You saved my life. Do not worry about me—concentrate on the battle," the warrior hissed, his voice thick with pain. "I will fight on." He wrapped his fingers around the haft of his spear.

"No," Esset objected. "I know burns, and yours are too bad—they'll get infected in this place, and you'll die. Go back to the city—we need reinforcements anyways. Get them for us?" Silver eyes looked at him for a moment—the warrior knew exactly what Esset was doing...and he was grateful for it. Besides, the summoner's words were true. The Nadra nodded and focused on the tunnel behind them for a moment before slipping through the battle back the way they'd come.

"Esset!" It was Nassata, at the forefront of their mortal group. "Larvae ahead!"

"Good," Esset growled. He knew what was coming now. The stone soldiers bashed aside the Reshkin swarm and created a narrow passage through their ranks. One incantation later, a panther ripped up the pathway and into the cavern.

As it turned out, the larvae were somewhat flammable. All it took was a brief touch from the intense heat of the panther to set them on fire. The fire spread slowly between larvae on its own, but the cat ran through the area, swiftly dealing with any opposition it met. Several Reshkin attacked to defend their young, but they fell to its claws immediately. Then the cat went after the few that tried to interpose themselves between the flames and the unscorched larvae.

The roar of battle drowned out the sickening snaps, flutters, and sizzles of flames burning the soft, sticky coating of the larvae. Esset's mind was so consumed by the task at hand that he didn't feel the sick sensation in his stomach or the burning in his chest; he simply fought and destroyed as the Reshkin roiled in the cavern. They didn't seem to realize that they'd already lost. About half kept attacking, but the other half futilely tried to stamp the fire out by dropping their bellies to the floor. The fire had gained momentum and was yet encouraged by the fiery panther; the Reshkins' attempts to save their young were in vain.

Soon the ceiling of the cavern was completely obscured with smoke, and even below it was smoky. Esset coughed a few times before grabbing his handkerchief from his pocket and tying it around his neck so he could pull it up over his nose and mouth. Toman didn't even have to free a hand—his handkerchief retrieved itself, tied itself around his neck, and provided a screen all on its own. The Nadra ignored the stench and smoke in the area and simply continued fighting grimly.

The group held off their position while the larvae burned out. Only once all the larvae were dead did the Reshkin retreat, granting their party a moment for rest. Although it made everyone restless and uneasy to wait on the battlefield, they needed the breather.

Esset was glad when they started moving again; standing still gave him too much time to think about this massacre as what it was: genocide. In order for this to work, they had to kill every single Reshkin—the bugs had to be forced into extinction. Esset didn't like that, so he had to force from his mind what they were doing so he could just do it. The longer they remained idle, the more his mind tried to make him face the horror of what he was doing; worse, it tried to make him remember every sickening sight, sound, smell, and sensation of this underground nightmare. He couldn't face it now—not if he wanted to continue. But they were moving now, and he could focus on the present again and hold the horror at bay.

The eternal night of the tunnels made it difficult to tell how long they had been fighting, but after forcing their way down innumerable tunnels and destroying two more caverns full of larvae, Toman, Esset, and the warriors were beginning to feel weary. By the time they found and destroyed the contents of that last cavern, Esset was beginning to feel like he was going to be ill. That sick exhilaration that battle brought was beginning to wear thin, and he had to wonder what position the sun was in aboveground. Then he realized that it had to be well past sunset— *how long have we been at this?* he wondered.

Their group had covered more ground than any of the others, since the others couldn't take care of the larvae caverns; even had they gone back for torches or built other fires, only Esset's summons burned hot enough and spread the flames fast enough to destroy a cavern of larvae before the Reshkin could rally.

In fact, Esset's group had passed through territory that other groups had traveled through in their circuitous search for the caverns. But hours upon hours in the underground battle had long since begun to get to him, and once the last cavern was taken care of, Esset wanted nothing more than to call it a day. A glance at his brother told him that he felt the same, despite the poker face that Toman was so good at maintaining.

"Okay, warriors! Formation change, we're going back to the city!" Nassata called to the group. With a feeling of great relief, the statues redistributed themselves around their group and they began the long trudge home.

"We have made good headway today," Nassata said as she came up between the two young men and clapped them on the shoulders. Esset stifled a wince as she hit a forgotten bruise. "Successive days should be easier, but I look forward to this all being over."

"Likewise," Esset replied. Toman just nodded his agreement.

Leaving enemy territory was always dangerous, especially after a successful day—the tendency to let one's guard down was great. The adrenaline was beginning to wear off, and the heightened senses brought by battle instead began to dull. It was far, far too easy to make a mistake, to miss something at a critical moment when heading back to safe territory. It was all too easy to feel that impending safety was safety itself.

That was one reason why Toman's animations were useful—they didn't suffer from distraction or inattention. In fact, as soon as all Nadran warriors had been delivered safely home, they would be going back into the tunnels to hunt Reshkin all night long. Still, the statues couldn't replace real warriors completely—they didn't always know how to react in a given situation, so the warriors needed to stay sharp until they were past the seal in the tunnel and safely within the city.

Once they were past the seal, Esset looked up at Tseka. Even that fierce, vibrant warrior was looking weary, her red scales stained with Reshkin blood.

"Warrior Tseka, haven't your people been working on a cure to Reshkin venom? Why did you kill your comrade this morning?" he asked. That terrible scream, brutally cut short, echoed in his mind.

"There is no cure—we have been unable to devise anything. We even gave some of the venom to the healer in the nearby human village, but she said the chances of finding a cure were slim. Besides, he would have died before reaching the city, even if there had been something waiting. Better to end his suffering early." Tseka sounded angry despite her weariness.

"But—" Esset began.

Tseka suddenly rounded on him, raising her torso up and looming down upon him menacingly, momentarily forcing the group to stop. "Don't argue with me right now, summoner," she warned.

Esset bit his tongue and nodded, and she moved away from him, as far as she could get without breaking formation.

There was no more conversation before they reached the city.

The next two days were spent combing the tunnels for Reshkin. Toman guessed they'd destroyed over half their numbers in the first day, not counting the larvae. Over the course of the second, he estimated the deaths of half of the remainder. By the third, the Reshkin were far less aggressive and more interested in hiding, which meant Esset spent most of his time looking through the eyes of a wolf or a panther to track the creatures down. They were far less thickly distributed, and most of the ones they found were individuals, not groups.

"How much longer do you think it's going to take to get them all?" Esset asked as they slogged their way back through the tunnels towards the city. The real question was one they were all wondering: whether it was *possible* to get them all. All it took was for a few to escape, and within a year they could easily be back up to their old numbers.

"Not less than a week," Toman replied with a shake of his head. He was thinking about the real question, but not responding to it. No one wanted to ask that question out loud—the thought was too bleak, and hunting in the tunnels every day was tough enough as it was.

"We'll just have to look forward to the celebration," Nassata said instead. "Once we reopen the entire underground city, we have a celebration planned, and you will both be invited."

"Well then... We'll just have to finish this all up as quick as we can," Toman said, rubbing his hands together with a wolfish grin, evoking smiles from those looking at him. Esset shook his head at his brother, needing the laugh, however brief.

"I gotta admit, I'm most looking forward to having open sky above me again and seeing the sunshine," Esset confessed.

"Oh come on, everyone knows you spend all your time inside anyways, with your nose stuck in a book," Toman teased. Everyone smirked—Esset had asked on a number of occasions about the Nadran library and when they might be able to visit it, but so far they'd decided to leave it sealed to protect it from the Reshkin.

"I like reading outside too," Esset said, raising his nose in a mock-superior fashion. "I am—look out!" He was the first one to notice the movement above them, but he wasn't fast enough. Part of the ceiling collapsed, and they all raised their arms to protect their heads from debris.

Toman felt something that wasn't a rock hit his shoulder and start to slide down his arm. His belts started unwinding from under his coat to defend him, but the thing snagged on his coat sleeve, and then he felt something cut into his arm underneath. It felt like a couple of knives stabbing into his arm. A second later, his belts were wrapping around the Reshkin, forcing its deadly mandibles away from him.

Toman stood and swayed for a second—the tunnel was chaos around him. Something glowing red narrowly brushed past him, and he felt the heat of its passing at the same time as he felt his blood run cold. Stone soldiers were making quick work of the few Reshkin that had attacked them, as were the warriors. Esset's wolf darted in and out between the fighters, catching those that were being driven back or trying to flee. Toman took in everything as a cold wave washed over him, then became distantly aware that he was falling. He didn't hear Esset yell his name, but he returned to himself when he hit the ground.

Suddenly the immediacy of the situation rushed back to him—every cell in his body screamed at him and it felt like his skin was on fire. His head throbbed, and he didn't know if it was from striking the ground or from the venom poisoning his body. One thing was for sure: the Reskin had bitten him, and now he would suffer the consequences.

"Toman! *Toman!*" Esset had seen his brother start to fall, but he hadn't gotten there in time to catch him. Now he was kneeling beside the animator, screaming his name. The Nadran warriors stood back, knowing he was already as good as dead. The ambushing Reshkin were all vanquished already, but the damage had been done. Esset briefly considered having his summon bite Toman's arm to cauterize the wound, but it wasn't really bleeding, and the poison was already in his system, so there was no point in making his injury worse. They needed an antidote now—they needed to move Toman, get him to help. He turned towards the warriors, only to see Tseka right there beside him with her spear point leveled at Toman.

"Hey!" the summoner yanked the spear aside and imposed himself between the red warrior and his best friend. "What do you think you're doing?" he raged, stepping forward and forcing her to put up her spear or stab him with it—she opted to pull it up.

"Summoner, he's as good as dead already. Don't make him

suffer before the end," Tseka responded levelly, physically moving back but not shifting her position on Toman's condition.

"No! We do not stop fighting for him," Esset raged—his ire was impressive, but in the eyes of the Nadra, futile.

"We have not been able to make a cure, Esset," Nassata said quietly from the side. Her words only gave Esset pause for a scant second.

"What about the human healer you gave the venom to? Anything she makes will be useless to you, but it could save Toman. We're taking him there." His eyes were too bright, and he twitched when he heard Toman groan and writhe in pain behind him.

"Esset, he won't make it that far—" Nassata said, trying to reason with him.

"We do not stop fighting!" Esset roared. There was no arguing with him, but he calmed enough to add, "You owe it to us to try." Nassata looked at him for only a moment longer.

"Tseka, Eska, get the animator, we're making time back to the surface," Nassata ordered them. Tseka shook her head at the foolishness but did as she was ordered.

"I just need help getting him onto horseback," Esset clarified. "I can travel fastest that way." He chanted an incantation and a fire horse materialized next to them. He mounted himself easily enough, but it took the help of two warriors to get Toman up in front of him. They passed the belts up too, using them to strap the animator to his brother so he wouldn't fall off. Esset didn't say another word and didn't waste another second—the moment Toman was secure, he set his summon into motion, leaving Toman's floppy hat on the ground behind him. Nassata picked it up and brushed it off sadly, and by the time she looked up again, they were gone.

The fire horse was a blur, streaking down the passages and leaving only ashy hoof prints and the faint smell of smoke where it passed. They had to pause briefly at the seal and wait for the snake to get out of the way, but there was nothing to stop them after that. They breezed past sentries like they weren't there until they reached the last set at the surface. At that point, Esset banished the horse, dropping the two young men to the ground, still strapped together. The sentries came up to them, looking very concerned as

Esset undid the belts.

"The closest town, which way?" Esset demanded.

The next syllables off his tongue were an incantation. The sentries just pointed and Esset nodded his thanks. A massive, fiery bird of prey had materialized next to him, its massive wings fanning tendrils of flame in the air. Esset climbed onto its back, leaving Toman on the ground this time. The bird sidled over to the stricken man on the ground and delicately took him up in its talons before launching itself into the air. It circled once, high above, then turned in the direction of the town.

CHAPTER 17

The fiery bird cut through the gusty night wind, but that didn't stop Toman's cries from reaching Esset. He couldn't close his ears to his brother's pain. Toman thrashed, unaware of the world around him, but the summon held him fast as Esset gritted his teeth and willed the bird to go faster. He told himself repeatedly that they had to fight—there was no giving up, they'd sworn it. The healer would have a cure, an anti-venom of some sort. They would make it in time. The things he told himself became like a mantra as he repeated them, an attempt to convince himself that he was doing the right thing. Tseka's way was never right; they had to fight for life. Toman wouldn't die. He couldn't die.

The cold night air whipped around him, but the heat emanating from the summoned bird was enough to keep him warm. The crescent moon didn't give off much light, but it was easy enough to see the village anyways. There were a few windows with candles, and the smoke from home fires betrayed it from a distance. Esset had feared that Nassata was right, that it would take too long to reach the town, but Toman's cries reassured him in a sickening fashion that at least he was still alive. Toman was human, not one of the Nadra; they only knew for certain that Reshkin venom was lethal to Nadra. Maybe Toman would live, even without an anti-venom.

Thanks to the bright, fiery wings of Esset's summon, everyone knew he was coming. They didn't know who or what was coming, however, so they hid. To them, it looked like a beast born of the Darkfires was coming to their town; a fiery demon swooped down below rooftop level and then back-winged to land lightly in the middle of the street. It stood upon a man crying out in pain— clearly a tortured victim of the winged beast. Those watching from behind curtains were bewildered when the fiery predator suddenly vanished, and another young man was visible for the first time.

"*Healer!*" he yelled at the cowering village. "Someone fetch a healer!" He knelt next to the body of the man crying out in pain, clearly very concerned.

Esset put his hands on either side of Toman's face and spoke, hoping his brother would be able to hear him through the fire of his agony.

"Toman, we're here, hold on, help is coming." He looked up again.

"*Healer!*" he yelled again before leaning back over his brother. This time, however, he stripped the gloves from Toman's hands. It was a promise he'd made a long time ago, one he had never wanted to make good on. If anything happened to Toman, Esset had promised that he would take the gloves and keep them safe, at least until Toman was able to look after them again. The gloves were too powerful to chance having them stolen when Toman was unable to understand what was going on. Fortunately, all of his animations would continue on as they had, unless a new animator donned the gloves and countermanded past orders. In the meantime, the gloves were safe in Esset's bag until the healer cured him. Esset forced himself to think in those terms—the healer would come, and the healer would help Toman. He would get better, and he'd get his gloves back. That was how things would go.

"*Where is the healer?*" Esset screamed again. Finally there was movement, with the nearest front door opening and a man rushing out. He was a common enough looking fellow with overalls and a scruffy beard.

"We'll have to take him to her," the man said, kneeling down to help. Together they ducked their heads under Toman's arms and carried him towards another house at the villager's directions. The door was already open for them, but they were a few steps inside before anyone greeted them.

"Oliver, right this way, set him on the bed," came a pleasant female voice. Esset looked to the side and his gaze followed the woman as she led them into a bedroom.

"We were helping the Nadra fight the Reshkin—he's been bit. They said you were working on a cure. Can you help?" Esset asked her as he and the villager—Oliver—laid Toman out on the bed.

"I hope so," the woman replied. "I've been working on a cure—one for humans, at least—but I haven't had a chance to test it." She walked quickly to a cabinet and opened it, her hand finding a vial without error before quickly closing the cabinet again. A moment later she had a syringe in her hand and she was drawing a pale liquid into it.

"Oliver, please hold him still," she requested. Esset stepped back out of the way. He was uneasy about the anti-venom being untested, but he was glad that there was an anti-venom at all. Since there was a good chance that Toman would die without any help... Well, it was all too likely that an untested cure couldn't hurt. He kept a close eye on her as she shoved Toman's sleeve up so she could get at the vein on his arm. Or rather, he was keeping a close eye on Toman to gauge his reaction. There was no immediate reaction, but then Toman's breathing began to pick up speed. Then he began screaming and thrashing, and Esset and Oliver had to pin him to the bed so he didn't hurt himself. It was pure torture for Esset to see his brother in so much pain. He couldn't say how long it was before Toman finally stopped fighting them and fell into a fevered sleep.

"Will he be okay?" Esset asked the healer after he and Oliver stepped back.

"I don't know," she replied, her eyes fixed upon her newest patient. "The anti-venom is untested. Tonight will be telling."

Esset was silent, staring at Toman until the healer spoke again.

"And even if he does make it through the night, it will be a long recovery."

"That's fine, I can wait for him," Esset replied. There was a chair beside the bed and he suddenly found it difficult to stand, so he sat down heavily on it. Exhaustion was crashing down on him now that the adrenaline was wearing off.

"You look like you could use rest. I will get a cot—" the healer began.

"No. I'll stay right here," Esset said. The healer pursed her lips but didn't seem inclined to argue.

"Very well. I have another patient I need to attend to—call me if his condition changes," she said. Esset just nodded, and she began to turn to leave the room.

"Healer?" Esset forestalled her. She looked back at him over her shoulder.

"Yes?"

"Thank you. For saving his life."

The healer smiled—Esset was only distantly aware that it was a beautiful smile—and left the room.

Esset came to with his forehead on his arms on the bed beside Toman. The summoner blinked owlishly and studied his brother, but nothing had changed—Toman was still asleep, not completely peaceful, but passably calm. Esset wondered how long he'd been out—he knew he'd kept himself awake at least an hour, keeping an eye on his brother before he'd put his head down beside him for just a moment, giving sleep the opportunity to ambush him.

Now Esset sat back and let the events of the past day wash over him. No—Esset noticed the window, and it was still very dark out. So it hadn't been the past day—probably still more like a matter of hours. Esset looked around the room then, the first time he'd truly paid attention to their new location. He was surprised to see the quality of his surroundings—this was no mere healer's house, it seemed. This looked more like a manor, the home of a minor noble or some such. The chair he was sitting in was very comfortable indeed, and the bed Toman was on was quite nice. The furniture was all of very fine quality, a combination of fanciness tempered with sturdiness.

It made Esset wonder—what was a noble doing in a tiny town like this? Was the healer the noble? His memory was too foggy to make an educated guess, he'd been so fixated on Toman's condition. Healing was an uncommon vocation for nobility; they didn't typically need vocations at all. Esset wrote off the question for later thought.

In the face of the luxury of the room, Esset was suddenly aware of how dirty he felt. Glancing around, he spotted a basin of warm water and a wash cloth, props that were fairly common in a patient's room. Esset went over to the washstand, and after washing his hands, he dampened the cloth and mopped his brother's fevered brow. There wasn't much else to do, so Esset washed his own face after that, then sat back down in the chair by the bed. Ten minutes later his face was planted on his arms again, and he was fast asleep.

Esset woke a few more times that night, but he didn't see the healer again until morning, although he had a feeling she'd checked in a few times. When she came in just after dawn, she woke him with the small noises she made taking away the basin and returning it with fresh water. Esset opened his eyes, then sat up slowly, his gaze finding her as she looked over at him and smiled.

"Good morning." He greeted her a bit groggily; she returned the greeting in kind. Esset glanced briefly at Toman—he was sleeping peacefully now, Esset was glad to see, so he turned his full attention to the healer. Now that he actually looked at her, he guessed that she was, indeed, the noble, her presence and vocation as odd as the house they were in.

She was a rather beautiful woman, with high cheekbones and lovely blue eyes. Her dark brown hair was very well-cared for and done up atop her head in a loose but pristine arrangement. Her clothes seemed simple for a noble, but too fancy and of a quality too good for her to pass as a commoner. Esset was guessing she was either minor nobility or the wife of a very rich merchant. He glanced at her hands, but there was no wedding ring on her finger. He took all that in in a second before realizing he didn't even know her name. He got to his feet and executed a little bow to her before introducing himself.

"I'm sorry, I just realized I never introduced myself. My name is Jonathan Esset, and the man you saved last night is my brother, Toman Atrix-Iiren."

"Pleased to meet you, although we both must wish it were under different circumstances. I am Lady Annalise Ateala, and I serve as healer for this town and anyone who needs my help," she said with a small curtsy back. She looked over at Toman.

"My patient seems to be doing well. It's tough to say for sure, but he should recover," she said. Esset heaved a sigh of relief as he watched her lay a hand on Toman's forehead to check his temperature.

"Excuse my surprise, but a Lady as a healer? That seems somewhat unusual," Esset said, hoping he wouldn't offend.

"There is nothing to excuse. My family reacted much worse to my disclosure, which is why I relieved them of my presence and moved here. Being a healer is my calling, no matter my birth, and my inheritance is my own, so I do with it as I see fit. This way, no one sees my family's 'embarrassment,' and I do not have to put up with their disapproving looks and remarks," she explained, moving about the room and getting another vial from the cabinet. Meanwhile, Esset chuckled at her comments.

"Well, their loss is our gain," he commented, already liking her and admiring her spirit.

"Indeed," Lady Ateala responded, flashing him a quick smile. "Now, Reshkin venom is a very potent and complex substance. It will take a long time to purge it from his system, so I will be needing to administer the anti-venom twice a day until he stabilizes, and once a day for a while after that. He will seem to get better and worse in waves for quite some time, but if everything goes well he will hopefully be right as rain in no time."

"That is great news, you have no idea," Esset replied, about as grateful as he could get. Lady Ateala just glanced at him and graced him with another one of those smiles. She filled a syringe with that pale liquid again and walked over to Toman's side.

"Okay, he shouldn't react so badly as last night, but he will react. Be ready to still him if necessary, please," she requested, taking Toman's arm to give him the injection. As predicted, he moaned and tried to roll a little bit, but Esset held him in place. It didn't take him long to move back into a restless, fevered sleep. Esset and Lady Ateala kept a close eye on him until he did so, and Esset let him go after he shifted into the somewhat calmer state.

"There we are. He may or may not wake up later today. If he does, please call for my maid, Tiffany, and she will fetch some soup. It's important that he eat something, and there's a bed pan under the dust ruffle. I doubt he'll be awake much longer than it will take for that. If you need anything else, call for me or my maid, as needed," Lady Ateala explained.

"Ah, Lady Ateala?" Esset forestalled her as she was about to turn. She paused to listen.

"What will we—do we—owe you?" She seemed to have enough money, after all, although money really wouldn't be an object, not after they got paid for this job for the Nadra. Lady Ateala smiled graciously.

"For now, nothing. Within the village, I trade my skills for the supplies and foods that I need day-to-day. For others, I ask only small favors or what can be afforded, if I ask for anything at all. Don't worry about it, we can figure it out later," she assured him. Esset smiled back.

"Thank you," he said. "Just let me know—anything at all you need, it's yours." Lady Ateala simply acknowledged his statement and his gratitude with another of her gracious smiles and a small nod before leaving the room.

A little while later, the maid brought Esset some food and showed him where the privy was located. Beyond that small excursion, however, Esset had no intention of leaving his brother's bedside. He was briefly forced to do so, however, when a "guest" came calling.

"Ah, sir?" chirped the maid at the door. Esset looked over at her and she continued quickly. "There is someone at the door for you." Then she abruptly fled. Esset blinked, glanced at Toman, and then headed out towards the front entrance. As it turned out, the guest was a Nadra—apparently the maid was afraid of the members of their race. She probably had to notify Lady Ateala too, but Esset was fairly certain it was more than that.

"Nassata!" Esset exclaimed upon seeing her familiar teal figure. He was very surprised to see her—she'd fought the whole day previous, after all, and must have traveled all night to make it to the town this early. A second, closer look did reveal her exhaustion; many of the signs that betrayed fatigue in humans were different, but at the very least, Nassata was leaning on her spear. Knowing that news of Toman would be of foremost importance, Esset didn't both waiting for a question.

"Toman's not doing great, but he's still alive, and the healer thinks he has a chance, at least," the young man reported, his own weary relief—and yes, still a bit of worry—showing through his demeanor.

"That is amazing news!" Nassata responded, looking very surprised indeed. Then she confessed, "I feared what state to find the two of you in."

"I thank Bright Hyrishal he's made it this far," Esset said. He added in a firm tone, "He's going to make it, and when he's well, we'll finish what we started. I'm sorry, but I can't go back yet, I can't leave him like this..." His tone lost its firmness at the end and turned apologetic.

"Do not worry about us. You won the war for us—the battles left we can handle, especially since the stone soldiers still fight.

When he is well again, we would appreciate your return, if only to do a final sweep to try to ensure the war is fully won, but we can delay our victory celebrations until then." Nassata appeared to mean her words, too, for which Esset was extremely grateful. He didn't like breaking—or at least bending—their contract, but he couldn't leave his brother in the state he was in.

"I came because I wanted to know what had transpired since your departure," Nassata continued. "And I thought you might want a few of your things." Only then did she flip her coils aside to lift the bags she'd brought with her. Sure enough, they were some of Toman and Esset's things, including Toman's well-worn, floppy-brimmed hat strapped to the top of a bag.

"Thank you, Nassata," Esset said sincerely, genuinely overcome with the unnecessary gesture from the warrior. On an impulse, he stepped forward and hugged the snake-lady. She reflexively returned the gesture. Esset was a little embarrassed when he pulled away a few moments later, but appreciative as well. The fleeting thought that maybe the Nadra were onto something with their tactile culture flicked irrelevantly through his mind.

"I can't believe you came," Esset confessed, feeling uncharacteristically emotional. "You must be exhausted, maybe I can see if the lady will let you—"

"Don't worry," Nassata forestalled him. "I did not come alone. I have another three warriors with me, and we will make camp outside town. We know some of the people here fear us, and we don't want to make anyone unnecessarily uncomfortable."

"Are you sure?" Esset asked. He couldn't shake the feeling that they were being turned away, and after the gesture he'd just received, that felt especially wrong.

"Thank you, Esset, we'll be just fine," Nassata replied with a smile. "Just worry about your brother—we will be well. I will come by early tomorrow to check in and see how things have progressed. I am glad Toman is still alive. Keep well."

"I'll give you an update when you come by again," Esset promised.

Nassata left, and Esset went back to the room again to keep watch over Toman. Another meal passed, and Esset kept an eye on Toman while trying to not let his own mind run away. To distract himself, he took out his summoner's tome and began flipping through. He read for a few hours, having the niggling feeling that there was something new there, but the new summon wasn't quite sticking in his mind. He glanced over at his brother, and he thought he saw Toman's eyelids move. He set his book aside in order to watch his brother's face, and a moment later Toman's eyelids fluttered again.

"Toman!" Esset called his name quietly but urgently, leaning forward and giving his brother's hand a squeeze.

"Come on, brother, wake up, just for a bit now," he urged. Toman's eyes opened partway, not able to compete with the light that was too bright against his tired eyes.

"Jonthn?" Toman mumbled.

"There we go, there you go," Esset murmured. "You're all right, you're safe. We're at a healer's. How are you feeling?" Toman squeezed his eyes shut for a second and then opened them a little further than the last time.

"Not so great," he groaned. Esset just nodded—that was to be expected.

"Do you think you can eat something? I'll help," the summoner asked.

"Mmm… maybe?" Toman hazarded. His voice was hoarse and raspy.

"Okay. Just wait one second, I'm going to call the maid to get you something," Esset said. He vanished from Toman's field of vision for a few moments before returning.

"She'll be back soon, and we can get some food in you. Is there anything you need?" Esset asked, hovering over Toman's bed. Toman shook his head slightly, then moved his hands on the mattress. The unfamiliar sensation of not having gloves on caught his attention and he lifted one hand enough to see the bare skin. He glanced a question at his brother.

"They're safe," Esset assured him. Then he averted his eyes. "Although that was one promise I never wanted to make good on."

"Sorry," Toman managed to reply hoarsely.

"Yeah, well, those bugs are going to be very sorry," Esset responded, his tone heated. Toman smiled slightly, then felt too exhausted with the effort to continue. Esset shot him a worried look, even though he knew that total exhaustion was probably to be expected. He was about to say something, but the maid came in with a tray just then. Within seconds of finishing his soup, Toman was back asleep.

Later that evening, Lady Ateala returned again and gave Toman another injection of the antidote. Once again, Toman seemed to get worse immediately.

"Part of the cure for the Reshkin venom forces the body to start actively fighting the venom. Otherwise, it's like the venom circumvents the immune system completely and kills the victim without being opposed at all," Lady Ateala explained unbidden. Perhaps she noticed Esset's obvious concern at his best friend's state. Esset's brown eyes flicked up to Lady Ateala, who was watching her patient carefully and did not return his gaze. "It only looks like he's getting worse because his body is suddenly being forced to react violently against the venom after doing nothing."

"Ah," Esset responded. "I was wondering." He hadn't been suspicious of her or anything, just very worried, but she seemed to understand his unspoken concern.

"It is only natural," Lady Ateala replied easily. Now she glanced at him. "If you don't mind my inquiry, how again did he come to be bitten by one of the Reshkin? They are problematic to the Nadra, I know, but last I heard, the Nadra were not overly welcoming towards humans. There have been few humans admitted to their city at the best of times."

"The Reshkin are the reason we were there," Esset explained. "They had become a bigger problem than the Nadra could deal with alone, so they went looking for help. Long story short, they found my brother and me, and we've been helping them for the past week or so."

"If you'll beg my pardon, you don't look much like soldiers," the lady put in. That got Esset's usual laugh.

"No, we don't," he agreed. "Our skills lie in magical areas rather than physical." Lady Ateala nodded.

"That would have been my guess," she responded. "What kinds of magics then? I could see you as a mage, but he," she gestured at Toman, "does not look like one to strive for the more scholarly magical pursuits."

"He's not," Esset acknowledged. "And although I am, neither of us is a conventional mage. I'm a summoner—some of the villagers saw one of my summons when I arrived."

"So I heard," Lady Ateala replied. "I've had to reassure many of our villagers that you weren't a demon-caller, nor the victims of one. I'm glad I was correct, and it will be good to have solid information to put their fears to rest that no demons will come calling," Lady Ateala said with a small nod. Esset rubbed the back of his neck self-consciously.

"Yeah... a lot of people seem to make that assumption. Despite fire being symbolic for both good and evil, Brightfire and Darkfire, somehow it's a widespread assumption that any fiery creature is from the underworld. But my summons are neither malevolent nor benevolent."

"What of him then?" she asked next, pointing her chin at Toman. "You said you were both...unconventional."

"Yeah, Toman's an animator. He can make things that aren't alive sort of come to life. It's not true life, of course, but they can do almost anything he wants," Esset explained with a shrug. "He can create things to animate, like a golem, or animate an existing object." Lady Ateala's eyebrows lifted in surprise.

"Fascinating," Lady Ateala said. "I can see how you could be very helpful to the Nadra. Inborn magical abilities are always so interesting."

"Any magical abilities are pretty fascinating," Esset replied, really warming to the conversation as it looked like it was turning somewhat academic. "Magic itself is fascinating—everything else in this world is governed by hard and fast rules, but magic can defy pretty much any of them."

"It does give those born with it something of an unfair advantage, however," Lady Ateala remarked.

"Well, yes, but like anything else, it's the luck of the draw. Someone born more intelligent or more athletic than those around him—or her—has an 'unfair' advantage as well," Esset pointed out. "Luck has and always will be checked and balanced by other forces in the world."

"Hm, yes, I suppose," the lady conceded.

"And magic seems to have its own rules too, if we can only figure them out," Esset mused.

"And then there's magic that comes from sources other than inborn abilities—like artifacts," Lady Ateala added.

"Oh yes! At the royal library back home, we have mage-lights that anyone can use. And of course there are magical weapons—staffs and swords. It fascinates me that people with absolutely no magical abilities can use them. It speaks to a pervasive force in our world—" Esset suddenly stopped himself with a sheepish expression. "Sorry, I just realized I was starting to go off on that. Toman always tells me no one's interested in stuff like that."

Lady Ateala smiled.

"Well, your brother would be wrong this time. I have always been interested in philosophy and the natural world, even beyond medicine." She waved generally towards her medicine cabinets. Esset was delighted.

"I have a question for you then," Esset said. "Since you mentioned them, are inborn abilities not fascinating too? Because it depends how you look at it—if you assume magic is the norm, then it's remarkable that people without magic can use magical devices. But really, they're just triggering a response in something that was created to give that response when triggered."

Lady Ateala jumped in and completed the thought for him.

"But if you assume magic is not the norm, then inborn abilities are even more unusual, for how does anyone access this inexplicable power we call magic?" she said.

"Exactly!" Esset exclaimed. Then he cringed at how loud he'd been and peeked at Toman, but his brother didn't stir.

"Exactly," Esset repeated in a more reasonable tone, his cheeks slightly red.

"I've always thought that magic is part of life, the energy of life, so I've always thought it odder that some people can't seem to access magic. And unfair. You say more intelligent people have a similar advantage, but what about those people whose magical abilities can set them up like gods? Yes, intelligence and hard work can go a long way, but can it compare to someone who could stop your heart with a thought?" Lady Ateala asked.

"You do have a point, but history shows that intelligence and hard work *can* make men—or women—that powerful. Akton the Cruel, for example. He built an empire and a religion around himself, and he was just a man. Yes, he recruited those with magic, but he didn't have any himself. All he had to do to kill someone was snap his fingers—someone else would do it for him. How is that any less of a power than having the magic himself?" Esset asked. "He learned to manipulate people to a level that could even look like magic when it wasn't."

Lady Ateala didn't look convinced.

"And remember," Esset continued. "Hard work is always necessary, even for those with magic. Even if someone has an inborn talent, they wouldn't be able to stop someone's heart with their magic unless they practiced and refined their skills first. Magic, intelligence, or any other inborn advantage still need to be practiced and nurtured."

"But..." Lady Ateala paused to gather her thoughts before launching a counter-argument. "But think of, say, healers." She waved a hand at her medicine cabinets again. "Imagine two scenarios. In one, a skilled healer, practiced in herbalism and surgery, comes across a man in the woods with a deep wound in his belly. In the second scenario, a young healer with raw, inborn healing talent comes across the same man. The inexperienced healer with magic will be able to save the dying man, but the other healer, without her tools, will not."

Esset shook his head.

"But with preparation and her tools, she could. It's analogous to the difference between Toman's abilities and mine. I can react to a threat instantly by summoning something, but there's a limit on the scope of my abilities. I can only summon so much. Toman needs preparation to react to a threat, time to create or seek things to animate. But given the time to prepare, his abilities, his power, far outstrip mine."

Esset didn't get the chance to see her reaction to his argument, for the maid poked her head in the door.

"Milady? You're needed," the maid said politely.

"Yes, of course," Lady Ateala replied instantly. She smiled apologetically at Esset.

"Excuse me. We'll have to continue our engaging discussion another time." She turned and followed the maid out the door after Esset nodded his understanding.

Esset found himself staring off the way she'd gone. He'd been surprised, but pleasantly so; he always enjoyed a good discussion with a learned person, and Lady Ateala definitely was that. Women less frequently pursued scholarly pursuits, especially women of noble birth. Esset didn't know why that was the case, but he certainly had nothing against woman scholars—he was more than willing to engage with any sharp mind.

Thinking back, he realized that the only female scholars he'd met previously had been older, either his mother's age or even older, with wrinkles and white hair. Esset turned pink again and found himself glad Lady Ateala wasn't there to see it. Speaking of unfair advantages…she was smart and pretty. No, beautiful. Definitely beautiful. Esset found himself looking forward to the next time he got to see her, and not just for the conversation.

It was late, and both Toman and Esset were asleep, Toman peacefully in bed and Esset fitfully in the cot. Lady Ateala paused in the doorway and watched them for a moment, a cat-like smile on her face. Then she entered the room and her gaze turned calculating as she studied Toman up and down, briefly laying a hand on his forehead, then his wrist. Then she went to the medicine cabinet and counted the little bottles of serum left in there. All the vials were marked with her own code; someone would have to know it before risking taking any of them. Lady Ateala reached into her pocket and placed two new vials next to the serums she'd been giving Toman, then ghosted back out of the room.

CHAPTER 18

Esset woke early the next morning, but he didn't try going back to sleep. He'd kept checking on Toman all night, but his brother had slept more peacefully than he. With an almost jealous glance, Esset took up a chair and pulled out his summoner's tome. He began perusing through it, going through familiar motions more than actually trying to read. His mind wandered, and soon he was staring at a page without even flipping it.

"You've been on that page for a while now," remarked a quiet, hoarse voice from the bed.

"You're awake again!" Esset exclaimed, stuffing his book aside thoughtlessly.

"Yeah. Water?" Toman requested. If the hoarse quality of his voice was anything to go by, it was no wonder he wanted a drink of water.

"Of course," Esset said, picking up the waiting glass of clear liquid from the bedside table where it had been left for just that reason. He helped prop Toman up before passing it over for him to drink.

"I forgot to tell you. Nassata came by yesterday," Esset said after that small task had been performed.

"How long was I out for?" Toman asked, surprised and sounding marginally better for the drink.

"Only one night, at that point," Esset replied. "I couldn't believe it either. She brought us some of the things I'd left behind in the hurry. Including your hat." The summoner grinned and lifted the hat from where it was sitting just out of Toman's sight; Toman had to smile at that.

"She said she'd be coming by again sometime today," the skinnier brother added.

"Tell her thank you," Toman replied, still smiling. That hat meant a lot to him—more than Nassata knew.

"I will. Who knows, maybe you'll be awake and she can come in and see you," Esset suggested cheerfully. "In the meantime, breakfast? It'll be more soup for you, but…"

"Soup works just fine. To be honest, I'm not sure I could keep anything else down," Toman confessed.

Before long, they had some soup for Toman, and Esset explained everything that had happened since their departure from Salithsa, including the news from Nassasta's visit. Toman was barely awake by the time Esset finished and Lady Ateala arrived to give him his morning injection.

"Toman, this is Lady Ateala," Esset introduced them when she walked in the room.

"Mmm," was all Toman managed, as he was quickly losing a battle with unconsciousness.

"She's going to give you some of the anti-venom. You're not going to feel so great right away, but it will get better later," Esset explained. This time Toman just gave the slightest of nods to indicate that he'd heard.

Toman was still marginally conscious when Lady Ateala injected the anti-venom in his arm; he froze, then started to sweat and moan as unconsciousness overtook him. Unconsciousness was no blessing, however—there was no reprieve from the pain; that much was obvious in Toman's unconscious reactions, twisting a bit in the bed as if trying to escape the pain within him. Esset hated seeing Toman suffer, but he couldn't bring himself to look away. Instead he took the seat next to his brother's bed and took his hand, helping him through it in the only way he could—just by being there. Lady Ateala lingered awhile, watching her patient— presumably to make sure nothing went wrong—before leaving them alone in the room.

An hour later, Toman had sunk into a less pained but still restless sleep, and Nassata came to call again. This time Esset knew what to expect when the maid briefly delivered her news and then vanished. He went to the door and invited her in, having asked Lady Ateala the day before if it was okay. Even though Toman wasn't awake to see her, he brought her to the room so they could speak there.

"How is he doing?" Nassata asked, her vibrant teal eyes coming to rest on the young man in the bed.

"He's getting better, slowly. He was awake for a little while yesterday and for a bit longer this morning. He said to say thank you, by the way, for bringing our things. Especially his hat," Esset said, a smile tweaking his lips.

Nassata smiled. "I am glad I thought to pick it up. He always had that hat on, even underground, so it seemed like so small a keepsake at the time."

"The previous animator took Toman in after Toman's family was massacred by Moloch," Esset explained. "The hat's from him. Toman's worn that hat every day since." That it had been left behind during their flight from Salithsa was a mark of how dire things had been.

"I am sorry none of us believed you—especially so for Tseka's misguided attempt at mercy. I hope you can forgive us," Nassata said, her hand reaching out to rest on Esset's arm. Having spent so long in the company of the Nadra, Esset no longer thought anything of the gesture.

"You couldn't have known—we have nothing to blame you for," he said with a small shake of his head. "And nothing to forgive you for. You were doing what you believed was right, as was Tseka. None of us had any reason to believe that things wouldn't have gone just as you thought they would."

"But you had faith, and you kept fighting. We will learn from that, I promise," Nassata vowed. "We are a people of peace, yet we were the ones pushing for the shorter, more violent end. We are of peace, and yet we did not fight for life as we should have. In your actions, you showed us we were wrong, and we owe you for that as well."

Esset wasn't sure how to take that. "I'm just glad he's going to be okay. When he's well enough again, we'll come back and finish the job. Actually, I was thinking that as soon as he's well enough to leave here, that we'd come. He won't be in fighting shape yet, but I will be, and with his army moving already, we can probably finish the Reshkin without him. He won't like it, and he'll be right when he argues that it'll be finished faster with him, but we can finish it just the same without him." Esset was feeling rather protective of his brother at the moment, and understandably so.

"That sounds fair enough," Nassata agreed. "How long, do you think, before that might be?" She was not being impatient, but the same couldn't necessarily be said for the council back home, and she had reports to make.

"The lady, Ateala, said it will likely be a week before he's conscious for normal hours, at the very least. She estimates two weeks for a majority recovery, three for complete. Although she was sure to stress that she was estimating only. Healing is complicated, with lots of variables that can go better or worse," Esset explained. Nassata nodded.

"Well, I will pass the report along," she said. "One of my people will take the message back to the city. In the meantime, I intend to stay here with two of my warriors. There will likely be little for us to do, but I convinced the council that you were too important as assets to risk." She grinned a little wolfishly, having gotten what she wanted. Her smile faded after a moment.

"Kessa was devastated to hear what happened," Nassata added, her eyes downcast. "She wanted to come, but I forbade it. She would not do well among humans, I think. Not without a little guidance, at least. We could not afford to be worrying about her here, not now. I know she will be glad to hear that Toman is still alive. I believe she has gotten quite attached to him."

"Yeah, they spent a lot of time together, didn't they?" Esset remarked with a smile. "But I hope Kessa realizes that we will leave when the job with the Reshkin is done. We may come back to visit someday, but we can make no promises. There…are things we need to do."

Nassata looked at the summoner curiously, but he looked like one who had been battered too often, too unfairly, and she couldn't bring herself to ask. Instead, she simply accepted his words.

"Well, we will start with Toman's wellbeing, but when we return, I will ensure that Kessa understands how things lie. I am sure she knows, on some level, the way things are, but I would not see her hurt if I can help it," Nassata agreed. Esset nodded his agreement—there was too much pain in the world already to add more unnecessarily.

"Well," Nassata continued after a brief pause. "I am going to go now. There is no need to make the people of this village any more nervous. But Esset—" She stopped until he looked up at her.

"Just promise me that you'll take care of yourself, too, while your brother heals. You look terrible."

Esset had to smile at that. "Yeah, I do tend to forget about myself a bit, don't I? Well I promise. I'll take care of myself too," Esset replied.

Nassata smiled back at him before letting herself out.

Esset passed a few boring days while Toman recovered, but then Lady Ateala's other patient—a woodcutter who'd nearly lost a leg in an accident—got well enough to return home, and Lady Ateala had more free time. Esset and the lady had more time for discussions on science, philosophy, ethics, and religion. Once Toman was strong enough to stay conscious for more than an hour at a time, Lady Ateala recruited Esset for errands in the village.

Armed with a quickly-sketched map of the village, a basket, and a list, Esset headed for the market.

"Good morning!" he greeted the baker cheerfully.

"Good morn'n," the baker replied more conservatively.

"Lady Ateala has requested that I pick up a loaf of bread and a dozen biscuits," Esset said, placing his basket on the counter. The baker looked surprised.

"Oh aye, I've got them ready for her. That makes you one of the lads came in here on that fire bird then, yes?" the baker asked as he fetched the requested items.

Esset nodded.

"My brother was bit and poisoned. The lady saved his life," Esset explained. The baker nodded.

"We're blessed to have her here," the baker agreed. "I don't know what we'd do without her. We were all worried for her when you two came in. Thought the fire bird was a demon!"

Esset gave a polite laugh.

"Never fear, no demons here," he reassured the baker, who nodded.

"So our lady said," he said. "You run along now, and tell the lady I'm making those lemon pastries she likes tomorrow."

"Of course. What do I owe you?" Esset asked.

"Owe?" the baker asked. "Why, nothing! We don't charge our lady nothing. She helps us, and we help her how we can. We can little afford to pay her, in a village this small, but this we can do."

Since Lady Ateala hadn't given him any money for the trip, Esset had assumed this was a way he was paying her back. But he found this symbiotic relationship heartwarming.

"Well, thank you. Have a good day," Esset bade the baker, who echoed the sentiment. Once Esset left the shop, the baker's expression went slightly blank.

"We're so fortunate to have Lady Ateala," he said to no one in particular. Then he shook himself and headed to check on the ovens in the back.

Esset stopped at a small farm at the edge of town next. He tapped on the door, but there was no answer, so he poked his head around the side of the house.

"Hello?" he called.

"Hello?" a female voice echoed from the barn. "Just a moment!" A minute later a farmwife in an apron emerged from the barn.

"Hello, stranger, what can I do for you?" she called when she saw him.

"I'm here to fetch some things for Lady Ateala," he called back. She stopped and smiled, then headed back into the barn. Esset was just debating whether to follow when she re-emerged. She had a glass jar of fresh milk cradled in one arm, one of the items from Esset's list, and a big smile on her face.

"We were all wondering about you two. I didn't see it, but I heard you made quite the grand entrance. Preacher William tried to stir everyone up with talk of Darkfires and demons, but Lady Ateala wouldn't stand for that nonsense. She has a way of talking people around, our dear lady does. Besides, you're nothing to worry about. Look at you, all skin and bones. You make sure to drink some of that milk—good milk, strong back, my ma always said! Now our good lady usually wants a couple other things too. I've got some fresh peas here I'll send with you if you'll pass me your basket. Was there anything else? Sometimes Lady Ateala wants some eggs or some other vegetables." She finally paused long enough for him to say something.

"Eggs, please," Esset said. He didn't have a chance to get a word more in edgewise as she took his basket and his arm and began dragging him over to the chicken coop, chattering about why her eggs were the best in the village, all thanks to the feed she gave them. Esset nodded occasionally, but she didn't appear to need encouragement to keep talking. Once he had the peas and the eggs as well as the milk, he slowly began backing towards the front of the house. Only once he reached the road did she stop.

"You take care, y'hear? And take care of our Lady Ateala, too. Bye now, dear!" She waved as he smiled and fled down the road.

The farmwife watched him go, and then her stare went blank.

"We're so fortunate to have Lady Ateala," she said to herself. Then she turned and went back to the barn.

The jar of milk was getting heavy in Esset's arms, but he had one more stop to make—a herbal tea to drop off to an elderly lady on the way back to Lady Ateala's. When he came up on the small farmhouse, he found the granny asleep in the rocking chair on the porch. Esset grinned at the irony—the tea he was bringing was supposed to aid sleep. He stopped at the bottom step and tapped on the railing.

"Good morning," he called softly, hoping he wouldn't startle her.

"Hm? Who's there?" The granny lifted her chin slowly from her chest and squinted in his general direction. Her eyes were filmed milky white.

"Jonathan Esset. I'm here to give you something from Lady Ateala," Esset said, stepping onto the first step.

"Ah, yes, that's wonderful..." The granny's chin sank back against her chest as her voice trailed off, and Esset hesitated on the bottom step.

"Granny?" he ventured.

"Hm? Who's there?" The granny repeated, her chin lifting as slowly as it had sunk.

"I have something from Lady Ateala." Esset wasted no time this time. He ascended the steps and pressed the packet of tea into her hands.

"Ah, bless you, bless our lady," the granny mumbled.   •

"Bless you," Esset replied, but the granny's chin was sinking to her chest once more, so he left quietly. His feet crunched against a dry twig on the walkway as he left, and she looked up one last time, her eyes blank.

"We're so fortunate to have Lady Ateala," she said. Then she gave a small snore and fell back asleep.

Lady Ateala was in to check on Toman's progress while Esset flipped through his summoner's tome, still chasing that new summon that seemed to be niggling at the back of his mind. When Lady Ateala was done, she gave Toman a pleased smile and a nod.

"I think we can cut you down to injections once a day," she announced.

"Awesome!" Esset exclaimed.

"*Thank* Bright Hyrishal," Toman said. Ateala laughed before glancing at Esset.

"It's been a week—why don't you take one of the other guest rooms, Esset? They're not being used," Lady Ateala suggested. Esset set his tome down.

"Nah, I'm okay," Esset said with a shrug.

"Really? The beds are far more comfortable, I promise," she coaxed him.

"The cot's not bad," Esset said.

"Really?" Toman piped up from the bed. "So that's why you thrash around all night on it?"

Esset scowled at him.

"Toman's well out of the woods now," Lady Ateala said. "In fact, a good night's sleep is the best thing for him, and if you're not sleeping well, neither is he."

"See? Doctor's orders." Toman was grinning now. Esset rolled his eyes.

"Fine then," Esset said. "If you're so bored of me, I'll get lost. Just remember, without me here you'll have no one to keep you entertained."

"It's not like you've been putting on puppet shows for me," Toman quipped.

Lady Ateala laughed. "I'll tell the maid to ready the room next door then," she said. "I have to go out for a bit, so you boys have fun."

"Bye!" they both bade her.

Once she was gone, Esset crossed his arms and looked Toman steadily in the eye. "Does this mean you want your gloves back?"

Toman sobered up at Esset's words. "No, hang on to them for now," Toman said. "I haven't any use for them right now anyways, and they'll be safer with you. I'm still sleeping too much, and when I'm asleep, I'm dead to the world. No. After I improve, I'll ask for them back."

Esset nodded seriously at the request. He didn't like Toman not having the gloves, but he had a point. Then again... "Why don't you just animate some stuff to keep watch? Y'know, if someone besides me, the maid, or Lady Ateala comes up to you when you're sleeping, they'll warn and defend you. It's totally doable!" Esset objected. "Carrying your gloves around for you is making me paranoid, seriously."

"Jonathan." Toman deliberately addressed him by his first name. Esset scowled.

"I get it, Jonathan. Trust me, this brush with death scared me too. You want me to have the gloves back as a sign that I'm better now. But I'm not better now. The odds that I will suddenly die from the poison after surviving it for this long are pretty low, but there are still odds for it, however small. I'm not better yet. I'm getting there, but I'm not there yet. Just...be patient. Please?" Toman's brown eyes were intense, and he used that intensity to lock Esset in place and keep him from trying to convince himself that the situation was anything other than what it was. The situation wasn't all bad, but believing it was all good could be dangerous too, and Toman didn't want to take that chance. There were too many other chances as it was.

"Yeah, I'll keep them for you a while longer," Esset said, looking away when Toman was done.

"And Jonathan?" Toman prompted, getting Esset to meet his eyes again. It was a lighter expression on the animator's face this time. Esset looked at him, already prepared to accept whatever he would say.

"Yes?"

"Thank you." Toman was the one to look down this time. Esset blinked for a moment, and had Toman still been looking at him, he would have seen the grin split his face.

"Brightfire, but that was unnecessary," Esset scoffed,

prodding Toman's pride. Toman looked up, a trace of surprise on his face, but he grinned barely a moment later too.

"Psh, there's no winning with you, is there?" Toman challenged him. "I don't thank you, and you call me ungrateful; I thank you and you call it superfluous! Honestly!" Esset turned his nose up, pretending to be snobby.

"Etiquette is a far more complex art than that!" he mock-sneered. "One would think you'd been raised in a barn, not in the esteemed household of the Esset family!"

"I grew up in a castle, thank you very much!" Toman retorted, mock-indignant. "A castle rightfully inherited and with a long legacy of greatness! My etiquette is unimpeachable!"

Toman and Esset stared at each other for a long moment, then burst out laughing. Esset collapsed in the chair and was holding his sides, he was laughing so hard; Toman wasn't faring much better. It was a while before they got a hold on themselves.

"Well, I'm going to leave you to your beauty sleep, for all the good that will do, ugly-mug," Esset said, getting up to leave.

"Well, at least I never have to worry about seeing a face like yours in my mirror, troll-face!" Toman called the parting shot as Esset walked out the door. Esset very maturely stuck his tongue out at his brother before closing the door behind him.

Esset now habitually helped out with housework and running errands. He was on his way out to deliver a prescription to the old lady on the edge of town when Lady Ateala caught up with him on the way out.

"Esset, wait up!" she called, trying to tie the ribbon from her bonnet under the chin as she hurried over.

"Your brother is sleeping like a rock, so he should be fine in Melanie's care until we get back. And if he tries to get out of bed again before my say-so, she can sit on him," Lady Ateala said primly as she caught up to him. Esset had to grin—yes, he could see the maid's rotund derrière providing ample threat to stay abed.

"And why are we both out at the same time?" he asked lightly, curious to know the answer. He thoroughly enjoyed Ateala's company and hoped maybe their paths would take them the same way for a while.

"Well, I found out just this morning that there's an herb I need that just began blooming. And since it's most potent at this time, I need to pick it now," she said coyly. She had a basket with her, and she held it with both hands, swinging in front of her. With her hair in a neat braid down her back, she looked perfectly prepared for a gentle herb-picking excursion.

"And, well, it's growing just past your little errand," the lady finished, smiling sweetly. "Might we accompany one another?"

"We might," Esset replied with a cheerful air. He extended his arm to her gallantly and she took it like the noble lady she was. She gave a spontaneous giggle, no doubt prompted by the loveliness of the day. The sun could not have shone more cheerfully, and birds chirped happily in the trees. People greeted them as they walked down the street. They chatted happily about little things: the weather and a few of the lady's most recent patients. Almost before they knew it, they had delivered the prescription and they were walking along the little path on the outskirts of town to where the herb the healer wanted grew.

"I'm sorry to take you away from your brother for so long," Lady Ateala apologized out of the blue as they headed down the path.

"Not at all, my lady," Esset replied smoothly, although he was a bit surprised by her unexpected words.

"Hm, m'lady," she echoed, almost wistfully.

"What was that?" Esset asked, not sure he'd heard her right.

"Oh, I was just thinking…occasionally it strikes me how different, how much better, my life is, now that I live here and not with my family. At home it was never 'Lady Ateala.' It was 'Silly Ateala,' or 'Foolish Ateala,' or 'Simple Ateala,'" the lady healer explained.

"Simple?" Esset repeated, astonished. "I find it very difficult to believe anyone could find you simple. It's not every day that I get to converse with someone as clever as you are, lady."

"Thank you for that, I appreciate it," Lady Ateala responded sincerely, looking a bit touched. She continued more sadly, recalling an unpleasant memory. "But back home I was not what my parents wanted me to be. I guess…since I didn't do the things they wanted me to do, or know the things they wanted me to know, that meant I was simple. I always tried to tell myself I was smart, but when everyone else says differently, it becomes rather difficult to believe."

"Well, clever Lady Ateala, I will never drop the 'lady' on you, and I will remind you whenever I can of how clever you are," Esset said, his smile a bit mischievous. "Don't ever doubt how clever you are. You saved my brother's life, and just look at all the people that you help every day. A simple person could not do the same job, that is for certain."

Lady Ateala smiled again.

"Thank you," she repeated. "It's funny—sometimes you just need to hear the words."

"Any time," Esset replied, pausing to give her a little bow. She laughed, charmed.

"Oh, there it is!" the lady healer suddenly exclaimed, spotting her herb ahead and rushing over.

"Okay, now we just need this bit here." She pointed at the leaves near the base. Esset partially missed her explanation of the herb's various properties and uses, so caught up was he in how she lit up when she talked. He didn't have a particular interest in medicine or herbs, but she made it interesting. They lingered as long as they could, gathering herbs, before returning to the house.

The next day, Toman wanted his gloves back.

"Really?" Esset looked at Toman, surprised. It had only been two days since their last conversation, after all.

"What I said before still stands, but...well, you had a point too, and not having them drives me nuts too. So give 'em here," Toman replied. He was sitting on the side of the bed, having just tried a little walk around the room. He still felt bone-deep weary, but it was doable, and he knew he needed to build his strength back up.

Esset happily dug into his side bag; he always had the gloves with him. He immediately passed them over, and Toman looked relieved too when he'd returned them to their rightful place over his hands. For fun, Toman animated his belt to zip off the dresser where it had lain quiet while he'd been ill. It wound up Toman's leg and settled back around his waist over the simple shirt and trews he'd been clad in while in Lady Ateala's home.

"Much better," Toman said happily, mostly referring to the gloves. He held his hands up and wiggled his fingers before dropping his hands back to his lap again. He glanced at Esset and smirked, spotting his relief.

"You're welcome," he quipped glibly. Esset smirked back.

"You're welcome," he retorted. They grinned at each other, but Esset could see that Toman was starting to droop a little bit. Taking the unspoken cue, the summoner got to his feet.

"Get some rest, Toman. We both might be sick of waiting and resting, but that's how you're going to get better, and the sooner you get better, the happier the Nadra will be," Esset said, shifting his side bag back once he was standing.

"Yeah, I know. And I know this has to be even more frustrating for you," Toman said, scooting further onto the bed so he could lie down and pull the covers over his cold feet.

"Hey, what're big brothers for but to look out for their littler ones?" Esset joked. It was a running joke with the Essets that Toman always seemed like the older brother, looking out for his younger, nerdier brother, so when the roles were reversed, they usually went out of their way to comment on it.

"Yeah right, ya pipsqueak," Toman growled, but Esset had already slipped out the door before he could finish the insult.

Later that day, Toman and Esset were playing cards in Toman's room. They'd borrowed a deck of cards and set up on Toman's blankets, since the animator was beginning to go stir-crazy with inactivity. He enjoyed reading occasionally, but it wasn't his favorite pastime either, so Esset had taken pity on him.

"I swear, you're cheating," Toman accused Esset, looking at his once again abominable hand. "You have to be."

"Oh come on, Toman. Of the two of us, it's far easier for you to cheat, and you know I have a lousy poker face. You and I both know I'm not cheating," Esset replied, playing another card. Toman scowled at the patterned piece.

"Yeah, whatever," he grumbled. "I'm just not feeling well today. More so than usual. That must be why I'm doing so bad."

He threw down his own card with a bit of ill temper, and Esset didn't argue with him.

"Esset?" Lady Ateala's musical voice came questioningly from the doorway.

"Ah, there you are. Hello, Toman. Do you mind if I steal away your brother for a bit?" the lady asked, stepping into the room when both looked up to greet her and see what she needed.

"Bah, go ahead. I keep losing anyways," Toman said, throwing down the rest of his hand. Esset winced when he saw his brother's cards—he hadn't lied.

"What can I do for you?" Esset asked, tactfully placing his own cards face down.

"I was hoping you could deliver a prescription," Lady Ateala replied, her demeanor a bit apologetic. "It's for Granny Ida. It's the tea she needs—she's out again already, and she can't sleep without it. She told me yesterday she only had a day's worth left, and she'd send her grandson by to pick it up for her today. But her grandson isn't very reliable... Something must have happened, or he forgot, so Ida doesn't have her tea. I just want to make sure she gets it."

"Of course," Esset agreed readily, getting to his feet. Toman glanced at his brother, then snuck his hand across the bed to peek at Esset's hand. He scowled when he saw it, then stuffed all the cards together and started shuffling them.

"You'll be okay without me?" Esset asked Toman.

"Oh yeah, 'cause losing at cards was helping so much..." he grumbled. Esset chose to give him the benefit of the unwell and not take offense.

"See you later then," Esset said instead, as if he had been given a more cordial response.

"Thank you, Esset," Lady Ateala thanked him as she stepped out of the way to let him out of the room. Esset just gave her a small smile and nod of acknowledgment—it was small enough payment for what she'd done for Toman.

"Well, I'm no good at cards, but do you want to play a game? I have other things I need to do, but they can wait a few minutes, and I could use a brief break," the lady suggested once Esset was out the door.

"I'd like that," Toman replied, cheering up slightly. He'd seen the eyes Esset had been making at her, but he wouldn't say no to a card game with the pretty healer.

"Okay then, shuffle those cards and deal me in." Swinging the door shut behind her, Lady Ateala headed over to the bed and took Esset's seat. They chatted a bit as Toman shuffled, dealt, and they played the hand.

"Now then, you've been having a rough day, I see," the lady healer said as they finished the hand—Toman had won despite his bad luck, so either Lady Ateala was being particularly nice or she really was that bad at cards.

"Yeah, I haven't been feeling so great," Toman admitted.

"Hm…" Lady Ateala said. "Why don't you lie down flat? I'll take a look at you." Toman obliged, shifting the pillows around so that he could stretch out flat atop the covers of the bed. Lady Ateala went to his side and gently pressed her fingers against his neck to measure his pulse.

"In what way haven't you been feeling well?" she asked, moving her hand to his forehead to check his temperature.

"Just…kind of a general unwellness," Toman responded. "Like I almost feel nauseous, almost have a headache…kind of achy all over, actually."

"When did this start?" the lady asked.

"I felt like this when I woke up this morning. It gets better and worse in waves."

"Hm… this could be part of the venom's work, or it could be the anti-venom. It's tough to say. It might be part of the natural process of getting better, or it could be a symptom of something else. I don't want you to worry, just to be aware," Lady Ateala explained as she looked him over.

"All right, now I want you to breathe evenly and try to relax. I want to feel your resting pulse, so just calm yourself. I don't want you to fall asleep, but I need you totally relaxed." Her tone was smooth and soothing, almost hypnotic, as he closed his eyes and followed her instructions.

"Just lie still," Lady Ateala murmured. Toman felt her fingers on the inside of his arm, opposite his elbow. There was a gentle pressure for a moment, then again on the same spot on his other arm. As he laid still and tried to slow his heartbeat through relaxation, he felt her fingers on his neck again, on the left, then on the right side. Then he had a sudden itch on his nose and he reflexively went to move his hand to scratch it. A cold shock ran through him when his arm didn't respond. His eyes snapped open and he tried to jerk, to move his body, any part of his body, but he was a stranger trapped in his own physical form, a mere passenger instead of an agent of his own movements.

Instinctively, he reached for his magic, and his thoughts—and thus instincts—reached for Esset first. At the same time, his open eyes now saw Lady Ateala over him, but he couldn't comprehend her smile. He couldn't see her hands, but her fingers had taken hold of the fingers of his gloves.

Less than a second later, before he could try to defend himself with magic, she easily slipped both gloves from his hands. His magic, his only defense, was gone, and someone had his gloves. His thoughts scrambled madly as he tried to comprehend what was happening.

CHAPTER 19

Esset had made good time getting the tea to the old lady, but once there, he was loathe to hurry back to the vague oppression of Toman's temper. The day was pleasant, so he meandered over to the town fountain. He greeted many of the villagers as he passed—thanks to Lady Ateala's errands, he knew many of them now, and his dramatic entrance was a distant memory.

Esset was thinking about how peaceful it was when every stitch of clothing he was wearing suddenly jerked. Esset staggered a step and then braced himself, thinking, *"What in the name of Bright Hyrishal was that?"*

"You know, when I started my little project with the Reshkin and the Nadra, I never dreamed that it would deliver me the animator," Lady Ateala crooned. She stood over Toman, looking at him with a somewhat dreamy gaze. The helpless young man lay rigid, screaming inside and fighting fiercely but futilely in spirit. He reeled from being cut off from every bit of physical and magical control he knew, so it was taking longer for the lady's words to sink in. They still didn't entirely make sense, even when he processed the words themselves. Toman froze internally, but the pieces began to fall into place with the name she spoke next.

"Lord Moloch... he will be so pleased," she purred, smiling maliciously. "He was pleased enough just hearing that I had you. I asked him if he wanted to have you personally, but he said I could have you if I wanted. It was so generous of him. But of course he wants your little gloves, so I had to wait until you had them again before making my move." She sat down beside him and began walking two fingers up his throat and chin to tweak his nose. "You were very careful with them...but not careful enough. You were so very trusting." Her smile was supremely superior and smug now.

She got up again and went to the cupboard. She opened the small door, happily swaying to some tune only she could hear. She withdrew a knife from the cupboard that anyone could easily have assumed was there for surgeries and other medical purposes. Toman knew that Lady Ateala now had a purpose in mind that had nothing to do with healing. If she were a pawn of Moloch's, it did not bode well for him.

"It was so much fun playing you—you and your so-called brother both. What a couple of bleeding hearts." She smirked at him and leaned in, trailing the flat of the blade along his cheek and whispering, as if telling him a secret.

"I was behind it all, you know, behind everything that brought you here. The Reshkin were my special project. I don't have a lot of magic, you see, but I'm very good with what I do have. I'm good at making little changes, so I made a lot of little changes in the Reshkin, over time. I made them bigger, stronger, and tougher. And, of course, I made them far more venomous—that was the easiest part! And then I coordinated them and sent them after the Nadra. The stupid snakes were clueless! I was delighted when they brought me some of their own kind, writhing in an agony that I was responsible for. I, of course, played the caring but helpless healer and inside, I rejoiced at the obvious success of my project.

"I thought, perhaps, I could exterminate those snakes completely. I was very put out when you and the summoner came on the scene, but when I discovered what I really had… Well, that was a different story altogether." Lady Ateala trailed the knife down the front of Toman's shirt, the sharp blade catching or slicing the cloth slightly in places.

"Do you know how many places a human body can be sliced or stabbed without damaging anything important? It's really quite remarkable. To do so, however, takes a very detailed and precise knowledge of human anatomy. Fortunately for you, I am a very good healer." She alternately teased and mocked in a disturbing fashion. Her fingers trailed along behind the blade, then moved around it to lead the way. She felt his chest beneath the cloth of the shirt and felt the gap between two ribs with her fingertips.

"Here, for example," she whispered. Toman felt the prick of the knife tip against his skin for a long moment before she exerted pressure on the handle. Very slowly, the blade sank into his skin and through his flesh until it had been buried hilt deep. Lady Ateala traced her fingers on his skin around the knife handle, but Toman didn't even feel it. All he could feel was the agony of the cold steel embedded in his body, the pain amplified by his helplessness and complete inability to control anything but his eyes. Even his throat was frozen, rendering him unable to do anything other than swallow.

"Just a hairsbreadth to either side of the blade are internal organs that, if pierced, would eventually kill you. But just here… very little real damage has been done. Does that not cheer you?" Lady Ateala smiled as she began to slowly withdraw the knife. Toman had tried to hold his breath throughout the whole ordeal, but it was impossible, especially with the pain of it. Each breath sent new agony ripping through his body as his flesh pushed against the blade with tiny movements, reminding itself of its pain. Blood began to flow freely from the wound once the blade began to withdraw, staining the clean white sheets of the bed and sinking into the mattress.

"But I'm not here to please you, I'm here to please me," the lady purred. "As I was saying before, the Reshkin were all my doing, and when you were delivered to me, I was very happy. When I learned that you were the animator that Lord Moloch both hates and desires so very much, I knew I'd gotten a lucky break.

"You see, Reshkin bites aren't lethal to humans if treated within a day or even two, and after a dose of anti-venom, the patient will be completely well again within three days. Yes, that's right, it's only thanks to me that you're still here, like this, right now. I've been poisoning you this entire time. If you hadn't received a single injection after the first, you would have been perfectly well right now. As I said…*so* trusting." With the emphatic "so," Lady Ateala had found a new spot for her knife and thrust it into his chest. Toman gasped and choked as another cold shock flooded his body.

"There we are," Lady Ateala crooned.

Why am I running? It's such a nice day, Esset thought,

slowing to a walk from his flat-out run. Then he paused to relish
the feel of the bright sunshine against his skin. This was too nice a
day to waste rushing about. Maybe he could somehow get Toman
outside to enjoy it too.

Toman. Esset shook himself and started running again. *I have
to get to Toman!*

Esset kept an eye on his surroundings as he ran, sharp for
obstacles, but then he noticed the courier riding into town. Esset
slowed and changed course.

I think Lady Ateala mentioned she was expecting a package,
I should see if it's there, he thought. He had jogged halfway down
the street before he caught himself again.

What's going on? Esset concentrated. Magic. It had to be.
Some small but persistent magic was distracting him from
returning to Lady Ateala's house, even though he was certain
something was wrong there. Toman was in trouble.

Esset stopped completely for a second and cleared his mind.
Then he concentrated on a prayer, asking for focus for himself and
protection for Toman. He prayed that he wouldn't be too late.
When he opened his eyes, he was fairly certain that the magic had
been cleared, and he set off running again.

"Lord Moloch found me just upon my sixteenth birthday, you
know." Lady Ateala was still talking; she twirled a curl of hair
around one finger as she illustrated the memory for Toman. "He
saw me for what I was, even though I yet struggled with it. And he
led me to see it as beautiful—glorious! My family disagreed, of
course. So I blackmailed them and took my leave. Now, here, I can
do whatever I want. I am well-funded, and I'm more than clever
enough to protect myself here.

"Those stupid townsfolk believe I'm some kind of saint, even
though I've had my way with almost every single one of them.
They don't remember, you see. Isn't that just delicious? Of course,
I nudge them towards worshipping me anyways, but it's really
quite superfluous." She giggled, curling her hands beneath her
chin, the knife blade sticking out at an angle.

"One farmer came in with a cough—just a simple cough. I kept him for three days. I ran a few experiments on him—I even tested the Reshkin venom—then tortured him at my leisure. At the end of it, I just tampered with his memory and sent him on his way, grateful that I had saved him from some rare disease I'd made up on the spot." She sighed happily at the memory.

"But I owe it all to Lord Moloch…and you are not my only reward for obtaining the animating gloves. No, Lord Moloch has promised me greater power, some accumulated magic to call my own. Just think of what I could do with something like that…" She stared off dreamily for a moment before looking at Toman like he'd said something surprising.

"But oh! You haven't really seen my work, have you? I mean, you know about the Reshkin, but they're a demonstration of my work secondhand. I amplified what was there already—the aggression, the hive mind, the venom, and the physical strength. I made tiny changes to massive effect. Unfortunately they're still very dependent on me for survival since their modifications, but in time, I will fix that. Regardless, those subtle modifications, amplifications—that is where I excel. Let me show you." Lady Ateala wiped the knife off on the sheets and then lifted the streaked blade in front of her. "Take this knife, for example. Already quite sharp, as you've seen. But it is sharp as an ordinary object is sharp. The physical edge is as fine as it can be, so it cuts well. But if I help it along a little…" Lady Ateala ran her finger down the flat of the blade and it gained something like a halo. She then held it out over the ceramic mug sitting on the bedside table and slowly lowered the blade. With very little exertion, the knife sank into the lip of the mug as if the ceramic were more like butter.

"Amazing, isn't it? How so little can go such a long way…"

Esset flew in the door and ran right into the maid, Melanie.

"Oh!" she exclaimed, grabbing his shoulders and stopping either of them from falling.

"Sorry!" Essest apologized, but he immediately began to tear away from Melanie to continue towards Toman's room. When he tried, however, he suddenly found that she had a very powerful grasp on him.

"Esset… you shouldn't be here." There was something very strange about her voice—it sounded empty, like she wasn't quite lucid. There was a lack of urgency to her words, as if she didn't quite care what was happening, but thought she should. Esset looked up at her, and her eyes seemed blank and distant. But he didn't have time to deal with her. He tried struggling again, only to find her grip got stronger the more he tried to escape.

"No…" Melanie murmured.

"I don't want to hurt you. Let me go!" Esset struggled. Now he knew, really knew, that something was wrong. He couldn't hear anything in the rest of the house, but that didn't necessarily mean anything. He knew something, someone, had gotten to Toman, and he couldn't stop until he found out what was happening. He didn't want to hurt someone innocent, but it was pretty obvious that Melanie was under someone's control. It didn't seem like he had much choice.

Esset went limp, and Melanie sagged forward a bit to compensate for the sudden dead weight in her hands, although she gripped him still harder. Then Esset suddenly jerked up, using his feet to propel him as he cracked the crown of his skull under her chin. The robust maid's head snapped back and her hands flew open to release him. Not stopping to make sure she was okay, Esset ran off down the hall to Toman's room.

"You know what I can't help but wonder about, with these gloves? Can you still use them with only one hand?" Lady Ateala asked, fingering the gloves with her free hand for a moment before looking back at Toman with her head tilted to the side.

"I mean, what if a would-be animator only had one hand?"

Toman felt his gut twist again, even past all the pain, as Lady Ateala held the glowing blade over his left arm. "What if something happened? An accident or…something?"

There was a horrible sensation of searing heat and aching cold as Lady Ateala rested the blade against the soft flesh of his upper arm. The knife began to sink through the meat of his arm with only the pressure of its own weight upon it. Outwardly, Toman was still paralyzed in place; inwardly, he was reduced to incoherent screams of pain. His eyes were open wide, streaming tears, but completely unseeing. There was only the insanity inside his own head as Lady Ateala added the extra pressure needed to push the knife through the bone of his arm as well. She stopped halfway, pausing for a moment.

"You know," she mused, holding the knife immobile in his arm, "you are helpless, and I made sure no sound can escape the room, so I might as well let you serenade me while we play." With her free hand, she freed him from the magic keeping him paralyzed, and she shivered with pleasure as he howled in agony while she finished cutting through his arm.

Esset's hand closed around the doorknob, and the eerie silence shattered as the soundproofing spell broke with the opening door. Esset felt a visceral reaction flood through him. Berserk rage and an incoherent need to defend his brother consumed his intellect. Even as his eyes took in the madness of the scene in the room, his lips were moving. Garbled, liquid syllables that he himself didn't recognize rolled off his tongue and he felt the heat of a summon surround him.

Fiery wings snapped open on his back, but didn't scorch their surroundings. A halo of heat surrounded him but burned nothing, and Esset was suddenly aware of a firm, fiery weapon that had appeared in his clenched fist. Some part of Esset knew that he had summoned the Guardian of Fire unto himself, in part becoming a summon to defend someone he loved who had been rendered completely helpless.

Esset lifted the flaming sword in his hand as Lady Ateala's beautiful eyes flew to the door, her mouth shaping into an "O" of shock. She had no defense that could stand against him: no reason or persuasive ability, no magic strong enough to aid her, and no physical might. He strode towards her, unmerciful, her pleading words barely audible over Toman's cries of suffering.

"No! How did you get past my precautions? How did you even *know*?" Lady Ateala raged impotently. She backed away from Toman's side, then thought to hold her enhanced knife in front of her. With a wave of his free hand, Esset sent a wave of blasting heat towards her. The heat melted the knife in her hand, and she cried out in surprise and pain as she dropped it; the heat hadn't touched her, only her weapon. Soon the lady was pinned against the wall, the flaming sword a scant hairsbreadth from her throat. The summoner's eyes were filled with fire, freezing her in place as surely as her spell had kept Toman paralyzed. Then those eyes flicked away from her, towards Toman as he rolled onto his side, clutching the stump of his arm as his own blood soaked his skin and clothes and the linens beneath him. There was a brief flare of fire, and Toman screamed again as each of his wounds were cauterized—his pain was intensified for the moment, but he now stood a better chance of surviving his blood loss.

"No, please…" Lady Ateala begged as those fiery eyes lit upon her again. She tried to edge to the side, but the white-hot sword point, flickering with flames, followed her. Seeing no mercy in those eyes, she suddenly went calm.

"Very well then," she said, standing straighter and putting her arms down by her sides. "If you will kill me, kill me." She waited, staring him back in the eyes. When the sword point withdrew slightly, she made her move. Hidden in the folds of her dress, she still had another knife, one she always carried concealed on her person. She drew it and her arm arced around—

With a gurgle, her arm suddenly dropped. The Guardian had impaled her throat with the point of his sword. Lady Ateala's eyes were wide in lifeless shock as the heat of the blade reduced her neck to ash; the invisible, consuming heat seared through the rest of her body a moment later, reducing her entire corpse to a faint sooty stain on the wall and carpet.

A second after, the fiery wings and flaming sword, the aura of heat and fire within all vanished, and Esset collapsed to his knees. Reeling a bit, Esset wasn't even sure what it was that he had just done. He hadn't consciously known about the Guardian before summoning it. He certainly didn't remember the incantation anymore. But the thoughts were secondary, almost ignored as they floated through his mind. Esset was too busy struggling back to his feet and to Toman's side.

"Toman! Oh Brightfire, please be okay. Toman, *Toman!*" The scene felt all too familiar; his brother writhing in agony, himself impotent to help. What could he do?

This was the hardest thing he'd ever done; it was almost impossible to think with Toman in this state. Normally, in times of crisis, Toman was the one who was good at thinking under pressure. Now, Toman was the one who needed him, so it was up to Esset to figure it out. Esset stopped his thoughts in their tracks and breathed for a second, calming his mind as much as he could.

Toman needed a healer, and the closest healer was among the Nadra; they may have been useless against the Reshkin, but wounds like Toman had now, he thought, should be within their realm of expertise. But Esset needed help to move him—he found himself strangely exhausted after summoning the Guardian, and he wasn't entirely sure he had the strength to get Toman outside so he could summon a bird to carry them back to the city. Besides, having another Nadra with him would grant him smoother entrance into the city. He needed to contact Nassata, and get her here as soon as possible.

Esset was unwilling to leave Toman's side to get the Nadra himself—he was not leaving his brother undefended again. So, he needed to send them a message. Esset pulled his side bag over his head and emptied it onto the floor. Then he grabbed a corner of Toman's bloodied sheets and tore a strip off. It was difficult tearing the slick red fabric, but he managed to extract a mangled piece and tie it to the strap of his bag. The Nadra would know that the bag and summon were his, see the blood, and come running. He just had to get it to them. He was forced to either leave his brother's side for a few moments or set the house on fire, so he opted for the former. He sprinted to the front door, passing Melanie on the floor, who was holding her head and looking around, extremely dazed— he would worry about her later.

Esset skidded to a stop on the front step and summoned the fire horse. It took him only moments to loop the strap of his bag over its neck and send it running in the direction of the Nadra. Esset went back to his brother's room and only then went briefly into a trance to make sure the horse met the Nadra . The horse practically flew when it ran full speed—it took less than a minute to reach Nassata, and he waited only until he saw them spot the horse before banishing the creature and leaving the bloody call for help on the ground.

Coming back to himself, Esset tore apart the room until he found bandages. The summoner's knowledge of first-aid was sketchy, but at least the bleeding had stopped. Toman was obviously in horrible pain, but Esset frankly didn't trust any of the medicinal items in Lady Ateala's arsenal—after revealing herself as an enemy, who knew what they could be. Hopefully the bandages weren't tainted at all—those, at the very least, he needed. A medic he was not, but Esset managed to at least cover and brace Toman's three wounds by the time the Nadra arrived. He'd left the front door wide open, and the three came in, spears bristling.

"Please, help me," Esset pleaded. Nassata immediately threw down her spear and slithered over to help.

"What happened?" Nassata was shocked by the scene, and no wonder.

"Just help me get him outside, please. I will explain, I will, but we need to get him to your healers." Esset recognized a hint of hysteria in his voice. He was losing his grip on the cool detachment that had allowed him to plan to this moment. Now he was beginning to falter, but he had to force himself to hold it together until Toman was to a healer.

"Out of the way." That was one of the other Nadra, a red-scaled male warrior who put down his spear as well and pushed Esset aside so that he could help Nassata pick up Toman in a way that wouldn't be excruciating to his stump of an arm. Esset found himself staring at Toman's severed limb and wondering if there was any salvaging it. But no—it would take a mage-healer to salvage it, and the Nadra didn't have any of those. It was lost, all too surely.

"Summoner, come on." It was the red warrior, giving his shoulder a little shake, and Esset realized he was probably going into shock. But not yet—he couldn't yet. He snapped back to himself and grabbed the animator's gloves from where they'd been dropped before moving to catch up to Nassata.

"Nassata, I need to fly to your city, can I ask you to come? One of my summons would have to carry you, and it won't be comfortable," Esset requested, an edge of a desperate plea to his voice. As he finished asking, they reached the front step and moved into the street in front of the house.

"Of course," Nassata replied, understanding. With two incantations and two bursts of flame, two giant, fiery birds materialized in the street. Esset climbed up the back of one and the Nadra helped him get Toman secured in front of him. This way, Esset could make sure Toman didn't lose a bandage and bleed out. Nassata, however, was too awkward to ride on the back of the bird—one would have to carry her in its talons.

Both birds took off, but then one swooped down to pick her up. The bird's talons were hot, but they wouldn't burn her. Still, the summon gripped her firmly, and Nassata's whole weight pulled earthward. Nassata clenched her teeth against the pain; her arms would be too wrenched for her to fight for a few days after this. But they got to the Nadran city of Salithsa far sooner than they possibly could have otherwise.

Somehow Esset managed to keep hold on his sanity long enough to get them to the entrance to the underground city. Toman had mercifully lost consciousness sometime shortly after they took off, although occasionally he moaned or reacted to a bit of rough air. The landing was rough too—Esset was completely exhausted and running on fumes at that point. Nassata shouted down the cave entrance for reinforcements; one Nadran sentry emerged and he and Nassata picked Toman up and began carrying him down the tunnel. Esset staggered along beside them; the summoner felt dazed and wasn't entirely aware of his surroundings.

Then the Nadran reinforcements arrived, and Esset was picked up and carried down the tunnel, the group making far better time on Nadran coils than stumbling feet. They went straight to the healer. Esset heaved a sigh of relief when Toman was finally in a bed and under the healer's attention, so relieved that he began to sway on his feet. Nassata took his arm before he could fall asleep upright and led him to another bed.

Esset didn't remember anything after that.

CHAPTER 20

Esset was shocked awake by a nightmare sometime during the night. He couldn't remember a single detail the moment he woke, but the feeling stayed with him. Unfortunately, his memory of recent events wasn't much better. Esset felt his stomach clench and his throat tighten as he frantically looked around the room.

"Whoa! Calm down, Esset, it's all right." Nassata was right beside him and placed a hand on his shoulder, trying to calm him. "Toman's right here." She looked towards his brother to point him in the right direction. Esset saw his brother then, asleep in the bed beside him. Kessa was on the other side of the bed, coiled around a large cushion. She perked up a little when she saw Esset looking at her, but she was clearly there for Toman, not the summoner. And Toman didn't look good. His skin was pale and a bit waxy, and his sleep was obviously drug-induced. But at least he was sleeping quietly, if not peacefully, and he had fresh bandages and clothes. The Nadran healer had looked after him, but there was only so much that could be done without the aid of time or magic.

"He's out of danger," Nassata assured Esset, knowing how bad the animator looked. "Thanks to you, he'll live. He'll get better."

"Oh Brightfire… How did this happen?" Esset buried his face in his hands and tried to get a handle on his emotions.

"Esset, what did happen?" Nassata asked gently, her hand still on his shoulder to comfort him.

"We trusted her…" Esset murmured. Nassata waited patiently for him to explain, and eventually he did.

"I don't know exactly what happened, but it was the healer, Lady Ateala. I, I didn't just trust her, I *liked* her. I thought of her as a friend. I don't know what happened, why it happened, but I'd left him alone with her. I'd done it before and nothing had happened, but this time he had his gloves." Suddenly he looked up, alarmed. Where were the gloves? They had to make sure they were safe, not in the wrong hands.

"The gloves!" Esset exclaimed, but Nassata was already withdrawing them from her braided harness, where she'd been keeping them.

"They're right here," she said, passing them to him. He instantly relaxed.

"Thanks..." he murmured in relief.

"You were in complete shock yesterday by the time we got the two of you down here. We couldn't figure out what the issue was with the gloves until Kessa came and explained it. I've been keeping them safe," Nassata explained.

"Thank you, Nassata. We owe you so much," Esset said genuinely. He was on the verge of an emotional collapse, and he struggled to control himself.

"We are only doing what we can." Nassata squeezed his shoulder to reassure him it was nothing. "Go on with your story." Esset took a deep breath and picked up the narrative again.

"She'd sent me on an errand, across town. When I was on my way back, my clothes jerked all of a sudden, towards the house. It was Toman—it was the only call for help he could manage, I guess, before Ateala took the gloves from him. He trusted her too. But he wasn't well. It was my job to protect him, to make sure he was okay." Esset was getting worked up again, but Nassata forestalled him before he could sink into a full, guilt-ridden tirade.

"Esset, he's going to be okay. Come on now, what happened next?" The teal Nadra coaxed him. Esset was so distraught he missed the steely anger deep in her eyes, the hidden ferocity directed at the one who'd dared hurt her friends.

"I tried to get back to him right away, but Ateala had some kind of magic keeping me away. I got through it, but I took too long. By the time I got there, she'd, she'd taken his arm—" Esset choked and couldn't stop tears from rolling down his cheeks. There was no stopping the flood of guilt, the feeling of failure. Across the room, Kessa gently slipped her hand under Toman's and held it.

"Go on," Nassata prompted gently, her compassion and sympathy towards Esset overpowering her anger at Lady Ateala. She placed a comforting hand on his shoulder.

"When I opened to the door to the room, she'd already... It was already too late. Somehow, I summoned something I'd never summoned before. The Guardian... I don't know how. But I killed her, and then I called you for help." He had failed, at the worst possible time, when he could not have been needed more. His brother had lost an arm, *because of him*.

"Esset." He didn't respond to Nassata this time—the story had been told.

"*Esset!*" She gave him a shake, not to be denied, and this time he raised his brown eyes to her brilliant teal ones.

"Esset, *you saved your brother's life*. Twice. He's alive because of you, and because of you, those gloves aren't going to be used for evil. You did that—you did all you could. She was smart, and she tricked you. She hurt your brother, but he will live— because of you. Without you, he'd be dead, and she'd have the gloves. Do you understand that?" Nassata demanded forcefully. Esset dropped his eyes from hers, and she gave him another shake.

"*Esset!*" When she had eye contact again, she continued.

"Say it with me—he's alive because of you. Say it."

"He's alive because of me." It was a half-hearted statement, said to satisfy her, to get her to leave him alone.

"Good," Nassata said, letting him go and letting him drop his eyes this time. "Now you work on believing that, okay?"

She waited until she got a half-hearted nod from him.

"Okay. Now lie back down and try to get some rest. I'll have some food brought in the morning, it's not too far away. Kessa or myself will always be here if you need anything, and we'll keep watch for you. No one will hurt you here, and they certainly won't get to your brother. Rest." She reached out to him again and this time laid a heavy hand on his shoulder to get him to lie back down.

Esset was in extremely low spirits the next day, although he did lend a hand to the Nadra by helping them hunt the remaining Reshkin. There had been a bit of a resurgence in their population, but nothing huge, and the Nadra made a bigger dent in their numbers than usual with Esset's support. Esset didn't actually leave the room, however; instead he summoned a wolf and used its body and senses to help the Nadra remotely.

Esset had banished his wolf for the day and was stretching after his body's long spell of inactivity when Nassata showed up at his room. She reached through the curtain and beckoned for him to come out. Tilting his head to the side, he obeyed. When he emerged, he found another Nadra, a rust-colored male, beside Nassata.

"I thought you'd want to hear this," Nassata said without preamble. "Terress, please continue."

Terress dipped his head and spoke.

"I've just returned from the human town. There was an uproar when the healer was discovered dead, so I and the other Nadra left there kept our distance. But then…it got quiet. Awfully quiet. We went to investigate, but the first few people either fled before us or were so disoriented that they couldn't remember their own names. A wider search determined that others had suddenly been struck with maladies. One woman we found dead. I came for reinforcements," he explained.

"We just came from the council—it was an easy decision for them to send a relief group. We need the good relations with the town, if nothing else," Nassata added. Esset knew the Nadra were also simply the type to help if they could.

"But what's wrong with them? What happened?" Esset pressed. He'd come to know and like a good number of the townsfolk.

"We don't know," Terress said with a shrug. "There is no sign. One spoke of it being the 'Hand of Bright Hyrishal,' repercussions for the healer's death, but no one looked particularly convinced."

"Do you think…" Esset looked away, leaving the sentence unfinished.

"What?" Nassata asked. Esset steeled himself, feeling obligated to answer.

"Do you think it was Ateala? She had us fooled, after all. What if she fooled them too? What if she…hurt them too?" he asked. The black guilt he felt for Toman's condition intensified as the harm inflicted on the villagers was added to it. How could he have been so blind?

"It's possible," Nassata said, her voice sympathetic. "Hopefully Toman can tell us more about what happened."

"Hopefully." Esset's voice was still bleak.

•

Toman opened his eyes again a day and a half after they arrived in Salithsa. Esset was eating lunch when Toman woke, but it was Kessa who saw his eyes open first.

"Toman!" she exclaimed happily, drawing Esset's attention. Toman immediately tried to move, but Esset had already dropped his food back on his plate and reached out to pin Toman's shoulders to the bed.

"Easy, brother, don't try to move," the summoner warned. Toman had already winced at the pain his attempt had caused, so he didn't argue.

"What—" Toman's voice cracked, his throat bone-dry.

"Ssh." Another late warning. Kessa picked up a mug from the table—it had a long, winding straw poking out the top.

"Here, drink some water. Through the straw now," she said, placing the straw right next to his lips so he could suck through it. A brief drink worked wonders.

Toman relaxed for a moment, then began looking around the room, taking in his surroundings. His mind was foggy, trying to catch up after being asleep too long; then it all came rushing back. He was in pain, in his side, chest, and arm.

"No!" he suddenly exclaimed—he'd tried to move his left arm. There was sensation, as if there were something there, but there wasn't actually anything. There was pain, but his limb was gone. He tried to sit up again, frantic.

"Toman! Don't sit up!" Esset had his hands on Toman's shoulders again, keeping him down. Toman felt the pain in his chest and side—and in his arm, too—as he struggled briefly.

"It's gone," he cried pitifully. It tortured Esset as much to see Toman now as it had to see him in his physical state in the first place.

"I know, brother," Esset said, bowing his head. "I'm sorry." He was suddenly overcome with the need to escape the room—his soul felt black with guilt, and he couldn't stand being in the small room for a moment longer. Toman stopped trying to force himself up into a sitting position, so Esset backed off, removing his hands and standing up. Toman was sweating in the pain he'd caused himself in moving, and Esset couldn't bear to see him suffering one moment longer.

The summoner suddenly turned away wordlessly and escaped the room.

Toman watched him go, wanting to call out to stop him, but the air seemed to stick in his throat. There were too many emotions to deal with, and the pain—he couldn't deal with it all himself. Kessa was there, and she was adorable, but she didn't know him—especially not the way Esset did. Toman's mind was foggy with pain and painkillers both, so it didn't even occur to him to wonder why Esset had left—all he knew was that he wanted his brother beside him.

"Kessa," Toman murmured, even though it was basically unnecessary to say her name to get her attention. "Thank you for being here."

"Of course," the little painted Nadra said. "Is there anything you need?"

"Please, could you bring Esset back?" he requested. She nodded right away and headed for the door. She pushed the beaded curtain aside and saw that he was still just right outside the entryway. She let the curtain fall shut on her tail and put a tentative hand on the summoner's arm.

"Esset? Your brother needs you," she said softly when he looked at her. "I'll wait out here." The rest of her coils slithered out of the room and into the hallway. Esset nodded, but he still didn't say anything as he turned and went back into the room.

Toman had never been great about opening up about how he was feeling, even to Esset. But he knew he needed to talk to his brother, if only to keep from thinking about his arm and panicking or letting the memories of what Lady Ateala had done to him in that brief time from playing over and over in his mind.

"What happened?" Toman asked. "Y'know, after she…" He averted his eyes. "After."

"I killed her," Esset said, looking away too.

Toman relaxed a hairsbreadth and looked back. "But, what *happened?*"

"Well, you must have managed to animate my clothes for just a second—they kind of jumped, so I figured you must be in trouble to do something like that... Anyways, when I opened the door and saw what she'd done, I summoned the Guardian."

"That's a new one," Toman said.

"Yeah...it was pretty powerful, but it sapped a lot of my personal energy, and the conditions I can call it under seem to be pretty limited," Esset semi-explained.

Toman waited, but Esset had nothing more to say. Toman frowned, recognizing that something must be wrong for Esset not to be all excited about a new summon.

"Come on, Esset. This Guardian sounds pretty cool, what'd it look like?" Toman prompted, feigning energy that he did not have. Esset gave him an unreadable look for a moment, and Toman didn't know if he was guessing his bluff or if he was surprised or what.

But Esset answered, so at least there was progress. "The Guardian wasn't like other summons... It was almost like I summoned it inside of myself. I had this huge, flaming sword in my hand, and..." He paused, and for a second, he seemed like his old self. "I think I had *wings*. Y'know, like in pictures of guardian angels? Except fiery. No halo though, that's for sure, but there was this kind of fiery glow around me. I remember the heat, but I didn't feel hot at all. It was bizarre."

"You mean *cool*," Toman corrected him. He still felt the weight of what he'd been through upon him, but for a moment, he was distracted. "Bright Hyrishal, Esset, you would've looked totally scary."

"I melted a knife right out of her hands," Esset put in almost as an afterthought.

"As I was saying: scary. Cool," Toman repeated. He was impressed, and although he didn't quite manage to force a smile in his state, he thought he'd succeeded in lightening the mood for a moment.

"But I was too late," Esset said, suddenly pitching forward and running his hands through his short brown hair. He pulled at the permanently messy mass, wracked with guilt. "Toman, I'm so sorry. I should have known, I should have come sooner, I should have never left, I—"

"Jonathan, you send those thoughts straight to the Darkfires where they belong," Toman said forcefully, lapsing back to using Esset's given name. Now he could read Esset's expression—that one was definitely surprise.

"You saved my life, Jonathan. She tricked us both, and an entire town of people, and more beyond that, no doubt. She used magic, too, small stuff that no one noticed, but stuff that got her what she wanted. There was no way we could have known, not either of us. And you saved my life not once, but twice. You saved me from the Reshkin's venom by bringing me to her, and then you saved me from her.

"Besides, we knew what we were getting into when we decided to go after Moloch," Toman murmured after a moment of silence. "She may not have had his power, but she was exactly his kind of weapon. We're just lucky he thought we weren't worth bothering with… This…time." With a massive sigh, he lapsed back into slumber the moment after he finished speaking, leaving Esset to wonder if Toman's words had still been lucid at the end.

When Toman opened his eyes again, he was absolutely ravenous. He looked around but saw Esset in a deep trance, no doubt helping the Nadra. When he rolled his head to look to the other side, he saw Kessa there. She'd found their sewing kit and was apparently taking it upon herself to fix the shirt that Lady Ateala had destroyed. Somehow the stains had been washed out of it, but repairing the cloth was proving more difficult. There was a rather mangled line of stitches along the tears, but she was intent on getting it right. Toman found himself looking at her face, creased in absolute concentration as she deliberately placed one stitch after another…in the wrong place. It was adorable, especially since it wasn't even his shirt—it had been a borrowed one that he'd worn while sick in bed at the false healer's.

"You don't have to fix that, you know," Toman murmured, his voice still a bit hoarse. She looked up in surprise and poked her finger with the needle.

"Ow! You're awake!" she exclaimed. She put the shirt aside, having forgotten it already. "How are you feeling?"

He opted not to answer. "That shirt should just be thrown out—it wasn't mine to begin with, although I do appreciate the effort," he said instead. Kessa looked over at the shirt.

"Yeah, I guess. I'm not so great at fixing it, either. Your brother made it look so easy," she said, a bit perplexed.

"Yeah, he does that," Toman replied, smiling slightly. "If it helps, I'm not so great at mending clothes either. Passable, but not great. I tease Esset about having lady-hands occasionally, but I make sure not to lay it on him too hard or he won't fix my clothes for me." Kessa had to smile.

Toman shifted and braced his hands against the bed to push himself into a sitting position, only to find himself moving unevenly. It was a shock to the system.

"Here, let me help you," Kessa said, but Toman leaned away.

"It was there. It felt like it was there," he said, disoriented. He looked down, but there was still just a stump where his second arm should have been. Heart racing, Toman let his head fall back into the pillow.

"What?" Kessa asked, withdrawing with a confused look.

"For a second, it felt like my hand was still there. It felt so real," Toman said. Kessa gave him a hug in lieu of knowing what to say.

"It's—" Toman abandoned the false start. "I remember talking with an old war veteran. He'd lost a leg. I remember him saying he had a 'phantom limb.' His leg wasn't there anymore, but he could still feel it." Toman clenched "both" hands again and squeezed his eyes shut.

"Did he ever come to be at peace with it?" Kessa asked.

Toman had to think before answering. "I guess. He learned to live with it, anyways." Toman tried to push thoughts of his missing appendage from his mind—well, mostly, anyways. Using his right hand, he checked on his other wounds.

"I don't think you should be doing that," Kessa said uncertainly.

"They're sore, really sore, but she just cut flesh and muscle." Toman didn't add aloud that Ateala, as sickening as she had been, really had known what she was doing. She'd missed internal organs entirely.

"They'll just take a while to heal," Toman added. His arm

would probably heal into a stump first, but he wasn't going to be moving around much any time soon. He really disliked that thought and wished that his power could work like Esset's so he could escape his body completely for short periods of time.

"I'll keep you company," Kessa promised.

"So's there anything around here that I can eat? I'm pretty hungry," Toman asked.

"Of course! We have some soup keeping warm—I'll go get some for you," Kessa said instantly, her coils already unwinding from their comfortable knot so she could propel herself towards the door.

Toman tried not to think about his phantom limb while she was gone—fortunately she was quick.

"Here we are," Kessa said, reentering the room carrying a bowl of soup. The Nadran guard outside held the curtain aside for her to entire, then let it fall shut on her coils. Looking up to watch her enter, Toman noticed that there were two of his animated soldiers in the room, standing guard. He didn't have that unconscious knowledge of their presence like he usually did, since he wasn't wearing his gloves. Fortunately Kessa distracted him before he could take that train of thought any further. She put the bowl down on the bedside table before studying him for a moment.

"Well, we ought to prop you up so you can eat some of this," she said. "If we go easy, it shouldn't hurt so much." Together they carefully maneuvered him until he was partially upright, at least enough that he could get the food in his mouth without making a mess and swallow the soup properly. Both were quiet while he ate. He hated being fed, but with only one hand, he couldn't hold the bowl himself as he ate, so they compromised—he operated the spoon, but she held the bowl out for him.

Toman didn't like his feelings of helplessness; he was tired of feeling helpless. He'd been bedridden for far, far too long, and he'd ended up in this state from being helpless in the first place.

"Thank you for all this," Toman said when he was done eating. "It can't be terribly exciting for you."

"I don't mind. We owe you much for what you've done. And…well, some of us care about you," she said, ducking her head slightly in the Nadran equivalent of a blush.

"I'm glad," Toman said, hoping his own color wasn't rising.

"Am I interrupting something?" That was Esset, startling them both a bit; neither had noticed the deep inhale and exhale that signaled him returning to himself.

"Brother," Toman greeted him with just the slightest hint of warning in his tone.

"Nice to see you awake and perky," Esset replied with a cheeky grin. Toman was glad to see that his brother was in better spirits.

"Well, semi-upright, anyways," Toman more-or-less agreed. "How goes the good fight?"

"Very well," Esset responded with a nod. "We've been killing every Reshkin we find, but we've been finding a good number of them dead before we even reach them, and without a single mark on them. We're pretty happy to see dead Reshkin, but we're not sure if we should be at least a bit concerned. I mean, if it's a contagion or something..."

Esset tilted his head to the side when Toman shook his head.

"They're all going to die, Esset. The Reshkin are going to go extinct now that Ateala is dead."

Esset blinked at Toman's statement.

"Uh... why?" Esset asked.

"Ateala was pretty talkative while... Well, she was pretty talkative," Toman said.

"I'm going to return this to the kitchen," Kessa put in, holding up the bowl and then ducking out of the room.

Toman felt kind of bad, but he was grateful too, since it was harder for him to talk about it with her there. He watched her go, and there was a bit of a pause; Toman was pretending Kessa's exit was more distracting than it was to buy himself some time.

"Wanna talk about it?" Esset finally asked when the silence stretched.

"Not really," Toman admitted. "It was pretty horrible." The understatement shielded him from the truth.

"Yeah," Esset replied.

There was another silence before Toman exhaled heavily, glanced up at his brother, then looked down at his hand and began speaking.

"She said she was just going to look me over, see how my recovery was coming," he began, trying to school his thoughts carefully so he wouldn't lose his self-control when his memories began flashing across his mind's eye. "She paralyzed me, with little magics. I couldn't have been an easier target. Before I knew what was happening, she had my gloves. I couldn't move. There was nothing I could do. I was completely helpless—"

The dam broke and his self-control dissolved. Esset did all he could; he listened well and spoke little. Whether Kessa had returned, listened from outside, and then gone again only she knew, but it was more than an hour later before Toman had told Esset the entire story and gotten a hold on himself again. Mercifully, sleep claimed Toman again after the ordeal.

Toman had taken to spending his long, bed-ridden days talking with Kessa while she practiced scale-painting on small tiles. On this day, she'd wanted to know his version of how they'd wound up doing what they did.

"And that's why we're traveling the world and honing our abilities to face Moloch," Toman concluded his life story. "Just think, if someone had taken him on a few years ago even, think of all the Nadran lives that would have been saved. Moloch doesn't just do the deeds himself—he fosters such things in others, like Ateala. There are more people like Ateala out there, I'm sure of it, just as I'm sure more atrocities will be committed by Moloch himself."

Kessa sat thoughtfully, tiles momentarily forgotten. She was quiet for so long that Toman spoke again, playfully this time.

"Do you understand, or are you going to give me your little frown again?" he teased.

Kessa smiled, but answered seriously. "I… I understand some. My heart still cries out you should find and keep peace, but…" Kessa's eyes watered and she brushed tears away. "But I remember those the Reshkin killed. That…Ateala killed, I suppose. And I don't know what to think, then." Kessa went quiet, but something about her poise suggested she wasn't done, so Toman held his tongue.

"There is something I don't understand," she finally said.

"What's that?" Toman asked.

"I asked Esset about your religion, and he said that Bright Hyrishal also preached peace. He said to turn the other cheek. To forgive. How does that fit with what you do?" she asked.

"I don't know," Toman admitted with a frown of thought. "Like I've always said, Esset's the religious one. I am too, I guess, but…well, to me, pursuing and stopping Moloch runs deeper than that. It's something that must be done. It's not just morality, it's duty, and…I don't know. I'm not sure I understand it myself. I won't lie, there is a desire for vengeance in there too, but it's far more than that too."

Kessa sighed a small sigh, and when their eyes met, she and Toman both realized they'd become frustrated with the conversation. Before he could be pulled into yet another bout of depression, Toman tried to lighten the mood. He gave her a rueful smile. "How did our conversations become so glum?"

Kessa smiled back. "It must be because you stopped falling asleep halfway through," Kessa teased.

Toman mock-winced. "The truth hurts," he said. "Thanks for keeping me company though. I would've gone crazy by now otherwise—"

Toman's gratitude was interrupted as Esset brushed the curtain aside, took five steps into the room, and faceplanted onto his bed.

"Long day?" Toman asked dryly. Kessa was giggling.

"Lots of walking, no fighting," Esset confessed. Toman studied him and decided that while Esset did look tired, it was nothing compared to some days.

"Haven't found any more live ones?" Toman asked, referring to the Reshkin.

"Just carcasses everywhere. A few here, entire caverns full there… It's creepy," Esset confirmed.

"Good riddance," Toman said.

"I find it disquieting, to be honest," Esset objected. "The loss of any natural species is a bad thing. It's a small consolation that this extinction wasn't of our doing. I just hope there won't be any unforeseen negative impacts on the underground ecology here due to the loss of the Reshkin. I know the changes made to them likely would have brought about the same damages regardless, but still."

Toman could only shake his head at his brother. "Always

complicating something simple," the animator said. "Good riddance."

Toman felt a black mood starting to descend and tried to distract himself. "Why don't we play cards? I've been teaching Kessa, and she's been kicking my butt, so hopefully she can kick yours too," Toman said.

"Bring it!" Esset crowed.

Four hands later, the animator suddenly threw down his cards and leaned back on his pillows.

"I'm done," Toman said spiritlessly.

"What—? You were winning!" Esset objected, unable to avoid seeing Toman's discarded hand.

"Hurray," Toman responded without a shred of enthusiasm.

"Oh come on, Toman. We need to pass the time somehow. Try not to think about it—think about the celebration the Nadra are planning! That'll be fun," Esset coaxed.

"Esset, we've been ignoring the one topic we should be talking about," Toman said with sudden aggressiveness, sitting up and leaning forward with intense brown eyes. Kessa pulled back a little bit, giving them space, but she didn't leave.

"It's not important yet. We can wait 'til you're better," Esset said, avoiding Toman's eyes.

"No, we can't. How am I supposed to fight Moloch with one arm? 'I'm a mage, not a fighter, blah blah blah.' Let's face it, we don't need a handicap like this," Toman hissed.

"Well, you are a mage, and it's not as big a deal thanks to that—" Esset began, but Toman cut him off.

"*As* big," he challenged. "That doesn't mean it's not a big deal. Come on, Esset. You know what a handicap it is to only wear one glove. What am I going to do, leave one glove stuffed in my belt? Gee, that's secure. Really, I—"

He cut off his tirade when Kessa made a little sound. It was a little sound like she'd tried to say something, then abruptly cut the noise off. It was a tentative squeak to gain attention in a room where she'd otherwise been forgotten.

"Aren't you going to make a new arm?" she asked, confused.

Both young men stared at her.

"I...thought you were just waiting for your arm to heal to do it," Kessa said, a little intimidated by the sudden, absolute attention she'd gained. There was a moment of silence and she squirmed a bit.

"No, that couldn't work," Toman finally said, shaking his head.

"Why not?" Esset asked. "Providing no one has the other glove on, you can still use animator magic with one glove. And if the other glove is on a replacement hand, it's more secure. Making it would be a lot more complicated than most of your stuff, but you could probably pull it off. Even if your sense of touch wasn't as good as a real hand's, it would still beat nothing at all, and it might even be sturdier or stronger than your original hand."

"But it's…" Toman's voice trailed off when he couldn't think of any real objection.

"Toman, that could work. Kessa, you are brilliant!" the summoner beamed at her. She perked up a little from her tentative stance.

"I had thought you'd thought of it already, else I would have brought it up earlier. I thought you were just waiting for your arm to heal," Kessa confessed, apologetic.

"No, I hadn't—" Toman began.

"You have to try," Esset interrupted.

"Yeah… I think so," Toman conceded.

"What are you going to make it out of?" Esset wondered aloud, his mind already turning over this new idea.

"It'll have to be sturdy—most fake limbs are made out of wood, aren't they?" Toman asked.

"I think so… but that's usually just a stick leg or something," Esset said. "Metal would be way cooler. Would that be too heavy? I mean, if you animated it, you should be able to work it so it's manageable, right?"

"That would be cool," Toman admitted, his mood getting lighter and more optimistic with each passing second. "I'd have to experiment…" His tone was very thoughtful.

"When do you want to start?" Kessa asked. "I should be able to get you materials to work with."

"Well I'd want to start on simpler stuff, just see if I can make something that would be like an extension of a limb," Toman said. "Just scraps of wood or rock—actually, working with rock would be smartest down here, and it would be a closer simulation of metal. I could test weights and stuff."

"You know, you don't even have to make it an arm," Esset was saying in the meantime. "You could have, like, claws."

The conversation devolved from there.

Drums reverberated through the tunnels, both heard and felt in every corner of Salithsa. The relentless pounding was a primal call to the body of each and every underground denizen to dance in whatever fashion matched their form as the Nadra celebrated the return of peace. Few slept for the three-day duration of the celebration, but for Toman's healing body, that wasn't an option.

"Victorious again!" Esset crowed as he walked into Toman's room and saw his brother awake.

"Won another puzzle game, did we?" Toman asked wryly.

"I don't win them all, but they're *fun*," Esset said, eyes alight. "Although Tseka keeps trying to get me to spar with her. Yeah, right, like being thumped around with a spear butt is fun." Then he spotted the piece of wood on the bedspread.

"Whatcha doing?" Esset asked.

"Just…practicing," Toman said, moving the piece of wood to the floor.

"How's that going?" Esset asked.

"Slow." Toman's frustration was in the clipped word. "It should be possible, and every so often I get far enough that I really believe it is, but… it's just so much more complex than anything I've ever done before. It has to be an extension of myself and able to deliver sensory information back to me. It has to behave so I don't even have to consciously think about it."

"You'll get it," Esset assured him. "But shouldn't you be taking a break? Resting, letting your arm heal?"

"Yeah, probably. I just—" Toman gave a huff. "It's driving me crazy. If I can't manage this, there's no way we'll be able to take on Moloch. Ever. And I have to know. I have to know if that's still something that's going to happen."

Esset looked away. "We might just have to wait to find out," he said.

"I know." Toman rubbed the skin above his stump in irritation.

"You know, after you were bit, there was a moment where I wanted to give up the chase for Moloch," Esset said.

Toman jerked and he flushed, opening his mouth to say something. At a shake of Esset's head, Toman's eyes narrowed and he closed his mouth.

"Let me finish," Esset said. "I was so afraid of what might happen to you. What could still happen to you if we kept on this road. As you're always reminding me, our lives aren't one of the old tales. There isn't always a happy ending. But it's the same as it always is, isn't it? Like after the Baliyan war. The things we saw…"

He trailed off, but Toman held his silence until Esset spoke again.

"Every time one of us has a brush with mortality, we question our path, but we always keep going." Esset squeezed his eyes shut. "This needs doing. Moloch has to be stopped. I don't question that." He opened his eyes again and met Toman's.

"If you decide you still want to chase Moloch, I'll follow you. Just like always."

"Thank you," Toman said, even though it didn't need to be said. Esset just nodded.

"So let's get you better. Once the celebration is over, we can go talk to Sergeant Warthog and tell her we won't be taking jobs until you're healed up, and then go see Mom and Dad," Esset said.

"They'll like that," Toman agreed.

"She'll freak out, seeing you like that," Esset said, suddenly grinning.

"Bright Hyrishal, she'll feed me until I explode." Toman groaned just as Tseka barged in.

"What are you groaning about?" her sharp voice asked from the doorway, but she didn't wait for an answer. "You two spend entirely too much time moping in here. Come on. Toman, Kessa's looking for you. We're celebrating! No sleeping." She slithered over and shoved Esset towards the door, nearly knocking him over.

"Hey!" he protested, but all he got was a poke in the back from her tail.

Tseka was already hauling Toman unceremoniously out of the

bed.

"Hey! Ow! Stop it, I'm moving!" Toman protested until she let him alone—that was only after he was on his feet.

"And don't stop," Tseka warned Toman as he moved very slowly and carefully towards the doorway.

"I won't. Sheesh, you wouldn't know I'd only been on my feet again for a couple days. I can't move that fast," Toman said.

Tseka ignored him. "The kitchen made some of that nasty sweet food you humans like so much, so you better eat it all. *I* certainly won't be touching it." She looked like she was going to give Toman an "encouraging" prod when Kessa poked her head through the curtain.

"You're coming! Good, the kitchen made cake!" she announced. She shot Tseka a wary look but wasn't deterred from going to Toman's side.

"Good, Kessa, you make sure these lazy louts make it to the celebration. No more slacking off," Tseka ordered. Kessa gave a meek nod before the scarlet Nadra slithered away.

"Yeesh," Toman muttered under his breath, and Kessa peered at him.

"She cares, doesn't she? She's scary, but she cares." Kessa looked a little confused.

"Yes," Toman answered simply. Kessa shook her head at the little puzzle of life.

"Oh, Esset, I just remembered," Kessa said. "Orisna says there's a new game for you to try. She seemed sure she'd beat you this time."

Esset grinned wolfishly. "Bring it."

After three solid days and nights of celebrating, the entire city collapsed into sleep for a full day before normal activity resumed and Toman and Esset prepared to leave. Leaving was more difficult than either could have imagined when they'd first stepped foot in Salithsa.

"Hey, I promise we'll try to come back and visit someday," Toman said, hugging Kessa back after she'd launched herself into his chest. It was obviously a one-armed hug, with his empty coat-sleeve stuffed with cloth and propped in a sling to hide the loss of his limb. He had yet to make a working replacement.

"Don't go yet," Kessa pleaded. "You're not better yet, you could stay a while longer..." She looked at him, her brilliant blue eyes watering.

"We're going to see our family," Esset said, even though she already knew that. "We'll be safe, and Toman'll heal up all right."

"I know," Kessa admitted reluctantly, snuggling into Toman's chest. Both of the young men had grown used to the Nadra's tactile inclinations, but even so, it was obvious that Kessa was clinging to him a little longer to delay their departure.

"Who knows, maybe one day, after everything's all over and done with, we could take you on an adventure, see some human cities," Esset suggested cheerfully, trying to brighten the mood in the tunnel. They had stopped to say their last farewells just inside the entrance to the tunnel that led to the city.

"It will be but an eyeblink to us," Nassata added to Kessa, reaching out to her cousin to draw her away from Toman and back to her own side.

"I will miss you both," Kessa said sadly, looking between the animator and the summoner.

"We'll miss you too," Toman responded.

"We owe you much," Nassata said, leaning forward and extending her arm. First Esset, then Toman clasped it in a warrior's grip.

"We owe you as much," Esset professed. "If you ever need us, the sergeant will probably know where to find us."

"And if you need us, you know where we can be found," Nassata responded solemnly. Esset nodded, and they smiled at each other.

"Well, we'd best be going. We'll be traveling the same way we came, and the sooner we get that over with, the better," Esset said. That small, bumpy carriage was boring, and spending days in it... he couldn't wait for it to be over. He was looking forward to seeing his family again, too.

"Bright Hyrishal keep you," Esset said by way of goodbye before turning and heading out the tunnel. Toman was a moment longer, meeting Nassata's and then Kessa's eyes and giving them each a deliberate nod before following his brother. He'd never been good with words.

"Peace be with you," Kessa whispered after them.

Once they were a few paces away, Nassata tugged her cousin's arm and pulled her back towards the underground city. "Come Kessa, let's go back."

Toman knew they'd be fine—he'd left his soldiers with the Nadra, and all the Reshkin were dead anyways. That wasn't why he glanced back to watch them go. Esset looked back too, and not just to see if Toman was coming. They'd both miss the snake-folk. But they had a job to do, and it wasn't done yet. They could look back, but they couldn't linger.

"Blueberries are in season now, aren't they?" Esset asked when Toman caught up with him.

"Maybe?" Toman hazarded—he didn't really keep track.

"Maybe Mom will have pie."

CHAPTER 21

Toman and Esset arrived at the Staggering Tankard early in the morning and ate breakfast while waiting for Sergeant Warthog's usual midmorning arrival.

"Sergeant!" Esset called to her, waving her over. Not that she wasn't heading in their direction anyways—they were both seated at the table always reserved for her.

"Boys," she returned their greeting more conservatively. "The Nadra are faring well again then, I take it?"

"Their problem has been taken care of," Esset confirmed with a nod. Sergeant Warthog drew even with the table and then noticed Toman's state for the first time.

"Had a little trouble, by the looks of it," she commented blandly.

"Yeah, we—" Esset was cut off by a sudden puff of black smoke that burst into existence in the center of the room.

A young man clad in black stepped from the smoke; he didn't press the element of surprise with an attack, but no one present liked the look of him. Sergeant Warthog whirled around, drawing a knife so quickly that it seemed to just appear in her hand.

Esset jumped to his feet, an incantation ready to spill off his tongue. Only Toman didn't move, trapped between Esset and the wall as he was. Not that he wasn't preparing for battle as well—he had touched almost every piece of furniture in the building at some point or another, and he was giving them instructions so that they would become animated at his whim. If this intruder proved hostile, he would find himself fighting every single object occupying the room.

The intruder was young, Toman and Esset's age or younger. He was pale and made paler by the contrast with his black garb. He wore a trim black suit and a sweeping black cape with a high collar. His black hair was pulled tight against his skull by a harsh leather band in a knot at the nape of his neck. Even his eyes were dark; Toman couldn't tell what color they were exactly, but they seemed to be a very dark shade of grey or brown. His expression suggested that he wasn't a very pleasant person, nevermind the fact that he looked like the villain out of any children's tale of heroes versus evil magic. His eyes fell on the sergeant, ignoring the others completely.

"You are the one known as the sergeant?" he asked her, almost disdainfully.

"Who wants to know?" she snarled. He ignored the question in favor of a demand.

"Meet at the eastern side of town. Half an hour." The black smoke lingering in the room suddenly condensed into a puff around him and multiplied. A second later, he was gone.

"Well that was special," Esset muttered darkly. The sergeant, meanwhile, was sheathing her knife and checking all her weapons.

"Wait, you're not going to meet him, are you?" Esset asked, surprised.

"I am," Sergeant Warthog replied evenly. "I think I'll slap him around with the flat of my blade a bit, and then, if he's properly repentant and not a total darkling, I'll hear him out."

"Are you sure that's a good idea?"

"His behavior was unacceptable. I can't have him setting precedent," the sergeant replied shortly, walking away from them towards the bar.

"Okay then, I'm coming with you," Esset said, following her. Toman sighed inwardly and braced himself to get up. There was no way he was being left behind.

"If you like, but stay out of my way," the headstrong mercenary agreed.

"I'm coming too," Toman said, following more slowly.

"You sure that's wise?" Esset asked. Toman glared at him and he subsided. The sergeant ordered a portable meat-pie for her breakfast and ate it quickly before setting off. Late morning found the dusty streets busy with traffic. Carriages, riders, and pedestrians navigated the broad streets easily. Everyone went about their business with a minimum of fuss between the low, simple buildings that made up the town.

Despite the generous amount of time still remaining, Sergeant Warthog set a good pace, and Toman was pale and sweating by the time they reached their approximate destination. When they stopped, Sergeant Warthog gave Toman another look over, her eye much harsher this time.

"You've got more than just a busted arm," she said flatly.

"Yeah," Toman said, not elaborating. He was also breathing a lot heavier than a quick walk through town should have warranted.

"You shouldn't be here," Esset said, his tone slightly sullen. Toman shot him another look, but Esset was pointedly looking away so he "couldn't see it."

"We early?" Esset asked, looking up at the sun. He and Toman had been inside so long that he couldn't track the time quite so easily. He thought they were probably early though.

"Not by much," the sergeant replied. "But he'd better show his skinny little—"

"There he is," Toman said. None of them had expected the black-clad young man to walk right up to them in an ordinary fashion, but that was exactly what he was doing. Sergeant Warthog had her hand on the hilt of her sword and an inch of blade cleared by the time he was close enough to speak.

"I'm sorry," he apologized immediately, his hands raised defensively, placating. The sergeant narrowed her eyes at him.

"Well, this is unexpected," she remarked. She didn't draw the sword any further out, but she didn't let it slide back into its sheath, either.

"I'm really sorry," he apologized again. Esset was still suspicious too, but when he looked the young man up and down, he couldn't help but notice a few other changes. The stranger's boots were clearly dusty, and his clothes were rumpled. His body language had changed completely; there were definite lines of humility in his posture, not the smug superiority that they'd seen before. It was almost as if this were an entirely different person, or...

"I had to approach you like that—people have to think I'm a bad guy. Please hear me out," the young man continued when no one seemed inclined to say anything one way or the other.

"Keep talking, kid," Sergeant Warthog warned, a definite threat in her voice. She kept that inch of steel bared.

"Um, it's kind of a long story..." he started hesitantly. The sergeant's expression made him start talking faster. "My name is Francis Martin, I'm the son of a merchant, but I pretend to be a

Dark Sorcerer so I can be with my true love, Princess Arabella, but I'm really a good guy and not very good at magic and please don't hurt me. Aarabella's been kidnapped and I need help getting her back."

Sergeant Warthog looked the kid up and down before letting go of her sword. There was a little snick as it slid home in the sheath, and the sergeant crossed her arms over her chest.

"I think you need to start at the beginning," she said. "The very beginning of all this." The young man relaxed a little bit when she let go of the sword and took a deep breath. Everyone sensed that this story was going to be an interesting one.

"Well, like I said, I'm just a merchant's son, and Arabella is a princess. Unfortunately, while successful, my father was never hugely prosperous, and Arabella is the seventh daughter of a king. With six sisters ahead of her, the king didn't really want to marry her off, because he didn't want to pay her dowry on top of the other six. He certainly didn't want her to marry a merchant's son... It just isn't done. But we're in love, and she didn't want to be shipped off to a convent, so we came up with a plan. Well, Arabella came up with a plan. Like I said, I have only a little magic, but the little bit I'm good at is illusions. I can only maintain them for about a minute, but it's good for a short bluff. It was Arabella's idea to dress me up and get me to pretend to be a dark sorcerer."

"Dark Sorcerer Francis?" Esset asked skeptically, smirking. It was hardly an intimidating moniker.

"Dark Sorcerer Martin is marginally better," Toman pointed out.

"Um, Dark Sorcerer Zaren, actually. Again, Arabella came up with it," Francis replied.

"Okay then, what next?" the sergeant prompted, shooting Esset a look to warn him to shut up.

"Well, she had me kidnap her when she only had a guard or two with her outside the city. I made some of my best illusions that day, some scary monsters. The guards took their stories back to the castle, telling of a powerful sorcerer who'd taken the princess, and Arabella and I fled. Her plan had worked really well. The king didn't send anyone after her, and no one came after us of their own accord, since the king didn't offer a reward. No one wanted to risk their lives against a sorcerer for a worthless princess—her words, not mine. I don't think she's worthless at all."

That last bit was said a bit defensively, and although Sergeant Warthog kept up her stern, stony demeanor, she found herself a little charmed. This kid wasn't stupid, but he wasn't all that clever either, and he was clearly devoted to this Princess Arabella.

"Anyways, just in case, we traveled through a couple kingdoms before finding a place to settle. There's an abandoned tower that we took over and made our home—after a few renovations. Arabella went into town to get the few things we needed every so often, but she told people that she was under a spell and had to return to her 'Dark Master.' It worked really well for a few years. Then...well, some bandits came across her on her way home yesterday and they kidnapped her, thinking they could ransom her. Please, I need your help getting her back. I don't have much to pay you, but I'll give you everything I have," he pleaded.

"How did you hear about me?" Sergeant Warthog asked. Having evil mages find her—even pretend evil mages—was a potentially serious liability.

"Before we settled, Arabella and I did a little information gathering to make sure we'd be safe. That was when we heard about you, before we took up our disguises and settled in," Francis replied. He seemed a little puzzled by the query.

The sergeant wondered if Arabella had also been making sure that there was someone in the area that she or Francis could run to if something went wrong. Probably. "Very well," she replied shortly.

Francis looked at her hesitantly and a bit hopefully—he wasn't sure if that was a "very well, I'll help" or just an acceptance of his last explanation. "You... You will help?" he asked tentatively.

"We'll help," Esset volunteered. Francis looked at him quizzically; he still didn't know who they were.

"I'm Summoner Esset, this is Animator Toman. I think a few bandits shouldn't be much of a problem. We might even be able to snatch your princess out of there before they know what's happening, and a nice show of force should keep them off your back permanently. Especially if we make it look like you did all of it," Esset said.

"We can keep your cover intact," Toman agreed with a nod.

"Some stone monsters and a couple suits of armor should do the trick, hey? You can do the snatching with birds if they're in the open and save your others in case we need some firepower." Pun intended.

"It'll be trickier if they're hiding in a building or cave," Esset remarked to Toman.

"Any idea where they've got her?" Toman asked Francis.

"I tried scrying, but I'm not very good at it…" he said, head hung low. Esset and Toman didn't dwell on it.

"We're gonna need supplies," Toman pointed out. "We should go back to the castle."

"Castle?" Francis asked, puzzled. "We can't waste time—"

"This'll save time, trust us," Esset assured him. "It's close, and there will be resources we need."

"Flying?" Toman asked with a wince.

"Aye," Esset replied apologetically. More lift-offs and set-downs wouldn't be good for Toman's healing wounds, but speed was clearly needed here.

"Sergeant, are you in, or are you leaving it to us?" Esset asked Sergeant Warthog then.

There was a pause before she finally caved. "I'm coming," she said, uncrossing her arms to prop her hands on her hips. Toman and Esset both grinned.

"Fair enough," Esset said. He chanted a particular incantation twice. A pair of massive fiery birds burst into existence before them, both mantling fiercely at first before subduing to Esset's will and standing calmly.

"Okay, welcome to Summoner Esset's Aerial Transport Service. Please mind your mount's beak and pinions; contact with either aspect of the bird could result in nasty burns. Sit in front of the wings with your weight on the bird's neck." Esset delivered the monologue in a uniformly cheerful tone as he gave Toman a leg up onto their bird.

"We haven't even started this thing, and I'm already doing things I'm too old for," the sergeant muttered under her breath, remembering her previous flights on stone mounts. Francis had actually started clambering up the bird's neck first. Sergeant Warthog was only a couple moments behind him.

The moment they were mounted, the birds launched into the

air. Pumps of their fiery wings sent them upwards with lurching jolts. Esset winced empathetically as Toman braced himself and bent over at the pain the rough flight caused. Fortunately their mounts' motions evened out once they reached a sustainable altitude; long glides were interspersed with swoops, lifts, and dives as the birds slipped from thermal to thermal and the scenery passed below.

Esset could see the castle as they approached, but he knew Francis and the sergeant would only see an empty patch of land. Esset kept his eye on the two, watching their expressions as they studied the "featureless" landscape below as they descended—and then the surprise when the walls of the castle abruptly appeared around them when the bird's feet touched the ground.

"Whoa!" Francis exclaimed suddenly—the sergeant started in surprise as well, but she bit her tongue. She, at least, had more practice at hiding her reactions.

Their mounts landed swiftly with a surprisingly gentle touch-down. Toman was well-used to Esset's summons, so when the bird crouched to lower its neck closer to the ground, he knew to brace himself. When the bird vanished, it was only a couple feet to the ground, which wasn't too bad if one was prepared. Esset purposely made his and Toman's bird vanish first for that reason. Sergeant Warthog and Francis were able to watch them and at least try to mimic the pair's movements. Francis staggered forward and windmilled a bit before the sergeant grabbed his collar to stabilize him. She let go as soon as he had his balance again, and he mumbled an embarrassed thank you. His near spill kept him from noticing the stone mastiff approach.

"Greetings, Master. How can I be of service?" Arxus asked.

Francis stared at the stone creature nervously after glancing uncertainly at everyone else. Toman and Esset, of course, were totally used to the animated statue, but the sergeant had never actually seen the castle. She'd known, at least approximately, where it was, but it had never been visible to her, and she'd certainly never been inside.

"We'll need supplies for four for a few days. We'll be flying, so keep it light," Esset replied. The mastiff didn't look at Esset, but since Arxus had been ordered in the past to treat the summoner's orders as if they were Toman's, he nodded and would obey. Arxus was the kind of creature to follow an order to the letter, but not necessarily in spirit. In a way, that was to be expected of a creature that was animated but not necessarily alive.

"That's—" Francis started, pointing at the stone dog. They waited for a second for him to continue, but he appeared dumbstruck.

"Francis, Sergeant Warthog, this is Arxus. He's... Well, he's the castle," Esset explained. It was an adequate explanation for the sergeant, who knew most of the story, but Francis looked a little confused. Since it was somewhat irrelevant to him, Toman and Esset didn't bother explaining further.

"Well, Sergeant, you're the senior officer here. What're your thoughts?" Toman asked. He was looking a little pale, which wasn't at all lost on Sergeant Warthog.

"I think I'm too old for this," she grumbled. "You boys take the lead, and I'll lend a voice if I think you're missing something. You know your own skills better than I do, so I'll leave this mostly to you. For now, we should take this inside and sit down. I want to talk to the two of you alone for a minute too and get a quick briefing on your last job."

"Of course," Esset replied. They started to walk towards the keep, and the massive wooden doors swung open to admit them without any apparent order or aid.

The hall glowed with majesty, each torch and chandelier placed to illuminate perfectly every tapestry and relief carving adorning the walls while still accenting the throne-like seat at the end of the room and the portrait that hung behind it.

Francis was all gape-jawed, which gave Toman, Esset, and the sergeant a chance to converse without him listening in. Three plush chairs waddled over to huddle together so they could sit down while they talked. Francis wandered a bit into the hall to admire the tapestries.

"Impressive place you've got here," Sergeant Warthog commented.

"Thanks," Toman said. He didn't elaborate, since this wasn't the conversation they were there to have.

"Okay then," the sergeant said, taking charge of the discussion. "First, Toman. If this weren't obviously time-sensitive and if I had someone else to take this job, you wouldn't be involved. You look like you're two heartbeats to passing out."

Yeah, that sounds about how I feel, Toman thought, but instead he said, "I'll be fine. I can take a back seat on this one, or at least a distant one. I don't have to be right in the middle of things to animate—that's just best for good reaction times if my creations need new orders. For something like this, I should be able to keep a good distance away. I can animate things to participate and keep out of the way myself. Getting there will be the worst of it for me." Sergeant Warthog narrowed her eyes at him—he wasn't fooling her, but both of their statements were true, so he was going along even if she disliked it.

"Okay, tell me what happened with the Nadra," the sergeant ordered. Esset summarized the entire ordeal in under five minutes, including the extent of the damage Toman had taken. It was a little glossed, but the sergeant was good enough at listening to briefings to get the full picture. She knew how close Toman had come to dying—twice. And it explained a lot about their condition and behavior now.

"The both of you are lucky to be alive," she warned them. "Just remember, this is what comes of messing with Moloch— except with him personally, it'll be ten times worse."

"We know," Toman replied, rock steady. For just a moment, Sergeant Gretchen Warthog's gaze flickered away from his. She was unnerved by his gaze. Yes, they did know what they were getting into, and not only were they prepared to look death in the eye, they knew what it meant to do so.

"That's why we're going to lay low until Toman's healed. Well, we will after this now," Esset amended.

"We probably won't even get paid for this," the sergeant grumbled, looking over at Francis, who was admiring a tapestry at the other end of the hall.

"Yeah, but look at him. He's pathetic. We have to help him," Toman pointed out. The sergeant *harrumphed* but didn't contradict him.

"Well then boys, you ready to rescue a princess?" she asked. The three of them exchanged looks for a second, then busted out laughing simultaneously. Like a traditional fairy tale, this wasn't.

"Oi! Martin!" Sergeant Warthog shouted to the young man. *At least she called him by his last name*, Esset thought. That indicated that she at least respected what he was trying to do. Francis hurried over, and they commenced planning. Half an hour later, they were in the air again.

"Darkfires take it, I was hoping for something more open," Toman cursed. They'd just found the bandits holed up in a large cave. Snatching back the princess would have been easy if they'd been in a field or canyon or under any open air at all—Esset could have simply had one of his fiery birds swoop down and snatch her up before the bandits knew what hit them. In a cave, the princess was that much more vulnerable to being used as a hostage.

"So we all were," the sergeant responded. "But we prepared for this too. We all know our parts. Let's do this." The three young men nodded and got into place.

"**Foolish thieves**." Toman was hiding at the mouth of the cave with a funny contraption that looked like a metal cone. When he spoke into it, it amplified his voice—and he was bellowing to begin with. He was also having a grand time with his allotted job. Francis sat in stony silence, letting the bandits assume that he was using magic to speak instead of deigning to speak with his physical voice.

"Return what you have stolen." Toman demanded.

Just as he finished speaking, the "Dark Sorcerer" and his "minions" suddenly "appeared" in the cave entrance. In reality, Francis had used his illusion magic to briefly mask their approach and then dropped the false image when they were in place. Francis and his "minions" needed no help looking fierce, however. Toman had animated three massive gargoyle-like quadrupeds for them to ride. They snarled silently and pawed the ground menacingly, leaving shallow furrows in the stony floor. Astride the lead beast was Francis, in all his black-clad, pasty-skinned glory. Somehow, he was actually managing to look somewhat menacing atop his fierce steed.

To either side of him were mounted matching suits of armor. Inside one suit was Sergeant Warthog—the other was simply animated metal borrowed from Toman's castle. Altogether, they made a fierce sight. They were all hoping to get the princess back without having to fight, but those wickedly curving claws and fangs on the stone beasts weren't all bluff.

Meanwhile, Esset was hiding behind rocks and slowly making his way around the side of the cave so he could get behind the bandits. At best, he would be able to extract Arabella with a fiery horse and a quick exit. At worst, he would be in a better tactical position to send some kind of fire creature into the fray if it came to that. Given the terrified expressions of the bandits at the moment, it was looking like it might not be necessary.

"You will pay for your hubris, puny men!" the voice bellowed. "Return my prize to me now or suffer the consequences!"

For a moment, it looked like their plan would work flawlessly, and the bandits would turn over the princess without any fight at all. Then the leader managed to regain his courage and rally his men.

"You bluff!" he yelled back. He waved a hand at one of his men to get him to grab Arabella and draw a sword on her threateningly.

"Bluff? You will pay for this insolence!" Toman roared into the voice amplifier. The stone beast with just the suit of armor lunged forward. It snatched up the nearest bandit in a clawed hand and raised it up into the air. The man screamed, a high-pitched squeal of terror, and uselessly battered his sword blade against the creature's stone arm. The gargoyle snapped at the man's face menacingly and shook him like a doll. The man dropped his sword and it clattered towards his mates. They drew back as if it were a poisonous snake. The gargoyle crashed back down to the ground and pinned the bandit to the ground under one gargantuan foot, its claws scraping the rocks gratingly. The bandit was slightly flatter under its weight, but he was otherwise undamaged.

"Stop! Move again and she is dead!" the bandit leader frantically ordered.

"Who is bluffing now?" Toman roared. "Know this—I am Dark Sorcerer Zaren, and you know not the territory into which you have wandered. This is your last warning: return my property or I shall destroy each and every one of you. If you damage my possession, death shall be the least of your fears."

Despite the seriousness of Arabella's situation, Toman was having far too much fun. In fact, that shred of seriousness was all that was keeping him from busting out laughing and ruining the entire thing. Not that this was a bluff—far from it. Still, they were hoping to avoid bloodshed. Meanwhile, Esset was almost halfway around the cave, level with the bandit leader.

"What kind of guarantee do we have that you won't kill us anyways?" the bandit leader shouted back. He looked worried— very worried, and his fear was legitimate. After all, Dark Sorcerers weren't exactly known for keeping their word.

"I will give you this guarantee only: return my possession in the next minute or you will all die. I can replace any possession I choose, but your lives are irreplaceable to you." Toman managed to growl menacingly while still amplifying his voice. It was quite intimidating.

The whole thing was a bit melodramatic for Esset's taste, but it was coming across as genuine to the bandits—at least half of them immediately threw down their various weapons and raised their hands in the air. The rest of them looked around at their comrades and quickly followed suit, the bandit holding Arabella included. Arabella immediately began running forward, but she had to pass the leader, and he snaked an arm out to grab her. She shrieked in surprise as he gained a harsh enough grip on her arm to bruise.

Esset was close enough—the simple syllables of the incantation rolled off his tongue and a fiery wolf materialized behind the bandit leader. The summoner didn't anticipate Arabella's next move, however. She balled her hand into a fist and punched the man square in the mouth. She wasn't strong enough to do serious damage—she was still a relatively small woman— but she startled everyone, including her captor, and he let go of her in surprise. The flaming wolf lunged and snapped its jaws around the bandit's now-empty outstretched hand. The bandit screamed in pain as his hand was simultaneously burned and crushed in the creature's jaws. The wolf vanished within a moment, but the damage remained.

Princess Arabella ran right up to the feet of Francis' gargoyle and flung herself onto the ground before him. She shook and wept so hard that Toman was worried that the woman had been permanently damaged by the experience. Then again, she had mustered up the spirit to punch the bandit leader. Was she *this* good of an actress?

"My lord, please forgive me my absence!" she wailed. "These

men stole me away—I never would have dreamed of stealing myself away from you! Have mercy, my lord, please!" She groveled in the dirt as Sergeant Warthog dismounted and walked woodenly over. Then the sergeant picked the princess up and unceremoniously slung her over one shoulder.

"You okay?" the sergeant murmured, almost inaudibly, to the princess.

"Fine," the princess peeped back, equally quietly.

"You are foolish, puny men," Toman roared. As he spoke the armor-bearing gargoyle reared up and clawed the air, freeing the bandit that had been trapped under its claws but menacing the rest of them. The bandits drew back, and some began pleading for their lives. Meanwhile, Esset was using the distraction to sneak back towards the rest of the group. The giant stone beast lunged forward and swiped at the air, causing the bandits to scramble back. Toman was fairly certain that they all thought they were about to die. He let them think that for a few moments before putting their fears to rest. Sort of.

"You are fortunate, you imbecilic meat-sacks, that I have other, more pressing matters to attend to. You may keep your lives, this time. If I grow bored later, perhaps I will seek you out for my entertainment," Toman added, making his tone almost bored. Francis and the sergeant turned their beasts away a moment before Francis put up an illusion of their absence, so they seemed to simply vanish. The other gargoyle menaced the bandits a moment or two longer before lunging out of the cave after the others. In that time, Esset had snuck past the illusion as well, leaving the bandits completely alone. In reality, Esset paused at the mouth of the cave so he and Toman could mount the gargoyle-like stone beast before all three of the beasts carried the princess and her rescue party away.

"Hey Esset," Toman said as soon as they were out of earshot—that wasn't difficult, since the bandit leader was still raising a fuss over his injuries.

"Yeah?" Esset responded, leaning into his brother's back to hear and be heard better.

"We just rescued a princess!" Toman laughed back.

"I know! I doubt this story will ever end up in the tales!" Esset laughed too. It was all totally absurd, really. The old tales were totally formulaic, and they definitely hadn't followed the formula. Yet at the same time, rescuing a princess did make them feel like a couple of giddy little boys living out a tale of heroes and dragons, good and evil. This little incident restored their faith in the world— just a little bit.

"Imbecilic meat-sacks?" the sergeant stated skeptically. Esset howled with laughter and almost fell out of his chair. They were back in the castle, in a small room sporting some comfortable chairs and a card table that they were seated around, having a bite to eat. After leaving the bandits far behind, they'd stopped briefly to make sure Arabella was okay and wait for the sergeant to climb out of the uncomfortable suit of armor. They'd introduced themselves to the princess but waited until they'd reached Arxus to give her the whole story. By then it was evening, and Toman and Esset had offered to put up Francis and Arabella for the night. At the moment, they were razzing Toman for the bits of his performance that they perceived to be overdone.

"I can't believe you used the word 'hubris,'" Arabella put in. "I'm fair certain they didn't know what it meant."

"Haha—I can see them now! 'Please, tell me what that means so I can avoid doing it again!'" Francis joked.

"Hey, that one was all Esset. When we planned the first bit, he said to say that!" Toman said, pointing at his brother.

"Oh come on, who doesn't know what hubris is?" Esset said.

"Not everyone likes to be up to their ears in religious literature, Esset," Toman pointed out. "And you don't find that word anywhere else."

"Nonsense," Esset huffed, pretending to be snooty about it. Only the glint in his eyes gave him away.

"Regardless, I'm sure they're still shaking in their boots," Francis put in proudly. "We owe you a great debt."

"Indeed we do," Arabella agreed, snuggling into her beau's side. "Thank you for helping this lug come get me."

"Lug?" Francis put in woefully before Toman and Esset could respond.

"Loveable lug," Arabella amended, sneaking a kiss onto the tip of Francis' nose. He was entirely appeased.

"It was nothing," Esset interjected, shifting awkwardly in his chair and deliberately looking away from the couple.

"Don't worry about paying us anything," the sergeant put in. She was in the business of favors, after all, and she knew that a favor could be worth more than any payment. Not that she expected to ever call in a favor on these two, but one never knew.

"Thank you so much. You are too generous," Arabella thanked them sincerely.

"Yes, thank you," Francis echoed. "I don't know what I would have done without you three." The rest of them knew that he probably would have gotten himself killed. Arabella too, probably. But none of them said it—he probably knew it already too.

"Well, it's been a long day—more than one day, for Francis and me. If no one objects, I think we should retire for the night." Arabella got to her feet and the rest of them rose only a moment behind her. Everyone bade their good-nights, and the princess and the merchant's son departed to their room.

"I should be heading out too," Sergeant Warthog said once the pair were gone. Toman was slowly sitting back down, trying to hide a wince as he did so. Both Esset and the sergeant noticed anyways, but they pretended not to.

"I'll show you out," Esset offered, stepping forward. "I know this place can be a maze."

"It might be small for a castle, but it's still plenty large," the sergeant agreed, accepting his offer. As it turned out, she had more than one motive for getting him to come along, but she waited until they were a ways down the hallway before speaking.

"I know you two are set on catching that mage, but I can't see you being okay with how things have turned out for Toman recently."

"No," Esset conceded, avoiding eye contact.

"I trust you've been giving this particular trajectory of yours some thought?"

"Of course," Esset replied, slightly defensive. He looked at her then, but only very briefly, with barely a glance.

"Just remember that you don't have to go after Moloch. Revenge is a dumb reason—" Esset tried to say something, but Sergeant Warthog forestalled him. "I know that's not why you're doing this, let me finish." She waited for a nod before continuing.

"And it isn't your responsibility to go after him either. I know you both feel it is, but there's still plenty of good you can do in this world without going there. You have to decide if this is worth your lives. I know you both think you've made that decision already, but you need to re-examine that choice and make sure you're sure.

"I hate to say this, but going after him will probably cost you your lives, or more, without any guarantee that you'll take him down. Plenty of powerful people have tried to get the better of him before and made not so much as a mark. Now, I've agreed to help you two if that's what you want, but… I'm asking you to reconsider. Don't answer me now—give it some thought. Promise me you will, and promise that you'll talk about this with Toman."

The sergeant physically confronted him then, forcing him to look her in the eye until he nodded.

"Good. Now, the main hall is just through that door, yes?" Sergeant Warthog pointed at the door up ahead, and Esset nodded.

Sergeant Warthog turned to go, but suddenly stopped.

"Oh, I nearly forgot. This came for you and your brother a week or so ago." The Sergeant pulled a thin, slightly crumpled envelope out of her vest pocket; it was marked with her courier's address, but had their names on it.

"Thank you," Esset said, curiosity piqued.

"I know the way out from here. Get some rest—you look like you need it. I'll see you two when you get back." With that, the sergeant resumed her quick pace, leaving Esset behind. Esset let her, slowing to a stop instead.

"Bright Hyrishal keep you." He automatically spoke the farewell at her departing back. She just lifted a hand to wave backwards before vanishing through the door.

Intrigued, Esset pulled the envelope from his pocket and opened it.

Jonathan, Toman,

Trouble at home. Please come.

Dad.

CHAPTER 22

Home.

Toman and Esset landed before the city gates to briefly check in with the guards before walking towards the Essets' home. This was Sedina, the capital city of Symria, a small kingdom that shared a border with Namara, where the Staggering Tankard kept shop. They both forgot their fatigue and Toman forgot some of his pain as they walked quickly down the streets to their childhood home.

Esset nearly ran the last few steps, so he was the one to tap on the door. Mrs. Esset answered the door, and she immediately flushed and beamed and flew out to greet her boys.

"Ed! Ed, our boys are here!" she shrieked. Esset was closer, so he was attacked with a massive hug first. Esset had a couple inches on his mother, but Mrs. Anita Esset's torso-crushing hugs were legendary. Mrs. Esset wasn't a very tall woman, but she made up her mass sideways. As usual, she wore a plain dress and the floral apron that she was rarely seen without.

Mr. Edric Esset was thin as a rake, but despite the few extra creases on his face and the spreading grey hair at his temples, he was looking well. The scholar was only a few steps behind his wife, but he couldn't greet his sons properly until they actually came into the house, given the small size of the entryway. He was beaming as he looked over his spectacles and down an overly long, thin nose at them. And he was always looking down—Esset came closest to his height, but still failed to meet it by a couple inches.

Mrs. Esset suddenly spotted Toman's arm in the sling as she pulled away from that first hug, and Esset found himself abruptly shifted aside and completely ignored by his mother as Mrs. Esset started fussing over their unofficially adopted son. Her eyes were wet as she hugged him very delicately.

"Good to see you, son," Mr. Esset greeted Esset, standing beside him and giving him a one-armed hug around his shoulders.

"You too, Dad," Esset said back. Both of them were watching Mrs. Esset and Toman as she made a large deal over the latter's state while also shuffling him towards the living room and into the comfiest chair there. There was much to be said between the two men, but little need to say it. Right then, it was enough for all of them that they were home.

Esset had intended to ask about his father's letter immediately, but he found himself taking a moment and just appreciating the feeling of home. Mrs. Esset was the kind who loved her creature comforts, and as a result, the house was always cozy and welcoming and there was always a large surplus of food to be eaten. It was a miracle that Mr. Edric Esset was still as thin as he was—that any of them were less than rotund.

"Come on, son," Mr. Esset finally said when Mrs. Esset had bustled off to the kitchen to prepare snacks. Esset flopped onto a chair while Mr. Esset sat more sedately on a couch and adjusted his glasses.

"So what was with the letter, Dad?" Esset asked. "I'm not sure I'd prefer the tome Mom would have written, but your note wasn't very enlightening."

"For a few weeks now, there have been attacks across the city. People have been vanishing. The city guards are stumped. I hate putting this on you boys, especially with everything that's happened—" Mr. Esset's eyes locked on Toman's injured arm.

"Toman might be injured, but I'm fine, I'll help," Esset said immediately. Toman just frowned.

"I'll help too," Toman said just as Mrs. Esset reentered the room with a plate of sandwiches and cookies.

"You're going to eat good food and get good sleep," Mrs. Esset said in her best Because-Mother-Says-So voice.

"Mom—" Toman began to object.

"Listen to your mother," Mr. Esset said. "We'll hear all that's happened and see how you're doing tomorrow." Toman frowned again but fell silent. Esset avoided looking at him.

"Does no one have any idea who's behind the attacks?" Esset asked.

"We're not even sure it's a 'who,'" Mr. Esset said. "They look a lot like animal attacks." A crease formed between Esset's eyebrows. Mr. Esset shook his head.

"But really, there's nothing to be done tonight. First thing tomorrow, we'll go to the city guard headquarters. They'll have all the particulars. Tonight…we'll just put aside what worries we can tonight, and you two can catch us up," Mr. Esset said. A long silence bespoke Esset's reluctance to let the topic go.

"Come, tell us what's happened," Mrs. Esset coaxed.

Esset started his monologue from the last time they'd visited their parents: several uneventful jobs before they'd met Nassata. Mrs. Esset fussed happily in the kitchen, planning meals and preparing even more snacks to stuff her family with. Even from the kitchen, she listened, and both she and Mr. Esset kept quiet while their son spoke.

Esset had only just begun describing Salithsa and their Reshkin problem when Mrs. Esset returned with food and caught Toman head-bobbing as he tried to stay awake.

"Enough!" she exclaimed, bouncing to her feet. "Toman, it's time you got some rest. I'm sure Esset can tell us the rest, or you can tell us in the morning." When she patted her hands against her apron, a little puff of flour *poofed* outwards. Toman waved away her help as he got to his feet.

"Okay, okay," he said. "I'm sure Esset can tell you everything." He walked normally, if slowly, towards the bedroom with Mrs. Esset in tow, offering everything from bedtime snacks to extra blankets to make sure her boy would be taken care of.

"I'm good, Mom, no thanks, Mom," came the mumbled replies.

Esset nibbled on a cookie while waiting for her to come back. He couldn't help but wonder if Toman had chosen his moment to excuse himself. Esset also wasn't sure if he was thankful for Toman's absence or wishing he'd come back.

As soon as Mrs. Esset returned, Esset told them about the Reshkin biting Toman. His mother sat down next to Esset then and wrapped her arms around him. Mr. Esset pursed his lips and a crease deepened between his eyebrows as he listened, but he still didn't interrupt. When Esset told them about Ateala, both parents shot multiple, worried glances towards Toman's room. Esset found it to be a relief to get the narrative off his chest and over with, but he still felt ashamed to tell his parents that any of it had happened at all.

"I'm so sorry I couldn't protect him," he finished, throat tight.

"Oh honey, you did," Mrs. Esset comforted him, cuddling him

as though he were still ten years old and not over twice that. "You did protect him."

"You boys are strong, Jonathan," Mr. Esset said to him. "We know you're both strong enough to keep coming home to us."

"You're home now," Mrs. Esset reminded Esset. "Just rest now, we'll take care of you."

"That's a relief," Esset admitted. He knew better than to think everything would be okay just because they were home, but just for tonight…he believed it anyways.

"Good. Now, I think we've all stayed up late enough. Time to go to bed," Mrs. Esset said.

"I'm not ten anymore," Esset reminded his mother fondly, teasingly.

"Tsk. Neither is your father, and I still have to remind him to eat and sleep most of the time. He'd spend all his time with his nose in a book otherwise," Mrs. Esset complained happily, rousing her menfolk and ushering them to their respective bedrooms.

Esset jolted awake as a large crash sounded next to his head. He bolted upright in bed and blinked frantically, adrenaline working to clear his muddy thoughts but failing. Toman sat on the bed across from Esset's, head in one hand, his stump dangling uselessly.

"What?" Esset asked muzzily. Then he spotted the wooden arm on the floor next to a knocked-over stack of books. *Ah.*

"I have HAD it," Toman growled. He looked up at Esset, eyes burning with anger. He tore his hat off his head, mangling the top of the floppy fabric in his fist. He almost threw it on the floor, then reconsidered and shoved it roughly back on his head.

Esset swung his feet to the floor and picked up the discarded attempt at a new arm.

"Sorry for waking you up," Toman muttered, still sounding more angry than sorry. Esset yawned.

"S'all right. Almost morning anyways. Did you sleep?" Esset asked. If Toman had, it hadn't been restful, judging by the dark circles under his eyes.

"Too much. I should be getting this arm made," Toman said.

"That'll be hard with your arm still sore. Maybe you should take a break, rest up for a bit," Esset suggested.

"I've been resting," Toman retorted.

"We have to wait until you're healed completely before we head out again anyways," Esset reasoned with a shrug. "And that will take weeks yet. You're not getting anywhere with this now, but if you just relax and ruminate on it, maybe something will come to you. Practice some other things, maybe. But right now, it's just going to take longer for your injuries to heal if you keep prodding at them like you have been."

"I hate being injured," Toman hissed vehemently.

"I know," Esset sympathized. "But that doesn't change the facts."

Toman exhaled loudly, his posture relaxing at least a bit. He nodded—he knew that, but he didn't have to like it. "I just feel like I'm wasting time," Toman vented a bit, but without the same degree of vehemence as before.

"I know," Esset said again. "But there's nothing pressing us to get back out there right away. We agreed to wait until we were strong before going after Moloch, remember?" Esset waited for Toman to nod before continuing. "So, rest. Heal, and get stronger again. You don't have to have your new arm ready for the second you're healed enough to head out again."

"I guess," Toman finally admitted, although he still didn't like it.

"And Toman..." Esset began, but then he let the words trail off. He wasn't sure it was a good time to bring this up. Then again, he wanted Toman to have plenty of time to think about it.

"What?" Toman prompted him when he didn't continue.

Esset sighed. Well, he had to bring it up at some point anyways. "Just... give some thought to what I have to say. Promise?" He didn't really wait for Toman's response before he continued. "Remember that this isn't something that we have to do at all—we don't have to go after Moloch. We can still do good in this world—perhaps, in the grand scheme of things, even more other good things—if we don't go after him."

"What?" Toman exclaimed, shocked. Esset could see the hint of betrayal in his eyes at the mere suggestion. "Esset, stopping

Moloch is something we—I—have to do! You know that! Aren't you with me on this?"

"Of course!" Esset snapped so quickly there was no way that Toman could doubt the sentiment. "You know that." That was a reprimand, no denying it, but this one Toman accepted. "But I want you to think, Toman, and not just act. I want you to be sure that this is what you want. You and I both know that one or both of us could die trying to stop him. If you want to go after him, I will be with you every step of the way, but I want you to be *sure*."

"I'm—" Toman began, but Esset cut him off.

"Toman, just think on it." Esset was far more subdued now. "Get better, keep working on your arm. We don't even have to talk about it again. You know I'll follow you no matter what you decide, but just think on it. Okay?"

Toman was taken aback by the fire in his brother's eyes, but after a long moment, he nodded.

Having said his piece, Esset withdrew from the room, fairly certain that Toman would keep his word. He'd think on it, and even if his decision remained the same, that would be a good thing.

"Ah, Jonathan, there you are," Mr. Esset said when Esset stepped into the hallway. "Are you ready to go?"

Esset glanced back at the bedroom, but "yeah" was all he said. He saw his father notice his tone and choose not to say anything as they grabbed their jackets.

"Jonathan!" his mother called as they were about to step out the door. They paused and waited for her to come bustling up the hallway.

"I packed lunches. And here's your breakfast." She pressed fried egg sandwiches into their hands. "Don't forget to eat! I know how you two get when you're working. Take care of each other."

"Yes, Mom," Esset said long-sufferingly, accepting the non-optional package and tucking it in his bag.

"Thanks, hun," Mr. Esset kissed his wife and the two men escaped to Sedina's cobbled streets.

Esset looked in the university's direction but it was hidden behind the tall roofs of the modest homes that cramped the narrow streets. He could, however, see the royal castle that the university nestled against, its fortifications towering over the city.

"So what's been going on at the university?" Esset asked as

they left the house behind.

"Hm... The usual, mostly," Mr. Esset began. "Korf is away, tracking a rumor that there's a traveling merchant with a rare scroll in the next town over. Haesher's daughter is getting married, and he's still in a tiff about the soldier who courted her." He lifted a hand to wave to a smiling neighbor.

"I thought they'd managed to convince him being a soldier was okay?" Esset asked.

"They had...until Haesher found out that the soldier's father was born on the Islands."

Esset winced. "And now Haesher thinks he's an Islander spy." Haesher was notoriously paranoid. A pair of children darted past, shrieking and giggling madly in play.

"And the drama continues," Mr. Esset actually looked rather amused by the whole situation. After all, the Islands were trade partners with Symria.

Esset shook his head. "Speaking of paranoia, what's up with Forris? Last I heard, a maid accidentally let a cat into his lab and it went after his test rats." Esset wondered if Forris had managed to get the maid fired. He hoped not; it was an innocent enough mistake.

"Forris...went missing. He was one of the first, actually. We haven't found his body, but he's not the only one." Mr. Esset looked away and Esset went silent. Forris had always had many radical ideas, and his paranoia, like Haesher's, had always been a source of drama and entertainment, but Esset had liked the man. Sedina's university had collected an eclectic assortment of rather brilliant scholars, and Forris had been among them.

"What about his work?" Esset asked after a long silence.

"The church officials still want it destroyed, but we're trying to get his research archived. After all, he revolutionized the study of healing. Who would have thought of generating and curing disease in animals and using the results to cure ailments in humans? Brilliant. Sure, results were only repeatable when magic healing was used, but it's only a matter of time before some of the results can be used to aid herbalism as well."

"I don't think the church liked his idea of using magic to augment humans with animal traits." Esset himself found the idea fascinating, but even he wasn't sure that would be a good idea.

"Well, no. That was a little extreme," Mr. Esset admitted. "But all the research is linked. It was only because he was researching hybridizing animal traits that he made the advancement in healing."

"I know. I hope you manage to persuade the church and the university to preserve…" Esset's voice trailed off as they turned a bend and saw a crowd up ahead, "…the research. What do you suppose is going on up there?" Esset changed their trajectory to investigate.

"Guardsmen," Mr. Esset noted as they drew closer. Sure enough, two men in uniform were trying to push back a crowd of twenty or so people. The expressions on the people's faces were telling: horror, curiosity, fear. The guardsmen looked grim.

"Guard Harn!" Mr. Esset called. The guard, an average-looking fellow with bulging biceps, glanced over at the call.

"Mr. Esset," he acknowledged them. His crowd was slowly dispersing, so he gave them his full attention. He appraised Esset for a moment and deducted who he was.

"Summoner."

"Guard," Esset greeted him back.

"Is it…" Mr. Esset glanced at the departing crowd.

"Another one." Guard Harn gave a curt nod. "Better come take a look."

Esset glanced at his father in time to see him steel himself and felt a wave of sympathy. Mr. Esset hadn't even done the same adventuring as Esset, let alone fought in wars. Seeing a dead body would be difficult for him—not that it was ever easy. The guard led them forward and Esset mentally added: especially a body like this one.

The victim was a young woman, and it looked like a wild animal had slashed her to ribbons with its claws. Her blue eyes stared sightlessly at the sky. She'd been dragged into an alleyway and left discarded next to a manhole and a pile of rubble from the building adjacent, which seemed to be under construction.

"It certainly does look like it was an animal," Mr. Esset said. Esset nodded, but something seemed odd. He knelt next to the body to study it closer. He reached a hand out and closed her eyes, knowing he would remember them later—he always remembered the staring eyes of the dead.

"Do you know who she was?" Esset asked, momentarily distracted.

Guard Harn shook his head when Esset looked at him. "I've seen her before, but I don't know her," he said.

"Tabby. Er, Tabitha," the other guard replied. "She was the cooper's daughter. Nice girl, always smiling. I didn't know her well, but I did help her out one night. A drunk was giving her trouble on her way home, so I walked with her."

Esset looked back down at her and spotted what was bothering him. "Look at this cut," Esset said. It ran straight down from just under her ribs to her navel. It was perfectly straight, and the cut was clean. Guard Harn crouched next to him.

"There's no way claws made this incision. Only a sharp, straight edge like a knife could cause this," Esset said. He debated whether to add another suspicion to that as well.

"That—" the guard frowned and inspected the wound more closely. "You might be right," Guard Harn conceded.

"Did someone defile the body after she died?" Mr. Esset guessed.

"I don't see how," Guard Harn said. "Our witnesses said they heard screaming and came running, but they found her like this. I don't see how someone would have had time to get to the body and do anything to it without being seen."

"Then it's either something supernatural or someone wants to make us think it's an animal or monster," Esset said.

"That seems reasonable," Mr. Esset agreed.

Guard Harn glanced between them.

"We just can't figure out how it's getting away so quickly. This alley dead-ends back there, but there's no sign of the killer," the other guard said. Esset glanced around the alley, and his eyes fell on the manhole cover. It was sitting slightly ajar, its lid caught on a rock.

"Have you checked the sewers?" Esset asked. Guard Harn followed his gaze and went over to the cover. The lid was heavy, but still easily moved by one man. An unpleasant—to say the least—odor wafted into the alley.

Esset went to peer down into the murky darkness.

"He'll be long gone by now," he said.

"Mmm," Guard Harn agreed. He dropped the cover back into

place and looked back at the body.

"The undertaker will be here soon. Once she's safely away, we'll assemble a squad and search the sewers," Guard Harn ordered. The other guard gave the manhole cover a look that was less than enthusiastic.

Esset found himself looking at the body again, particularly the long abdominal cut. "You don't suppose…" he began. Then he had to continue, because Guard Harn was giving him a curious look.

"Why the abdominal cut?" Esset asked. "The rest of this just looks like an animal attack, inflicted to kill or subdue an opponent. But a cut like that is specific, probably made after death. If people were coming in a hurry, why take the time?"

No one had an answer.

"Could we… get a healer to look at her?" Esset requested.

"She's dead."

"I know, but maybe more was done than just the cut. Maybe something was…removed. Could it hurt to look?" Esset coaxed. He thought he heard the other guard mutter something about defiling the dead—and Esset did sympathize—but after a long, thoughtful look, Guard Harn nodded.

"Very well. We're still waiting for the undertaker to get her, but we'll have a healer look at her before she's buried."

"Thank you," Esset said. "What about the other victims? How many have there been?"

"We've found three bodies, all mangled like this one." Guard Harn paused and studied the body a moment longer. "No," the guard corrected himself. "They've been getting worse, little by little. I couldn't tell you if they all had that particular cut though. I never noticed. No one did."

Esset had guessed as much, but he kept that to himself. Apparently he'd learned more than he'd thought while he'd been hunting various monsters with Toman. "What about missing people?" Esset asked, remembering his father's words.

"Four people have been reported missing, but one of those we suspect is just a runaway. Depending on what kind of people this monster goes after, we might not have heard. Like people from the corner district," Guard Harn said. The corner district was the undesirable part of the city—beggars and criminals tended to congregate there.

Esset nodded his understanding. He was about to ask another question when the clop of hooves and creak of wooden wheels signaled the undertaker's arrival. Esset had to keep his lips from twitching into a smile at the man's stereotypical appearance: black garments, pale skin, and a long, drawn face.

"Guard," the undertaker greeted Guard Harn as his horse and cart pulled up.

"Undertaker," Guard Harn replied with a nod.

"Esset, why don't we head to the guard house now?" Mr. Esset suggested. "They've a map of where victims were found. Maybe we can see if there are sewer entrances near all of them."

Esset nodded.

"I'll join you there soon," Guard Harn said by way of farewell.

Mr. Esset waited until they were a respectful distance away before patting his son on the shoulder.

"I'm proud of you, son," he said.

Esset shot his dad an odd look. "We haven't caught the killer yet," Esset said.

"I know, but you've already helped the investigation along," Mr. Esset replied. "They called me in to answer questions about Forris, but I fear I wasn't very useful. You're far more like the summoners of old, helping the kingdom in times of need. I'm just a scholar."

"You do valuable work," Esset objected. "And the original summoner was a scholar too."

"I know," Mr. Esset said, smiling. "And I have no regrets with my path in life, but when I can't summon anything past a horse, I hold the summoner's title in name only. But you—I'm proud of you."

Esset flushed a little. "Uh, thanks."

Mr. Esset patted him on the shoulder again and when they rounded the corner, the guard house came into view.

The stone building hummed with activity; guards and civilians bustled in and out, dealing with everyday disputes and squabbles. The guard at the desk recognized Mr. Esset and, like Guard Harn, recalled that Mr. Esset's son had been called to help. He waved them through without pausing in his discussion with an irate merchant. They headed for a man with greying hair in a small office; the door was open.

"Captain," Mr. Esset greeted the man. "This is my son, Jonathan."

"Good to meet you, Jonathan, I'm Captain Carlson." The captain rose and leaned over his desk so he could shake Esset's hand.

"The honor is mine," Esset replied. "Guard Harn filled me in on some of the details of the case, but said you'd have more."

"You met Harn?" the captain asked, eyebrows rising.

"We ran into him as he reached the latest victim," Mr. Esset said.

"Ah. Well, it's good you've seen things firsthand and spoken to Harn then. He's lead investigator. I'll get you caught up on what we have," the captain said. "Where would you like to start?"

"The victims. Are there any connections between them?" Esset asked. The captain shook his head.

"One old woman—a drunk—a foreign merchant, and a carpenter. And now a girl," the captain said.

"A cooper's daughter," Mr. Esset supplied, and the captain nodded his thanks for the information.

"None of them seemed to know each other. As for the missing...well, there's a boy, but we figure he's just a runaway who hitched a ride with a merchant caravan. The others are a scholar, a housewife, a butcher, and a kooky old nuisance who sold cure-alls." The captain relayed the information matter-of-factly, except for that last bit, which had a hint of "good riddance" to it. Esset imagined there was history there.

"What about where the bodies were found?" Esset asked. The captain waved at a map on the wall, one marked with red and blue pins.

"The red pins are where the bodies were found. The blue ones are the residences and work places of the missing folks."

The pins appeared to sprawl randomly.

"Do you have any maps of the sewers?" Esset asked, but the captain shook his head.

"No, why?"

Mr. Esset and his son explained what they'd noticed at the crime scene.

"Hm." The captain stroked his beard as he stared at the map.

"If I'm recalling right, there are sewer access points near all of bodies except this one. The merchant. He was the first." The captain pointed at a red pin.

"Has anyone caught so much as a glimpse of the killer?" Esset asked. The captain shook his head grimly.

"There's been rumors that it's an angry ghoul or some such, but…" The captain shrugged. "We're at a loss."

A tap sounded at the door, and they all turned to see Guard Harn there.

"I've assembled a squad. We're ready to take a look in the sewers," he said. He waved for them to follow, already turning to go.

"Good luck," the captain said.

"Thanks…" Esset wasn't looking forward to delving into the city's foul-smelling underbelly, but if that was what it took to find the source of these attacks, that was where he was going.

The stench was so bad that even breathing through his mouth didn't help. Esset and most of the guards had secured kerchiefs around their mouths and noses. Refuse flowed around their feet, following the slight downhill slope to—Esset didn't actually know. He wondered where all the waste went for a moment before pulling his attention back to his immediate surroundings.

The liquid and muck covered the toes of their boots, and Esset was glad his had been treated to repel water. One guard wasn't so lucky, and he was groaning and lifting his feet with rude squelching sounds.

"This is just gro—" The guard was cut off by falling refuse; the pile of feces shot down an overhead chute and splattered against the back of his neck. Snickers echoed around the sewer as the other guards moved closer to the walls, where the refuse couldn't hit them.

"Quiet," Guard Harn reminded them in a soft voice, and the snickers and complaints faded.

"It doesn't look like there's any surface we could track prints on," Esset said, his voice soft enough that it wouldn't echo down the tunnels.

"No," Guard Harn agreed grimly.

Esset frowned at the liquid muck.

"I was going to summon a wolf, but standing in liquid will

force them to banish before I can do any effective scouting," Esset said quietly to his father. Plus there was nothing around for the wolf to fight, not even one of Toman's animations. "Too bad Toman's not here. He could create something to navigate this mess," Esset murmured.

"A sewer would be a very bad place for healing wounds," Mr. Esset reminded him, and Esset winced. He hadn't thought of that.

"I can still summon a bat," Esset suggested. He'd hoped for the wolf's keen nose, but the sewer probably would have foiled any scent-tracking anyways.

Guard Harn moved closer to them so he could hear. "Shall we move out?" he asked.

"I might be able to save us a trip through the muck. I can summon a bat that can navigate the tunnels and hopefully spy out our killer, if he's down here," Esset said.

"That...would be preferable," Guard Harn said after a moment.

Esset automatically looked for a place to sit, but he quickly realized he wasn't going to find one. Somehow, he was going to have to do this standing. "Okay, watch my back," he said, spreading his feet apart and clasping his hands behind his back to get balanced.

Foregoing speaking the incantation, a little bat materialized in front of Esset and he tried to submerge his consciousness into it. He almost succeeded, but at the last moment, he felt himself falling backwards and jerked back into himself. He didn't even get as far on his second attempt, but on the third, his mind slipped into his summon and it darted away down the tunnel, along with Esset's consciousness.

The slimy walls crawled with flames, and the water looked like churning lava. Every time waste came flying down an off-shoot, the bat swerved wildly, even though Esset kept the creature high in the center of the tunnel to avoid it.

The sewer split several times, and Esset mentally marked which way he went each time, backtracking when he went too far to keep from getting lost. He was starting to wonder if he shouldn't have the group move forward so he could banish and re-summon from scratch, but he wasn't finding anything at all. With liquid on the floor, there were no tracks to follow, and Esset hadn't even spotted any irregularities on the walls.

He did see rats swimming in the sewage a number of times, however. Esset had no particular dislike for rats, but he did shudder when he saw them, mostly at the thought of swimming in all that waste. He was backtracking yet again when he saw yet another rat swimming—and then two more. Thinking back, he realized that all of the rats he'd seen had been headed in the same direction. It was only when he'd followed the one branch that he'd seen them— whenever he followed a bystream, he wouldn't see them anymore, unless they were headed to that one branch. Thinking it odd, Esset started to follow the rats. Maybe they knew something he didn't.

Something struck Esset's physical body back with the group, and Esset jolted back to himself to find himself falling. He flailed and his hand slid against the slimy wall, but he caught himself and managed to keep from falling into the sewage.

It was chaos as Esset tried to catch his bearings. Men were shouting and moving, including the man holding the lantern, throwing firelight helter-skelter around the tunnel.

That was when Esset realized that he didn't see his dad.

CHAPTER 23

Toman stood on the empty hillside, having trudged on foot to the spot. When Mrs. Esset had been busy, he'd snuck out to do something both she and Esset would heartily disapprove of: relocate the castle.

He'd almost said something to Esset about his plan, but then Esset had said what he had about stopping Moloch... Toman pushed that thought away. Esset would say he was still too sick to move the castle, too drained. He would think Toman was being rash. Well, Esset needed to think less sometimes.

Toman felt weary and sore all over, and for a moment—just a moment—he wondered if Esset was right. Then stubborn pride took the fore: he could do this. He had to prove that he could. After all, if he wasn't getting better, he couldn't build an arm, and if he couldn't make a new arm, he couldn't fight Moloch.

Toman closed his eyes and exhaled slowly, reaching for that particular spot in his mind, that spot right "beside" his animator magic.

Here. Come here, he thought, and the castle materialized before him. At the same time, Toman felt the energy leave his body in a great rush, like water pouring from a cup tipped over. Black splotches danced across his vision. Just before consciousness left him, he admitted to himself that both he and Esset had been right. He was capable of moving the castle, but it hadn't been a wise move.

Toman collapsed, unaware than his cheek was pressed up against a muddy little spot on the ground. The door of the castle opened and a stone soldier came out and carried the animator inside.

Esset glanced around frantically, trying to find his father. He felt panic rising when he still didn't see him, but then a cough came from behind him. Esset whirled around and found his dad on one knee in the sewage. Slime was smeared all over his back, and there were long slashes down the sleeve of his coat.

"Dad!" Esset moved to help his father, but Mr. Esset waved him off, and Esset realized there was only damage done to the coat—no blood or injury.

"Watch out for that thing, son, it might come back," Mr. Esset said, not looking at Esset but past him, searching the tunnel for signs of whatever had attacked them. Esset immediately began scanning their surroundings too, but he didn't see anything.

"What was it?" Esset asked.

"Don't know. Big. Fast," Mr. Esset replied. He was on his feet now, alert.

"Anyone get a good look at it?" Guard Harn asked the group, but everyone shook their heads. They all had their backs to each other, ready for a second attack…but none came. There was no sound in the tunnels beyond the splash of new waste entering the sewer.

"What happened?" Esset asked once it became clear that whatever had attacked was gone.

"Whatever it was, we barely heard it coming," Guard Harn said. "There were a couple small splashes, some scratching sounds, and then something *big* came at us out of the darkness. It went straight for you, but your father yanked you out of the way."

"It took a swipe at you, but it only caught my jacket," Mr. Esset put in. He looked a little pale, and he fingered the damage to his coat. It would need some serious patching—it was a miracle that the claws hadn't caught flesh. Esset turned to look at the damage.

"Thanks, Dad." Esset looked his father in the eye and nodded.

"Of course," his father replied.

"May I see?" Esset reached out to his father's sleeve, and Mr. Esset held out his arm. Esset poked his fingers through the rips; they were ragged. Had they been clean, Esset would have suspected knives, not claws, but the ragged tears were consistent with the claw wounds on the dead body he'd seen.

"Well, at least we've likely found our killer," Esset said.

"So it would seem. But what was it?" Guard Harn asked. Esset shook his head.

"If you'll watch my body again, I'll take another look. I have an idea where to go this time," Esset said. All the guards exchanged looks, but Guard Harn nodded.

"Go ahead. If it comes back, we'll be ready."

Once again, it took Esset a couple tries to submerge his consciousness into the bat while standing, but soon he was flying down the tunnels again. The bat swooped about, keeping a close eye on the sewage below and pausing to flit in a small circle whenever it caught a glimpse of a rat swimming below. Then it darted ahead until it either reached an intersection or saw another rat. The hunt gained pace the further Esset went—he saw more and more rats, all swimming in the same direction. Esset was just reaching his limit for remembering all the turns and branches he'd taken when he caught sight of something ahead.

The bat's echolocation bounced off something large and moving quickly. Esset urged the little bat along, but whatever it was seemed to be adept at keeping just ahead of the bat, and Esset couldn't identify the source of the movement. He didn't doubt that it was whatever had attacked him earlier. .

Esset lost track of the creature before long, and the bat fluttered in a circle before a branching tunnel, chittering angrily. He tried to track it by the splashes it made in the sewage, but the sounds echoed too much and there was too much waste incoming into the sewers to pinpoint which tunnel the creature had gone down. Esset had to choose between two forks; instead of just picking one at random, he waited until he saw a rat and followed it.

The bat darted forward again until another anomaly appeared in the tunnel ahead. This time, the large object didn't move, so Esset approached more cautiously. Whatever it was, it was larger than the creature he'd chased earlier, and Esset guessed what it was before the bat's strange senses could confirm it. He'd found the missing bodies.

The little bat flitted closer as Esset tried to determine how many bodies were there. The corpses were piled together, and in the muck, it was difficult to tell which limbs belonged with which body.

Suddenly, something large lunged at the bat, and the last thing Esset saw was a long pair of jaws snapping shut. The bat exploded into a small puff of sparks and ash, and Esset's consciousness jolted back into his body.

Esset sucked in a massive breath of fetid air as his heart pounded wildly, echoing in his ears. He started to lose his balance, but Mr. Esset braced his shoulders to help him stay upright.

"What did you find?" Guard Harn asked before Esset had caught his breath.

"I found—" Esset sucked in another deep breath. "I found the bodies. And our killer. He ate my summon." Esset hoped the creature enjoyed its burnt tongue.

"You okay?" Guard Harn asked, looking him up and down.

"Yeah, fine. It was just…jarring," Esset said. His heart was still calming, but his breathing had returned to normal already.

"Good. Let's move out," Guard Harn said. He immediately took the lead, although Esset would have to direct them as soon as the tunnel branched. Guard Harn assigned positions while they moved, guarding their rear and keeping the two Essets in the protected center of the group.

Everyone was tense as they navigated the sewers. Their sloshing steps filled the quiet, interspersed with the squeaks of rats and splashing of new waste. Esset counted off the branches in his memory, although there were still swimming rats to lead them if he forgot.

"We're getting close," Esset finally murmured. Another turn and they were in the tunnel that held the pile of bodies. A guard held his lantern higher to cast the light further, and the mound's large shadow was just visible. So was the shadow moving just beside it.

"No, you can't have it," a garbled voice rasped from ahead. The group stopped dead, and Esset and his father exchanged looks. Guard Harn made a small motion with one hand and the group edged forward again; all of the guards held their swords at the ready. The shadowed form moved closer. First, the lantern-light caught on animalistic eyes, reflecting red. Then it started to illuminate the rest of the creature.

It had been human once, but now it was a twisted mixture of human and rat. It had patches of fur interspersed on its human skin. Its figure was lopsided; one arm was mostly human, but at the wrist it twisted into a rat's paw, except the thumb was still opposable.

The other arm was overdeveloped at the shoulder and longer than it should have been, its forearm and fingers over-extended. Vicious claws extended from those fingers, too long to be useful as anything other than weapons.

The rest of the body was modeled similarly, so twisted that it was miracle the creature moved as efficiently as it did. And the face was a horror. One ear was placed higher on the head than the other, and the face had been obscured in part by the patches of fur.

"You can't have it. I won't let you take my research." Bristly whiskers sprouted around the lopsided nose, half muzzle, half human mouth. The speech was garbled because the jaw now housed too many oversized murine teeth, sharp and yellow.

"Forris," Mr. Esset whispered, pale and wide-eyed.

Esset did a double-take, but he could barely fathom how his father had made the connection. Forris's research into augmenting humans with animal traits, the rats he'd kept for his research, his being the first disappearance, and the whispers about his research being taken away, as the church had always threatened to do: it made sense. Still, this creature didn't look anything like the Forris Esset had known.

"Forris?!" Esset exclaimed incredulously.

"The reeking one knows me, the one who smells of ash and fire and *evil,* how does he know me? How?" the creature hissed, drawing closer. The group shrank back, except for Mr. Esset, who stepped forward.

"Because he's my son," Mr. Esset said. "Tobias, is that really you?"

"Ah, Edric, it's you." All of Forris's attention fixated on Mr. Esset. "Yes, it's me. I came here to continue my work before they could take it, they were going to take it, like they've come to take it now. But you won't let them. You were my friend. Why are you with them?" The creature—Forris—drew forward, then back, then forward again, clearly agitated and indecisive.

"I came to find you," Mr. Esset said in his best soothing tone. "I was worried about you. All the scholars are. When you went missing, we feared you dead, like the other bodies we'd found."

"Dead?" The creature's eyes darted back and forth nervously, looking for the killer.

"Yes, someone killed them," Mr. Esset said.

"That's terrible. I hope the city guard catches the killer. Thank you for warning me. I will keep an eye out, but few people venture down here. I mostly stay here, to research." Forris was almost starting to sound lucid.

"Tobias, what happened?" Mr. Esset asked, trying to get answers while keeping Forris calm.

"I was warned, warned that they were coming to take away my research. So I did what I always should have, what everyone was too scared to let me do. I carried out my experiment and it was a success! Just look! I improved my frail human body with traits from my rats." Forris reared up on his hind legs and spread his arms as if his twisted form were proof of a great victory. The soldiers twitched in response, but they held their ground, and Forris didn't seem to notice.

"Yes, I...see," Mr. Esset replied, a crease between his eyebrows. "They kept it from the rest of us scholars, that your research was going to be taken away. Who warned you?" Mr. Esset asked. His concern was genuine, if not for the reason Forris assumed.

"Ah, that would be my new patron. He's a brilliant man, and rich, but secretive. He only ever spoke to me as a shadow, but with his help, I made such advances! He encouraged me when everyone else quibbled and argued about controversy. Pah!" Forris spat into the sewage.

"I'm jealous," Mr. Esset said, speaking words every scholar secretly wanted to hear about his work. Forris preened. At the same time, Esset glanced at the soldiers; they were starting to get antsy, but this approach had so far proven effective.

"It's too bad all are not as clear-sighed as you, Edric," Forris said. "But people ever fear change. That's why I've been staying down here. It's not so bad, and I can research in peace."

"No," Mr. Esset agreed reluctantly. "So what kind of research have you been doing? What advancements have you made?" That seemed to be the right question, for Forris's jaw gaped open in a grin before he bounded towards the pile of bodies.

"I have been working on making an assistant. I have yet to create a living specimen, but I've been progressing in leaps and bounds." Forris's voice came amidst splashes and squelches in the sewage, and he returned shortly with a misshapen form dangling from one mutated hand. It was twisted in a fashion similar to Forris himself, only in reverse; it appeared to be a rat that Forris had tried to mutate into a human. It was the size of a child, but its form was bent at unnatural angles, stiffened in death in a position of agony.

Mr. Esset swallowed hard and barely managed to speak. "Impressive. How did you do it?" Mr. Esset asked faintly. He didn't really want to know, but he had to ask.

"I borrowed from some of the city-folk. All you need is a piece, and when you meld it—miracle!" Forris crowed.

Esset felt sick.

"This has been excellent practice for future volunteers who want to be improved," Forris continued, oblivious to the angered and sickened expressions on the soldiers' faces.

"What did you borrow?" Mr. Esset asked.

"Their organs," Forris replied, as if that were perfectly reasonable. "I tried the heart first, then the liver, then other organs, but none seem to be doing the trick."

"Tobias, you're killing people," Mr. Esset whispered. Forris's misshapen face twisted further in confusion.

"No, I'm doing research," he said.

"There are eight people dead, and you killed them," Mr. Esset persisted. Forris shook his head.

"No, I haven't killed anybody. I'm just doing research, down here where no one will bother me."

"Forris, you cut people open and took their hearts and livers. People can't live without their parts!" Mr. Esset said, his voice growing stronger.

Now Forris seemed to be detecting the distress in his voice. Esset glanced between them, fearful that Forris would grow violent towards his father if this dialogue continued.

"No," Forris said, shaking his head again, but his eyes were unfocused. "No."

"Tobias, look behind you. Those are bodies there. Dead bodies. People you *borrowed* from," Mr. Esset said. Forris's head whipped around, and he stared at the corpses. Then he started backing up towards the group, forcing the soldiers to give ground.

"No. No, no, no. This can't be," Forris said. He turned to look at Mr. Esset again, then finally seemed to see the rest of the group. "No," Forris whispered at their expressions of anger, horror, and revulsion.

"What have I done? The shadow said, he said..." His voice trailed off. "I can't, I didn't—I didn't mean... What have I done?" Forris shook his head, then nipped his own arm with sharp teeth, as if it would wake him up from a terrible nightmare.

"I can't—no! This is, is, NO!" Forris began to thrash around and the group backed up further yet. Then he went quiet and stilled, his head bowed.

"Kill me," he whispered, but the group kept their distance. Mr. Esset opened his mouth to speak, but Forris cut him off. "Kill me. Please, kill me!" He advanced on the group and the men steeled themselves.

"KILL ME!" Forris roared, and he leapt. Esset shouted an incantation, and a flaming wolf materialized and intercepted him mid-leap. The pair were propelled away from the group, the wolf's jaws locked around Forris's throat.

They splashed down onto the far side of the sewer tunnel, and the wolf was banished by the quantity of liquid that washed over it. But the damage was done. The group approached cautiously, but Forris was already finished, his eyes unblinking in death. Mr. Esset looked away, and Esset rested a hand on his shoulder.

"I'm sorry," Esset murmured. Mr. Esset just shook his head and rested his hand atop his son's, giving it a squeeze.

"Well, I'll survive, but I think I'll leave adventuring to you boys," Mr. Esset said as they started home. They'd finished their reports to the captain and used the guard house facilities to clean up a bit.

"I'm sorry about Forris," Esset blurted.

"You did what had to be done. Forris was clearly mad. Whether it was his own experimentation or something else that did it, when he realized what he'd done and what he'd become, he didn't want to live anymore. You saw that as clearly as I."

"I know, I just...hate taking lives," Esset said.

"That's a good thing," Mr. Esset said.

"I know," Esset replied. They walked in silence for two blocks before Esset broke it again.

"Am I bad person for... Well, I was thinking of trying to convince Toman to not go after Moloch anymore, but after this...? I'm not so sure anymore. This made me want to go after him more."

"I don't see how any of that would make you a bad person," Mr. Esset replied reasonably. "But how so?"

"When Forris was talking about the "shadow," his new patron, I just... Well, it occurred to me that that sounds an awful lot like something Moloch would do. It's probably just paranoia, but after Ateala, I just don't know. And even if it wasn't him, it's still the kind of thing he has done and will keep doing, and he needs to be stopped."

As he was wont to do, Mr. Esset took the time to mull over Esset's words before replying, and they walked in pensive silence for a block. "'Just because you're paranoid doesn't mean someone isn't trying to kill you,'" Mr. Esset quoted. "I don't know if it was Moloch either, but I think you have reason to be paranoid."

Mr. Esset sighed.

"I'm an old man, and I just want to see my children safe. So part of me does wish that the two of you would give up on Moloch. However, I also know that would go against both your natures, and you know I would never advocate that. If you boys need to do this, do it."

They walked in silence for a while longer.

"Thanks, Dad."

Mr. Esset just nodded.

When Toman woke up in the early afternoon, still laid up in his castle, his thoughts immediately turned to Esset's words from that morning.

"We don't have to go after Moloch. We can still do good in this world—perhaps, in the grand scheme of things, even more other good things—if we don't go after him."

Toman exhaled heavily. Esset wasn't always right about everything, but he was right about a lot of things, often enough that his words deserved weight.

Jonathan doesn't want to die, he realized. He's afraid of death. Immediately following those thoughts came the obvious, fortunately. Well, yeah. I don't want to die either. I certainly fear death. But there are things I fear more, and just because we're afraid to die doesn't mean we're not willing to die for the right things. He reflected on that for a minute, uncomfortable with it, yet somehow sure.

Is pursuing Moloch worth it, then? That was the question, and that question was linked deeply to a firm belief that he held: *If anyone can beat him, we can.* Unfortunately, that belief didn't mean that they *would* beat him. Toman knew quite personally how much suffering Moloch could inflict, and thus how much suffering the world would be spared if Moloch were removed from it.

Of course Toman wanted revenge, too, but he knew how pointless that was. That wasn't *why* he wanted to go after Moloch. With the power he'd been given, with the power that he and Esset had combined—he felt obligated, to some degree, to use it to help people. But more than anything, he wanted to prevent what had happened to him from happening to anyone else.

But if we can do more good doing other things, because we're not dead from chasing Moloch? Toman considered that. Part of him had always felt that he would die doing what they were doing, one way or another. He had a mission, a job—they helped people with their magic. It was what they did. If Moloch didn't get them, someone else would. But, he realized, it probably *would* be Moloch.

What if we did live to middle age, or even old age? He realized that Esset was different—he *hadn't* assumed they'd die young. Toman wasn't relishing the thought of death any more than Esset did, but Toman realized that he accepted its eventuality—even immediacy—and Esset did not. Not to the same degree, anyways. Esset probably had thoughts of what would happen after, later. Even if they didn't die, there would come a day where they wouldn't go out and actively help people like they had been doing. Esset probably had plans—dreams, even—for that possibility. Toman didn't, so he stopped to reflect on it.

A wife? Kids? A job? That all seemed incredibly foreign. He liked women well enough, but he'd never actively chased them.

There'd always been too much else to do. Having kids just seemed weird. Having a job seemed weird too, but slightly less so. What would he *do* though? *Sculpting?* Maybe. He could create something with his magic in great detail, so why not? He could probably make really good money off it, and it took him far less time to do it his way than an artisan with tools and no magic.

Could I live with myself if Moloch were still alive? Now there was a good question. He wasn't sure he could answer it, but given how much trouble he was having right now just resting when he needed to get better…that spoke volumes. Toman sighed aloud and rested his head back, closing his eyes.

My decision will determine Esset's future too. That was the hardest part. He couldn't do this without him, and they both knew it, but Esset was the best kind of brother anyone could ask for. Esset would never use his own plans for the future against Toman, and Toman wondered if knowing that and letting it affect his own decision was wrong. But it wasn't an easy decision, so maybe not.

I'm willing to sacrifice my own life for some things, but what about Esset's? he wondered. If I could right now exchange my life for Moloch's death, straight across, then I'd do it. But what about Esset's?

Esset's words echoed in his head: "Don't say that. If we came face to face with Moloch right now, would you trade my life for his death? I will tell you my answer: no. I fight, Toman. We fight. If we die, we die, but it's not because we give up." Esset, at least, knew his answer.

And Toman supposed that was his answer too then. It wasn't a satisfying one, not by any stretch, but it was the answer. Toman didn't want to die, and he wanted Esset to stay alive even more. He hoped they'd make it, that they'd do all the good they could in this world and worry about the next when they got there.

They were going to stop Moloch.

CHAPTER 24

New resolve and a newly crafted arm brought Toman and Esset back to the Staggering Tankard a month later. It was getting late in the day when they arrived, but the sergeant was still there.

"I was beginning to wonder if you boys had changed your minds about coming back," Sergeant Warthog said to Toman and Esset by way of greeting. "I know you said in your letter that you were going to, but you sure took your time."

"Nope, we're committed," Esset assured her with a smile. "We just had a few things to take care of."

"Well it's good to clap eyes on you again... intact," the sergeant commented. Toman raised both gloved hands and wiggled his fingers at her.

"Impressive," the sergeant said wryly at the finger-waggling. "Considering Esset told me you'd lost the arm."

Toman removed his glove to show off. Silvery metal moved like warm, living flesh, as naturally as his other hand. Sergeant Warthog could only shake her head in wonder. Toman slipped his glove back on, keeping the supernatural arm discreetly hidden under his clothing.

"Do you have anything for us?" Esset asked.

"Well, I'm getting close. I don't want to say anything 'til I'm sure though. I should know within a couple days. I'm just waiting for word back," the sergeant said.

"You were a little vague in your letter about what exactly you're doing for us," Esset said, taking a seat across from her. Toman took the chair beside him. The sergeant, as usual, always sat on the side of the table facing the door, and in the outside chair, so she couldn't be blocked in.

"There are some things I'm looking for. You're both mages, yes, but not in the conventional sense, so there are a few areas where you would be at a disadvantage. I want to minimize those disadvantages for you. Most of what I'm looking for can be gotten in the form of enchanted objects—amulets are usually the most common and convenient. A few general protective enchantments, I'm thinking, and some to allow you to detect magic in various forms. There's one other kind of item that will be very tricky to obtain, but I've got enough strings to pull to get my hands on a pair of them. I've also been digging up some intel on Moloch, but I don't want to say anything on that front until I have a full picture."

"As much as I'd like to have every scrap of information as soon as I can get it, I suppose that makes sense." Toman respected her enough to not press the issue.

"What is that other kind of amulet you were trying to get?" Esset was curious to know.

"Amulets of immunity," the sergeant replied. "That's what they're most commonly called, anyways. They're quite powerful, and as such, they are exceedingly difficult to come by."

"Immunity from what?" Toman asked.

"Magic." She forestalled any response by raising her fingers slightly from their resting position. "They work in a particular way. Typically there is a spell locked in a breakable amulet; in breaking the amulet, the spell is released. Its effects work upon the breaker, making it impossible for any new magic to affect the user for a set amount of time. How powerful an individual amulet is determines how long the effects last."

"So we can still use our magic…" Esset prompted.

"Yes. Since you're not conventional mages, it'll work even better for you than for most. You can't cast spells on yourselves anyways, after all. You'll just want to make sure that any other beneficial magical enchantments are in place before you activate the immunity. They'll continue to work—only new magics and spells will be unable to touch you."

Esset was surprised that something so powerful even existed. Then again, there was probably a catch. Or two.

"Keep in mind, this won't make Moloch helpless against you," the sergeant warned. "It'll still kill you if he uses magic to pick up a mountain and drop it on you." Toman and Esset exchanged a look—catches indeed.

"How long will the immunity last for, typically?" Esset had to ask.

"Like I said, they vary, but I'm after one that will last longer than ten minutes—at the least," the sergeant said. Toman and

Esset's eyebrows collectively rose. "Moloch won't go down without an extensive fight."

"Rare...and expensive. We'll owe you for this," Toman said.

"Big time," the sergeant agreed. "Especially since I've been calling in favors of my own just to try and find a pair. But we'll worry about that later. After all, you will have already gone a long way towards clearing that debt if you manage to get rid of Moloch."

"Get rid of Moloch, eh? Well nah, there's a lofty goal indeed," a familiar male voice drawled from behind Toman and Esset. Sergeant Warthog gave no hint of surprise, but Toman and Esset both stiffened and Esset ground his teeth. He was getting tired of being ambushed at the Tankard.

"Erizen." Sergeant Warthog's tone wasn't very welcoming. "You have a demon's luck, as usual, walking in just in time to hear what you shouldn't."

"Oh, it's hardly news," Erizen said, inviting himself to sit down at their table. He flicked a hand and a chair slid itself over from the adjacent table so he could sit. His smarmy smile contrasted against the other expressions around the table, ranging from indifference to irritation.

"I had a spell set so I'd know when your little do-gooders showed up. And if you're looking for immunity amulets, our interests once again align. I wish to hire you again!" Erizen made a grand gesture that garnered no response whatsoever.

"I can see I have your interest," Erizen continued. "As you all know, I'm part of a council of dark mages. As one would expect, relations tend to be less than perfectly stable between various individuals, but as long as everything is relatively discreet, no one much cares. At least, we don't interfere in each other's business. Normally I stay well out of such politics in favor of my personal entertainments, but my one neighbor, a Mage Lord Atli, has been making a nuisance of himself. As it happens, he is in possession of a few amulets of the variety you are interested in. I am proposing that I give you the intelligence you need to successfully steal those amulets and a few other small items, and we split the prizes." Erizen sat back and folded his hands in his lap to let them consider his offer. There was silence around the table.

"Boys, I need a moment with Erizen," the sergeant said. Esset frowned but stood, remembering the same request from last time. Toman's expression was perfectly schooled into a neutral mask.

Sergeant Warthog leaned forward once the pair was out of earshot.

"You have grown *soft*," she accused. A brief sneer of revulsion flashed across Erizen's lips at the suggestion.

"Nonsense," Erizen snapped.

Sergeant Warthog smirked. "Oh? Then why send them in alone? Once upon a time, you would never have left such a venture to others. The excitement alone would have ensured your participation, nevermind the satisfaction of revenge first-hand."

"Well, one must learn *some* lessons over the years. But you have a reason to bring this up." Even when his temper was provoked, Erizen was astute.

The sergeant suddenly grinned wolfishly. "Oh yes. But first, tell me: What is your opinion of Moloch?"

"I think I would rather not have him as an enemy." Erizen's smile vanished for the first time.

"But he is not an entirely desirable ally either, is he?" the sergeant prodded.

"He is volatile, unpredictable. He is powerful, and not just in terms of magical strength. He plays his politics well, and he is cunning," Erizen replied guardedly. This was high praise, coming from Erizen.

"It would probably be beneficial, or more convenient, if he were not around, yes?" Another gentle prod. Erizen watched her, still guarded and clearly not intending to respond, so she continued.

"And clearly you don't feel up to the task yourself, or you would have acted by now," Sergeant Warthog continued. Erizen's expression darkened and his pride goaded him into speaking.

"It is simply a matter of risk-to-gain analysis," he put in dismissively. "The potential benefit is simply not worth the likely cost."

But the sergeant's suspicions were confirmed. "And if the risks could be all but negated?" the sergeant asked, seeming to turn her attention to her fingernails. One was tearing, and she raised it to her teeth to carefully chew it off.

"What are you saying, exactly?" Erizen asked—it was close

to being a demand.

"You've grown soft, Erizen," the sergeant accused again, this time scorn dripping from her tone. "You used to revel in any challenge, relish even the thought of a potential one! Now? Feh."

Erizen was frustrated, and it showed—he had forgotten how well she had once known him—still knew him, since he had changed so little—but there was still little he could do but rise to her bait. "I do not *fear* Moloch, if that's what you're implying," he snapped. "But I am wary of him—only a fool would not be."

Sergeant Warthog grinned a slow grin. "Yes, I know," she replied, watching with pleasure as he grit his teeth. In all actuality, he had not changed much over the years since they'd known each other, but she had, and it was giving her the advantage, however slight. And she was playing that advantage with great ferocity. "But I wonder, will the Erizen before me now consider my proposal? Once, the Erizen I knew would have leapt upon it."

"You have not changed so much," Erizen replied, deflecting the indignity of her interrogation. "You are still insufferable. It is only the way you are insufferable that has changed."

The sergeant only smiled and waited. She knew he would succumb to her challenge eventually, and she knew he knew she knew it. That was what made this victory so delicious.

"Very well. I will hear you. No more games," Erizen conceded.

The sergeant smiled a moment longer before conceding also. She had what she wanted now, after all. "These boys," she said, indicating briefly to Toman and Esset, who waited by the bar, covertly watching them but unable to hear anything. "They're stronger, smarter, than they look—you know that—and they're bent on taking down Moloch. I've thrown in my lot with them. I think they have a chance—just a chance, mind—of actually succeeding." She could tell from Erizen's expression that he still had doubts, but that was only to be expected.

"Your proposal?" Erizen asked. It was obvious that he would require some convincing.

"They want Moloch gone. You want Moloch gone. Your goals align. There is much you could do to help them indirectly. Intelligence, mostly. You undoubtedly have valuable, *current* information on Moloch. Your involvement could be minimal, risks even fewer. But the potential benefits…vast. You and I both know it."

"Gret—" Erizen began, still not favorably inclined, but Sergeant Warthog cut him short with a slight shake of her head and a lifted hand.

"That was not the proposal," she said. "That was simply…something to consider. Later. The proposal is this: Go with them, work with them against this enemy of yours. Do a little more damage than originally planned; be the old Erizen again. Challenge yourself. Then you'll get a real look at those two, and you can consider what else I have told you." Now she stopped, and now she awaited his response with folded hands.

"Oh, mah Gretchen," Erizen drawled heavily. "Run away with me? I could make you young and beautiful again, and we would be madly in love."

Sergeant Warthog laughed harshly. She didn't actually know if he was serious or not, but it didn't matter—her answer was the same either way. "Your ego assumes much," she replied. "But then, it always does. Now, my proposal?"

"Will you marry me?" Erizen drawled. Now he was definitely joking. She drummed her fingers on the table once, pointedly, making him laugh. It was the only answer that she dignified the "proposal" with.

"For all the physical youth I have retained, it cannot make me feel so alive as you can. You invigorate me, Gretchen. How could I deny you? Whistle for your puppies, and we can discuss our plans." Erizen was smiling sardonically, at ease again. Ignoring the condescension, Sergeant Warthog raised a hand to summon Toman and Esset back to the table.

"Well! It appears we shall be working together," Erizen drawled at them once they were within earshot. Esset scowled and shot the sergeant a look, which she ignored. Toman didn't show his emotions. Erizen immediately commandeered the conversation again.

"Your dear sergeant has persuaded me to come along on our little venture to Atli's treasury. Now, I can't have anything connecting us to pull this off, so I will simply have to meet you there. I can give you directions, of course. So, here's the general plan: meet in the city beside the castle, wait for nightfall, depart for castle, break in, get our prizes, go our separate ways—like I said, I can't have any known ties to you. We'll meet back at my castle so I can give you your share of the loot. All the breaking in and planning of the theft, I will leave to you. Pretend I'm not there. Do not count on my skills—plan only around your own. Think of me as a bonus." He smirked at them. "Agreed? Swell. Now, I shall be on my way—pressing engagements and all that."

Erizen held out his hand to shake. Esset automatically reached for it, hesitated, then braced himself and shook it. Like the first time, Erizen used the contact to send the jolt of information to Esset, everything they'd need to know for the mission.

Erizen rose smoothly as Esset tried to regain his bearings. "Ta!" Erizen bade them as he sailed out the door, and it was only another two seconds before Esset was scowling again.

"Okay, this should go without saying," Sergeant Warthog said. "But stick to the mission. No taking down any more members of Moloch's council. It could alert him to the threat you pose or goad him or the other lords into hunting you actively. Besides, with the setup they have, odds are any replacement will be as bad or worse than the one you kill."

"Of course," Toman said. Esset nodded his agreement, although he was inwardly wishing he could wipe out the lot of them—Erizen included.

"I know you're not happy about this, but his help has become vital to your success," Sergeant Warthog said, eliciting surprised expressions from both of them.

"How so?" Esset asked.

"Moloch has a Greymaker."

CHAPTER 25

Hard flying brought Toman and Esset back to the kingdoms governed by the dark mage lords swiftly. Now the sun was beneath the horizon and darkness encroached on the landscape. A couple hours earlier, Toman and Esset had switched from the conspicuous summoned birds to massive stone creatures animated by Toman so they could fly invisibly by night.

A faint smudge on the horizon marked a town, and Esset signaled Toman to fly closer.

"Town. We'll be inside Atli's kingdom by now, shall we take a look?" Esset shouted. Toman simply nodded.

The evening was overcast, helping to hide them in the sky. Their stone mounts would be a bit more noticeable if they flew close enough to see ground activity clearly, but seeing one of Atli's towns would be informative, and it would be worth the risk.

They soared high above the small huddle of buildings clustered in the middle of sprawling farms. Wisps of smoke trailed from chimneys, but the buildings were small and in poor repair and there was very little activity, even though darkness hadn't fully fallen yet. Toman spied three uniformed soldiers patrolling even in this small a town.

Toman pointed at one house, and he and Esset swooped down to take a closer look. Finally, a resident: a woman in a tattered dress pumped water from a well next to a house. Toman and Esset hovered above the building to study her; she looked healthy, if a bit thin.

The woman suddenly jumped and looked over her shoulder, and for a moment, Toman thought she'd sensed them there. But no, she wasn't looking up; she shrank in on herself as a soldier walked up to her with a predatory smile on his face. They spoke, but they were too far away to hear.

Toman felt sick as he watched the scene unfold, knowing that interfering would be a bad idea. The soldier moved in close, ignoring the woman's fear and obvious desire to flee. When the soldier reached out to grope the woman, she shied away, eliciting an angry bark from the soldier. The soldier raised his hand to strike her when someone burst from the house. The man wasn't large, and he didn't try to fight the soldier, but he did put himself between the soldier and the woman and make placating gestures with his hands.

Toman's hands clenched into fists when the soldier struck the man to the ground. The man didn't try to fight back, even when the soldier kicked him while he was down. The woman fled into the house, and the soldier yelled but didn't pursue. He kicked the villager one last time, then stalked away. Toman forced his breathing into an even pattern to keep himself from going after the soldier. As they continued to hover, the woman crept back out of the house and helped the man to his feet and back inside.

Toman finally tore his eyes away to look at his brother, realizing, belatedly, that he probably should have been paying more attention earlier. His brother's impulsive streak could have gotten them in trouble there; sure enough, Esset was sitting stiff, his outrage displayed clearly on his face. Before he could decide to do something, Toman pulled the mounts up and left the village behind them; they'd seen all they needed to see. They knew what kind of ruler Atli was.

They landed in a small copse of trees as the sky began to lighten with the first rays of morning.

"You sure we can't dethrone this guy?" Esset muttered as they dismounted.

"I know the feeling," Toman replied, but they both knew they were moving forward as planned. They each pulled out their sleeping rolls and began spreading them on the ground.

"It does make Erizen look not so bad, though. At least his people had enough to eat. Both those villagers were thin," Toman commented as he laid down in his bedroll.

"Hm," was Esset's only response. After a silence, he added, "But what about him giving Moloch a Greymaker?"

"That doesn't rest easy," Toman confessed. "But it does make sense."

"How so?" Esset asked, disbelief and contempt in his tone.

"Erizen is playing a tricky game. He has to keep Moloch and

the other dark lords convinced he's on their side. Especially Moloch. *Not* giving him a Greymaker might have incited an attack."

"Hm," was Esset's response again.

"Once Moloch is dead, let's come back," Toman said. "Then we can eradicate every single one of these monsters."

"That I can agree with."

"I thought you'd like that. So what are we up against here? Erizen gave you the information, not me," Toman said.

"Well, I've got a bit of the layout of the castle and the town, and an estimate of Atli's manpower, but not a ton else." Esset cast about for a twig and started sketching in the dirt. "If you animate some stuff *here*, I'll do some scouting to verify our intelligence. Then we sneak in. I won't summon anything unless we're found out, since my summons are a little...obtrusive. With Atli's resources, it's best if we get in and out before he knows we're there. If we raise the alarm, there's a chance we won't get out, not with the number of mages he has under him."

"Good to know," Toman murmured, already considering what kinds of creatures he'd need to make.

"It'll be risky," Esset said.

Toman nodded.

"But if the sergeant says we need these amulets, we need them. We need every edge possible to defeat Moloch. He's clever, and we need to anticipate as much as possible, because it'll be the thing we don't think of that he'll exploit."

Esset let out a huff of breath at Toman's words.

"You're right. Once Moloch's done with, we can fix the rest of this."

Their meeting place was a dingy little inn located in the city next to Atli's castle. They reached it in the early morning and stayed sequestered in the tiny, dingy room all day, night, and day again, keeping a low profile.

"There's no way Erizen would ever stoop so low as to spend a night in a place like this himself," Esset complained, squishing a bug that was meandering across the floor.

"It is an unobtrusive kind of place to stay," Toman said. "But I do imagine he's getting a kick out of making us stay here." Their confinement was wearing on them both as they waited for Erizen to arrive.

"To say the least. Your creations are waiting. Even scouting through my bat's eyes has gotten old," Esset said.

A tap sounded at the door. Esset rose to answer it, speaking as he walked. "You know, we could always go without him." He opened the door, but no one was there.

"That would be rather inconsiderate of you. Especially since I've come all this way." That was Erizen, of course, but Esset was a little confused before he realized that the man must have a way of turning himself invisible.

Not wanting to give Erizen any satisfaction for his ploy, Esset turned away from the empty doorway and grabbed his bag. "Fine, let's go then. You're just going to trail along behind us, invisible, then?" Esset asked. Something in his tone suggested that Erizen was a freeloader and a coward if he chose to do so. Toman, for his part, simply got up and headed for the open door.

"I may or may not intervene as needed," Erizen said in a smug voice.

"That's nice," Esset said. He could tell Erizen's general proximity from the sound of his voice and footsteps—apparently the spell only worked to obscure vision, not sound or the other senses. Which meant that any of his summons would easily be able to locate him, if necessary.

Good to know.

The two brothers seemed to wander as they headed towards the outskirts of the city. They lingered in the marketplace for a while, then moved on. They had been unable to detect anyone paying them any undue attention, so they figured they were safe from suspicion for the moment. It was full dark by the time they were outside the city.

Toman's creations, disguised as lumpy boulders strewn about

the terrain, came to life at Toman's command. Foremost were the stone griffons they would use to surpass the tall walls that surrounded Atli's castle. There were seven of them, and they could carry passengers—including other, non-winged animations—and also be used to fight once they got there.

It was a short flight to the castle. A small stone bird, a lookout and scout, flew up to greet them and then led them to a momentarily deserted location in the courtyard. They were working between the gaps in the guards' patrols—Atli didn't shirk on his own personal security, being smart enough to know that when someone ran a kingdom the way he did, many people would want him dead. As such, they had to move as swiftly as possible.

Toman's stone griffon landed only long enough for its rider to dismount before taking off again. Esset's griffon landed a moment later, and Erizen's the moment after that. Unlike the first two, Erizen's griffon didn't depart—it stayed with them, their backup for the time being. The others could be called upon for outside help, but they would be left waiting, circling the castle in the darkness in case they were needed. Toman and Esset hid in the shadow of the wall as a patrol of two soldiers went by. Only after it was past did the other griffons swoop down low enough to drop their burdens before winging away into the darkness. It was fortunate for them that there was only a sliver of the moon in the sky, not nearly enough for the enemy to see them by.

"There, servants' entrance," Esset whispered. Toman snuck over to the sturdy door and crouched in front of it, releasing a thin but long chain onto the ground. It slithered like a snake into a tiny gap and a chunking sound came from the other side a moment later. As Toman opened the door, Esset joined him swiftly, and after a few animations had followed them in, they closed the small but heavy door behind them. Fortunately, no one was waiting for them on the other side, although Toman knew their luck wouldn't hold forever. They found themselves in the kitchen, and they had to be very careful navigating their way to the other door—there were bodies lying, asleep, by the hearth. Too cheap for beds for all the slaves and servants, many members of the kitchen staff simply slept on the kitchen floor.

To Toman's surprise, the door from the kitchen into the rest of the castle was locked as well. Not that such a thing would stop them; out came the chain snake again, but this time it slid its "head" into the lock and manipulated the links of its body until it matched the keyhole. Then Toman twisted the handle open and the snake withdrew so he could open the door to admit them.

They nearly ran right into a patrol. Toman quickly pulled the door shut, but he was still careful to be silent. He kept his grip on the handle, which would click loudly as it closed. He held his breath as the patrol went by, praying they wouldn't check the handle. Their mission would surely fail if they were discovered this early on.

The patrol's muffled voices came through the door, talking about...a card game? They carried straight past the door. Once their voices faded, Toman cracked the door slightly, letting an animated stone rat scurry past his feet into the hallway first to scout the way. A second one scurried out after it, but it split off in the opposite direction to check the other end of the hall. It only took a moment for both rats to reach the corners of the halls and give a little nod, signaling that the way was clear.

"Okay, time for you to do your bit, Erizen," Esset said from behind Toman.

"That's *Lord* Erizen," the mage corrected him.

"Get to work, Lord Erizen," Esset replied, swallowing a nastier comment.

"Go right," came the smug little reply. Erizen clearly enjoyed pushing Esset's buttons. Repeatedly. Toman found himself wishing they'd both forgo their respective attitudes and just get the job done as quietly and efficiently as possible. Or maybe that was anxiety making him irritable. He didn't much care for stealth missions.

The brothers followed Erizen's directions and made their way downwards in the direction of the treasury. They'd accidentally managed to time their entrance so that they followed the first two guard patrols at a safe distance before having to split off in other directions. Really, it was the safest place to be; since they knew where the closest patrol was, and the patrols rarely overlapped, they didn't have to worry much about being surprised by another. Erizen continued to give them quiet directions from behind Esset and just in front of the stone griffon that stalked after them.

Toman couldn't believe it when they made it to the safe

without having to confront a single guard—quite honestly, once they'd descended, he had begun to think that it would be impossible to avoid them. The interior of the castle seemed maze-like, the route to their destination long and circuitous—and Toman suddenly realized something. Erizen had deliberately led them on that trail. If he'd somehow learned the routes that the guards took on their patrols and mapped out a long, circuitous path around the castle, they could get in without detection. It had taken longer than anything Toman and Esset would have done, but there was less risk his way.

Toman just hoped that once Erizen had what he wanted from the treasury, he wouldn't bolt and leave them to try to find their way out themselves. There was no way Toman would be able to remember the way to the exit, and even if he did, it wouldn't be the direct route. Uneasily, he wondered if that were part of Erizen's plan as well.

"This one."

Toman raised an eyebrow at the nondescript door that they'd stopped in front of. It looked totally ordinary—not the kind of door one expected to protect a room full of treasure. In fact, if Erizen hadn't pointed it out, he might not have noticed it at all.

"No guards?" he asked suspiciously.

"Shields, booby traps, wards..." They could practically hear the shrug in his voice. "Would a guard really help at all?"

"Whatever," Esset muttered. Toman just shrugged and stepped forward, extending the chain snake to pick the lock like he had before. The knob glowed red hot, melting the chain in an instant; the liquidized metal dripped from the keyhole until no more was left inside. Toman blinked at it.

"Oh." He thought for a moment, then walked several paces to the side. If the lock was enchanted, then the whole door probably was too. That meant that the strongest part of the entire treasury was probably the door, making it a foolish place for them to focus their attention. Therefore, the wall was his target. Toman placed a glove against the wall and concentrated. He wanted to make a golem—a large, clunky golem, with whole blocks as body parts. It was actually quite easy, since there was a minimum of shaping the material needed to accomplish that goal. With a few minutes, a grating sound, and a momentary struggle, a rough humanoid-shaped set of blocks drew out of the wall and stepped into the passageway, leaving a man-shaped hole in the wall. Toman and Esset grinned at each other. They called the griffon inside and then had the wall-golem step back into place; from the outside, there was no sign of a breach, just two small, stone rats keeping watch and ready to scuttle out of sight if necessary.

Inside, it looked exactly like they'd imagined a treasure room to look when they were kids. Crowns, jewelry, gold-and-jewel encrusted armor, and enchanted weapons had been arrayed around the room, with chests of coins and great bars of precious metals arranged against the walls and on tables. They'd seen treasure before—heck, Arxus had come with a sizable inheritance—but this was so *flashy*. Erizen was already moving.

"Ah, here we are," they heard him say, and a nearby necklace suddenly seemed to levitate off its display place. A moment later, it swooped downwards and vanished. "Leave this part to me, gentlemen—I know what's worth taking."

After looking around for a moment, Esset began to reach towards a jewel-encrusted sword that was nearby.

"I also know what's booby-trapped," came Erizen's droll voice. Esset glared in the voice's general direction, but he withdrew his hand and didn't try to touch anything else. The pair waited with their arms crossed, watching an astounding number of items vanish.

"How exactly are you carrying all that?" Esset couldn't help but ask. They hadn't all been small items, either, nor light ones. Really, there was no way Erizen should have been able to move after picking up that many items. Magic. It had to be.

"Some of us have *useful* magical abilities," Erizen mocked condescendingly.

Esset's expression went from curious right back to extremely irritated. Huge fiery animals weren't exactly great for stealth missions; Esset already knew that, but the comment vexed him anyways. He resisted the temptation to summon a wolf to bite Erizen on the rear.

"Are you quite finished?" he snapped instead.

"For the moment." Esset could hear Erizen's irritating smile in his voice.

Esset tried not to let it get to him. "I mean are you finished collecting things? The longer we stay, the more likely we are to get caught."

"Quite." Erizen's voice was closer this time, right beside them. "Do lead the way." Toman turned back to face the wall and had it step out to admit them back into the hallway. The stone rats darted out to check the halls for people, but it was already too late; a mage had stepped around the corner, and he saw the golem in the hall—not a patrol, just bad luck.

"Hey!" he yelled, calling out an alarm as he saw Toman and Esset stepping out of the treasure room into the hall. "Intruders! Intruders in the treasury!"

If the mage-robes hadn't been hint enough, the blast of pure energy that shot from his hands was a pretty good hint that their discoverer was a mage. Esset threw himself forward on the ground, an incantation rolling off his tongue as he fell. A smoking crater was blasted into the wall directly behind where he'd been standing the moment before. There was a muffled curse from Erizen as the stone griffon bounded from the treasury to run abreast of the fiery wolf that streaked towards the mage.

"Come on!" Toman grabbed Esset's arm and hauled him to his feet, momentarily safe in the knowledge that griffon and wolf would keep the mage occupied long enough for them to get a head start. The plan was theft, not warfare—normally they would have fought, but they'd already agreed that if fighting broke out, flight would be their priority. Fortunately, however, Toman and Esset's skills made them good at doing both at the same time. Outside, on the opposite side of the castle, two stone griffons were suddenly attacking the guards, drawing some attention on that front—and keeping it away from their break-in.

Not that the distraction meant no guards would be coming. The treasury was pretty important, after all. The clunky stone golem ran ahead of them, so when a guard patrol appeared ahead, it slammed through them like a battering ram. Esset uttered another incantation, and a fiery wolf was among them. Esset kept it from going for the kill, but it still did a great deal of damage to the guards. Even though the guards worked for a mage, that didn't mean that they were used to fighting stone giants and beasts of fire; they quailed the same as any other mortal.

The wolf bit a sword arm, then whirled and leapt at another

guard, landing on his chest and rebounding off him to follow its master. The stone giant, Toman, Esset, and presumably Erizen just kept running.

"Which way?" Esset called to Erizen as they skidded to a stop at the end of a branching corridor.

"Right. Then up the first stairs we see," Erizen's voice replied. So he was still with them. Esset didn't like that he couldn't physically keep track of the man, but then again, Erizen had said not to worry about him, and Esset wasn't quite sure he'd feel guilty if the arrogant mage were left behind. Then again, the directions helped, and he did have the treasure.

The group took off down the right corridor, and sure enough, there was a set of stairs after they sprinted down the hall. There was also another guard patrol. The giant rammed through them again, and the fiery wolf made sure none of them got their bearings until the three of them were past. With the screams of pain from the guards, Esset knew that they'd be encountering more opponents soon—there was no way they were going unheard. They needed to get out as soon as possible. Regular men weren't too big an obstacle, but mages could be very troublesome, and even if Atli himself didn't show up, he had plenty of other mages in his employ.

It was as though his thought had summoned them; they'd just reached the top of the steps and started to run down the left-hand corridor that Erizen had called out when the stone giant was stopped by a mage-shield. Sparks and bits of stone sprayed to the sides and back, forcing Toman and Esset to skid to a stop and throw up their arms to protect their faces. Esset was too slow and found himself rewarded with a few small cuts on his face from the flying stone chips. The golem was considerably worse for wear— its entire front was scorched and battered, but fortunately the end effect was smaller. The golem started to bash at the shield, sending more bits flying.

Toman and Esset crouched to make themselves smaller targets, and Esset grinned when he saw two mages beyond the shimmering surface of the shield; they were in the same corridor, down a ways. Banishing all the summons he currently had with him, he incanted a new chant, and a massive, fiery panther appeared—on the mages' side of the shield. Their faces went white when they saw it, and their shaken concentration weakened their shield—a second later, the golem smashed through. About the same time, the two mages had personal shields thrown up to protect themselves from the blazing beast that pounced at them.

The panther roared in fury as it mauled their mage-shields, its voice the sound of a whirling maelstrom of flames. Not even air could escape the devouring hunger of fire, and one mage collapsed when the panther shattered his shield. Esset prevented his summon from killing the man, instead turning its attention to the other mage as the group sprinted past. The second the panther hit the second mage's shield, the man's resolution failed, and he turned and ran. The panther pursued a few paces before Esset called it back. With a snarl, the fiery cat obeyed and whirled to bound after the group instead.

They barreled through two more groups of guards, and after the last, Esset murmured a prayer as he ran—the panther had escaped his control for a matter of scant moments and managed to do more damage to a guard than he intended. The man wasn't dead now, but the summoner wasn't sure he'd survive, either. After the brief prayer and a swift lockdown on his control of the creature, they rounded a corner and saw the kitchen door.

"There!" This time there was no lock-picking or attempts at stealth. The golem bashed the door down with a single stomping kick and they flooded into the room. The sleeping servants screamed and pressed against walls or hid under tables as the group ran past, ignoring them completely. Esset restrained the panther from attacking them, steering it up behind the golem instead. The golem smashed through the outside door next, and stone griffons met them there. Guards were rushing forward, but the panther sprang to meet them, buying the trio enough time to mount up and take off.

The darkness of the night sky was their friend as the stone beasts winged them away from the castle, carrying them far upwards and over the city. They landed in a different location from where they'd taken off originally, on the off chance someone may have seen something. Esset was only too glad to land; his heart raced and his blood was hot despite the cold flight back.

"Well, did we get what we came for?" Esset asked, looking at Erizen's griffon.

*

There was no answer.

"Erizen?" Esset asked. After a second and a flash of irritation, he tried again: "*Lord* Erizen?" Still nothing. Concerned, Toman and Esset went over to the stone beast, and that was when they saw the scrap of cloth tied to the creature's ankle. Toman freed it and spread it over his hand. Black letters spelled clearly; "Good work, pups. See you later."

"Figures," Esset snarled, turning away.

"Well, it was part of the plan to part ways almost immediately after escaping and meet him back at his castle," Toman pointed out. He wasn't entirely happy either, but he wasn't as ready as Esset was to assume the worst of the mage.

"We'd best make use of what darkness remains," he said, pushing down his anger as best he could. Getting any angrier would be too much like letting Erizen win.

"Looks like," Toman agreed. "Come on, let's go. We have a long trip ahead of us."

They flew through the night and hid in a canyon next to a stream as dawn broke. They were both exhausted, but once they were camouflaged and in their bedrolls, Esset found he couldn't sleep.

"Hey Toman," Esset said quietly to get his brother's attention.

"Mhmm?" Toman responded without looking at him.

"I'm pretty sure that guard didn't make it."

Upon Esset's words, his best friend looked over at him. "Who?" he asked.

"You didn't even see him, I don't think. It was when we were pushing through one of the patrols—I lost control of the cat for a second. It mauled a guy...really badly," Esset explained. He still stared at the rocks, and his voice was flat, but Toman knew better than to think that meant his brother didn't care.

"We were fighting, Esset. It couldn't have been helped," Toman said, trying to reason with him. But he knew Esset wouldn't accept that.

"It should have been," Esset argued.

"No one's perfect," Toman said quietly.

Now Esset finally sat up and turned his head to look at Toman. "No, but I'm strong. Remember what Dad said, before we set out the very first time? We're strong, a lot stronger than ordinary people. And that means we should be able to afford to do things right. We are strong enough to fight without taking lives."

Toman let Esset's argument stand for a moment, because it was true. "But not always," Toman said softly. "We can only do our best. But we knew going in that we'd end up with blood on our hands. We were lucky the Baliyan war was mostly against undead, but even then there were times that we couldn't avoid taking lives."

"I know," Esset said, looking away. "But this time—good grief, he was a guardsman. For all we know, he didn't even want to be there. For all we know, he was a good guy, with a wife and kids who'll never see him again. And I killed him."

"Come on, Esset. You don't know that—you could be borrowing trouble here. You don't know he was a good guy; it's just as possible he wasn't. And it's possible he's still alive."

Esset snorted at that attempt at reassurance. "Yeah, maimed for life, and so crippled he's an invalid."

"Esset—" Toman could see he wasn't getting through at all; Esset had set his mind on being guilty about this. Toman was about to make him listen. "Esset," he tried one last time. Then he reached out and grabbed the front of Esset's coat and yarded him forward, putting them both in the sitting position.

"Listen up, Jonathan," Toman began forcefully. "You need to get it through your thick skull that you're human. You're not some flawless hero from an old tale, unable to step a single foot wrong. You're strong, but you're not perfect. Is your hubris so great that you think you are? You know what the Book of Bright Hyrishal would say about that. No, you're not some hero of tale, you're Jonathan Esset, son of a scholar, a mere mortal who's trying to make a difference for the better in this world." He let go of Esset's jacket with a little shove, landing his brother back in his seat with a soft thwumpf.

Esset was quiet.

"You know I'm right," Toman pushed after a moment of silence. He had every intention of bullying an answer out of the summoner.

"Yeah," Esset finally admitted softly. After a few moments, he added, "But that doesn't mean it's good, or right, or that I have to like it."

Toman sighed. "No...I know." And it wouldn't get any easier, either.

CHAPTER 26

Toman and Esset flew nights and kept out of sight even after they'd crossed into Erizen's territory. When they reached the castle under the cover of darkness, Esset flew in close first, looking for the boy whose face Erizen had implanted in his memory. He finally spied him wearing a page's uniform and playing with a cup and ball in the garden inside the castle walls. Esset made another pass just to be sure he had the right person, and then he waved for Toman to follow him down.

The kid didn't see them until they were almost atop him. The boy's eyes widened and he jumped back, but he was soon grinning at the stone griffons, craning his neck to watch them when they took off after depositing their burdens.

"Okay, this way," the boy whispered, waving Toman and Esset into a shadowy corner. A little gargoyle perched on a pedestal, and the boy walked straight up to it, patted it on the head twice and kissed it on the nose. A shadow shifted in the corner as a passage opened silently in the flagstones next to them. Esset rolled his eyes at the "key" to open the passageway. Erizen. It figured.

The boy scampered over to the edge of the trapdoor and waved for them to go down ahead of him. Toman ducked down first, shimmying down the ladder into the darkness. From the coolness of the tunnel, he knew the walls would be stone, and a quick touch confirmed the guess.

The boy hopped nimbly down behind them, and the tunnel went pitch black as the hidden entrance slid silently shut behind them. A moment later, the boy lit a small lantern—Toman didn't know where he'd gotten it—illuminating the passageway ahead. Fortunately, the boy was small enough to dart by them and lead the way down the tunnel.

Toman and Esset had to jog to keep up with him and his bobbing lantern. The passage had a few forks and offshoots, but the boy never hesitated. Finally they reached a set of stairs and a peephole. The page blew out the lantern and set it down, then pressed one eye up against the peephole before triggering some unseen mechanism, prompting the stones to slide out of the way.

They emerged from behind a plush tapestry and into a hallway. The boy put on a very well-mannered behavior and led them sedately into the hall as if they'd entered the castle in a perfectly legitimate fashion.

It didn't take long before Toman recognized the hall leading to Erizen's study. The page walked them right up and tapped on the door, which opened to admit them.

Erizen reclined in chair behind his desk, two books open on his lap.

"Ah, you're finally here," he remarked, moving the books to the desk and waving the page away. Toman and Esset stepped inside and the door closed quietly behind them. Erizen picked up an ornate wooden box from his desk and held it out to them.

"Your portion of the spoils," Erizen said.

"Thank you," Toman said, accepting the box and peeking inside to make sure there were, in fact, two amulets inside. There were: two relatively non-descript stones on strings. The stones were black and very thin. Toman had no way of verifying that they were, in fact, immunity amulets, so they had to take Erizen at his word.

"Now, you've decided to work with me, and I with you, so let's get down to business." Erizen came around the front of his desk and leaned back against it. "Our dear Gretchen was right. It's high time Moloch was dealt with.

"Moloch is a nasty piece of work, and he's politically powerful as well as magically powerful. He's cruel, unpredictable, and cunning besides. What makes you think you stand the chance of a rain drop in a bonfire of beating him?"

That was direct, but Toman found he liked it. It was refreshing. "Moloch bears a special hatred for animators—I believe we can lure him away from his political power base and some of his resources. If we can make him come to us, that should level the playing field somewhat," Toman explained.

Erizen snorted. "Not enough. He has a Greymaker," Erizen said.

"How much of a difference does that make?" Toman asked,

knowing full well that they didn't have enough information about Greymakers.

"Imagine someone who wants to put out a fire, but only has water from a well. They can pump up water, but it takes time, and there's only so much water in the well. That's your average mage. With the Greymaker...well, imagine a dam, holding back a mountain lake. All we have to do is open the floodgates. Not only will the fire be put out, the entire city will be flattened and the memory of fire erased." Erizen appeared pleased with his analogy.

"That's how much power the Greymaker generates?" Esset asked, surprised.

"The other lords mocked me for taking over a large, mountainous territory with few tenants. They didn't laugh so hard when they found out how much power I could get from just land, using the Greymaker. They looked downright unhappy when I built the mines, too." He wore a smug little grin.

"So how do we destroy the Greymaker?" Toman asked, pinpointing that target as the first order of business. They couldn't allow Moloch to have that much extra power at his disposal. Even the immunity amulets wouldn't help them if he were that strong.

But Erizen snorted. "You can't."

"So what, you're telling us to give up? I thought you said you were with us on this," Esset challenged him.

"Don't test me," Erizen warned. "All I said was that *you* can't. *I* am a different story. I built the Greymaker; I can destroy it, easily. Although I don't intend to. Simply disabling it will be sufficient."

"If being able to take the Greymaker offline is such a unique ability of yours, won't Moloch know immediately that you did it?" Esset asked reasonably.

"Oh yes. But not if I accuse him first," Erizen replied with a sly smile.

"What?"

"I will pretend to be enraged and go to Moloch to accuse him of tampering with *my* Greymaker. If anyone other than me could do something like that, after all, it would be him, as the only other owner of a Greymaker, the only other person privy to its particular workings. I would have to shut down my own Greymaker temporarily, which is undesirable, but I am confident I can stockpile enough power that I would have something to fall back on if something goes wrong.

"Anyways, I accuse him of disabling my Greymaker, so when his goes down, the rumor will already be circulated that there is someone else capable of such a feat. I will mention that you two were sighted just before the damage of my device, so it will be a logical conclusion for him to assume you were the culprit of his machine's downfall as well." Erizen folded his hands before himself, concluding his part of the plan.

"That…could work," Toman conceded.

"Clearly," Erizen replied arrogantly.

"If we prepare everything else beforehand, that can be our catalyst for getting him to come after us in our stronghold, too," Esset put in. "Can you cut him off from any reserves he may have from his Greymaker, or is that beyond the scope of your abilities?" Esset asked Erizen. He deliberately played to Erizen's pride in his wording.

"Unnecessary. The Greymaker's resources are too vast to catch and hold without the Greymaker spell structure to hold it stable. He would need days of preparation to horde the power," Erizen replied primly. Esset hoped he wasn't just saying that so he wouldn't lose face. "Now, what about your side of the plan?"

"The simplest plans are usually the best—fewer things can go wrong. We were going to take a direct approach," Toman began.

"We have a location in the mountains where I've been building an army on and off for years. I have a good number stockpiled, but not enough yet."

Erizen's eyebrows rose. "You'll need soldiers in the thousands to make any kind of difference against Moloch."

"I know. And if I can take some dedicated time, I can create that many. We aren't ready quite yet, but we will be soon."

"We'll have to set up a signal for when to spring the trap then," Erizen commented. Toman nodded before continuing.

"So we lure Moloch to this location. Can you make it seem that the Greymakers were somehow disabled from our location?"

Erizen nodded.

"Good," Toman continued. "Then all you need to do is disable the Greymaker and send him in our direction. We'll do the rest. Not even Moloch can stand against a stone army in the thousands."

Erizen pursed his lips and tilted his head from side-to-side in a maybe, maybe-not gesture.

"He could with a Greymaker."

"But you're taking care of that," Esset reminded him strongly.

"Indeed."

"I also have some animations for our defense. Add a few more amulets, like ones the sergeant is getting us so we can sense magic, and we'll have the edge we need to beat him." Toman crossed his arms and waited for Erizen's response.

"Relying on brute strength against Moloch... It will be a gamble," Erizen said after a thoughtful silence.

"Going against Moloch at all is a gamble," Toman replied. Erizen nodded pensively.

"Well!" Erizen was suddenly his sharp, showman self again. "The risk to me is minimal. Even if you fail, I won't be discovered if *I* play *my* cards right. Which I will. I will wish you luck. After all, it will benefit me greatly to have that condescending menace no longer looking over my shoulder. I have a few ventures that would be much more lucrative without him cutting into my business." He looked pleased as a cat with cream on its whiskers.

"Now then, come look at my maps so I know where to send Moloch..."

Toman and Esset stood at the base of a small tower perched on a mountainside far away from any civilization. The mountainscape was dotted with hundreds upon hundreds of boulders and rocky formations, that is to say, with Toman's creations disguised as such.

"One month."

Esset tore his eyes from the spectacular view to regard his brother.

"One month, and I should have everything prepared," Toman said.

"That's not that long," Esset said, studying his brother. Esset wanted Moloch dead for many reasons: ethics, morality, for what he'd done to them and others. But he knew that for his brother, it ran even deeper than that, and he worried about Toman's wellbeing this close to a confrontation. *The* confrontation.

"No. And yet I wish it were sooner. But to be fully prepared, it'll be one month of animating soldiers, no distractions." Toman sounded calm and collected.

"Do you think Moloch will fall for Erizen's act?" Esset asked.

"I wouldn't worry about Erizen—he seems like the type who can take care of himself," Toman replied.

"Yeah, but what if Moloch catches him and Erizen gives us up?" Esset asked. He didn't necessarily think that—he just needed to talk away these thoughts.

"Honestly? Unless Erizen joins the fight against us— doubtful—I don't think it'll make a difference. Moloch hates animators, right? I think he'd come after us regardless. It's just a matter of time, and we've made sure that he'll learn where we are," Toman replied.

"Yeah, you're right." Esset conceded. Something was going to go wrong—he knew it. Every time he read his summoner's tome, the phoenix summon practically jumped off the page at him. But he couldn't tell Toman that, just as he couldn't suggest they back out now. He knew Toman wouldn't change his mind.

The phoenix… He really hated that summon. He hated the fact that it even existed, that it was even an option. Its mere existence changed everything. To trade one's life for brief but incredible power—no.

What about the Guardian? He'd summoned that once before. Surely, if things got desperate, he could do it again, to save Toman. The only problem was that the incantation for the summon seemed to have erased itself from his mind completely. He couldn't even remember the precise conditions under which it could be summoned.

All summons had conditions, a contract between summoner and summoned that had to be followed. Esset knew the conditions of all his summons—but not the Guardian. He supposed it was possible that it was a one-time thing. Or maybe he could only remember under the conditions that the summon required. Somehow, that wasn't reassuring.

Why was the phoenix so prominent in his mind? Was it simply because he was so worried about Toman, and himself, and Moloch's demise? Surely that was it. That had to be it. That his knowledge of summons tended to come to him just when he needed it was purely coincidental. Now if he could just calm down so that he didn't see the incantation for the phoenix written in fire every time he closed his eyes…

"You're not having second thoughts, are you?" Toman asked suddenly, studying his brother. He knew something was wrong, but that was to be expected—it was entirely too possible that they were facing imminent death. He just wasn't sure there was anything wrong beyond the obvious.

Esset locked eyes with Toman. "None," he lied with perfect confidence.

After all, they were brothers.

CHAPTER 27

One month had passed, and the signal had been posted; it was time to set their plan in motion.

Erizen knew how thin a line he would be walking, but he also knew that this was the most minimal risk he could take and still have a chance at that reward. Blast Gretchen, she was right—he liked this. Nothing could make his blood sing more than a true challenge, a true risk. On the other hand, he'd never had this much to risk before, back when Gretchen had known him. He felt a sneer play his lips; honestly, what was he thinking? He was also more powerful than he had ever been, and he had never allowed his own cunning to dull.

He twisted his lips into a malicious smile instead. No, Moloch would get his comeuppance, finally. And the prize Erizen would get was security; he had no interest in governing territories larger than what he had now, or hording more treasure or power. He had a secure base here, and enough power to hold his own against anything—anything except Moloch. Moloch, that unpredictable menace, who could choose to destroy Erizen just for the thrill of it—and probably would one day—or who would certainly turn upon him if Erizen were deemed a threat. It would be worth the risk to remove Moloch from the face of the earth.

Erizen tweaked his spell so that if things went sideways in his confrontation, he could trigger it to slingshot him right back to his castle. He didn't think anything would go wrong on his end, but he was still alive among a nest of dark mages because he was careful, almost to the point of paranoia. Not that it was paranoia if everyone really was out to get you. But he missed the reassuring presence of the Greymaker—he'd already disabled it, to be sure that everyone would notice its absence before he confronted Moloch.

Erizen ran scenarios through his mind, trying to rouse a bit of genuine anger in himself—unrelated anger, to be safe—to make his performance more genuine. He just hoped that the two puppies that Gretchen had such faith in would be able to pull this off. If not, he had preparations in place to flee. He hoped they realized that if this went sideways, he was going to cut them loose. Then again, chances were, if this went sideways, they'd be dead pretty quickly. There wouldn't be anything he could do anyways.

Ruby, the current favorite of his harem, stepped into the room. She knew better than to disturb his spell-casting; she simply waited for him, although she posed herself against the wall in a way he rather enjoyed. Yes, there were definitely perks to cultivating loyalty in his subjects. Especially the women... Erizen directed his attention inwards again. Transportation spells were typically complex at the best of times, but the number of fail safes he was building into this one made it all the more so.

It's too bad I won't be there to see Moloch's face when those two scrawny puppies take him out. Now that would be entertaining. Unfortunately, not so much so that it would be worth the risk. *Such is life.* He finished the final touches on the spell and relaxed, creating a loop in the magic so it would sustain itself until he chose to turn his attention back to it.

"Ruby, love," he purred to the woman clad in less than two square feet of red cloth.

"My lord Erizen," she breathed back. Erizen was possessive of those who he saw as belonging to him, and that possessiveness was apparent as he kissed her, claiming her for his own. She melted against him, perfectly willing to succumb to whatever he had in mind for her. Even if it were nothing at all.

"Mmm, you tempt me at a most inopportune moment," Erizen chuckled.

"I am at my lord's disposal," she replied, her dark brown eyes gazing at him.

"You know to take care of things in my absence," Erizen replied. He let her go, his mind already consumed with his project again. Pleasures of the flesh were enjoyable, but they could distract him only momentarily from his true joy—challenges of the mind. And this game—this game would be the game of all games.

"Yes, my lord," Ruby replied from behind him. "I will see to everything. Good luck, my lord."

Erizen laughed haughtily. "I don't need luck." He stepped into the center of the room and triggered the spell. The game had begun.

"WHAT ARE YOU PLAYING AT, MOLOCH?" Erizen roared. There was an automatic retaliation when his transportation spell penetrated Moloch's barriers, but his shields absorbed it easily. It was difficult to make a damaging spell that triggered automatically, so mostly they were just used to distract and make sure that at least an intruder didn't go unnoticed.

"Lord Erizen, you are out of line," Moloch said in perfect calm, folding his hands in front of his body. Erizen had landed in his great hall, and Moloch was standing there, receiving some audience—not mages, Erizen could tell immediately, and therefore of no consequence.

"You are the only one with any knowledge of the Greymaker's workings—you cannot convince me that you are not responsible for the disabling of mine. I see *yours* is still in working order," Erizen hissed, narrowing his eyes.

"I will resume your audience later," Moloch said, waving his hand dismissively towards the people he had been speaking with. Once they had turned to leave, the powerful mage directed his attention at Erizen.

"Now, my friend, won't you tell me what has incensed you so?" Moloch was the picture of poise.

Dark Lord Moloch was a well-groomed individual, his angular features clean-shaven, serving to accentuate his narrow eyebrows and short black hair. His emerald eyes were sharp, keenly watching even the slightest nuances of Erizen's behavior— and anyone and anything else in the vicinity. He was a man who missed very little, and those unaware of that fact tended not to last very long. He wore mage-robes, sweeping expanses of deep red fabric that fell just short of the floor. The only adornments that Moloch indulged in were rings; he wore several bands of varying materials. The rings were all very simple, and most who knew him would guess that they weren't for decoration—they held complex spells that Moloch could release and use in an instant if the occasion called for it.

"Two days ago, my Greymaker was disabled. I was not suspicious at first, but the problem has eluded my ability to fix it. I know of only one person who might know enough about the Greymaker to create a problem like that," Erizen snarled.

"Please calm yourself," Moloch requested, unconcerned by

Erizen's anger. While the red-robed mage's ire was a force to be feared, it was fortunately not easily stirred.

"What's your game?" Erizen demanded, although he outwardly made an effort to compose himself. He made a convincing display of being unwilling to back down.

"No game, Lord Erizen. I am not responsible for the malfunction of your Greymaker. If you are sure your device has been sabotaged, then you must look to another as the culprit," Moloch explained calmly.

"I'm not convinced," was Erizen's steely reply.

"What would be my motivation to remove your Greymaker from the equation?" Moloch asked reasonably. "One would presume I would be making a move to attack you, but such a measure would be unnecessary on my part. Why would I give you warning of an imminent attack, if that were my desire? You are a clever man, Lord Erizen, consider that."

Erizen narrowed his eyes at the other mage, as if doing just that. He'd always been careful not to show the true extent of his genius to the other mages. As a result, the Lords all knew he wasn't stupid, but none of them thought him particularly clever, either. Most assumed he'd stolen the Greymaker spell from someone else. They all thought him a fool, wasting his time on women and other pleasures. Not even Moloch was onto him, Erizen was sure.

"If not you, then who?" Erizen asked suspiciously.

"I am afraid I do not know."

Erizen made as if to object, but Moloch raised a hand to silence him, and the mage wisely obeyed.

"I don't know, but I have been looking into it. I made note of your difficulties as soon as they occurred, and I have been gathering intelligence on the matter. I do not know for certain who has sabotaged your Greymaker, but I have my suspicions," Moloch explained. "I will aid you with your search—it is the least I can do." Erizen knew that Moloch liked him—or rather, he saw him as a useful source to cultivate—as Erizen had been sure to make himself a useful pawn to the more powerful mage. That was why Erizen wasn't surprised by this reaction, or Moloch's offer to help. Erizen's act told a different story, however.

"Seeking the best way to lay the blame elsewhere, eh?" Erizen challenged him, pretending to be impressed with his own astuteness.

"As I said before, such subterfuge would be unnecessary on my part, if you were correct and I were working against you," Moloch pointed out.

Erizen narrowed his eyes at him again before visibly concluding that Moloch was probably not guilty. "Very well, I accept your help. What have you found, Lord Moloch?" Erizen asked, adding the title to his name to signify that he now accepted Moloch's explanation.

"I have been tracking the movements of an old enemy of mine who has been wandering around our territories for nearly a month," Moloch explained. "He calls himself the animator—a hereditary position, incidentally. His predecessor inconvenienced me greatly before I killed him, and it appears that his whelp has come to growl at me as well. It seems the foolish boy thinks that he can threaten me by going after the rest of the council members. You are aware of the assault on Lord Atli's castle, I am sure."

Erizen nodded. It would have been strange had he not been, even in the persona that he was playing for the mage council.

"I believe that was his first attack, ineffective though it was. Lord Atli lost a few possessions, but nothing of great import, according to our peer. No, I'm thinking it will be a simple matter to exterminate this whelp and move on. I already have a lead on his whereabouts." Moloch appeared quite confident in his assessment.

Erizen had to wonder if he knew about the immunity amulets—that could change things if he did, although the plan was to go ahead regardless. "Then what are we waiting for?" Erizen asked impatiently.

"All in good time, my friend. I will confirm the lead, and then the whelp will be dealt with. Remember, vengeance is best served cold. When one has absolute control, after all, one can exact the most pain." Moloch's grin wasn't pleasant; then again, neither was the one Erizen gave him in response.

"You are correct, as usual, Lord Moloch," Erizen deferred. Moloch inclined his head to acknowledge the compliment.

"In the meantime, why don't you accept a guest room here in my castle? I am hoping for confirmation within the day," Moloch suggested.

"Yes, I think that would be most amenable," Erizen agreed.

A long time ago, Erizen had discovered that if one subtly cast a spell while in the presence of a person, without showing any sign of spell-casting, it simply didn't occur to that person that he could possibly be the caster. Mages, of course, could sense when a spell was being cast, but there were ways around that, and Erizen had learned to use that to his advantage.

For example, in mid-sentence, Erizen had triggered the spell he'd prepared the night before, utilizing the "back door" he'd built into Moloch's Greymaker. Moloch would sense the spell, but it would seem to have originated somewhere in the mountains, where Toman and Esset waited for Moloch to come to them. Erizen doubted anyone else would even be able to sense it. Certainly no one would suspect Erizen, standing right in front of Moloch in that moment, for Erizen gave no sign of having done anything but accept Moloch's invitation to stay. Moloch only batted an eyelid very briefly, but it was enough to let Erizen know that Moloch felt his Greymaker go down. Not that Erizen gave any indication that he knew that.

"Excellent, I will have rooms prepared for you immediately. Would you like to entertain one of the girls?" Moloch asked.

"That would be delightful," Erizen replied, licking his lips. My, what a difficult job he had here. This was all even part of his cover!

"I will have one sent to you. Now, if you will excuse me, I have some business to attend to. You understand."

"Of course, Lord Moloch. I thank you for your understanding. I was not rational when I first came to you, but all is clear now." Moloch just smiled without showing his teeth as he gestured for a servant to lead Erizen away.

Erizen went willingly. His part here was all but done. Now all he had to do was keep sharp in case things went sideways.

The brothers waited. They read books. They exercised. They played cards. They sparred.

Esset chafed.

They had the amulets. They had magical immunity. They had thousands of Toman's animations lying in wait. They had Esset's summons ready to go. They had home ground and high ground. They had every advantage they could get.

So why did it feel like something was wrong? Why did it feel like they were facing their doom? Esset was on edge from seeing the phoenix's summon scrawl across his vision every time he opened his summoner's tome—it had not relented. Had they missed something? Did they even have a chance?

Erizen had sent them no messages, but that was according to plan. They began to wonder if Moloch really was coming, although they kept sharp anyways.

"I wish we'd been able to practice more with the magic-sensing amulets. Or been able to test-run the immunity amulets," Esset said, picking a card from his hand and laying it down on the table between him and Toman. They sat in the ground floor of the tower, near the door.

"We did get the immunity amulets tested, and they're legitimate," Toman said. Esset wished he felt as calm as Toman sounded, even though he knew Toman probably didn't feel that calm either. "And we simply don't know enough mages to test the amulets around different magics. Plus we don't want to use them up."

"I know. I just wish… Well, I guess this isn't something we could ever feel one hundred percent confident about," Esset said. Toman shrugged, but when he briefly met Esset's eyes, Esset saw a burning fervor smoldering there. No, Toman wasn't calm either.

Almost intimidated—and a little ashamed by his own lack of conviction—Esset changed the subject. "So what do you want to do after this? I mean, after we beat Moloch, what's the first thing you want to do?" Esset asked, speaking confidently to try to boost his own morale.

"Make doubly sure that Moloch is dead," Toman replied.

"Yeah, but after *that*," Esset said. Toman blinked slowly at him.

"Nevermi—" Esset jumped mid-word as the magic-sensing alarm warned them like an electric shock.

Moloch's incoming transportation spell had tripped the alarms. Toman and Esset jumped to their feet and took a second to pinpoint where Moloch had landed using the feel of the spells. Then they snapped their immunity amulets and exited the tower to stand on the cold, rocky mountainside. Spotting Moloch was easy.

They'd expected Moloch to try invisibility or some such, but instead he walked calmly towards the tower, as if out for a pleasure stroll. He was totally unafraid of them. Esset glanced over at Toman—they were supposed to launch their attack the moment they set eyes on Moloch, but the animations were still.

Moloch stepped around a boulder and kept closing the distance between them, stopping only once he was within easy earshot. Toman simply stared at Moloch, hatred in his eyes.

"I just wanted to say, this is a lovely location up here," Moloch remarked casually. "It's not often I have the occasion to leave the kingdoms anymore. I really must thank you. But you know, you never should have come after me. There was really never any way you could have won." He spoke as if the battle were already over.

"Toman, what are you waiting for?" Esset murmured to Toman, unwilling to take his eyes off the mage. Time was ticking—it would take time to wear Moloch down and stop him for good before the amulets wore off. But Moloch kept talking.

"What I do is something like farming. It is so rewarding, after sewing so many seeds, to see one come to fruition. And this one— well, Animator, your seed I sewed a long time ago. No one escapes me, you know. It's only a matter of time. Those amulets protect you from new magic, but this magic has been waiting inside you, Animator, since before I destroyed your predecessor. On the day I destroyed your village, I made sure no survivor could ever be a threat. I simply waited until the right moment to bring my seed of power to life." Moloch laughed, and Esset felt himself go cold all over. *What was he saying? No!*

"Toman, attack!" Esset urged his brother desperately. "What are you waiting for?" He risked a glance at Toman, who seemed frozen in place.

"Me," Moloch said. Esset could hear the laughter, the mocking, condescending laughter in Moloch's voice.

"He's waiting for me, for my order, for my *permission*. I planted a geas in him a lifetime ago, and now he is under my control."

The Guardian, *the Guardian*—Toman was helpless, he needed

protection, surely he could summon the Guardian! But it was lost to him, and Esset knew that his other summons would be sadly insufficient.

"Come on, Toman," Moloch mocked, beckoning to the animator. Toman obediently walked to Moloch's side, and the mage snatched the immunity amulet from Toman's neck. Esset could only watch.

"Why don't you attack? Him." Moloch pointed at Esset. Sweat broke out on Toman's forehead, but the boulders began to move—his animations were coming to life, and they were going to kill Esset.

"And since you have no chance of escaping this lovely mob of statues, we'll be going now." Moloch's smile was sickening— Esset couldn't breathe, but he could feel the weaving of a transportation spell around Moloch and Toman. Moloch was taking Toman—he would use him, torture him, and kill him. And the gloves would be in Moloch's possession. Esset was powerless to stop him, and that incantation burned in his mind.

We fight, Esset thought, echoing the sentiment he'd believed for so long. But now, faced with *this*... Bright Hyrishal had sacrificed himself to save the world. In life, sacrifices great and small were necessary. Now, *this* sacrifice was necessary.

That incantation burned in his mind.

As Esset spoke, summoning symbols began to burn in the air around him. Time slowed—literally slowed—and a visceral knowledge of what he was calling and what it would do dawned on everyone present. No foreknowledge was required; the phoenix granted that understanding to everyone involved.

Inside, Toman howled. *No, Esset, no! Don't do it, Jonathan!* Even Moloch paled and tried to build his spell faster.

Fire bloomed around Esset, forming floating arcane symbols. Wings unfolded behind him, then separated from him as the long, elegant neck of the phoenix stretched up towards the sky. It wasn't so much summoned as born, brought into life right then and there on their plane of existence. Then it was whole, and it swept its wings forward. Moloch screamed, his voice cracking in agony as a streak of blinding red-orange light pierced his chest. But

Moloch's spell, his escape route, was complete—with a blink, Toman and the mage vanished, suddenly leagues away from the site where the phoenix unfurled and stone giants advanced on it and the summoner.

Toman's mind had gone berserk, but he was frozen in place, unable to move as he was transported back to Moloch's kingdom, into what looked like the mage's inner sanctum. Moloch was on the ground, writhing in agony, but he wasn't dying; Toman knew because his spell wasn't loosening its grip. Moloch's screams pierced the palace, and his minions came running, only to hide in the surrounding shadows, unwilling to risk helping their master. They knew him—he would lash out at anyone near. He wasn't dying—he would live.

Moloch wasn't dying. Esset would die. Moloch would live. And Toman would be Moloch's prisoner, to live, die, or be tortured for lifetimes upon the dark mage's whim. Toman raged, knowing the cost of his best friend and brother's summon.

It was all for nothing.

Esset's soul seemed to have split into two. One half was frantic and screaming; he had failed to stop Moloch, and now Toman was in his hands for good. The other half was perfectly calm and serene, as if he had drifted far away from worldly concerns. His body stood on the mountainside, surrounded by advancing stone foes. It didn't matter though—the fire around the summoner was so hot it melted them before they could come close.

A scream—a screech—rent the air. Esset's mouth was agape, but his scream was drowned out by a larger sound. The louder cry was from the unfeeling agony of his surroundings as the sudden, intense heat radiated into the rocks and trees. The frailer plant life simply disintegrated into ash. The sap in the trees boiled instantly, causing the ancient plants to explode with a resounding crack. The earth itself fared no better; some stones squealed and then exploded while others were split asunder or melted into glassy puddles. Everything was scorched and blackened, leaving nothing recognizable behind.

With a flare, the fire expanded, and a full league in every direction was immolated—a hole of melted stone was carved in the mountainside. The tower, the animations: everything was gone. Esset felt his feet lift off the ground. He hung there, cradled in heat. No, not cradled—that brought to mind gentleness, and the pain was not gentle. Esset was at the very center of the inferno, consumed yet untouched. The fire around him was white, so hot it was colorless. Every muscle in his body was extended and rigid—his arms were stretched from his sides, his fingers spread. His head was tilted back, his feet inches from the ground.

Magic whipped like wind around him, lifting his hair and the edges of his clothing for a moment. Then it whirled around him again, this time carrying ash with it, crystallized flecks of blackened stone. The air spun around him like a vortex, sucking flame and ash inwards to implode upon the summoner. The ashes glowed red-hot then, turning Esset into a being of liquid fire, encasing him completely. One intense flash of hot white light later, there was nothing.

The mountainside was empty, featureless but for the crater and a slim, egg-like pedestal in the middle. It glowed red hot, but slowly faded to a glossy back. It stood there, alone, in the epicenter of the destruction. A cold mountain wind descended around it, but it was untouched, a monument to the life—and death—of the summoner.

END OF BOOK ONE

AFTERWORD

Thank you so much for reading my debut novel! If you loved this book, please leave a review wherever you purchased it. If you'd like to read more, you can track me a number of different ways:

My website (including my blog): http://stephaniebeavers.com/

Twitter: @St_Beavers

And I have a mailing list at my website; sign up to receive updates for my new releases!

Comments or questions? Shoot me an email at StephanieNBeavers@gmail.com.

I hope to get the next novel, Fire Within, published soon! In the meantime, there's a free short story on my website. It's a brief prequel/teaser set before the events of this book. Check it out on my website!

ACKNOWLEDGMENTS

A first book is a huge accomplishment. For me, it's the culmination of years of reading and writing and the passion for both. I know I couldn't have done it without so many people.

First, Mrs. McCutcheon, my fifth grade teacher who got me hooked on writing in the first place. There have been so many other teachers since then, too, who have encouraged me in my writing.

Of course, I must thank my family, who read my book despite not being fantasy readers (or in my dad's case, not even a fiction reader), and who supported me in finishing the manuscripts for this book and the next.

I must thank my wonderful editor, Brenda Errichiello, for transforming my writing in such a way that my story has now been told the best it possibly could be.

And I must thank Damon Za for the brilliant cover art!

Last, I need to thank Kristen Lamb. I have followed her blog and read her books on craft and business, and I have learned so incredibly much; I honestly don't know if I ever could have gotten published without the resources she provides.

So to everyone—friends, family, supporters, and mentors—thank you.

ABOUT THE AUTHOR

Stephanie Beavers always knew she wasn't from the *real* world. That was why she spent so much time daydreaming and living in various fantasy worlds created by others and herself. Stephanie knew she was actually supposed to have been born as a dragon or a cat—or at least someone who had magical abilities. Now grown, she appreciates the beauties of the real world too, but saves herself from sanity by spending as much time in magical, or at least fictional, worlds as possible.

Stephanie shares her mind with a myriad of characters, most of them not human, and most of them possessing magic or special abilities. When they get too loud inside her head, she writes them out or drowns them out by submersing herself in the fiction of others. For those who love magic and adventure, she offers you an outlet so you can escape reality too.

Made in the USA
Lexington, KY
03 December 2014